PRIMAL REAL ESTATE

SHIFTERS

NICHOLAS WALLS

Primal Real Estate

Cover design by Anca Gabriela of BRoseDesignZ.
Interior design by Francis Nguyen.

ISBN-13 978-1-7328016-2-2

Dedicated to all the people

who helped make this dream a reality.

You know who you are.

PRIMAL REAL ESTATE: A SHIFTERS NOVEL

CHAPTER 1

The Wolf dreads the Pitfall, the Hawk suspects the Snare, and the Kite the covered Hook.

-Horace

SHRIEKS OF JOY SPLIT the air, lovers whispered sweet nothings in one another's ear, and the smell of hot dogs and cotton candy suffused the glittering bacchanal. Another balmy night at the San Dominguez boardwalk.

It was a pity the man running across the moonlit beach couldn't enjoy the evening's festivities.

Rupert Turo's breath came out in desperate gasps, lungs burning as he powered across the sands. Blood fell from countless cuts, his clothes sticking to him more by sweat and vitae than any remaining cloth, wet patches of sand left behind him like crimson breadcrumbs. Each time Rupert fell, terror pushed him to his feet and drove him onwards, clinging to a desperate and forlorn hope for survival. The sand sucked at his feet, kicking up in great plumes as he ran from his tormentors. The lights and laughter of the boardwalk faded behind the fleeing accountant until only a sliver of moonlight peeked through the clouds to watch the panicked prey flee.

Brilliant Luna was the only witness to Mr. Turo's end as his harriers tired of their game.

A growling snarl erupted behind the panting man, close as his own shadow. Rupert turned with a shout, arms thrown up in a futile gesture as he fell beneath a nightmare of claws and fang.

His screams in the dark were swallowed by the crashing waves and lost amidst the joyous revelry in the bright waterfront arcades.

Seagulls swung lazily in the blue sky as waves gently crashed against the sandy shores of San Dominguez. The dawn sun barely crested over the horizon; half a golden disc mirrored on the water. It might have been a picturesque setting, fit for any hackneyed greeting card, except for the bloody corpse lying in the sand. A sheet covered it, the wet cloth more ruby than ivory. Red patches dotted the sand in a ragged trail towards the brightly lit boardwalk in the distance, its rides and lights dim and silent in the early dawn.

Two men stood vigil over the body in the morning stillness. A raggedy fellow with a haggard face anxiously puffed away at a cigarette and fiddled with a police badge hastily affixed to his windbreaker. His companion, a stocky man whose gray sweatshirt strained across anvil-wide shoulders, knelt by the corpse.

Lifting the sticky sheet took some doing. It clung wetly to the body, what precious little of it remained. Curved swathes of wine-dark sand arched away from the mauled cadaver, geometric arcs of violence. Thick gouges marred the body, gaping holes where chunks were simply missing, torn away with terrible force. The victim died hard. Judging by the red trail, he took a while doing it.

Lieutenant Jerry Reiger indulged in a final drag on his cigarette, chucking it to join a growing pile at his feet in a gross display of crime scene contamination. *Like I give a damn.* The tired cop felt he'd earned the nicotine filled treat. Reiger and his crew had been on scene for hours, ever since a panicked late-night call from two lovers out for a romantic moonlight stroll led them to the gruesome remains of Mr. Turo. Reiger's people had been doing damage control and making sure no bystanders got too curious. *Not that it matters. Forensics is going to make some bullshit cover story anyway.* The lieutenant was more concerned with the state of his habit. *Half a pack before breakfast is not a good way to start the day.*

"It's too damn early for guessing games, Brock. The suspense is killing me." Reiger said.

Brock Macintyre didn't much look like a Macintyre. His stoic features owed more to the sun-kissed descendants of Egypt and North Africa than it did the people of the Celtic isles. Brock's face might have been carved from stone, but the smoking law enforcement agent could read the big man's mood well enough. Brock was pissed. And when people like Brock were pissed, other people died.

"Definitely the work of the Furies," replied Brock. "They carved their mark into the victim."

Despite his better judgment, Reiger peeked under the sodden rag. Sure enough, amidst crimson viscera and shredded meat, an arrow shaped furrow had been dug into the body, while a cracked ivory curve lay over it in the shape of a bow. The lieutenant recognized the sign of the Cull of Actaeon, rebel shapeshifters commonly known as the Furies. They were not a friendly bunch, as the late Mr. Turo could attest. *Christ, they used the bastard's own ribs to mark their kill.* The officer drew in a shocked, nicotine-tinted breath while Brock reflexively rubbed his side. Jerry knew four pale scars bisected the soldier's ribcage. Both men were uncomfortably familiar with the damage those monstrous claws could do.

"Eighth victim since the peace talks started. The Truce between the Court and Senate has gotten the Cull worked up. Another victim to lay at their feet. I'm afraid the body count keeps rising." Dropping the sheet, Brock stood and scanned the beach. Reiger's men had cordoned off the area; red and blue lights flashing, deflecting undue inquiry into the incident. They needn't have bothered. Despite the hour, no surfers rode the waves nor were any couples sauntering merrily down the beach, enjoying the quiet morning.

Reiger sullenly glared at the tide as if it were responsible for the lieutenant's current situation. "Shit, here I was hoping it was just a loose jaguar or something normal, like a roving band of cannibals. At least that way I could get back to sleep." Rousted from bed by a call from his private backers in the middle of the night, the lieutenant desperately needed coffee.

Then again, Jerry couldn't act too surprised. He knew damn well what he'd signed up for. As liaison for Brock's "people" and the shadowy power brokers that ruled them, the ever-quarreling Senate and Court of Raptors all of the "weird cases" came straight to Reiger's desk. No delay. Lieutenant Reiger lived in a world of secrets and nightmares, any hope of being a good civil servant coming in a distant second to running damage control for two competing groups of shapeshifting secret societies that, for all Reiger knew, had afternoon tea with the Illuminati.

The jaded defender of public order grunted and took another drag on his cigarette before dropping it to join its fallen comrades. He'd be out a pack by sunrise. *Worse than I thought.* Reiger generally measured problems by how many cigarettes they took and things looked grim.

"Looked at the files while you were en route, Brock. The freaks are getting bolder. Turns out this poor bastard was Court, a representative working for Arkadas, working on the Beachfront deal. You know, the property case big enough to get your friends to stop killing each other for three minutes?"

Brock grunted disapprovingly. "The Houses are wise and noble, Reiger. You shouldn't make light of their honorable actions."

The dutiful spiel made Reiger snort. "Don't hand me that shit, Brock. The only time they stop spilling blood is to find some other way to screw each other. I've cleaned up too many of your messes to believe anything's noble about the Houses. Court or Senate, it's all the same. A gang war is a gang war, even if the members are a bunch of shapeshifting psychos."

It belatedly dawned on Reiger that he was speaking to one of those psychos and a high-ranking officer in the ranks of the Senate's foremost killers to boot. Fortunately, Brock was the bigger man, figuratively as well as literally. The fact that Brock didn't burst into a ten-foot-tall wolf-faced murder machine and eviscerate Reiger was testament to that.

"My House, the noble Senate, is doing its best to uphold peace and order in San Dominguez. You know as well as I do that casualties happen, despite our best efforts." Brock's tone softened a fraction. "We can't save everyone. You know that, too."

Reiger grunted noncommittally, earning a frown from his broad-shouldered companion.

A puff and a heartbeat later and Brock spoke again. "Do you know if the victim was Kin?"

Reiger took another drag on his cigarette before giving a brief head twitch of denial. "Naw, just a thin blood working through the firm."

Brock inclined his head a fraction, something Reiger figured passed for a relieved nod from the man. "Good. The Senate and Court won't be looking to shed blood over lost honor over a thin-blood. Better chance of maintaining the Truce."

Neither took much solace in the fact. Hard to feel relieved with a mutilated corpse lying in front of you.

Reiger idly kicked sand over his discarded cigarettes, an ignoble burial for the used-up stubs. "You really think the Truce is gonna hold? The Houses aren't known for playing nice with each other."

Brock's eyes fixed on the bloody sheet, his craggy features pensive. "Our leaders will call upon us to hold to honor, but it won't take much to shatter the peace. Tensions are running high as it is. The Furies aren't the only ones getting antsy. The Cohort and the Court's kill teams are itching for blood. It's getting difficult keeping the rank and file from each other's' throats. News of this getting out isn't going to help."

"Thought you and your crew were supposed to be on top of this?" Reiger gestured stiffly toward the boardwalk with his cigarette, glowing ember waving over the bloody mess like funerary incense. "Look at that. The Furies took their time on this. This poor stiff died hard. Where were you and the rest of the Cohort? Some defenders of the Senate. I can't keep filing 'animal attacks' in our reports. The press is having enough of a field day as it is."

Brock, stiff-backed and tight jawed, glared at his companion. Jerry flinched. The officer couldn't help it. He'd seen first-hand the apocalyptic mess that Brock could make when he let the wolf slip. Whenever those freaky golden eyes turned on him, Reiger felt the Reaper's shadow pass by. *Every time.*

"The Sunset Cohort are the best, Jerry. We offer no quarter to those renegades. However, the Furies are cunning. They know how we fight. Many of them were previously Cohort, after all." The admission seemed to pain Brock.

Reiger wisely kept a sneer off his face and a joke locked behind his teeth. The lieutenant had known the Houses and their enforcers too long to have anything approaching loyalty or reverence for them. *Killers are killers. The Cull just happens to do it without the Houses' permission. Either way, people die.* Still, Brock was a friend, so Reiger tried to be polite.

Brock paused, measuring his words. "There are other considerations as well. We've been pulled back these past few nights. The Senate are reigning us in while they engage in talks with the Court. Both Houses are serious about the peace talks and don't want a scuffle ruining it."

Reiger nodded tiredly. "Guess that confirms the rumor going around the cooler. Word is that the Houses are bringing in some outside help for the Beachfront case. A neutral third party, some legal hotshot from back east." The slender man paused and took a final drag, sending another cigarette tumbling to join its fallen comrades. "I heard he's Kin, but barely. Distant relative. Thin blood."

Brock grunted, amazed but unsurprised at the speed at which gossip traveled in their seaside community. "In other words, someone no one will miss." Rolling broad shoulders with a crack, the stocky soldier mulled the situation over in silence. Reiger watched Brock work through the political ramifications. Reiger tried to give enough of a shit to contribute but he was too tired. *I just want to be done with this and get some sleep. The shapeshifting bastards don't pay me enough for this bullshit.*

"You know how this works, Brock. Shit rolls downhill. If the Houses are playing patty-cake and actually talking to one another, it figures they'd bring in some sacrificial lamb to cover their asses in case things go sideways. The great and infallible Houses love their scapegoats."

For all his loyalty to his House, Brock didn't gainsay the crass lieutenant for the slight. The soldier cast one more look at the mauled remains in the soaked sand. "For their sake, I hope the poor fool is smart enough to stay away."

{—}

With a jangle of keys and muted grunt, Jonathan Augustus Doe strode across the threshold of his beach front property festooned with precariously balanced luggage to survey his new domain. California sunlight flooded into the empty house; dust motes cast about by the gentle sea breeze sifting through the open door. Jon Doe looked about his abode and nodded in satisfaction. A less kind soul might have called it smug gloating.

A modest two-bedroom affair, the house's white walls and dark hard-wood floors may not have impressed Jon's former Harvard classmates, but to him it was a palace. It was *his*. When the blue-eyed college graduate looked around, he saw much more than a bare house. No, the recent law grad saw the beginnings of an empire. *His* empire.

Kicking the door shut with his heel, Jon tottered over to the kitchen counter and unceremoniously deposited his luggage, more by momentum than intent. Once the many suitcases dropped, they revealed a tall, immaculately dressed young man smoothing his pressed dress shirt and silk tie for any wrinkles. Jon had packed just the essentials for his sudden move: dress shirts, well-polished shoes, a mere six ties, and enough hair gel to supply a stylist for a year. Thus unburdened, the dapper fellow set off on a self-guided tour of his new *Casa de Jon*, sleek phone out and dialing before he'd taken two steps.

By the time the all too familiar voicemail message kicked in, the young consultant had covered half of the house and moved on to the master bathroom.

You've reached the Doe residence, too busy on a yacht or spelunking who knows where, leave a message, etc. etc. Nothing new to Jon. He hadn't actually been expecting to reach his parents anyway. *Why change the patterns of a lifetime?*

"Mom, Dad, hi. This is Jon. You know, your son? The one whose graduation ceremony you didn't attend? I'm still alive, thanks for checking up on me. Now don't fret, I'm not asking for any more cash. I've already landed a sweet gig for myself, working for none other than the esteemed Decks and Domes Incorporated and Rising Sun Development."

Jon paused for dramatic effect at the name drops. The theoretical dramatic effect if his parents ever got to the message, at any rate. *Two of the biggest real estate development companies in the U.S., notorious industry rivals, and they both want the D.*

"Some local company went belly up, freeing up a hot new piece of beachfront property onto the market. Seems there was a bit of a paperwork snafu and both D&D and RSD are calling dibs. Nothing new, right? Except this time, they called in a third party to settle the dispute. That third party is none other than baby blue-eyed wunderkind, yours truly! Already moved out to California, don't worry, not mad you missed my moving party. Your loss, anyway. It was epic. Now I'm out here on the West Coast, soaking in the sand and the sun. The bigwigs even covered the cost and set me up in a sweet little beach bungalow. Now, if you will excuse me, dearest Mum and Dad, I'm going to go work on my tan."

Jon thumbed off the phone and sat back with a grin only the most charitable soul wouldn't call smug. *Maybe this time I've shaken them up enough to get a call back. Miracles do happen, after all...*

Though the newly-minted lawyer would never admit it to his parents, or anyone else for that matter, the whole thing seemed beyond bizarre and set off more than a few warning bells in Jon's sandy blonde head. Giants like D&D and RSD kept armies of lawyers on the payroll for just these sorts of occasions. Hell, the two loved scrapping with their rivals in the opposing firm. An old rivalry, matter of honor, or some such, neither willing to yield an inch no matter how much it cost the companies. Their legal battles were the stuff of legend. Attorneys swapped dark tales of their grueling cases around the water cooler.

The economic powerhouses tended to be pretty exclusive about who got into their inner-circle. To have both corporate juggernauts reach out to Jon, barely three months out from passing the BAR, skipped right past unusual and straight into Twilight Zone territory.

Jon's shit-eating grin melted into a frown the more he considered the situation. Jon Doe might be a bit prideful, but he was no one's fool. When he'd gotten the letter, he'd passed it off as a sad attempt at a prank. As a consummate prankster himself, Jon felt a bit insulted. *Like I'd fall for something so obvious.* But when he'd called his fellow interns out on it, his legal compatriots treated the invitation letter like a dead rat.

A diseased dead rat.

Everyone warned him off of it. *Everyone.* Even the elderly Darius Bewford called Jon into his office for a "friendly word." Another gesture which pissed the young graduate off.

Figures the only way the old bastard would give me the time of day is to cut me off at the pass. Just thinking about it got Jon angry all over again.

"Now see here, young Doe." Holding a comb under his nose to mimic the octogenarian lawyer's prodigious mustache, Jon squeakily pontificated to the empty home. "This may appear like a good deal, but things aren't always what they seem. Take my advice and let this one go." Scoffing and rolling his eyes at the memory, Jon gently set the comb down and fastidiously finished unpacking his clothes.

Mocking his former boss boosted Jon's spirits. *If Old Man Bewford and his cronies kept true to form, they probably wanted me out of the picture to shake hands and have some backdoor meetings with their buddies, making sure all parties were on board and no feathers got ruffled. Well, I'm not worried about stepping on any toes. Not when, if I play my cards right, I might be running my own firm in under a year.*

The vindictive thoughts only fueled Jon's already overwrought fantasies. *First job and I'm already working with Arkadas & Associates.* Getting in with one of the oldest law firms in North America would kick his career into overdrive. Jon would be the youngest full staff member. Ever. *Daring. Bold. Inspired. How very me! At this point, all I need to do is figure out if I want my name filigreed in gold or silver on the office plaque.*

Daydreaming about his inevitable success, Jon heard the movers' truck pull up outside. Grinning ear-to-ear and with visions of shimmering name plaques in his head, the young man walked out to supervise the furnishing of his abode.

A few hours later, with the sun just sinking into the sea, Jon felt utterly invincible. He adjusted the hallway mirror as a final touch, taking a moment to admire his reflection before gazing at his newly furnished home.

The move went off without a hitch. His expensive Baker couch sat squarely opposite an entertainment center that wouldn't have looked out of place at NASA, all sleek lines and modern finish. A queen-sized mattress awaited him in the bedroom, and the fridge stood well stocked. Tucked between the couch and the kitchen stood his pride and joy; an oaken work desk he'd won from Harvard Professor Kao on a bet. It'd been a hell of an effort to talk the stingy coot into taking the bet and even more work to pull it off, but the sour look on the professor's face made it all worth it. Thinking about it still brought a smile to Jon's face. One more reminder of his own invincibility.

Perfect. Flush with victory, Jon decided to reward himself with a night on the town. The sun had just set and the stars winked down at the world. With practiced speed, Jon showered, dressed, and dashed out the door to conquer the evening.

§——§

Even as the thudding bass washed over him, the young buck knew he'd picked the wrong club. Having set out from his newly settled home, Doe prowled the nightlife of San Dominguez, judging the clubs and scenes. Like a dashing and Adam's-appled Goldilocks, he searched for one neither too packed nor too empty, but just right.

Howl seemed to fit the bill. An old renovated brick warehouse, something about the crimson scrawling script of the old school luminescent sign called to Jon. The beautiful ladies gliding inside in tight little nothings may have played a factor in it. So, with a wink and nod to the living wall of muscle masquerading as a bouncer, Jon slipped inside.

This time it seemed his bachelor senses, finely honed amidst un-counted college frat parties, pub crawls, and one-night stands, had led Mr. Doe astray.

"Club," it turned out, meant something very different out here in Pacifica. Back east it meant high end shirts, short skirts, and flawless hairdos. Here, fishnets, torn clothes, and piercings ruled the floor. Leath-er masks and harnesses adorned more than one patron, and thudding Industrial music roared aggressively from speakers half the size of Jon's car suspended on chains.

Standing there in pressed slacks, designer silk shirt, and immaculate-ly styled pompadour, Jon stood out like a sore thumb amidst the sea of leather, latex, and denim.

Damn. Swing and a miss. Jon gave a little mental shrug, undeterred. *Might as well get a drink.*

Brushing past several scantily clad club goers, Jon weaved through the heaving bodies to reach the bar just to the side of the sunken dance floor. Bellying up to the bar and slapping down a wad of cash, Jon bel-lowed out his order.

"Hey, barkeep! Let's get this party started right! Rum and Coke and keep the tab open!"

Bald, tattooed, and utterly unimpressed with Jon's bravado, the bar-tender swept the money into his apron like a magic trick and fixed Jon's drink. Almost as quickly as the cash vanished, Jon's drink appeared.

Kicking back the booze, Jon noticed a far more fetching companion than the barkeeper. Slim, nearly albino with winter white hair, her lips as brilliantly neon green as her licentiously short skirt, tiny waist coat, and white-fur trim platform shoes. She just so happened to be eyeing the newly arrived bachelor with interest.

Well, well. Glad the flash impressed someone. Let's see if any other pat-ented Doe moves translate coast to coast.

"Why, hello there, beautiful. What's your sign?" Wiggling his eyebrows, the sheer ridiculousness of the delivery sold the line.

Her laugh turned out to be as cute as the rest of her. Infectious, too. She held up one hand to her mouth to cover her flood of sniggering, flashing a white rabbit tattoo that glowed in the club lights. "Oh my god, that's terrible! Does that actually work?"

"Nope! It's awful! Atrocious! Bad, even!" The cheesy Snagglepuss voice set the fluorescent-lipsticked woman into another fit of giggles. Jonny boy liked what it did for his potential romantic conquest.

Wow, honest to God dimples. The night is looking up.

Feeling fairly merry himself at this point, Jon leaned in closer. "But it makes a terrific ice breaker for talking to gorgeous women. How's it working now?"

The object of his affections shook her head at the cheesy pick-up lines and playfully swatted at Jon, hand lingering just a moment on his arms.

"Seems like a success." Smirking, he moved to plant a kiss on her hand, playing the gallant gentleman. Just before his lips greeted albino skin, the emerald lipped beauty snatched her hand back, hopping away. For a moment, Jon swore her eyes were crimson in the flashing club lights.

"Smooth moves, hair gel, but not smooth enough! You'll have to be quicker to catch me." Pulling out an old-fashioned watch on a chain, from her vest, she posed and made a show of looking at the antique timepiece. "Hello, goodbye!" With a wink and wiggle of her nose, she darted away, white-furred boots flying.

Jon moved to pursue, only to find himself held in place by a very large, very insistent hand.

"Watch the shirt, pal. It's worth more than you are."

Shaking off the hand, Jon spun to face the guy eye to eye... and adjusted his gaze upward by some distance to find them.

The newcomer towered head and shoulders above Jon, skin like burnished copper with a crown of platinum dyed hair, nearly as wide as he was tall. Not an ounce of it was fat.

Holy steroid abuse, Batman. I've seen concrete softer than that.

"Don't." The laconic command instantly set Jon's teeth on edge. He'd heard judges and drill instructors with less steel in their voice. It was clear this meat-head bass-stereo sounding son of a bitch took their authority for granted.

And that pissed Jon off.

Jon flashed a dazzling and pointedly insincere smile. "Yeah? What makes you say that?"

Spike-hair only pointed in the direction of the vanished lass. "Not her. Talk to other people."

Blinding smile on full blast, Jon stepped forward to stare down the giant, chin to forehead. "Right. Got that part. Now, one more time, for those in the back. Why?" He drawled out the question like he was talking to a six-year-old or some of his Harvard sports team buddies.

"Taken."

Wonderful. Very specific. The disyllabic response did little to ease Jon's temper.

"Didn't see a ring buddy. Believe me, I was looking. Real hard." Jon leaned against the bar with a leer, half expecting the big man to take a swing on him.

Instead, the snow crowned mountain of muscle walked past Jon, lazily pursuing the subject of their philosophical debate. He looked back at Jon, pointing to his tree trunk neck. "Collar." Apparently considering the matter tabled, the big fellow turned and vanished into the heaving crowd.

Shaking, Jon sat back against the bar and downed his drink in one gulp.

What the hell was I thinking? That guy could have folded me in half with one hand. The law school graduate ruefully shook his head. *My weapons-grade mouth, at it again. Almost expelled at Harvard and now almost dead before I even start my new gig. Good job, me!* It wasn't just the running mouth that had Doe out of sorts. Despite his gift for gab routinely getting Jon into trouble over the years, macho posturing wasn't par for course.

Should've had the guy eating out of the palm of my hand, gotten him to pay the next round of drink. Jon was quite fluent in meathead. He'd long become adept at playing the Harvard Crimson sports teams like a fiddle. All of them, from basketball to lacrosse. A dirty joke and a winning smile turned enemies into accomplices. Looking down at his empty glass in disapproval, Jon marveled at himself. A sense of being off-kilter nagged at Jon.

Okay, it might just be culture shock but something about this place is... *weird.* Jon tried to put his finger on it but couldn't pin it down. *Hell, maybe I'm off my game. A good carpenter doesn't blame the wood. Might be the smoke drifting around the club. Finest in all the Shire, right guys?* Snickering at his internal witticism, Jon flagged down the bartender, trying to salvage the night and ignore the unfamiliar and unwelcome tightness in his gut.

Some pantomime, a bit of yelling, and more than a few glasses later, Jon stood at the edge of the pit nursing a bruised ego and an overpriced mixed drink.

And people call my profession unethical. Sipping the fruity beverage, Jon watched the frenzied gyrations on the floor. A stocky woman, all curves and ample charms, enthusiastically jumped up and down, ignoring the beat with flagrant disregard. Furry stockings covered her legs above some kind of New Age hoofed shoes. A horned headdress curled around her auburn locks, swaying to the beat. Here and there, larger straight-edged head ornaments pierced skyward, worn by massive men and women that towered above their partners. Some kind of body builder kinksters convention, best Jon could figure. *Yep. Definitely ranking on the weird scale.* Though, the longer Jon looked at them, the more the Harvard graduate developed a creeping impression that the horns actually sprouted from their heads.

And the more he watched, the more convinced he became, and the more he considered the very real possibility someone slipped him a little extra something in his drink. Lifting the glass to the light to peer at its suspect contents, Jon's attention became distracted by a dancer on the floor, uttering an appreciative curse under his breath.

She stood out like a beacon, even among the wild crowd. Decked out in a black leather jacket and torn jeans, she thrust and bucked with the beat, riding the music like a wild animal. Built like a scrapper, all lean muscle and attitude, the punkess blazed through the dance floor without restraint or regret. She was a warrior, a force of nature. With every step, she conquered the floor and made love to it at the same time.

Spiked red hair, chased with streaks of green and purple, stabbed the air as she bobbed and weaved. As if sensing his gaze, the dancer looked up. Mismatched green and amber eyes shone in the strobing lights, looking over a delicately pointed nose, which looked like it'd been broken more than once. Locking onto Jon, the asymmetrical Venus grinned like a fox in a hen-house.

Oh shit. That look. Jon knew that look. The "gotcha" look of a thousand lawyers about to close a case. When she cocked her head in invitation, the red head might as well have pulled a chain.

Downing his overpriced drink, Jon shouldered his way into the pit, determined not to let this fey creature escape. As soon as they met in the pit, Jon opened his mouth, ready to enchant and bedazzle with his silver tongue. Instead, the dancer grabbed him by his tie, pulling him into a passionate kiss. She claimed his mouth, silver tongue and all, as thoroughly as the dance floor. Although one hand gripped his tie, her other hand gripped a bit lower than that.

The satisfied growl that vibrated through Jon's mouth indicated she liked what she found.

Fighting through his bliss and shock, Jon rallied and broke the kiss, designer shirt catching on the assorted metal studs and spikes from the jacket. "That's a hell of a hello." Her hands remained where they were, proving a delightful distraction. "What, oh wow ohhhh, wha...what's your name?"

"Name's Magda. How about you, little buck?" A touch of brogue colored her question.

Irish? Boston transplant? Oh hell, who cares!?

Stunned with the forcefulness of the unorthodox greeting and rather distracted by the hand caressing his swelling member through silk boxers, Jon's blood starved brain fell back on rote habit. "Doe, Jon Doe, practicing legal consultant." Feeling the need to brag to this enchanting creature, Jon mustered up the brain cells to carry on. "Currently representing Rising Sun Development and..." Before he could continue his spiel, his dance partner's face flushed with rage.

"Rising Sun? Those stinking carrion eaters?" Jon winced as Magda painfully gripped his poor manhood, anger and thickening brogue coating her words in equal measure. "They've caused much grief to me and mine over the years." Her eyes blazed, and Jon frantically tried to protest his innocence and beg clemency for his threatened anatomy.

"Hey, I'm just the hired help. Passed the BAR and managed to land a job. I'm freelance, I'm not *with* them!" The frantically struggling lawyer knew about Rising Sun's shady reputation, but he'd never run into it personally. Seems the accusations of unethical dealings carried more weight than Jon thought. *You don't see this kind of heat unless something heinous happened.*

Of course, only a fraction of Jon's brain ruminated on his employers' shady reputation. Most of him was immediately focused on a situation and certain piece of anatomy at hand.

When the pressure still didn't let up, Jon's mind frantically ran through options. Since fight and flight seemed limited with her neon purple painted nails holding his family jewels hostage, the lawyer attempted negotiation. Managing a weak smile, Jon croaked out, "Don't blame me, I just work here."

A few tense moments passed where Jon feared an unexpected career change singing soprano lay in his future before Magda relented. Jon sighed, as the hand ready to take his better half returned to massaging it.

"Well," Magda purred, "Your employers have screwed a lot of people around here." She leaned in close, warm breath tickling his ear "Seems only fair one of 'em gets screwed in return." Her mouth greedily found his as she pulled him deeper into the din and madness of the club.

CHAPTER 2

ROSY-FINGERED DAWN CREPT through venetian blinds, sending bars of light dancing across the room as Jon clawed his way to consciousness, drawn by the sweet smell of coffee and the sound of running water. Blearily, he looked around and realized he wasn't in his house. He certainly owned more than a well-used mattress and some dumbbells.

Spartan by way of Sex Pistols. Blech. Pass. Untangling himself from the covers, he smiled as last night's festivities came back to him. The evening passed in a blur of heaving bodies and passion. They'd danced until his legs nearly fell off, pressing feverishly against one another on the floor. Her hands rarely left his body, roaming every inch of him like an explorer charting new land. Jon had eagerly returned the favor. They'd lustfully grappled on the dance floor, caressing and teasing, sliding past jeans, leather, and silk to tease, touch, and taste. It became a dance within the dance, seeing how much their partner could take.

A whole hell of lot as it turns out. Jon chuckled and rubbed his temples. Any other club they'd be thrown out for indecent exposure, damn near boning on the dance floor. Seemed to be just another night at *Howl* since the crowd had danced on around them without missing a beat. Finally, Jon drove the two back to her place, Magda claimed she didn't have a car, their tongues locked damn near the whole time.

Good thing the cops didn't pull us over. Be a hell of thing to talk my way out a ticket with my junk out like a flag pole. Salute, my good officer!

As soon as the door shut, Magda had shucked her clothes except for her leather jacket, and mounted her new boy-toy, riding him hard, studs and zippers rattling. It'd been all Jon could do to keep up. His universe began and ended at Magda's hard, tight body. Eventually, an exhausted and satisfied sleep claimed Jon with Magda resting beside him in a tangle of sheets and sweat.

As the passionate night came back through his thawing brain, Jon buried his face in his hand with a rueful laugh. *Yep. Definitely slipped me something in the drink. Doing all that, right on the dance floor. With a total stranger. And then back to her place!*

Jon was no stranger to the hook-up scene, but never anything like that. Too...spontaneous.

I calculate, plan, and strategize, dammit. I freaking improvise at least! No one takes the D by surprise. Strangely, despite his impulsive decisions, regret was the farthest thing from his mind. Hunger, for example, took first place. His stomach rumbled loudly at the mere thought of food.

The shower stopped, and Magda sauntered into the room in just her birthday suit, and all thoughts of breakfast fell away. Jon stared, Ogled, even. Sure, he'd had a front row seat last night, but he'd been a bit pre-occupied. Small metal studs gleamed at her nipples and a ring glinted in her navel. A small tuft of fiery red hair framed the crux between her thighs. *Huh, natural. What do you know?* Then Jon noticed the scars. Mostly small, uneven slashes and lighting strike lines. One large prominent scar stood out; a flared oval of off-colored tissue just above the piercing in her toned core.

Damn, she's been through hell. On other people, he'd have looked away and ignored the scars. Blemishes like that freaked him out, anyway. Not Magda. On her, the healed wounds didn't seem out of place. The scars suited her somehow, like badges of honor. Magda certainly didn't do anything to hide them. Nothing in her posture suggested she minded the roaming eyes tracing their lengths.

Magda grinned as Jon stared, toweling her hair dry.

"Morning, buck. Jon, was it? You look like death warmed over. Don't worry, pot's near done brewing." Water droplets falling to the carpet as she exited the room with a fencer's grace.

Honest, at least. Jon followed his gracious host to a small kitchen, gathering up his clothes as he did. A pot of life-giving nectar bubbled away. Magda poured herself a cup of coffee, added a dash of whiskey, and took a sip, relishing the reinforced black liquid nirvana. Jon's blood rushed southward despite the bedroom athletics of the prior evening.

Wow, hell of contender for first place in my top ten of one-night stands. Should probably focus on breakfast. Might be good to get to know the woman, stranger really, who threatened to crush my gonads. Fully intending to get right to it, his shuffling caught Magda's attention.

His red-headed host noticed his standing ovation and smirked. "Well, seems someone doesn't need coffee to get up this morning."

Mug in hand, Magda strode to him imperiously, a panther stalking their territory or conqueror claiming their prize. Downing the scalding liquid like a shot glass, she leaned against Jon. "Why don't we see if that tongue of yours is as silver as you claimed?" With a sweep and hip check, Magda took Jon to the floor, sending the loosely gather clothes flying and straddling his head.

Despite the rough treatment, Jon's vigor remained undiminished, pointing proudly to the ceiling. *Thank God for soft carpets. Not the break-*

fast I was thinking of, but why waste a golden opportunity? Jon grinned up at her between the valley of her thighs and set to his duties with gusto.

Tongue dancing agilely, Jon's labors pulled a hungry growl out of Magda. "Ohhh, that's the spot. Right there!" She gripped Jon's hair and ground against him furiously, the fiery-headed beauty riding him to the first of the morning's crescendos.

They carried on for some time. When Magda finally kicked Jon out the door, with only an ice-cold cup of coffee as consolation and pinch of the rear as a goodbye, Jon was absolutely famished.

§——§

While Jon went off to breakfast, Magda went to work. The second her boy toy was out of sight, the redhead broke into an easy lope. Worn shoes pounded a steady rhythm on the concrete as she dodged by passers, trashcans, and even cars. What Magda couldn't dodge, she bowled over.

Their own fault for not paying attention.

Sick of the slow-moving morning commuters, Magda cut off the sidewalk and darted through alleyways and backyards, bolted between narrowly packed downtown buildings, and dodged through quaint little beachside suburb strips. *Buses, cars, hah! Nothing wrong with your own two feet. I remember we got by just fine before all these metal boxes clogged everything up.*

By the time she set eyes on the *Hard Times* fitness center, she'd worked up a pretty good sweat. Set into a strip mall surrounded by a slice of suburbia, its clientele consisted of would-be meatheads, yuppies, housewives looking to rekindle the magic, and househusbands looking to burn off the gut. All of whom knew to fear Magda on sight.

Padding through the front door and munching on a half-melted protein bar, she idly waved to Max at the front desk. She was slightly taken aback when the lanky-haired string bean got up and chased her to the cubicles in the employees' section. *What's got him in such a fuss?*

"Magda, there you are!"

"Aye, Max, so I am. What's got you bent out of shape?"

"We've been waiting for you. Your doctor came in and dropped off a note for you."

Mismatched eyes blinked slowly. "My doctor? Is this a joke? Are you pranking me? I honestly didn't think you had the stones for it."

"No, seriously." Max looked sickly at Magda's proud grin but defiantly waved a sticky note at the new arrival like a holy charm. "Big guy, shaved head, muscles like he ought to work here. Looked like Luke Cage and Sargent Payne's illegitimate love child. Seemed nice though. The guy said it was urgent but he couldn't get ahold of you through your cell."

Max trailed off with a grumble, sharing the common frustration of the *Hard Times* employees in getting ahold of Magda. She'd "accidently" lost, forgotten, or smashed any cellphones that found their way to her which made it a pain the ass for her co-workers to get ahold of their wayward trainer. Part of the reason she remained part time despite her reputation as a deviously talented workout instructor.

Jupiter's balls, Brock's serious. "Give it here, I'll take a look."

She flipped over the card, halfheartedly scanning the words. Brock Macintyre, Ph.D. Requesting her timely presence at the usual meeting spot. Magda's immediate superior in the Sunset Cohort and a constant pain in her ass.

Godsdamit, I've had suitors less persistent. Nothing for it, then. Have to go.

Magda noticed Max worriedly looking at her and grinned. It did nothing to reassure the man. "Thanks, Max. It's fine. Not my doctor but I know him. Bit of a gag between us."

Max looked unconvinced but shrugged, more than willing to let it go. "If you say so."

As soon as Max went back to the desk, Magda angrily shoved the paper into her bag. Slipping into her workout gear, Magda went out to the floor where her fitness class awaited their trainer's arrival. The redhead grinned wickedly. *Oh good. Victims. I know just how to improve my mood.*

"Hello, ladies and gentlemen. Welcome to hell. I don't want to hear any whining. If you're brave enough to sign up for one of my classes, you know what's in store. I'm feeling particularly piqued today and you all get to suffer for it. Let's get started, shall we?"

§——§

It's amazing how quickly one's day can change. Jon pondered this simple truth in his current situation. For instance, Jon had found himself in a pretty good mood, leisurely strolling down a San Dominguez beachfront neighborhood. Having landed a great job, had some of the greatest sex of his life, and enjoyed a delicious crab cake omelet at a local cafe, Jon felt fairly unstoppable.

Of course, this was all before the abduction.

A black bag over the head and being unceremoniously thrown in the back of a van understandably dampened anyone's day.

With all the aforementioned in the "pros" column, being strapped to a chair, trapped by parties unknown, and a foul-smelling sack sticking to his face all weighed heavily in the "cons" column.

Each of his rapid breaths dragged the cloth wetly against his mouth. He could taste the foul cloth, a potent cocktail of sweat and rubber. Damn near hyperventilating, Jon struggled against the ropes for what seemed like the hundredth time.

The thump of footsteps behind him froze the legal counsel in place.

"Welcome, Mr. Doe. We appreciate you taking time out of your busy schedule to attend our little meeting." Spoken calmly, as though welcoming a VIP to a business meeting rather than speaking to a bound and gagged abductee, each word was crisp and enunciated. A faint English accent pushed through, though with something else behind it. The hooded legal consultant was suddenly and incongruously reminded of the SAE fraternity brothers back at Harvard.

Hazing was never this bad!

Light pierced his eyes as the hood was torn away. Blinking away spots, Jon looked around. His current prison consisted of a narrow room lined with metal racks holding various construction gear; bright orange cones, yellow netting, and PVC piping to one side with rebar, mallets, and bags of concrete to the other. In front of him, a slender fellow in a tight black suit loomed, features obscured by a black ski mask. Only his eyes shone through, gazing with hawkish intensity at the bound figure in the chair. Dust and cement hung in the air, motes dancing in the hazy light of the swaying overhead lamps.

Jon's nose noticed this fact scant moments after his eyes. As he began to sneeze violently, goblets of phlegm flying, a frown touched the corners of his host's piercing eyes. The standing man shook his head with a long-suffering sigh.

"Well now, that simply won't do. Gentlemen, kindly clean up our guest." Gloved hands grabbed Jon from behind and ungently swabbed the snot from his face. Satisfied his "guest's" needs had been met, the severe looking man languidly waved away the help. Hands and cloth receded as the hawk-eyed fellow drew a wickedly curved blade, silvery steel wrapped in worn leather, light dancing along golden filigree. Jon's heart hitched at the sight of it.

"Your actions are of great concern to us, Mr. Doe." He paced back and forth, his voice matching his stride in a measured, even cadence. "The high and noble Court chose you with deliberate care. Of many potential candidates, we selected you for this singular honor. Yet rather than show gratitude, you repaid us with contempt. We expected better of you, Mr. Doe. We expected results." Jon's kidnapper pronounced the last word with all the finality of passing judgment upon the condemned. Profile cast half in light, half in shadow, his piercing gaze fell upon the seated audience of one, demanding a reply.

Dazed, confused, and more than a little worried for his continued health, Jon fell back on his best trait; insouciant obsequiousness or, in layman's terms, kissing ass. *I might be a bastard, but I can be a charming one.*

Sniffling back the last of his snot, the legal counsel launched his pitch. "Gentlemen, I'm sure this is a big misunderstanding and we can come to a position when everyone's concerns are suitably addressed. I hear your points, and they seem completely valid. Moving forward on this, I'm sure we can find a suitable solution to satisfy all parties." Jon gestured, hands open as he attempted his best trusting pose. The bonds, and sheer terror, may have undermined his efforts somewhat.

His host strode behind him to confer with his esteemed mook colleagues. *Okay, dialogue opened. Good first step.* Hope bloomed in Jon's chest. *Not my finest, but not bad considering what I'm working with.*

When his kidnapper's mutters changed to quiet laughter, Jon's relief became confusion. As the quiet laughter became raucous, mocking guffaws, Jon's confusion sank to full blown despair.

Talker, as Jon thought of his most communicative abductor, strutted back into the light, smug even through his ski mask. "Oh yes, I am quite certain that you have our best interests at heart." The hawk-nosed man's voice turned merciless as steel. "You speak to one raised amongst the Lawgiver's Halls. I've sat in judgment over the highest lords and parsed grains of truth from mountains of falsehood. Know that you seek to deceive the Inheritors of the Sun. Brought into being by the Words of Undying Light, we alone do battle in shadows and remain untouched by the foulness there. Such pathetic deceptions as yours are pitiful. Lies are our meat and half-truths our wine. Do not try to mince words with me again. The results *will* be unpleasant."

Raising a knife, Jon's abductor smoothly cut away Jon's tie before proceeding downwards, slowly cutting open his shirt. Each sliced button sent muted shocks through Jon, as he struggled not to flinch too hard and risk impaling himself as Talker slashed through Jon's club shirt. The shimmering blade trailed along the lawyer's waxed and spray-tanned abs to stop just below his navel.

"You shouldn't have spurned our offer, Mr. Doe. A polite refusal we could have understood but to lay with the wolf…" the voice *tsked* softly. "That is an insult we cannot abide. You made promises, Mr. Doe, and we expect you to keep them."

Deciding that the time for reasoning with crazy people had passed, Jon went with the only other choice; begging.

"Wait, wait, hold on just a second! What are you talking about? What promises? I didn't get an invitation to anything! I'm sorry someone missed your birthday party or whatever the hell you're ranting about but I swear it's not my fault and has nothing to do with me!" Jon's voice rose in panic as he plowed forward, desperate to hold off the blade's kiss.

"I just moved here. New place, new job, new everything. For fuck's sake, I haven't even been in the office yet! I don't start until Monday!" Angry, bitter tears welled in Jon's eyes. "You bastards abducted me off the street. I've only been here two freaking days." Hissing out the last words, Jon squeezed his eyes closed, unwilling to watch his life end at the hands of a masked lunatic. When the expected stabbings didn't come, Jon cracked his eyes. Talker seemed to weigh Jon's desperate plea as he idly toyed with the strangely curved blade.

"Are you denying that you have worked with the hated enemies of the Sun?" Talker emphasized the question by resting the blade edge on Jon's throat, causing the immobilized lawyer to strain backwards in the chair.

Jon gritted his teeth, disbelief warring with panic in his blitzed mind. *Sun? As in Rising Sun!? First Magda nearly castrates me for working with Rising Sun and now I get abducted by guys with a grudge against Decks and Domes. I just can't win.* Swallowing nervously, Jon hastily presented his defense to the knife-wielding psycho jury.

"Decks and Domes co-hired me as a legal consultant with Rising Sun Development. Both of them, dammit! I didn't make any decision, haven't even looked at the paperwork yet." The blade pressed forward, and Jon nearly snapped his spine trying to lean away from the gleaming edge. "It's the truth." He croaked out the words through a dry throat, painfully aware of the blade at his jugular. Jon twisted away from the glinting gold and steel blade, tears spilling down his face.

His captor glared at him a moment more, scrutinizing Jon like a bug under a magnifying glass. Satisfied with his examination, Talker nodded to himself, intricate blade vanishing in the blink of an eye, as the black clad kidnapper flowed upright.

"We appreciate your honesty, Mr. Doe. Again, thank you so very much for taking the time to attend our meeting. I am glad it proved so productive. My associates will see you out. Fear not, we will keep in touch." As the descending hood expunged all light from Jon's world, Talker's eyes haunted him into the dark.

{—}

The bag stunk just as bad the second time around. It clung to Jon's face, stale and stagnant. The rocky van ride conspired with the damnable cloth in its plot against Jon's roiling gut. Having his hands bound behind him didn't make things any more comfortable for the terrified lawyer either.

Never been a fan of blindfolds. Always hated those stupid piñata parties my nannies set up. Didn't even care for it when Bethany wanted to experiment. Come to think of it, Jennie's blindfold surprise ended badly for everyone also. Did I ever ask for another guy in the mix? A man spends a little more than his girlfriend on hair products and suddenly she thinks he wants some extra sausage.

It took the shaking lawyer a moment to recognize his mind was rambling. *Okay, need to stop thinking about exes and start thinking about how to get out of this.* Even though Talker's threats seemed to indicate Jon living past this point, he didn't really want to entrust his well-being to the largesse of ranting maniacs.

Right. Think. I've talked my way out of bad situations before. Revisiting college triumphs sparked a bit of defiance in Jon. Anything to get away from the helplessness and fear.

It's like freshman year all over again. Only these guys aren't Harvard Crimson boys and they have guns rather than hockey sticks and baseball bats. No, no, don't focus on that. Focus on the human element. Exhibit A; Flunkies. Used to taking orders. More muscle than brains. Okay, time to revisit "How to mess with Mooks 101."

Half-baked plan at the ready, Jon put on his best Hah-Vahhd accent and went to work with ounce of his blue blood. "Thanks again for the clean-up earlier. I must say, you seemed well-practiced with those hands. Nice and soft. Very delicate technique. Tell me, do you wipe for your boss as well?"

The reply was immediate, curt, and irritated. "Shut your mouth and keep quiet. We have nothing to say to the likes of you."

Engagement with a hint of anger. Now we are getting somewhere. Seizing the opening like he was back in the debate hall, Jon pressed on.

"Oh, I'd be surprised if a cretin like you had anything to say at all. Forming all those difficult words into actual sentences must be terribly tasking for you. Congratulations by the way, I'm sure the rest of your family is happy to see you expand your circle of friends with kidnapping. Keeping up the family tradition... well, the *other* family tradition." The law firm aspirant paused theatrically before continuing. "World's Oldest

Profession, am I right?" Though they couldn't see his wiggled eyebrows in the bag, there was no mistaking the leer coating his voice.

An angry grunt and the sound of leather gloves straining told Jon his barb drew blood from at least one of the mooks. "Watch yourself, grazer, or I'll punch your teeth down your throat."

Ok, he's angry. Need to get him sloppy. Time to talk meathead. Jon screwed up his courage and did his best impression of a cheesy action hero. "Say it to my face, punk!" Jon was suddenly grateful for the bag. It hid his grimace. *Great. Real macho. Except for the squeaking.*

Regardless, it seemed to do the trick as the next thing Jon knew, the goon ripped the bag away with a curse. Jon could practically see the veins bulging in the bulky man's neck. The goon dragged Jon upright, face to snarling face.

"Big talk for a punk ass wolf-fucker." A wave of halitosis and spittle rolled over Jon like a hammer-blow.

Your breath hurts worse than your weird ass insults, dipshit. Is this some kind of West Coast gay slang? I've heard of a bear but what the hell is a wolf? The incoherent raving at least gave Jon more to work with. *Sexual hang ups. Easy pickings.*

"Don't be jealous just because you can't get any." Jon smiled lasciviously at his kidnapper. "I'm sure we can hook you up with a nice bear to cuddle with." He batted his eyes as the man's jaw worked furiously and his eyes bulged.

If I'm lucky the dumb bastard will blow a blood vessel and I'll escape while he strokes out.

The more the mook got worked up, the better Jon felt. It was good to back in his natural habitat; hoodwinking idiots and making folks dance to his tune. Jon almost forgot the sheer terror that twisted his guts into knots.

"Hey, I have a great idea. San Francisco is just a hop, skip, and a jump up the coast. Forgot about the kidnapping thing. Road trip! I mean you've got the sleazy van, the hood, and the handcuffs. I'm sure you can find a nice hairy friend who's into that sort of thing."

The big guy slammed Jon against the wall of the van, eliciting curses from the driver. Jon didn't care much for it either.

"If you don't shut your mouth, I'll kill your sorry ass!" Spittle flew into Jon's rictus grin.

This guy looks ready to pop. If things weren't so serious, I'd be enjoying myself. Time to go full grade school.

"Whoa there, buddy. It wasn't my ass we were talking about." Jon cocked his head as though pondering a difficult question. "Oh! I know! We can just ask your mom about the best places. I hear she gets around."
Dance, puppet, dance!

"My mother was a saint! A High Sworn woman! She'd never lay with a stinking forest-hopper like you! She's pure, you hear me? PURE!" Damn near frothing at the mouth, the big man slammed Jon repeatedly against the van side, punctuating his sentences with bone-jarring force.

Head painfully bouncing against metal, Jon's fear came crashing back. *Oh crap, pushed too hard. I needed him angry not unglued.* Even as his teeth rattled and the taste of pennies burst in his mouth, Jon tried desperately to get a handle on the situation. Unfortunately, panic and head trauma impeded his efforts. Instead a dim sense of unfairness joined the pain. *They must have the wrong guy. I mean, yeah, my parents' sense of humor sucked when they named me, but it's just a name, a bad joke!*

Dazed, Jon noticed ranting stopped. So had the beatings. The masked giant hunched in the van, breath coming in short gasps as he glared at Jon with murder in his eyes. The bruiser's fingers twitched several times, clearly itching to blow his annoying captive's brains out. The internal debate ended. Just as the brute reached for his gun to do just that, several things happened at once.

First, Jon panicked, screamed, trying in vain to push his body through the van.

Secondly and arguably more importantly, Mook Two, quietly laughing as the debacle played out, grabbed the bigger fellow's arm. "Calm down, our orders are to keep him alive."

The final and most important action in preserving the obnoxious lawyer's life happened when the driver, more focused on the fight than the road, swerved violently to dodge an impatiently merging car. The van jumped up onto the curb in a confused symphony of shouted curses and squealing tires, slamming to a halt on an unsuspecting light post. Both mooks went tumbling, along with the big guy's pistol.

Right toward Jon.

The lawyer lashed out with a kick and nailed the big mook in the nuts, curling him into a ball. Jon jumped for the lose pistol, twisting around and pointed it awkwardly at his kidnappers. Jon wasn't exactly a gun nut and zip locked hands behind his back made for strange poses at the best of times.

Still, the barrel of a gun aimed one's way is persuasive, not matter the odd angle.

"Drop your gun!" Jon shrieked out. Mook Two, eyes wide behind his mask, shakily set his piece down and backed up against the side of the vehicle with hands raised.

"We were never going to kill you. Court's honor! Just a talk, to make sure you knew the stakes." Even with the big mook's groans to corroborate his claims, the frantic reassurances didn't exactly make Jon feel better.

Screw this, gotta go, gotta move, now! "Open the door. Do it!" Jon kicked the downed bastard's ribs for emphasis. As Mook Two, second of his noble lineage, awkwardly squeezed past Jon to pop the van doors, Jon crab-stepped over to the other gun and scooped it up, getting his hands in front of him. The pistol armed lawyer hopped over the still groaning abductor to burst out the van doors.

Blinding daylight greeted Jon as lazy afternoon traffic drifted past. When the driver opened his door, he enjoyed a face-to-face meeting with both barrels of Jon's newly acquired toys.

"Keys." The barked order sent the driver fumbling and the shining ring of keys landed in a jangle by Jon's feet. Jon snatched them up in an awkward stoop and got his hands in front of him. The next moments proved a difficult juggling match of trying out keys, sometimes with the aid of his mouth, and waving guns to keep the kidnappers at bay until the cuffs gave way with a click. Jon slowly backed away, stolen pistols held in front of him in trembling hands, before turning and running, full tilt, into the city.

CHAPTER 3

"GOOD WORK, everyone! See you all next time. Remember, pain fades but results stay!" Waving to her class, Magda shucked on her leather jacket with a metallic jangle and strutted out the door of the *Hard Times* fitness center.

Following her usual sadistic routine, Magda had run the class through a brutal mix of cardio, weightlifting, martial arts, and good old fashion suffering that defied any easy categorization, partly because Magda changed it up according to her mood. The only universal constants in class were that you sweated like a pig and it hurt like hell.

Heh. Poor Lambs. Still, I warned them what they were in for. Not that I'd have let them leave if they tried.

A good day, even with Brock's nagging message. After kissing her boy toy goodbye this morning and stealing a pinch of that cute little butt of his, Magda inflicted untold pain on her noon fitness class. The thought still made her laugh. *Proud warrior of the Cohort, slayer of beasts, and I still have to pay bills.* The stipend of the Senate covered next to nothing. *Cheap bastards. Ah well, making these poor souls sweat gives me something to do since the Senate has declared a ceasefire with the Raptors. Besides, it isn't really work if you enjoy it, right?*

Magda kept grinning, the sight enough to send a young couple crossing the street. She paid them no mind. Happened all the time. The warrior's mind lay on her recent conquest and her upcoming festivities.

Surprisingly good lay for a thin blood relative. Guess the buck line still holds true.

The knowledge that Jon Doe worked for the Court of Raptors and their puppets in Rising Sun made her conquest all the sweeter. The red-headed warrior couldn't care less about property deals and understood even less of business stocks, but Magda was proud Cohort, servant of the Senate, and that loyalty extended to the House's proxies in Decks and Domes. This meant her hatred for the Court and their feathered hides fell onto Rising Sun as well.

Both Rising Sun and D&D currently squabbled for the lucrative Beachfront property at the behest of their Mythic backers. The Houses wanted the land not only for the profit it could bring in but also to deny their rivals any scrap of advantage in their ancient contest. Knowing she'd gotten first dibs on their new hired help made Magda briefly consider tracking the young Mr. Doe down again and come back for thirds.

Eh, too much trouble. Maybe later. Besides, duty calls.

"Duty" in these times of wretched peace meant meeting up with her fellow Cohort soldiers and grousing about the lack of heads to bash. Especially now that Brock went out of his way to hold her hand and play at being her keeper.

Bastard, Magda thought good naturedly. *You'd think by the third time I "accidentally" smashed one of those little cell phones Brock's so keen on, he'd have given up.* Brock was nothing if not determined. She'd known rocks that got tired before he did.

It still felt like a cheat that the Cohort officer left a message with her mortal work to wrangle her in. The dingy little fitness center didn't exactly have a well-staffed front desk but when a well-spoken jar-headed wall of muscle came in and slapped a notice on their desk, they damn well payed attention. They'd passed the memo on with dutiful speed, letting Magda know the second her leather jacketed ass stepped through the door.

With no excuses left, off to the pub Magda went.

After a brisk jog through back alleys and over fences, Magda wasn't even breathing hard, though she did chuckle at the shocked look on the elderly couple's faces when she tumbled over their fence and into their petunias. *Still don't see why some people get upset at a jaunt through their yards. Just passing through. Figured they might be more neighborly.* Whistling merrily, she arrived at a place more home to her than her own place; the Den.

From the outside, the Den was a sorry excuse for a drinking establishment. A blunt concrete block of a building, the exterior's peeling neon paint a hallmark of a thankfully forgotten '80s aesthetic. One more ugly bit of ageing urban architecture. None of it belied the storied past to the pub.

The location itself had been a watering hole for over a hundred years, ever since waves of English, Spanish, and French explorers first arrived and settled in for the long haul. Various pubs, eateries, and dens of licentious entertainment continually cropped up in the same spot. Each time one burned down, collapsed, or just plain blew up, another would take its place.

In recent decades, the squat box housed a cocaine fueled discotek, followed by a cocaine fueled workout center, full of tight spandex and drugged up yuppies sweating their brains out in the age of neon and excess.

Now it was the Den, a pub specifically catering to shapeshifters, mythological creatures, and other not-quite-human folk. It kept a selective clientele, aided by some scary looking bouncers. Flanked on either side by properties that remained perpetually unsold, for Magda and other long-toothed veterans of the Sunset Cohort it served as a place to fraternize, play, and unwind.

Or stir things up, depending on how many drinks the shapeshifting warriors had.

With a cheerful nod to Ursus, a shaggy mountain of muscle masquerading who ensured only the right kind of folk made it into the Den, Magda Lahm Dearg, Bannersworn and decorated veteran of the Sunset Cohort kicked open the padded double doors and strutted inside to drink with her people.

Her good mood lasted as long as it took for the doors to swing shut.

Something was wrong. The Cohort was family and you could always tell when something was wrong with family. Rowdy at the best of times, soldiers of the Sunset Cohort sullenly nursed drinks, muttering and snarling at one another. A pall hung over the Den like a wet shroud.

Damn, looks like a funeral in here. The thought brought a snarl to Magda's face. *If those Court bastards broke the truce, there will be hell to pay.*

Before any imagined dire wrongs could be righted, Magda's belly reminded her she needed food. She'd worked up an appetite making her victims at the gym suffer. The punk-haired warrior stalked up to the bar and waved down Columella, proprietor and head waiter of the Den. He also happened to be a priest of Bacchus, god of wine and all things debauched and fun. The portly barkeep came bounding up, tiger print apron flapping and ivy vine laurel nearly toppling from his head.

The devotee of Bacchus smelled of the vine, face glowing merrily. *Good to see he's keeping up with his libations, holding to his faith while others lose theirs. Must be nice getting drunk in the name of your god.*

"Magda, you little minx! Couldn't resist having another taste of me, eh?" Columella laughed, pulling a paper and pen from his garish apron, tone deaf to the mood of the room.

Magda bared her teeth in something only a fool could've mistaken for a smile. "I don't care for pickled ham, you old sot. I'll have the slop you call breakfast, if you think you can manage it. And the hair of the dog that bit you, presuming you haven't finished it all yourself."

Columella roared with a drunk's delight, slapping his ample belly, while Magda glanced about the room. Few of her line mates acknowledged the new arrival and fewer still raised a cup to toast her banter. *Gods, how bad can things be?* Fear and worry gnawed at Magda. The Cohort raised insults to an art form. Her need for a drink kept pace with her worry.

Oblivious by choice or by too much indulgence in his religious duties, the bar proprietor and priest of Bacchus sauntered off to fulfill his duties as host and holy man of the vine.

Even as the jolly booze-slinger left, Magda spotted one of her squadmates in trouble. Her keen senses deduced this because she saw his mouth moving. *Whenever Niall talks, trouble follows as surely as night follows day or flies follow shit.*

Rocking an oversized leather jacket and frayed jeans like an extra off the set of Grease, Niall Taggerty looked the complete opposite of his current unwilling debate partner, one Gerald "Deimos" Stark, a veteran centurion in a much-patched plaid shirt and weathered work boots. The two sat across from one another, locked in heated debate. In truth, neither sat so much as hovered above their chairs, caught up in their argument. The boy's spiked mop bobbed about as he gestured emphatically. Deimos' face grew redder and redder, sun-beaten skin almost the same color as his ruddy beard.

Navigating the tables like a ship through shallows, Magda entered ear shot just as Deimos lost what little temper he had.

"That's enough, you ignorant pup! Our ways have kept the House strong for centuries. We earned our position through the blood and sweat of your betters. So cease your soft-headed bellyaching!"

Niall didn't so much as flinch in the face of the stocky veteran's rage. Impressive considering Deimos was broad as a barn and half again as tall as Niall. *Have to give the boy credit for courage, if not for sense.* Magda moved up to restore order in the ranks as Deimos continued growling at the young man.

"There are terrible things in the world that the humans have no idea about. Those little bastards depend on our strength for protection. One more missing isn't going to matter. What matters is that the House stands and our enemies fall."

Niall leaned back, arms crossed contemptuously as he glared at Deimos' cherry red face. "Not sure the dead guy's family sees it that way. Some protectors we are. Sitting here in a circle jerk while innocent people die because some our own kind go off the deep end."

Deimos slammed both hands on the table, looming over the mouthy lad. Niall rose to stand, not quite eye to eye, with the older warrior. The veteran's body swelled as the beast within surged in time with his anger. Another button popped free of his plaid shirt, yielding to swelling pectorals. "Kid, if you don't shut your damn mouth, I'll rip out your tongue and leave it for the crows. You haven't seen half the shit I've seen."

Magda's palm hit the table like a comet, startling Niall and Deimos. The squabbling idiots looked up to meet Magda's flinty gaze. Deimos' face paled, red draining away and body shrinking to his normal bulk. Niall had a queasy look of awe and, perhaps something more, on his face.

"I've gutted twice the shit you have, you old bastard, and I say back off of the pup." Magda's words were harder than steel. "Deimos, you're a veteran of the line. I expected the iron-hearted Bane of Anpu to set a better example. Get your head out of your ass, quit throwing a tantrum, and balance your fucking humors!"

Deimos flinched at Magda's tone, the sharp snap of a commander that brooked no argument. Deimos reflexively pounded his chest in salute, fist to heart. "Apologies, Bannersworn." The veteran jerked as though burned when he realized what he said, fist unclenched and held at his side like a disobedient child.

Too late. Deimos couldn't take back the words from the air. The old air of command, familiar though long faded, made the centurion utter the discarded title. Magda's nostrils flared and her own hands balled into fists. Even as Deimos deflated, her own musculature swelled. Bitter memories rose with the mention of her old rank, old wounds flaring inside Magda. Only for a moment, then the storm of pain and hurt quieted.

"I gave up that rank, Deimos. I'm going to excuse that slip to being too far in your cups. Get lost. Now."

"Sorry. It's just... you sounded like you used to... I forgot myself." Barely stopping himself from snapping off another salute to the former Cohort officer, Deimos quickly retreated to join a dice game in the back of the Den.

Magda never took her eyes off of Deimos' retreating bulk, even as her hand came up to slap Niall upside his head, a move so honed with regular use she could do it blindfolded.

"Ow! What was that for?"

Magda turned mismatched eyes on the young man. "I'm only going to ask nicely once. What did you do?"

Niall rubbed his head and glanced down guiltily. "What makes you think I did anything?"

Magda planted her fist into the greaser's gut, driving him into the chair and followed Niall down, her oft-broken nose inches from Niall's soon-to-be-broken nose.

"Because you're you. What. Did. You. Do?"

Niall flailed a bit in his chair, only to choke off his protests when Magda snarled back with a shove. "Don't give me any shit, Niall. I'm not going to be so gentle next time."

Niall let out a deflated sigh of defeat and stopped squirming.

Good lad. Shouldn't have to discipline him twice.

"There's been another murder. Damn Furies keep killing people and all anybody seems to care about is 'wounded pride,' 'showing weakness,' or some other high school locker-room horseshit. No one mentions the dead guy or his family. No one cares. Some poor bastard who didn't have half a snowball's chance in hell of fighting back gets ripped apart and none of the great and mighty Cohort seem to give damn just because he's not a Shifter!" Niall's voice grew in confidence as he picked up speed, half a decibel from shouting. Foregoing niceties, Magda clamped down on his flapping jaw, ramming Niall's teeth shut so abruptly they barely missed chomping down on his tongue.

Magda rubbed her temple with the hand not occupied by keeping Niall blessedly silent. *Jupiter's balls, I am not drunk enough for this. Where is Columella with my drink?* Failing to see the portly barkeep, Magda stole Deimos' cup, abandoned in his haste to escape his faux paus, and drained half the cup.

"Merciful fates, Niall. Casualties happen. It's tragic, yes, but the simple truth is that people die in this conflict of ours. Been that way since Rome's eagle stood over half the world. You of all people ought to know that, what with Sean, bless his soul, being a centurion and all." Niall's eyes flashed with grief at the memory of his brother's death, lost in service to the Senate and Cohort. "Sean saw it. Everyone here has seen it. Too many times. You'll see it too. Then you'll understand that sometimes sacrifices have to be made."

The muted Niall glared defiantly, silently refuting with all the valor of youth that he'd ever become as jaded as the rest of the Cohort. Despite herself, Magda couldn't help but smile.

Plenty of courage, not a lick of sense, all piss and vinegar. Now who does that remind me of? Despite herself, Magda nearly smiled. Fortunately, her exasperation with the vocal pup won out.

"I swear, Niall. If you cannot find trouble, you make trouble."

"An interesting statement considering the source, Magda."

The duo turned at the gravelly voice to greet their last squad-mate, Brock. Hands clasped behind his back, he looked every inch a drill-sergeant.

"Niall, learn to read a room. Look around. The Cohort's pride is stung. Fierce warriors one and all. However, the wise and powerful Senate have ordered them to reign themselves in while their lessers..." seeing Niall's face flush, Brock held up a hand, forestalling any outraged protests, "... that is to say those they protect are being killed. The Cohort knows one purpose in its long existence; battle. Now, with the Truce in place, they can't retaliate and that is all most of them know. Spilled blood demands blood spilled."

Brock paused, waiting for Niall to offer a rebuttal. To the surprise of his elders, Niall held his tongue without Magda's forcible assistance. Satisfied he held the lanky youth's attention, Brock continued.

"Even worse, many of them understand where the Furies are coming from, to a point at least. They fought alongside them, after all. While none would be so foolish as to openly declare themselves, many are former brothers and sisters in arms. Some of them were like Deimos, Cohort to their core. Worse, many likely dwell in our very ranks." Despite the gravitas of his words, Brock's voice never lost its level tone. A casual observer might think they were discussing the weather, rather than a radical splinter group of militarized shapeshifters.

The thought of the Furies amongst our own Cohort makes me sick. Damn traitors, claiming divine favor even as they commit atrocity and spit on the

Senate' own gods-granted authority. Magda hunted down some more booze as Brock lectured their sulking companion.

"Here stands the Sunset Cohort, a host of potent killing machines who can't fight the enemies they want to tear into and instead are set to hunt their comrades." He fixed a steely gaze upon Niall and Magda. "People are angry, just like you. Spoiling for a fight, just like you. If you aren't careful, you might be the next target. You may want to be more politic in how you act for the time being." Brock's gaze took in both of his line mates.

Niall had the good sense to at least look abashed, but Magda wouldn't have any of it. She hocked a glob of phlegm onto the floor, sharing her opinion on the matter. "Stop making the Furies out to be our long-lost kin or tragic lovers in a shite romance novel. Monsters, madmen, and traitors, the lot of 'em. I'll not coddle any fool who doesn't know where their loyalties lie."

"Not everyone shares your views, Magda."

"I'm a warrior, Brock, I won't mince words or play politics."

Brock met her anger stoically. "And I'm an officer, Magda. Same as you, until you stepped down."

Magda's eye brows shot up in shock before she flushed red. Niall leaned back in his chair, putting as much distance as he could between himself and his elder line mates without making himself a target. *First Deimos and now Brock. Definitely not drunk enough for this shit. Push it a bit further, you jarheaded jackass, and I'll knock you down a peg.*

Niall tried to inch back the chair without being noticed, making tiny hopping motions as best he dared.

Brock continued over her warning growl. "We have a responsibility to see the bigger picture. The situation's a powder keg right now. The House is our life and our livelihood. The Senate may be dense at times, but they are ancient, wise, and lead us best they can. So, right now, I need you to remember your duty to the Cohort and the House."

Magda fought the pounding in her temples and reigned in her temper. *Damn him, he's right.* That level head was the very reason he represented the Senate in the region. Many others in the Sunset Cohort, herself included, held longer service with the Cohort than Brock. Some by decades.

The key difference was in attitude and perspective.

I spoke true when I said I was a warrior. Magda had marched and fought and bled alongside her brothers and sisters of the Cohort. *Fight or die. Pure and simple. The way I like it.* She considered the dusky officer before her. *Brock thinks beyond the glorious din of battle.*

Cold, calculating, and focused, he'd never lost sight of the larger picture, even in a blood red haze. She trusted him to guide her blade in times like these. *I am a warrior.* Magda repeated in her head, clinging to it. *Perhaps one day, I'll be a leader again.* The echoes of past glories and pains echoed in her mind as she remembered the burden of command, the blood on her fallen comrades on her hands. It still burned in her soul. *But not this day.* She swigged the last bitter dregs of her purloined drink in a hurry to douse that fire and drown the pain. She studiously ignored Brock's raised eyebrows and Niall's frown.

Brock drew out a slip of paper from his back pocket, breaking her reverie. "At any rate, I've got some good news. Lieutenant Reiger's forensics department thinks they have some leads on the Furies' activity. It's in the labs now, but once they have anything, we will be first to know.

Magda grinned savagely. "Which means…"

"… we get first crack at them," Niall finished with significantly less gusto than the veterans.

"As representative of the House, yes, I do." Brock's subtle emphasis on the singular wasn't lost on either of them. "I'm choosing you two to be my honor guard until this situation is resolved. We keep our heads down and our ears primed. I've gotten word that there's a High Meet going down at the Curia in a day or two. All are expected to attend. Formal garb. No exceptions."

As if on cue, both Brock and Magda glared at Niall, whose attempts at innocence and feigned nonchalance crumbled rapidly under his elders' gaze. He groaned in defeat, head thumping on the dinner table, hand raised in defeat. "Message received. Bathrobes and towels it is."

CHAPTER 4

JON BOLTED into his new home, roughly jamming his shoulder into the pastel wood in his haste to get inside. Slamming the door shut, Jon slid the lock home and leaned shakily against the sturdy wood. He was exhausted and, even worse, filthy. Jon's expensive club wear was covered in sweat, dirt, and other unmentionable things he'd picked up in his mad dash to escape. Jon peeked through the eye-hole, heart still pounding, watching for any pursuers. After a few agonizing minutes, Jon stepped away from the door and collapsed onto his couch, sweat-soaked shirt sticking to the fine leather. Any other day, that would have sent the dapper young man running for the laundry and cleaning supplies. Right then and there, Jon couldn't work up the will to care.

His panicked escape replayed in his mind's eye like a broken film projector; a haze of hopping fences, darting through back alleys, taking blind twists and turns without ever looking over his shoulder, afraid he'd see his kidnappers right behind him. In his panic-filled haze, Jon ditched the guns in a dumpster behind some restaurant.

It's what they do in the movies, right?

Trembling, Jon rose from his overpriced repose and staggered to the shower, fumbling out of his clothes and dumping them into the bathroom mini-hamper. Turning on the heat as high as he could stand it, Jon stood in the blasting water and let the scalding liquid wash over him. He stood there trembling, letting the water lobster his skin. A metallic clank from the front door sent him bouncing off of the wet tiles, jumping reflexively with nowhere to go.

He froze pressed against the shower wall, a soft skinned cockroach, listening intently. When no sound of breaking glass or other burglary followed, Jon let out a breath he didn't know he'd been holding and eased off the tiles.

Just the mail. No knife wielding abductors. Jesus fucking Christ, this is ridiculous. I have to get it together.

Forcing himself out of his steamy sanctuary and toweling off, Jon cracked open the door, furtively glancing out at the street as he snatched his mail from the rusted box hanging by the front door so quickly that the thing swung and swayed noisily.

Standing at the kitchen counter, cold linoleum cooling his pinked skin, Jon performed the simplest, sanest task of his day; he sorted his mail.

First and foremost, the sleek congratulatory letter and package from Arkadas & Associates, the legal firm he'd be working with for the duration of the Beachfront Case. Frowning at the bulky package and folder of paperwork, Jon set it to the side. His previous pride smothered, the package lacked its prior luster.

Kidnapping does take the shine off. Fear surged in him at the memories of knives and cruel hands but the Harvard graduate focused on his mail, fighting it down.

Lift. Read. Sort.

Sifting through the advertisements, credit card offers, and ladies' undergarment magazines, Jon found one other item of interest.

The letter came sealed in a crisp ivory envelope. Spidery hand writing graced the front with a golden foil sunburst seal pressed upon the back. *No stamp. No return address. This is a personalized delivery.* Curious and afraid, Jon tore open the envelope with shaking hands. It only took him two tries.

Inside, a letter written in the same spidery handwriting cordially invited him to a gala at New Edfu estates. Furthermore, they appreciated his acceptance of their offer and wished him to join them in celebrating his good fortune and become better acquainted with his backers, the Family Aegolius. No plus-ones, invitation only. Formal attire required.

By the end, Jon's hands shook out of rage, not fear. *Those lunatics in the masks mentioned an invitation. This certainly fits the bill.*

Everything about the elegant letter screamed aristocratic, old-world arrogance. People without fear, more money than god, and no respect for anyone they viewed as beneath them, which meant just about everyone. Nothing new, Jon ran into plenty of them during his stint at Harvard. *Hell, we're practically cousins. Probably why I can't stand them unless they're offering booze. Too familiar by half.*

For the first time that day, the beleaguered lawyer's spirits lifted. The invitation changed everything.

Kidnappings and cryptic threats? Unfamiliar territory for Jon. He didn't know the rules, didn't' know how to deal. Haute couture and petty politics? This game he could play. This game he could win.

Let's see how far down this rabbit hole goes. Folding the letter primly, Jon went to prepare for an evening out.

§—§

An early moon, full and luminous, loomed overheard as Jon thread-ed his BMW inland, away from the coast and its city lights and into the wilderness. Sea and surf turned to foothills and woods with alarming speed. The dirt road wound lazily back and forth through the crowding trees, aged reminders of older times, times when man huddled in stone huts and pretended it was only the wind howling outside. Above the tree line, lights shone in the distance, half glimpsed will-o-wisps in the dark. Plunging through the dark, Jon brought the sports car to a halt.

A massive and overwrought iron gate blocked any further progress. Thick stone walls stretched out to either side, discouraging casual visi-tors or pastoral wanderers. *Holy shit, I'd need a tank to get in! Bad news for the Girl Scouts in the area.* A valet stood at the gates, more soldier than servant as she stood at crisp attention.

A brief chat, a flash of his invitation, and Jon passed the gate though it still took several minutes to reach the estate itself. Parking his car between a Porsche and a Ferrari on a finely landscaped garden masquer-ading as a drive way, Jon couldn't help but be impressed.

The mansion loomed imposingly against the twilight horizon. It dwarfed the ancient trees around it and even in the dim evening its ivo-ry façade gleamed impeccably. Light poured from its many windows, a glowing sea holding back the night beyond. Stained glass sparkled from windows beyond the main hall, each wing and tower a lighthouse in the dark. More than merely ostentatious it was a statement; civilization im-posed upon the heart of the wilderness.

A marble fountain cast in the overly muscled likeness of Neptune with trident raised aloft, burbled away softly as Jon stepped onto the soft gravel of the expansive walkway. A shining marble staircase lead to the oaken doors of the entrance. *Here I thought Mom and Dad were loaded.*

A butler in full uniform offered to take the new arrival's coat as Jon entered the shimmering house. Politely deferring Jeeves' best attempt to strip him, Jon deftly snagged a glass of champagne from another attendant and pretended to sip the bubbling amber liquid as he used the habits refined at a hundred high society parties he'd attended growing up. Mr. Doe cased the room with professional detachment, eying the party with the same clinical evaluation he reserved for clients, courtrooms, and legal opponents.

In short, he treated each and every one of the guests as liars. *Takes one to know one. Thing is, I've got an edge. I'm a professional. I do it for a living.*

Soft strains of violin and piano drifted through the hall, the party goers' murmur punctuated by gentle clinks of glass and quiet laughter. Crystal chandeliers hung from lofty ceilings, their light reflected on the polished gray marble floors like matching suns. Amber accents ran along the walls while white panels mimicking ancient columns marched in stately fashion, matched by the golden wallpaper the color of a new dawn. Flame shaped sconces dotted along the walls assisting their sister suns in lighting the airy chamber.

Everything was as finely manicured as the invitation letter. Even the guests matched the estate, completing it like pieces on a chess board.

Tuxedo touting sirs mingled with madams in elegant evening gowns, figures moving in slow orbit throughout the warmly lit foyer. Features varied wildly from pale ivory to dark mahogany. The variety took Jon by surprise. In Jon's experience, such events tended to be monochromatic affairs for exclusive cabals.

Chalk the diversity up to the West Coast scene. Doesn't matter, their blood is still blue.

Examining the guests, a surreal sensation took hold of Jon. Dotted amongst the party were a riot of talons, feathers, and razor-sharp beaks. Fingers and vicious talons plucked hors d'oeuvres from passing trays. Brilliant plumage sprung from a low-backed dress. Glancing at the incandescent feathers, Jon's mind narrowed in on the important things;

wardrobe. *Those colors work fabulously with that dress. I'm glad my halluci-nations have some taste. Are all the drinks in this town spiked?*

His lack of shock shook Jon more than the upper crust rendition of Animal Farm taking place around him. *Should I be worried, that I'm not worried?*

Jon clinically re-examined the room. *No, of course I shouldn't be worried. People don't just sprout feathers. That's stupid. It's just a theme to the party. I've seen weirder. This is nothing compared to Julie's "crystal girl" birthday party and that "recycled clothing" thing. Still don't see how wear-ing cleaning products makes anyone socially conscientious. At least I know I rocked that saran wrap toga.* Jon mentally clucked to himself for not pre-paring to mingle. *Kidnapping is no excuse not to do my homework.*

As an avid subscriber to the likes of W Magazine and Vogue, Jon seethed internally at being left behind the curve. *Dammit. First the club and now this. I'm missing the hottest trends.* Still, upon reconsideration of the latest fashion craze, Jon was unimpressed. *Horns and feathers, really? Must be a West Coast thing. New York would never be so crass. For now, business at hand.*

Studiously ignoring the feathers, Jon stepped forward to mingle and figure out the stakes of the game. In doing so, he accidentally brushed past a fan of emerald quills protruding above a delightfully plump derri-ere, to a breathy and indignant gasp of the owner.

"Pardon me. I didn't mean to disturb your exquisite plumage. It must have taken a lot of effort to get those feathers so glistening."

Anger gave way to bemusement in the face of such bald-faced flat-tery. Dark eyes glinted with mirth. "Young sir, a gentleman usually asks before ruffling a lady's feathers." With a dismissive sniff and a slight smile, the woman went back to mingling.

Despite dressed in last year's fashion and enduring the brief faux paus, the charming Mr. Doe nodded and shook hands, exchanging mean-ingless pleasantries, empty words passing through lying smiles, soft as lace and sharp as daggers. Names and faces passed by even as his ears picked out details from a host of conversations. Jon found the party's murmur a cat's cradle of lies, double meanings, and conspiracies, each conversation carried sinister hidden undercurrents.

A den of vice and sin. Excellent. Worst fears, confirmed. Still nothing regarding an abduction, or acquisitions, or other cute pseudonyms for violent street snatching reached Jon's ears as he mentally sorted the din. *Okay, Alice, deeper down the rabbit hole we go.*

Finishing his circuit, Jon passed the violin quartet next to a grand piano when a vision nearly blasted all thoughts from his mind. She walked with the utmost poise, her piecing amber eyes took in the room and weighing it in a glance. Stately legs strode unerringly on heels beneath a sharply cut ivory dress cinched with a shimmering sable belt. Scintillating gold earrings, bracelets, and necklace accented burnished copper skin. A golden coif pulled umbral tresses back in a smart tail, framing high cheekbones and full lips. The Mediterranean goddess turned to smile at Jon and he returned it in kind, recognizing the drawn blade of a politician's smile.

Every one of the lawyer's instincts screamed at him to beware the earthbound angel before him. Despite that, Jon fought a traitorous urge to like the woman.

"Good evening, I do not believe we have had the pleasure, Mr...?" A finely manicured hand accompanied the prompt.

Jon took the proffered hand and tried very hard not to focus on her flawless skin. "Doe, Jon Doe, practicing legal consultant."

Her amber orbs widened momentarily, the tiniest slip, and her smile went from bright to radiant. Jon found himself swimming against her charisma, wanting to relax in spite of the dangers. "Mr. Doe! How good of you to come! I am so pleased you have agreed to meet with us. I am Selina Aegolius."

"Thank you, Ms. Aegolius. I'm grateful for this chance to meet such a lovely hostess." Though the circumstances certainly dampened his enthusiasm, Jon found himself meaning every word.

"Well, I see you learned some skills at Harvard." Her eyes glinted challengingly behind the polite mask.

Well, I never could turn down a challenge. Let's see if she shocks easily. "Silver tongued flattery and brown nosing, two of the specialties picked up from a delightful stint at college."

A full-bodied laugh escaped Selina's lips for half a moment before good breeding and practiced manners choked it off.

That might be the first honest thing I've heard all evening.

"Mr. Doe! Don't lawyers burst into flames if they speak the truth?"

"No, that's only when we refuse to take a bribe. It's in the Faustian Bargain we all sign to get our practicing licenses."

He took a drink to hide a triumphant grin while Selina visibly struggled to suppress another laugh, nose crinkling. Against his better judgment and all prior experience, Jon decided to enjoy the interaction. *He who dares, wins, right?*

Even as Jon decided to cross the Rubicon and mix a bit of pleasure with his business, a new face joined the discussion.

"Dearest sister, how tasteless of you to monopolize our guest." The refined voice came from an equally refined gentleman. High cheekbones and regal bearing matched a flawless bronze complexion. Midnight hair joined his high-necked suit of matching hue. Walking toward Selina and Jon with a flute of champagne in hand, the unwanted interloper flashed a smile Jon knew from personal experience required extensive practice in a mirror.

Selina let out a barely audible sound of exasperation, somewhere between a sigh and paint blistering curse. "Brother of mine, you know full well my duties as host entails ensuring guests enjoy our hospitality as much as ensuring our mutual goals are on schedule. I've only just begun discussing matters with Mr. Doe." The muted "without you" hung in the air as she turned to Jon with another almost-honest smile.

"Allow me to introduce my brother, the esteemed Aahmes Aegolius," Selina continued. "Aahmes, this is Jon Doe, our most recent addition to the team for the Beachfront Case." Something about her emphasis on the last words seemed to capitalize both letters, like a bad CIA codename.

Selina's brother smoothly shifted his drink with skill born of long practice, extending his hand. "Charmed, though Mr. Doe and I have met before, albeit in a more informal setting."

Red flags rose in the back of Jon's head as he shook hands with Aahmes. Something about him set Jon's teeth on edge. When Jon's baby blues met burnished gold eyes, everything clicked into sickening clarity.

"Talker!" Jon yanked his hand back from the newcomer as though burned.

Aahmes raised a sardonic eyebrow as his sister's eyes glittered with mirth. "I beg your pardon?"

Wiping his hand on his jacket, Jon's head snapped between the two siblings, trying, unsuccessfully, to watch them both at the same time, suddenly feeling like a cornered rabbit. "Your brother abducted me, blindfolded me, and... and... ruined my breakfast!" Righteous outrage earned Jon a smirk from the brother and a skeptical glance from the sister. *No appreciation for the most important meal of the day. Monsters, all of them.* "I had to jump out of a goddamn van!"

Aahmes gave an imperceptible shrug. "And yet here you are. Clearly it wasn't moving too quickly."

"Aahmes! You told me your team *spoke* to the intermediary." Selina looked scandalized at the news.

One immaculately groomed eyebrow arched skyward again. "So they did, Selina. With my supervision, of course. I merely tired of waiting on a response and upped the time table of our meeting." His hawk-like gaze returned to Jon. "My apologies for ruining your meal, Mr. Doe. If you'd like I'd be happy to arrange a more personal meeting, perhaps over dinner instead. We could discuss breakfast after." Hunger infused the aquiline features.

Jon panicked inside but squashed the emotion as fast as he could. If he had learned one lesson in his years at Harvard it was to never let them see you sweat. His face a politely neutral mask, Jon spoke in a reassuring timbre designed to woo even the most stubborn jurors. "Apology accepted, Mr. Aegolius. We can chalk it up to a simple misunderstanding. I had no idea that kidnapping a complete stranger and raving about invisible enemies passed as sound business practices here in California. Duly noted."

Unfazed by the barb, Aahmes merely cocked his head. "Your proclamations of innocence are both astounding and impressive, Mr. Doe, considering you played Barry like a finely tuned fiddle. You even fooled me into thinking you knew nothing of the Houses. A masterful play." He raised his drink in salute, a fencer ceding a point.

Barry? Who the hell is Barry? Jon's mind frantically replayed the kidnapping. *He probably means that hotheaded guy who threw me around in the van and nearly killed me.*

"Barry's an idiot."

His riposte earned a soft chuckle. "Be that as it may, you still have my congratulations and admiration. There is less prey in you than your namesake led us to believe." He straightened and something imperceptible changed in Aahmes, the smirking dilettante transformed into something greater.

"A word of warning, Mr. Doe. We are very proud of our heritage. Barry may not be the brightest among us and may have some strange ideas about what gods we pay homage to, but he fully accepts we are the sons and daughters of divinity. The One-on-High charges us with a noble role." The words flowed from Selina's brother like honeyed wine and glowed with the warmth of a true believer. Gone the jaded aristocrat and in its place stood a judge or priest, speaking with the power of ancient days.

Selina's exasperated sigh cut the sermon short. "Dearest brother, I think that is quite enough proselytizing. We can extol the virtues of the Court and our lineage another time. Let Mr. Doe enjoy the party. Our esteemed colleague will need time to fulfill his duties."

"Of course, dear sister, of course." With a final predatory grin, the senior Aegolius gracefully turned to mingle with other guests.

Jon frowned after Aahmes before turning to Selina who stood utterly unperturbed by the odd exchange. "I have to give you credit. I can't remember the last time I met my abductor at a formal event. Much less received an invite for a dinner date from them."

"You must have terribly boring dates in Massachusetts." Selina's playful tone robbed the words of any poison and just like that, Jon once again found himself honestly enjoying himself. More a moment at least. He liked this half of the Aegolius duo far more than the other.

Still, it doesn't change the fact that I am dealing with some deranged, frightening people. Realizing he was well and truly up the creek, Jon decided to power through, relying on the wit, charm, and daring that got him out of being expelled from Harvard more than once. "I must say if that is the quality of your staff, I'm less flattered by your invitation after meeting my coworkers."

Selina turned dark eyes upon her guest, eyes that burned with secret fires. "I assure you, Jon, that you were selected after careful measurement in a variety of attributes." Something in her gaze, a veiled challenge or interest, sent Jon's blood racing. "We expect you to perform to the best of your abilities."

"I'm more than happy to give a demonstration of my many talents."

"Is being a silver-tongued devil one of them?" Selina replied dryly.

"Certainly, but at double the usual rates."

Playful banter bounced between the two as they walked to a long table lined with culinary delights. As Jon tasted the delicious smoked salmon rillettes, he realized how his charming host was playing him. Selina had nearly gotten him to forget her brother's little kidnapping stunt.

Oh, she's good. I have to be better. Jon attacked the deviled eggs and caviar with a vengeance to fortify himself for their renewed verbal joust.

Selina changed track as she loaded her plate with various cheeses of dubious color and sweet fruits. "You demonstrated great courage back there. Very daring. However, take care in fencing with my brother. Aahmes is exceptionally observant. He always knows when you are lying. Always."

A wry smile tugged at Jon's lips. He recalled a piece of advice from an old friend at Harvard; if everyone thinks you're lying, it probably means they're already doing it and expect the same courtesy from you. "I meant what I told your brother. I didn't push any buttons with Barry, I read the poor dumb bastard as a high-strung meathead and took a gamble. Almost caught a bullet for my troubles. I really have no idea who or what Aahmes was ranting about. I still don't."

His host's eyes bored into Jon, weighing him with the same intense scrutiny as Aahmes. Jon stifled a shiver. "You really have no idea, do you, Mr. Doe?"

Having won results with unorthodox tactics at his entrance, Jon tried a move virtually unheard amongst lawyers and politicians; honesty. "No, I really don't. Why don't you enlighten me?"

Their meandering course brought them through a set of delicately etched glass doors onto a small patio. A speckled Grecian marble bannister framed the edges, pillars standing sentinel to the night beyond. Carefully manicured hedges provided a screen against any casual onlookers while the gentle burble of a fountain thwarted eavesdroppers.

Jon leaned on the bannister and picked at his plate while his evening guide considered his question. Selina looked radiant in the soft golden light flooding out of the Mansion. Time and again, Jon found himself wanting to trust Selina, despite knowing better.

Every time her piercing gaze turned on him, so much like her brother's, Jon was brutally reminded of the razor-sharp intellect and ruthless resolve displayed by his new partners. *Dropping my guard isn't an option if I want to live through this.*

Silently taking his measure, Selina came to a decision. "Very well, Jon."

Again, only the barest hitch in using his first name. Jon appreciated the effort of fighting a lifetime of ingrained manners for his benefit, though he also suspected it to be a ruse to gain his trust. The Harvard graduate chalked it down to both. *A little of column A, a little column B.*

"My brother and I represent an old family. Extremely old. Rising Sun Development is simply one of our many interests. Our ancient rivals back D&D. You are caught in a conflict older and grander than you can comprehend. The contest over the Beachfront property is simply one more field of battle, another contest. Unfortunately, it seems you are less of a player and more of a pawn." Something that might be have been kindness or admiration touched her eyes. "Which makes your actions thus far all the more commendable, Jon. Very few of your kind survived encounters with the Blood."

There's that emphasis again. Back to CIA code names. She couldn't have made the capitalization clearer if she'd written it out. Her patronizing tone set Jon's hackles up and veiled hints of shadowy conspiracies made him even less credulous. He actually felt a little offended, having actually tried honesty for once in his life. *I'm not gonna get suckered and roll over for cheesy B-Movie writing.*

"Ah. The Blood. This is where you reveal you are actually a 'vuhm-pire' and 'vant to suck my bluuuud!'" If Jon wasn't so irritated and stressed, he might have been embarrassed at his terrible voice impressions and use of toothpicks held in front of his face for fangs. "If" being the operative word, of course.

Selina's shook her head sharply, earrings glinting like tiny stars in the moonlight, a moue of distaste on her lips. "No, Jon, I am most certainly not one of the walking corpses of the Old World, though some of them are in my employ."

Jon wasn't sure what creeped him out more; her deadpan talk of vampires as if they were real or that she didn't bat an eye about employing blood-sucking undead. *I guess it's not too different from hiring lawyers.*

Her voice took on the same fervent tone as her brother's earlier speech. "My kind are Shifters, sprung from the union of primordial forces and mankind. My brother spoke the truth when he said we are descended from the gods. Our clan are the offspring of Horus, kin to falcons and, as held in our most sacred texts, charged with divinely ordering the cosmos. We are related to humanity and have coexisted with your kind for millennia, but we are very much distinct. Elevated, one might say."

Jon suddenly felt very grateful for the champagne. Downing the drink gave him a moment to hide his disgust. "I understand honesty is unpopular in our circles, but you didn't have to insult my intelligence at the same time."

Selina's hurt expression might have actually cut Jon to the core, in more pleasant circumstances. "I spoke nothing but the truth."

"Well, that might be worse. It's good to know I'm working with people with such delightful delusions of grandeur."

"Jon…" Whatever else his host intended to say was lost as a terrible howling erupted from the hedges behind him.

Throwing Jon to the ground with surprising strength, Selina stepped between her guest and the keening thing behind him. The howling cut off with vicious crack. Something warm and wet splattered across Jon's back. Twisting around, Jon gaped at the impossible scene before him.

Selina stood silhouetted in the moonlight, elegant legs braced wide, a furred nightmare impaled upon the brazen claw that replaced her hand. The monstrous digit was buried in the chest of the snarling creature. Its lupine muzzle chomped at the air, blood forced from ruined lungs in a heavy mist, the vitae coated Selina's dinner dress in a carmine spray. Impaled on the end of her talons, its claws futilely scratched furrows in the metal as it thrashed about. With a final flex of her oversized talons, Jon's protector ended the monster's struggles with a gurgling rasp and gush of ruby viscera.

Even as Selina dropped the beast, its features blurred and ran like melting wax and smoke streamed from the body as it shrank, until only a shocked looking teenager in ruined shirt and torn black jeans lay slumped on the ground.

Prone upon the cold balcony, Jon stared in horror at his host's blood-soaked claw. Inhuman talons glistened with the guts of the would-be assassin. With a flick and a shake, the grotesque bronze appendage blurred and shrunk, replaced by a delicate human hand once again. Picking at the ruined sleeve of her previously impeccable dress, Selina frowned down at the cooling body in annoyance before turning to her stunned guest.

"Consider this a teaching moment, Mr. Doe. This is the world you live in now." She gestured breezily at the gory tableau. "You likely have questions. Speak with the esteemed Arkadas. Given what a night owl he is, you might still find him at his office. If you have not already received your packet on the Beachfront Case, Arkadas can fill you in on your duties. I'll call ahead for you." Selina paused for a moment, the killing hand delicately tapping pursed lips. "I apologize for your clothes. Our servants will attend to the cleaning." Without another word, Selina turned and strode briskly into the mansion's waiting light, already moving onto another piece of business on her phone.

Even as his host departed, Jon slowly realized he sat covered in blood next to a dead teenager. He jerked away from the cooling body and its spreading puddle, crab walking around the fountain frantically. Jon offered no resistance as the servants arrived and calmly began clearing away the mess. They took his coat and provided him a spare jacket, promising to return his original cleaned and pressed within a few days. Numb, Jon allowed himself to be led to his car, where he sat for several minutes trying to control his shaking hands. Eventually, Jon started his car and slowly drove off into the night, leaving the continuing cheer and music of the party behind him.

CHAPTER 5

A FULL MOON SHONE in the sky above the domed Curia, its marble facade echoing the splendor of ancient Rome, an auspicious sign for the warriors of the Senate. The Sunset Cohort gathered in full ceremonial regalia, purple tunics with sashes of russet gold, proudly displaying their noble colors.

Such nobility was lost on certain attendees.

"I feel like I need a pipe and fuzzy slippers to complete this getup," Niall complained as he fidgeted with the loosely hanging robes. "Remind me again why we're dressed up like discount Hugh Hefners?" It was well known by his line mates that the younger Shifter fancied himself a stand-in for James Dean, but the purple smock robbed any hope for Niall emulating the movie star, turning "smolder" into "pout" by the magic of ancient and absurd bathrobes.

Brock herded his line mate toward the Curia, assisting with his disheveled robes and laboring under the impossible take of keeping Niall out of trouble. "Tradition. We don this garb to honor our ancestors and strengthen ourselves in the style of old. Now stop squirming."

While Niall struggled with the traditional garb, Brock looked every inch at ease, a dusky bodybuilder in royal purple, though his blunt features lacked a patrician's grace.

Niall reached skyward as Brock adjusted his sash. "Didn't know bathrobes made you tougher." He grunted as Brock tightened the russet strip a bit harder than necessary.

Sneaking up behind them, Magda slapped Niall upside his head by way of greeting. "Shut up and do as the officer commands, pup."

In contrast to Brock's immaculate garb, Magda wore her toga in the loosest sense, wrapped around her waist like a skirt with sash tied in a rough knot to hold it. It lacked any of the decorum of her esteemed peerage, though Niall appeared to appreciate how it showed off her pale legs. Magda feared the youth may have been too busy drooling to pay attention to her reprimand. *Thought I cleared up that little crush a few months back. Ah well, another instructional beating won't hurt him. Permanently, anyway. Niall could always use another "learning experience."*

Brock grunted, somehow compacting a great deal of professional disgust into a single sound. "Sloppy uniform discipline and dress code violation all in one. If this were my old Army unit, you'd be doing laps until you puked."

"Brock, I hunted Fomorian Mourn-Brays while you still were still figuring out what to do with your dick. Fuck off."

"Magda, please. Not only are you barely thirty years my senior, kindly recall that I served in Vietnam before I ever became a centurion."

Magda threw up her hands. "That's not the point. My seniority stands. Which lets me wear this." She waved a hand at the haphazard toga. "It's loose, functional, and leaves me able to fight if need be." A wild grin sprung to her face. "Besides, Celtic blood runs in these veins. Snubbing our noses at thrice-damned stuffy Roman traditions is a proud part of *my* heritage."

Niall's head bobbed stupidly as counterpoint to Brock's unflappable expression, stoic even in the face of his teammate's playful posturing.

"Even though our Cohort, our House, claims the founders of Rome as ancestors?"

Magda laughed at her fellow warriors, happy with her little band. *They might be flawed, but they are family.* You accepted your family as they were, warts and all.

"Fine, fine. We'll compromise. You can use Niall as your Barbie doll and I'll laugh."

Magda waited indulgently until Brock judged them as close to presentable as possible, and they filed into the open square of the Curia and took their place in the ranks of their fellow Cohort warriors.

Not all were marked equally. Though all attendees wore togas and all bore the symbol of the Sunset Cohort, a disc half sunk beneath a horizon, a panoply of other honor markings decorated the host, denoting the ranks and worthy deeds of each member.

The number of badges and awards would have a Boy Scouts troupe green with envy.

Here, clustered lightning bolts denoted a veteran raider. There, a shattered sword proudly claimed a warrior battling beyond impossible odds. Magda's grin faltered at the sight of the shattered sword. *I'd be wearing that myself, if I still claimed the title of Bannersworn.* She glanced at the bare cloth she wore. When she gave up command, Magda had surrendered the titles and rights that went with it. It seemed a bitter thing, but far less bitter than betraying the memory of her dead line mates by wearing glory where they wore only funerary cloths. *Better this way. Better not to remember. I don't want to see any more friends die. Even if the*

Senate claims it a victory, the price was too high. I won't shirk my duty but I won't claim glory simply for surviving.

At the edges of the mustering grounds, an honor guard styled after the ancient Roman Legions stood at full attention. They were the Triarii, pride of the Cohort and most elite warriors the Cohort could muster.

Brock and Magda exchanged worried glances at the sight of the armored elite. The slovenly clad Magda leaned over to her stone-faced companion. "Since when do the proud Triarii mingle with us common folks? Aren't they too busy climbing the social ladders and kissing ass to bother with us lowly plebs?"

Brock's worry lines creased harder at Magda's flippancy. "It is true the Triarii are often too busy with the affairs of the House to attend, but this is a High Meet. All Cohort members not on special assignment or essential duties are expected to attend. Rank grants certain privileges, but it doesn't grant that much privilege."

"Don't bullshit me, Brock. I'm not some wet nosed punk like Niall." Niall's sputtered protests went ignored by both senior Cohort warriors. "The Senate values them too much to risk letting them off the leash, even with a High Meet, and they certainly don't attend parties in full battle gear."

Brock sighed, the most expressive Magda could remember him being in a long time. It did not raise her spirits. Suddenly, Magda felt a desperate need for a drink. *Things are worse than I dared dream if Brock is feeling worn down enough to show it.*

"Recent issues with the Furies and the sensitivity of the Truce demanded a statement be made, a show of strength to remind the warriors of their proud legacy and remind their enemies why they should fear them. Hence, the Triarii," replied Brock.

The Triarii formed two proud rows, stiffly facing one another across the large square, framing a small stage. Beyond, the large dome and portico covered entrance of the Curia rose proudly. A small forest and park surrounded it, ensuring privacy for the nighttime ritual. Hired security, on the Senate's payroll, ensured sure any unwanted guests kept a wide berth.

Signifer Marius took to center of the stage, grey of hair and garbed in the same armor as the Triarii. He bore the *signum*, standard of the Sunset Cohort. Three bronze discs climbed the stout oaken length, topped by a broad half circle affixed at its peak. Copper inlays on the demi-disc aped the rays of a resplendent dawn.

A simple item but it represented the heart and soul of the Cohort.

Many of the Shifters would die to save it. Still more would willingly slay to protect it. Marius had done so on many a bloody occasion. Wolf pelt mantle of office draped about his shoulders, the scowling taskmaster looked upon the sea of purple and gold.

"*Salve,* brothers and sisters, inheritors of Rome and wielders of its divine Imperium! Be proud this night, for the blood of gods and heroes runs in your veins. Be grateful, for you still draw breath and may enjoy this world's bounty. Be humble, for it is only through the sacrifice of our forbearers, living and dead, that we maintain our dominion of the Earth."

As one, the Triarii slammed gauntleted fists to their chest plates in salute; a martial cacophony of clashing metal. Despite her earlier misgivings, Magda's heart soared with pride at the sight.

Niall leaned over and elbowed Brock in the ribs with a snicker. "Laying it on a bit thick, eh?"

Brock's expression never changed, but the cable taunt muscles in his shoulders belied his inner fuming. "*Cuilibet fatuo placet sua calva.*"

"Huh?"

"It roughly translates to 'Shut up, Niall.'" Magda breathed through the corner of her mouth.

The old veteran's ears might have overheard the exchange, as his scowl deepened before his stentorian voice boomed again.

"In honor of the gods, I shall recount a tale of origins this most auspicious of nights, that all may remember whence we came and draw strength from the past to forge a prosperous future."

"Long ago, there dwelt a noble house upon the headwaters of the Alpheois. Lycaon, King of Arcadia, sought to challenge the gods. The king wished to test their wisdom and their vigilance, and so he and his house slew Nyctimus, one of his own sons, blood of his blood, feeding the cooked flesh to Jupiter when the thunder-bringer graced his hall. Enraged at this act, Jupiter hurled his mighty bolts and slew Lycaon's brood to a man. Having snuffed the kinslayer's line, the Leader of Fates then cursed Lycaon with the form of a wolf and set the former king running into the wilds." The Signifer paused to glare at the crowd.

"Yet Jupiter was not yet finished with the House of Lycaon. The Banisher of Ills raised Nyctimus from the grave and blessed him with the gift that had been a curse upon his father. The resurrected Nyctimus was granted the secrets of form-change, switching 'twixt the guise of wolf and man. Olympus grants him provision to continue his gods favored line with the lady Nonakris."

Niall blanched, looking between his teammates. "Wait, wasn't she Nycti's mom? Good thing the gods are down with keeping it all in the family. Still, dude's ripping off Oedipus' gig. Guy should sue."

The boy's ramblings ended abruptly as the Signifer slammed the banner against the stage, voice full of fire and wrath. "But like the condemned Lycaon, some seek to betray their own family, to slay and devour the flesh of their brothers and sisters. I speak of the Cull of Actaeon, the so-called Furies. These vagabond scavengers seek to subvert our righteous authority. They foolishly reject the wisdom of the venerable Senate as weakness. The Senate represents us; it has our voice and speaks for us all! These maddened creatures mock us all by their actions. They must be brought to heel!"

Marius visibly gathered himself before continuing in a voice as hard as tempered steel.

"Yet our House is both prudent and merciful. It laments bloodshed between brothers, and understands our enemies deceive the noble with lies and half-truths." He slapped an open palm upon his breast plate. "It the potency of our divine blood, our wild *thumos* which leads to passions unbalancing humors and corrupting our good sense. Thus, in their wisdom, the Senate justly offers amnesty to those that recant their misdeeds and return to the side of the righteous."

The Signifer's proclamation sent a ripple of murmurs about the crowd. Brock and Magda exchanged knowing glances.

"This is bad."

"Very."

Niall's head whiplashed between the two. "Thanks for being cryptic and all, but how is that bad? This ought to help get the killings to stop, right?"

Brock hissed the answer through gritted teeth, as though it pained him to even utter it. "The Senate would never have offered mercy from a position of strength."

Magda nodded sadly. "Marius's speech is the Senate's acknowledgment of Furies existing in the Cohort itself. The old bastards knew members of the Cull would be here. In our ranks. Word is sure to reach the ears of the rogue Shifters. We'll see if they come to talk." As she spat the words out, she craned her neck to look at her fellow warriors. *They might come to the bargaining table, but damn me if I let them walk away unscathed. Niall might be a young fool but he was right about one thing; those bastards owe us a blood price.*

"If they continue to refuse such mercy and deny the justice in our decrees, we shall be left with no recourse. We shall unleash our virtuous strength, and in *Bellum Iustum*, fall upon them tooth and claw." The dire tones of the proclamation left no question as to the terrible intent of the decree.

This didn't stop Niall whispering furtively to Brock once more. "Wait, what? bell am? just am? What was that about?"

Brock frowned. "It's Latin. *Bellum Iustum*. It means a just or holy war. A stick to balance the carrot. Now, for the last time. Shut. Up. Niall."

"Oh good. As long as we are keeping up with the classics." As snarls erupted from around him, Niall wisely took his superior's advice.

Upon the podium, the rite master continued his tirade, as such as a preacher preaching fire and brimstone. "No enemy may stand before the House united. We shall cast down our foes and stride forward triumphant! Our glory shall not be denied! *AVE SENATUS!*"

The armored Marius raised his arms high, *signum* hefted skyward, as howls and cheers poured forth from the assembled throng.

With that, the high ceremony ended, and the fun stuff began.

Marius departed the stage and attractive men and women wearing tunics a hair's breadth from being scandalous roamed the crowd with food and drink. Caskets of rich red wine rested beside tables of meats, breads, and fruit.

Bless the wisdom of the ancients. They knew a public ritual without food or, horror of horrors, without wine was no proper ritual at all.

Their worries forgotten for the moment, the Cohort set to the proffered feast with gusto.

Magda laughed, drank, boasted, and wrestled with her battle brothers and sisters. *Gods, it feels good to be among comrades.* This was her family. The rituals never failed to remind Magda of that. Even in the darkest times, this camaraderie and kinship fired the scarred warrior's soul. *If drinking, fighting, and fucking ever lose their appeal, gods take me swiftly.*

Magda watched as Niall blushed and pointedly looked away as a serving girl sashayed by him, his bad boy routine cracked wide open and his youth laid bare. Magda clucked in disapproval. *Boy's young. A few years with the Cohort and he'll learn. Got to take your joys where you can. Life is short. Too short. You never know when the Fates may take you.* Memories of fallen soldiers rose in her mind, bringing with them a crashing wave of melancholy. Magda drowned it all with more rich, sweet, red wine. The spirits kept the darkness at bay, as it always did. Catching Brock's worried eye, she flashed him a rude salute before she turned away with a rough laugh.

Flush with wine and good cheer, Magda tore one final chunk of hard dark loaf, pinched a passing server's rear, and climbed the steps to the Curia to pay her respects. Rubbing the final crumbs from her hands as she entered the portico, Magda dipped her fingers into a dish of holy oils and touched forehead and heart. Sanctified and anointed before the gods, she entered the Hall of Victories.

The colonnade stretched from entrance to rear, trophies displayed between the towering pillars. Magda walked past tattered banners from fallen friend and foe, the worn cloth stirred gently by an air-conditioned breeze. Broken blades, split shields, and other relics of battles past proclaimed the glories and victories of the Sunset Cohort. Magda stopped before a broken and charred spear, its pieces resting upon a marble plinth. Melancholy arose even through the sweet buffer of her drink. Pride and sorrow warred within the red headed warrior at the sight.

Magda touched the round puckered scar above her hips, mind drifting to battle where she'd earned it. Fragmented memories of fog, tentacled horrors, and the inescapable smell of sea brine. Try as she might to fight it, a flood of memories rose on a tide of pain and remorse.

Those bastard Fomorians came out of the sea under cover of mist, blanketing the valley with a murky fog. We stood but we stood alone. Our reinforcements never arrived. The damned Court of Raptors never showed. Faithless cowards. Left us to face the horde ourselves. Only Magda and her line mates stood against the freakish descendants of Atlantis. She'd been Bannersworn then, guardian of their standard and commander of her own squad. They were but a handful against a horde. *But by the gods we still held!*

The battle was a blur, a gallery of nightmare images and horrendous sounds, monstrous foes emerging from the blinding mist. Wave after wave of the monsters, unyielding as the tide. Magda's squad fought with all the savagery within them, elbow deep in brackish blood, staining the rocks with cursed Fomorian vitae.

For all their desperate bravery, the Cohort had been forced back, their numbers dwindling with each new wave of deep-spawned monstrosities. None of the shapeshifters died easy. Magda's eyes misted as the memories played on, an unwilling audience to her final battle as Bannersworn.

Sweet fates, I could hear Alonso screaming not an arm's length from me and all I could see was that blasted grey soup. I only found him when the blood sprayed over me. Red and gray and purple ichor, oh gods, I tried to save them, I swear. I gave everything I had.

Magda's line had made their final stand amidst the rocky coast near San Francisco. The enemy war leader, coral armor dripping with foggy dew and Cohort blood, broke their lines with a flanking maneuver. Magda's hands clutched at the puckered scar at her waist in remembered agony. *The coward struck me from behind with his damned spear.* Magda'd been pinned to the ground as his freakish bodyguards tore her final line mates limb from limb. *Jenny, Octavia, Ventus, Samuel. The gods took you too soon.*

As her comrades fell beneath twisted claw and chitinous blades, Magda's vision faded in a red-dimmed tide. Snapping the bastard's spear from her gut, the Bannersworn rammed the foul weapon down its deep spawned monster's throat. The Fomorians unnatural storm magic turned upon them when a bolt from the heavens roared down to strike the spear shaft, frying the sea-borne fiend. Seeing their champion struck down by their own weather-working, the spirit of the undersea creatures broke.

. Magda didn't remember much after that. *They say I was half alive and swinging blindly at enemies long fled, covered head to toe in blood. My enemies and my own.* She did remember the war leader's burned corpse affixed to the charred spear like a battle standard. *Aye, we won. But only I survived*

Since that day, Magda refused command and stepped down into the rank and file, unwilling to order others to their deaths. *I'll shed blood and be bled in turn, but I won't have others die for me.*

Shaking off her dark mood and angrily scrubbing unshed tears, Magda continued through the airy hall. Ducking through a door at the rear, the hall gave way to a great dome. Ancient deities of Rome adorned the chamber roof while closer to the floor, small alcoves lined the walls. *Aedes* filled each niche, statues of the divinities in their own private shrines. The augurs tended to them regularly and ensured the holy icons suffered no neglect. The gods' current silence and withheld favor from the Senate and Cohort's pleas did not preclude their continued worship. In truth, it only strengthened it. The cries of the faithful grew shrill and numerous in these dark times. Some screamed their pleas and offered more desperate tribute.

The Cull of Actaeon. The Furies.

A small but growing band of malcontents, railing against both the Senate and the Court, who claimed to be the true servants of the gods. They offered up blood, bones, and bodies to the gods. *The fools bellow that the Senate and the Court have lost their way, forgotten their purpose and enfeebled by modern ways, blaming them for the gods' silence. Maniacs and zealots. As if spilt blood will win back the gods' favor. It isn't the Olympians who demand brothers and first born.*

Shaking matters of faith from her mind, Magda passed from the temple to the best part of the Curia; the heated baths. If the Hall of Victories honored reflection and the Dome turned one's thoughts to prayer and the divine, the baths were made for fun.

Elegant and luxurious, the bath system contained a variety pools full of heated water. The largest of them, the Prime, took pride of place in the center, roughly half the size of an Olympic swimming pool. Lesser pools rested in side alcoves, purple drapes allowing for more private rendezvous. Like with the rest of the Curia, the Senate wasted no expense with the baths when it came to displaying their wealth and power. Keeping their warriors comfortable at the same time proved a nice bonus.

Carelessly dumping her noble robes on the marble floor, Magda dove into the water. Touching off the bottom, she swam its length, front to end, lazily floating along. Drifting, Magda luxuriated in the bath's warmth, seemingly oblivious to the world. In truth, the red-tressed floater listened. *Bless their lusty little hearts, the Cohort are loose lipped in their cups and their baths.*

Office politics existed everywhere, even in military forces like the Cohort. Especially in military forces like the Cohort. And, as with their Latin ancestors, politics almost always took place in the baths. Even deep in her cups, Magda had noted who slunk off from the party early. *As if any centurion of the Sunset Cohort would miss a chance to wine and dine when someone else is footing the bill.* She'd fought beside most of the warriors, knew their hopes, their temperaments, even their lovers. If the Cohort centurions snuck to private rooms, once you removed the possibility of romantic interludes, only conspiracy remained.

Believing themselves in a safe place, the centurions aired their grievances, bellyaching and moaning in the tried and true traditions of soldiery the world over. And their grievances were many. She listened as several of the old guard, grizzled veteran Deimos among them, fumed at the current ceasefire. They feared the Senate had lost its teeth, disgusted with the House leadership's unwillingness to unleash them upon their ancient rivals or even the renegades. Magda sympathized.

No argument there. I don't have the faintest idea what the old bastards are thinking, holding us back from our due vengeance. Even with all the sound and fury, Magda dismissed such complaints as the rumblings of warriors with no outlet for their frustrations. Those, she understood. She'd heard such bellyaching from her warriors since she'd entered the Cohort. The other, quieter whispers made the former officer's blood run cold.

A few, very quietly, wondered if the Furies' cause held merit, that perhaps the time had come to march against the Senate and erect a new system. Thankfully, the others quickly silenced such sedition. Few of the Sunset Cohort seemed ready to rebel against the Senate, at least for now. Magda rubbed her head and deeply yearned for more wine.

Damn his eyes, Brock was right. Plots are afoot, maybe even a risk of a coup. Damn him for convincing me to spy on my own. Damn him for being right to do so. Magda despised politics and skullduggery. She knew full well politics and military went hand in hand, being a proud Roman and therefore Cohort tradition.

She just didn't like it.

A cleared throat interrupted Magda's eavesdropping. A serving lad stood nervously, the steam causing the intentionally minimal white tunic to cling to his form in very interesting ways. Magda liked what she saw. Judging by the tented tunic, the young man enjoyed the view as well. She grinned and swam over, fully intending to take advantage of the situation to release some tension. *Might as well have some fun with my business.* But as she moved toward him, she noticed his hand extended, index and pinkie pointed down.

"Your meal is ready, honored centurion. As you requested."

Frowning, Magda waved off the messenger and slipped out of the baths. Moments later, clad in thick robe and dripping on the cold marble floor, she met with Brock and Niall under the shadow of Hermes within the Curia's airy dome.

"The servant signaled properly. Message received. What's so damn important that you dragged me out of the baths? I was there doing your skullduggery, after all."

"We just received word from one of our scouts. They tracked the new legal talent, that 'stag boy toy' you bragged about during dinner, to the Edfu estates. Seems the Court decided to host their own festival."

Gossip travels faster than light, especially among soldiers. "You're riled up because of that? He hasn't declared for either. If Doe wants to enjoy free champagne, good for him. Even better if it's at the Raptor's expense. If you're worried about him being wooed with wine and good times, get him down here to the baths. The boy will change his tune."

Brock grimaced, his usually stony front cracking further. "That may no longer be an option. My sources spotted him speaking with Selina Aegolius herself."

Niall let out a low whistle at the revelation. The younger of the Aegolius siblings, Selina had already etched out a reputation for intelligence and ruthlessness in the board rooms. The Amber Falcon had snatched more than one prize from the hungry jaws of the Senate on the corporate battlefield.

"One of our young bloods got antsy and tried to assassinate Ms. Aegolius, violating the terms of the Truce," Brock continued. "Worse still, he failed. Things are going to get messy. The Senate is asking you to use your prior connection with the lawyer, however tenuous, and do some damage control."

Magda cursed soundly and at length as the statues of the gods looked on. The Senate didn't ask; it meant an order. Dire situations called for the most desperate measures, forcing her to resort to that most hated of tactics.

Diplomacy.

CHAPTER 6

STARS TWINKLED merrily in the night sky, uncaring of the desperate scrambling of earthbound mortals below. A fact which Jon found rather rude as he stumbled up to the offices of Arkadas & Associates, covered in blood and desperate for help. Jon slammed the owl face knocker on the heavy doors, the wood and iron an anachronism in the modern age. The knocker fit the looming buildings aesthetic, a twisted love affair between a medieval cathedral and asylum.

A blocky central building sat, stately and imposing, with two heavy wings jutting from its sides. Thickly paned windows gazed out like baleful rows of unseeing eyes from a brick façade, brackish with age and the unkind touch of the elements.

Fluted chimneys marked its gabled roof like grave stones to merry hearths long past, all of them still and cold save one. The solitary plume of billowing smoke might as well have been a lighthouse to Jon's fevered mind. *Someone's in there! Someone who might be able to make sense of this insanity.* Iron knocker banging on aged wood, the blood-speckled lawyer held to that thought like a life raft, trying not think about the impossible nightmare he'd witnessed.

Jon's mind still struggled to grasp the horrors he'd seen at the Aegolius Estates. It consumed his mind as he drove from the solitary mansion, numbly following the pleasant voice giving directions from his phone.

Jon thought he'd known the game when he confronted Selina. He expected backdoor deals or maybe mob connections. Dark rumors always hung around the legal giants, but the young Doe always dismissed the more fanciful stories. You didn't exactly take slurred third-hand rumors by drunken fraternity pledges swearing they'd heard it from their best friend's roommate's second cousin, as gospel.

What Jon witnessed at the mansion dropped his world out from under him.

Selina's arm, bronze and bloodied, as it tore through flesh and bone. He'd heard the howl, seen the body shrink as his beautiful host dragged her clawed hand out the attacker's chest. *All that blood.*

Then Selina, with her guests and staff, carried on as though nothing out of the ordinary happened. The party continued merrily, hidden behind rows of trees and polite requests for your invitation, never mind the bodies and blood stains. *Maybe that's why their floors are all marble and hardwood. Easier to clean up the mess. Sorry for the trouble, Jeeves, didn't mean to bleed all over.* A strained hiccup bubbled out of him. *My poor jacket. Awful polite of them to give me a loaner while they dry cleaned.* He tugged at his pristine borrowed garment. A murderer's coat. *What a rip off, Judas got some silver and all I get is a loaner. It's not even my color.* More hiccups came, faster and faster, as Jon's stomach heaved.

No sooner did a tired looking attendant open the door then Jon vomited onto their finely polished shoes. Spitting bile and regurgitated crab cake from his mouth, Jon looked up with a weak grin. "Jon Doe, practicing legal counsel. Here to see Mr. Arkadas."

One disgusted look and vomit scented apology later, the door man ushered Jon inside, now looking less tired and far more irritated. The interior wasn't any more inviting than the exterior. Cheap fluorescent tubes hummed overhead, washing the room in cold light and bleaching any color from the minimal furniture. A scattered handful of haggard looking plants did little to liven the place up. Sea green wallpaper hugged the walls. A handful of chairs and end tables, uncomfortably reminiscent of a dentist's waiting room, clustered off in a corner. Black and white checkered linoleum only underscored the aging, clinical feel of the place. An intimidating receptionist desk sat and front in center like a linebacker.

Shell-shocked as he was, Jon's mouth continued on autopilot. "Love the décor. Very early Bedlam. Did it come with the place or did you hire Dr. Frankenstein as your interior decorator?"

The disgruntled fellow walked around the large desk to pick up an old corded phone, another archaic remnant in the place, leaving Jon to fend for himself. Jon steadied himself on the plastic of the chairs, trying to ignore his protesting stomach. The dizzying tile pattern and hazy luminescent lighting wasn't help him keep the food down. As Jon struggled not to throw up, he eavesdropped as best he could on his charming concierge. He caught snippets of his chaperone's one-sided conversation. "Yes sir. No sir, definitely not bleeding, though he does rather look like one of those winos on Third street."

The part of the Harvard graduate not in shock took immediate offense to such slander to his immaculate sense of style. *You deal with shapeshifting monsters brawling at a party and see how you hold up.*

The attendant nodded and hummed a few more "Yessirs" before hanging up.

"Mr. Arkadas will see you now. This way, please. Try not to make another mess."

My dear desk jockey, next time I hurl I'm aiming for your shirt. The guide led the bedraggled lawyer down the black and white hallway, spirited up a spiral staircase with wrought iron railing, emptying them onto the third floor. The new hallway traded in its black and white tile for a floral pattern carpet in the same delightfully sickening sea green as the wallpaper. It nearly made Jon puke again at the sight. *He dares judge how I look surrounded by this gaucherie? Those in hideous houses should not throw stones.*

They trotted along flanked by scowling pictures of heavily joweled men until Jon's guide stopped by a heavy wooden door, an intricate carving of an oak covering its entirety. Even Jon's shell-shocked mind could appreciate the beauty, particularly given how grotesque the rest of the place looked. The roots seemed to coil into the carpet as its leaves brushed against the frame. Small woodland animals hid amongst the leaves, watchful owls a singularly reoccurring motif. Amidst the delicate woodwork, an embossment proudly proclaimed "Arkadas."

With such an ostentatious display, there could be no doubt whose office they stood at.

His guide gave a polite double rap on the door, announcing them without actually entering or saying a word. *Professional and discreet staff. Thick heavy paneling. If I see a painting wink at me, I'm bolting.* Jon got the sense that a lot of back door deals went on beyond that oaken portal. The esteemed Mr. Doe tried very hard not to think about how many secrets, and how many people, never left Arkadas' office. A booming voice called them through.

His escort waved Jon in and shut the door, never once looking inside. Despite the room's spacious size, it managed to feel oppressive and small. Cigars, brandy, and old wood weighed heavily in the air. A single light blazed overhead, muted by a stained-glass Tiffany fixture. Groaning bookcases lined the room, packed to the brim with legal books, ancient texts, and artifacts from around the world. A statuesque grandfather clock ticked away, tucked between two bookshelves. *Museum, library, and trophy gallery.*

The door behind Jon seemed to be the only way out. Some might call it a fire hazard, some might say secure. Others might just say paranoid.

A roaring fire blazed away within a fireplace, its cherry distressed oaken mantle mirroring the bookshelves. An unnecessary affectation, given the frigid air conditioning but it performed its true purpose. It made a statement. *More wealth, more power.*

Three figures turned their eyes on Jon as he entered the room and he got the impression he'd interrupted something important. Suddenly, Jon wanted to be anywhere but in that room.

A tall man sat by the blazing fire, long legs folded in one of several plush dark leather chairs. Though wearing a classic three button business suit, it defied tradition with a garish color scheme. Brilliant crimson jacket and trousers, an equally carmine tie, coupled with a yellow button-up vest shining underneath. Instead of coming across as Ronald McDonald at a boardroom meeting, the man projected a tangible sense of dignity and restraint. A knowing smile rested easily on his terra-cotta face. He reminded Doe of a thousand carved Buddhas the world over; serene and patient. A particularity impressive feat given his very loud getup. *Gain enlightenment, lose fashion sense I guess.* Jon couldn't believe it was a fair trade.

Despite the serene man's garish outfight, the lady, and there was no doubt she was aught but a lady, held her own.

She stood with regal poise, back to the fireplace wall, in a simple black suit, comfortable and utterly utilitarian. Her burnt gold complexion needed no shiny bauble to compete with it. A wickedly curved sword sat at her waist, its shining hilt dazzling against its owner's stark attire. She possessed an air of casual watchfulness, a hunting cat at rest. Amber eyes ceaselessly scanned the room, taking the newcomer in at a glance, before continuing their endless circuit. In contrast to her relaxed lethality, her seated companion remained an isle of calm.

The third inhabitant filled the room by his sheer presence. This was the owner of the building and everything in it, Arkadas himself.

Seated behind a handsomely cut wooden desk, a timeless classic adored by executives and insecure power mongers alike for its projected masculinity, the large man glared at the vomit scented lawyer. Clouds of cigar smoke curled past thick salt and pepper mutton chops. Arkadas' bald pate shone in the dim light. Bushy brows lifted and fell with each puff of his stogie as owlish eyes glared at Jon with patrician arrogance, a man used to giving orders and being obeyed. Jon mistrusted him on sight. *Bastard could be Old Man Bewford's brother.*

Wearing a severely cut burgundy suit, Arkadas seemed as anachronistic as his building, a relic from a time when the Industrial Revolution was the hottest thing on the block and Britannia ruled the waves. Jon incongruously envisioned Arkadas plastered on a World War I poster, pointing imperiously at any passerby. *I want YOU to do something for ME!*

Shaking out a bit of his cigar into a china ashtray, he waved Jon in with a meaty hand.

"Mr. Doe, I presume? I am Archibald K. Arkadas." It sounded like an imperial pronouncement or title of office. "You keep some odd hours, my boy. We expect our employees to arrive early, but you beat them all." The stout smoker guffawed loudly at his own joke. "Have some tea. It is an ungodly hour."

Jon blinked, only now noticing an elegant silver pot sitting on a mirrored tray surrounded by diminutive cups. "Tea? Uh, sure. Thank you."

Red turned in his chair to smile at his standing associate. "Betai, since you are already up, would you be so kind as to assist our guest?"

The silent warrior flowed from the wall to pour tea, one hand lightly resting on the hilt of her sword the entire time. Without spilling a drop, she passed Jon a cup one-handed, making the entire process one interconnected dance, each movement performed with lethal grace, economy of motion, and confidence.

I've seen professional bodyguards with less poise. Jon decided in that instant that he never wanted to see her use her sword.

"Thank you." The silver cup shook in Jon's hands, scalding tea spilling onto the little saucer. *Damn. Thought the shakes stopped a while back.*

Three sets of eyes watched as Jon drank down the bitter steaming liquid as tried to get his nerves under control. He didn't need years of legal training or the cutthroat halls of Harvard to know he couldn't show any weakness. *Any blood in the water and I'm as good as dead.*

Arkadas' piercing gaze bored into the beleaguered consultant, measuring him for a suit or sizing him up for a coffin. Apparently satisfied, or at least less displeased, Arkadas thumped the desk with a meaty fist.

"Allow me to introduce my associates. The lamppost is Siddartha Vanara. You can just call him Ganesh." Jon winced at the tasteless remark.

Rather than take offense, Siddartha smiled and shook Jon's hand. "Ganesh is fine by me, young man. It's worked so far, why stop now?" He chuckled warmly, as though laughing at an old joke. "This is my companion and bodyguard, Betai Ka Bagha. She does not shake hands." Ganesh took in the Harvard graduate's incomprehension as his lips tried to form the unfamiliar words. "Betty is perfectly suitable."

Sheepishly grateful, Jon smiled back.

With a great harrumph, Arkadas commandeered the conversation again. "With the niceties out of the way, let's hear why you showed up here looking so bedraggled. Judging by your appearance and the hour you stopped by, to say nothing of a phone call from one of the famed Aegolius siblings telling us to expect you, I presume you have quite a tale to tell us."

Jon took a deep breath and launched into his tale. Despite back tracking, stuttered stops, and breaks for tea, Jon felt much better afterward. It sounded so ludicrous when spoken out loud, Jon had half convinced himself it couldn't be true. *Must have been something in my drinks. A staged kidnapping and props at the party. Any moment they are going to laugh and tell me this is an elaborate hoax. Hazing the new guy.*

Arkadas' thunderous guffaws quickly destroyed that forlorn hope. It wasn't the temperate giggle of an incorrigible prankster. It was the hardened caw of a Wall Street vulture that mocked others' misfortune and saw opportunity in their woes.

"An assassination attempt? At the Raptors' estates? Congratulations are in order, my boy! You've only been on the job a few days and you've already cocked it all up." He lit another cigar, puffing noisily. "When Ms. Aegolius called, she didn't mention anything about that. Hah! At least I don't have to pay for the dry-cleaning bill this time around. Bodies always cost extra." Arkadas' casual acceptance of the bloody murder and clinical dismissal of the cover up and disposal of the corpse, set Jon's hands shaking all over again.

The overtaxed Mr. Doe clamped his hands down on the cup until his knuckles were as white as the porcelain. He knew those in his profession tended to be ruthless, that it was a dog eat dog world, but nothing in Jon's experience prepared for him for this. *I thought the old guard at Harvard were cold-blooded. Callousness, apathy, and greed, the holy trinity of the dollar bill, nothing new. I get that. Hell, that's my profession. This is something different. Something darker.*

Picking up on the young man's distress, Ganesh reached over from his seat and gently removed the cup from Jon's hands before it cracked. Ganesh frowned at Arkadas, a teacher chiding a schoolchild on a lesson. "Compassion, old friend! Mercy and patience belong to great minds."

Arkadas forwent the advised mercy and instead loosed another great harrumph of pungent cigar smoke. "Hogwash and nonsense. Time is money and mercy is the last plea of the incompetent. At least a blood bath on the hill explains the Aegolius siblings' calls for an emergency meeting. I'm supposed to be seeing them…" he pulled an elaborate golden pocket watch from the vest of his voluminous coat, "…shortly. Hmmph."

Arkadas lifted his bulk from the capacious chair and pressed one large finger to the intercom on his desk. Lined in brass, it looked old as the house. He pointed with his cigar, embers glowing like a baleful eye. "I'll deal with this situation. One which, I might add, you put on my plate, Mr. Doe. In the meantime, you can speak with our resident representative on this case." The big man scowled harder, which struck Jon as somehow physically impossible. "The little shit is an attaché, a loaner if you will, so any idiotic thing that comes out of his fool mouth may or may not represent my firm, understood? Good." Ringing the buzzer impatiently, Arkadas yelled through the desk communicator. "MARC! GET YOUR PASTY ASS IN HERE!"

It consistently amazed Jon how sometimes manners and decorum only went skin deep. *All the money in the world and not an ounce of refinement. Maybe he only keeps up the old money airs around clients.*

"You called, Master Hedwig?" A short fellow entered the room, a stone's throw over five feet. His expensive suit hung loosely and looked like it'd been slept in. Lanky jet-black hair framed a face designed for insouciant grins, demonstrated by the one currently plastered across it. A tint of darker undertones clung to his pallid skin, faded echoes of a tanner complexion. The pallor seemed unhealthy, speaking of too many hours in front of a computer screen and an avid and insistent avoidance of the sun. Dark eyes glittered with intelligence, alert and sharp despite the hour. Something about his slouch and smirk seemed aggravatingly familiar, but Jon's wearied mind couldn't pin it down.

The new arrival sized him up in the same way, eyes darting up and down momentarily before a wide smile broke across his face, showcasing brilliantly white incisors. "Bravo, Jonny Boy. You really stepped in it this time."

Jon's jaw dropped nearly to the floor. *Now I recognize that shit eating grin!* "Marc? Marc Sipskos, it is you, you gangly bastard!" Forgetting propriety at the sight of a friendly face, especially one the lawyer never thought he'd see again, Jon Doe abruptly embraced his Harvard partner in crime. Marc responded with all the warmth and social grace Jon remembered; an awkward a double pat on the back for the long-separated co-conspirator.

Glad to see success hasn't changed him much. Jon thought ruefully as he pulled back, rubbing where his old friend hit him with unexpected strength. The lanky-haired technician felt like a wire rack, all knobby hard edges and zero yield.

Ignoring the touching reunion, Arkadas wound an expensive looking scarf around his neck and shrugged into an oversized coat. "You know each other. Good. Maybe now Marc will move his ass. Sipskos, grab the Beachfront files and bring the newbie up to speed." Arkadas paused at the door to nod to his friend, scowl thawing fractionally, confirming Jon's suspicion that manners only applied to social equals.

Hired help doesn't rank high enough to bother.

"Vanara, we'll continue another time." Granting a perfunctory "ma'am" to Betai, Arkadas vanished out the door.

Taking the stodgy businessman's departure as his cue, Ganesh stood as well. "My friends, our host has the right of it. The hour is late, and it is best to rest and restore a weary mind and body when confronting troubles. Jon, a pleasure to meet you and I wish you the best. Marc, a joy as always."

Marc tipped his chin in acknowledgment. Betai opened the door and glided through after scanning the corridor. Ganesh followed a few steps behind.

Jon looked his friend up and down as the door shut. "Marc. Marky Marc! Wow, how you been, man? Wait, no, scratch that. Important questions first and only, I remember the rules. What are you doing here?" Jon stopped and scratched his head, concern and confusion warring inside him as his mind tried to catch up. "For fuck's sake, Marc, *where* have you been?"

Marc shrugged and turned his head a bit, unkempt locks screening his face. "To answer your questions in order; I'm fine, office monkey work mainly, and it's a long, long story." Something about his old college buddy's tone made Jon shiver, despite the roaring fire. "Follow me, let's get you caught up."

CHAPTER 7

MARC WALKED in front of Jon, barely a shadow in the dim light. Jon's found-again friend walked them back down through the spiral staircase, heading farther back into the aging house. The two emerged into a large hall, a concave of paneled glass braced with ancient iron framework looming above, a window into the starry dark. Industrial metal cabinets stood in regimented lines. Smaller wooden ones, beaten and worn, dotted the area at irregular intervals, orbiting the desks which sat as lonely islands in the mess.

Fax machines, printers, and copiers sat wherever room existed and sometimes where there wasn't. The resulting mass of cords made a snaking tangle on the ground, terminating in overworked power strips. Strange shadows criss-crossed the expanse, mismatched lamps making a puppet show of desks, chairs, and rolling chalkboards. It reminded Jon of the Ludwig Von Drake from the old Disney cartoons.

The old quack would fit right in.

It looked like the office of mad scientists, some experimental mash up of Feng Shui and Chaos Theory and nobody remembered to clean up the mess.

An eerie stillness and deep chill hung over the workspace. Only Jon and Marc moved in the empty space. *Feels like a morgue in here.* Jon shivered in his jacket.

They arrived at what could only be Marc's desk. Rubik's Cubes, sliding puzzles, and a lone yo-yo sat next to piles and piles of notes, leaflets, and colorful sticky-note pads. Tiny sticky notes sprouted around the computer screen, turning it into a multi-color sunflower.

Yep, success definitely hasn't changed him. Jon looked again at his old friend, his stomach tightening in knots. *Then again, maybe it has.* Beyond the pallor, something indelible had changed in Marc. Something in the absentee genius' eyes, hunched posture, and the way he never seemed to move. Something that made Jon want to run for the door.

An awkward silence passed between then as Marc shuffled from cabinet to cabinet, gathering up a small mountain of folders and files. The stack met the desk with a weighty thump.

Jon cocked an ear. *Huh. Echo, echo, echo.* He smiled, hand to ear, half expecting Marc to jump in on the joke, like in their Harvard days. His pale amigo did no such thing, much to Jon's increasing discomfort.

"This is it, the sum total of the Beachfront case." Marc tapped the pile, eyes locked on his desk.

"Thanks" Jon eyes bounced from the stack and up to his friend. "So. Been a while, buddy. How have you been?"

Marc's nose flared as if smelling something tasty, a strange look came over his face. Jon swore he looked almost… hungry. "Not bad."

Struggling with the verbal short shrift, Jon tried his damndest not to fall back on the old conversational standbys of compliments and idle banter. *Not with Marc. I remember how much he hated small talk. "Wasted air" he used to call it. Probably why he was never the life of the party.*

"That's good." Jon paced and looked about the place. "Not exactly the friendliest of office spaces. You guys should call your union."

Marc shrugged. "I've never been too concerned with superficial matters."

"Yeah, like hygiene or fashion sense." Thinking back on Marc's deplorable habits as a roommate in Harvard brought a wistful grin to Jon's face. "You haven't changed much since you fast-tracked out." Jon tried not to sound bitter about his friend's hasty exit from Harvard. Jon almost succeeded. Almost.

Marc gave another non-committal shrug behind his lanky hair and kept his eyes locked on some invisible spot on the desk. "Well, given my current condition, I'm not likely to change much."

That perked Jon's ears up. "Condition? Are you okay? It's not the Big C, is it?"

Marc's head jerked up and he barked out a cannon-shot laugh, harsh and short. "Cancer? Hah! I don't think I have to worry about that. Not anymore."

The blue-eyed wunderkind blinked in confusion but didn't comment. *Shit, for all I know, Marc thinks he's figured out how to avoid cancer with some weird vitamin mix or something. Wouldn't be the first time.* Jon shuddered as he thought about some of Marc's more ill-advised health short cuts. *Never seen anyone go through so much work to avoid working out and eating healthy. Hope this harebrained adventure doesn't end with him getting his stomach pumped.*

"Hey, mind if I eat? I'm famished." An odd question coming from the ill-mannered geek from Jon's Harvard days. Almost as odd as the twitch and odd glint in Marc's eyes that came with the question.

Could be he's one of his weird diets or, small miracles, he's learned some manners.

Jon gave a bemused thumbs up. "Yeah, sure, go for it."

Marc smiled, almost relived. Reaching into a mini-fridge under the desk, he pulled out a thick clear plastic bag, viscous red liquid pooled inside. Forgoing a straw, scissors, or anything else, Marc chomped down, noisily slurping out the contents.

Ick. Nope. Still no social graces.

Jon's poor stomach did a few flips as his friend vacuumed the liquid down. Even as Marc hummed happily around the bag, an odor hit Jon's nose, reminding the lawyer of doctor's visits, scraped knees, and childhood fist fights. The familiar copper tang forced Jon to confront a creeping suspicion. "Holy crap, Marc, stop! Is that blood?!"

Contentment drained away from Marc's face, replaced by confusion and surprise, flaccid container hanging from a corner of his mouth. Irritation cropped up on Sipskos' face even as Jon's words echoed in the room

"Well, yeah. What the hell did you think this was?" Snatching the emptied remains of his meal, Marc waved the drained pouch about, crimson tinted droplets spaying.

Images of the dead teenager at the manor flashed in Jon's mind and he flailed frantically at his friend's hand, desperate to push the bag away. Marc's arm hardly budged under Jon's efforts. *It's like shoving concrete around!*

"I don't know, a novelty energy drink or some crap. I stopped trying to make sense of your eating habits after your eel-juice and pomegranate smoothies. I just figured it was you being...you. The old you, I mean."

"Jon. This is the old me." Marc's eyes widened at his friend's befuddled look. "I've been a vampire since college." Still no metaphorical light bulbs of realization blinked on above Jon's head at the blunt reveal. Only dull shcok. Lights certainly flared in Marc's eyes, though.

Bright, angry, lights.

"You didn't notice? We roomed together for damn near a year and you couldn't tell?" Sharp fangs protruded over Marcs thin lips as he picked up steam. "Jon, you rarely paid attention in class, but I thought you cared enough to pay attention to me. Were you really too busy chasing skirts and acting out to get Mommy and Daddy's attention that you couldn't figure it out?!"

Jon held up his hand, palms out, placating, trying to slow his friend's tirade. "Figure out what? That my roomie and best friend became a blood sucking Dracula nerd? No! That option wasn't even on the table! Who thinks that?" Pissed and defensive, Jon fired back. "What about you? Why didn't you say something? You never told me any of that stuff, not even when you up and ran off!"

Disappointment and anger rolled off of Marc in waves. "I figured I didn't have to. That you already put it together. Remember senior year? When I got really sick?"

Jon nodded cautiously. "Yeah."

"And then changed all of my classes to night courses?"

More cautious nodding followed. "Sure."

Marc pinched the bridge of his nose. "You didn't find it strange that you never saw me eat normal foods or that I slept in the closet until I ordered black-out curtains?"

Cheeks burning hotly, Jon rallied. "Hey buddy, 'normal' is relative in your case. Remember your Tofu and Peanut Butter Surprises? Doesn't really fall on any culinary spectrum of normal I know of. And, might I add, the closet thing wasn't beyond the realm of possibility either. I thought you had calculated that to be the most efficient way of sleeping and giving me my space whenever I snuck a lady home."

Marc's eyes grew distant as he pondered his friend's impromptu defense, mind turning and churning away at the hypotheticals. "Not a bad thought. You aren't entirely wrong...but that's beside the point." The pallid attaché's gaze zeroed back on Jon. Marc flopped back into his chair with a deflated sigh. The resulting wash of air stank, an underlying moldering staleness, like air pushed out of a tire or an old balloon. "I suppose I figured you cared a bit more."

Silence reigned as the two friends stared at each other over a distance made vast by time and resentment.

Jon took the first faltering steps bridge that gap. "Marc...I did care. I still do! You were my best friend. Hell, my only friend! Us against the world, back at Harvard. They didn't like you because you weren't exactly Ivy League material and they hated me because I wouldn't shut up and play ball. Then you just vanished! How do you think I felt when my one amigo left without saying a word? You abandoned me." Jon suddenly grew fascinated with the floor, more than a little uncomfortable with all the emotional 'sharing' going on.

The vampire looked down, fiddling with a fountain pen. "That wasn't by choice. There was an...adjustment period." Shadows of pain crossed Marc's face for a moment, hands twitching, the pen reduced to a ruined mess of ink and metal in an instant of remembered pain.

The sight of his friend, who struggled with opening jars of mayonnaise at the dorms, accidentally crush a metal pen hit Jon hard. *Damn. What kind of shit has Marc been through? Screw it. Undead blood sucker or not, but he is still my best friend.*

"Marc. I've been a jerk. I should have asked about you. Called, or something. It just, dammit, it hurt too much. My best friend, the one guy I could trust, up and left without a word. It hurt." He took a deep breath. "I'm sorry."

The dead man's eyes went from his ink stained hands to the warm-blooded fellow across from him. A heartbeat passed. Then another. A dopey grin slowly crept onto Marc's face. "Don't make this weird."

Jon's choked snort echoed in the dark chamber. "Yeah, because being on an episode of 'My Accountant is a Vampire' isn't making it weird."

As the two snickered like school boys, the years fell away, if only slightly, for the estranged friends.

"If you're going to do your job and hope to make it out in one piece, listen and listen well. I have to bring you up to speed and we have no time to waste." Snatching up a yo-yo, the dead man looped a complex series of patterns as he lectured his former roommate, same way he did in their Harvard days, catching Jon up on whatever class the lout skipped, flirted, or slept through.

"Point the first; your employers aren't human. Well, some of them are, but not the ones pulling the strings. Both Decks and Domes and Rising Sun Development are fronts for the interests of two ancient powers. First, the Senate, which you can simply think of as Senate because I know you failed our Latin classes. They back Decks and Domes. Our second contestant is the Court of Raptors, backing Rising Sun. Both Houses, as the power blocs are known, are part of a loose alliance of Mythics, which is what non-humans like to call themselves, known as the Western Concordat. The greatest and most powerful Mythics came together under a loose agreement with codes of ethics and honor detailing..." Seeing the glazed look in Jon's eyes, familiar after dozens of Harvard lectures, Marc shifted gears. "Doesn't matter right now. Big picture, short version." Marc's yo-yo spun in complex loop-de-loops as he continued.

"Long, long ago in a galaxy far, far away, by which we mean the Mediterranean sometime when Athens was the place to visit, the various supernaturals and things-that-go-bump-in-the-night decided they liked the perks of human society, such as wine, fine foods, and indoor plumbing and wanted in on the action. It wasn't a terribly radical concept in and of itself. They'd been living alongside humans for most of recorded history."

Jon cocked his head, eyebrows pinching quizzically, waiting for the other shoe to drop. Then he realized his friend wasn't kidding. "You're telling me I work for monsters, creatures straight out of Grimm's Fairy tales, and that those same slavering beasties run the two biggest legal firms in the Western Hemisphere?!"

"Correct. And before you ask, no. Old Man Bewford wasn't a Mythic, only an asshole."

Jon fumed for a minute, struggling to fully come to terms with Marc's matter of fact revelation that things not only went bump in the night but they also wrote his paychecks. "Wait, back up. So these fanged monsters one day decide to buy real estate in ancient suburbia and it just happens? Really? That's it? I call bullshit. These big bad critters visit one dust covered hut in ye olden times and decide, hey, maybe we should set up shop and nobody bats an eye?"

Marc nodded. "Sure. All the ancient myths and legends always involve two parts; the human and the monster. Granted, the way human folklore goes, the business end of a sword was usually involved and terminated the monster part. Hmm, come to think of it, monster folklore kind of agrees. Anyway, the point stands. We've always been neighbors, always will be."

Jon couldn't tell which part Marc meant when he said "we." *I think I'll let that part of the lesson be ambiguous.*

"Mythics simply had to adapt their methods to blend in. Your particular employers trace their roots to the ancient Mediterranean. They saw what many humans working together could do and wanted to emulate that success. Their ancestors, some few of whom are still alive today, decided to get involved in a truly evil thing; politics."

Jon snickered and Marc grinned. Just for a second, a spark of the old days flickered brightly. *Damn, good to see something of my amigo is still there, fangs and all.*

"The old creatures worked in the shadows, using their abilities to accrue wealth and power in ways no mortal could. They could command the waves, haul great stones from the earth with ease, even spy upon and murder political rivals. Hard to claim "assassin" when it looks like a pack of wild animals did it. Some of them, the shapeshifters, had a natural edge over their more obviously monstrous kin when it came to blending in with humanity. They've set their roots in deep, getting involved with the big names; Rome, Greece, and Egypt. These Shifters integrated themselves into all aspects of human society. And, as before, they fought tooth and nail, making damn sure no one found out about their bloody little shadow war."

Jon blanched as images of a mutilated teen and spreading crimson puddle surged to mind. "Seems like things haven't changed much."

"It hasn't. These Shifter Houses are ancient, ruthless, connected, and concerned with three things: Power, Power, and Power. Face is important to them and they will never forget a slight." Marc sighed and Jon jerked back to avoid another nose full of graveyard. "Which, regrettably, brings us to our current fiasco."

"The Houses are always looking to expand their territories and holdings. They had been pressuring Quarks Inc., a local software company that bought up some prime beachfront property a while back when the buying was good, to sell to the Houses. One snag in that plan. Ramses Higgs, the founder of Q-Inc, refused to sell. Seems he and the Shifters had a bit of a history."

As Marc picked up steam in his story, the yo-yo spun faster and faster. Jon couldn't tell what struck him as more surreal: the ancient conspiracy of bloodthirsty monsters or his vampire buddy doing tricks with a child's toy.

"Higgs hated both of the Houses. He ran into some Mythics back in his MIT days. Thought they were pricks back in college. Still thought they were pricks when they asked him to sell, years later. He was one of the few pure mortals to stand up to the Shifters."

Jon's low whistle echoed in the dark workspace. "Sounds like a real badass."

"Yeah, he was."

Jon cocked an eyebrow. "That is a very ominous 'was' there, Marc."

"As you are learning firsthand, the Houses don't usually take no for an answer. Quarks Inc. challenged them multiple times and carved out a sphere of influence out here in the West Coast. So, the Houses started eyeballing Higgs' business. They applied pressure, both legal and otherwise, and stymied his every effort to develop the land. They pulled out every trick in the book and eventually drove Q-Inc into bankruptcy."

"All because the guy wouldn't sell? That seems a tad excessive."

Marc shook his head, frowning. "Actually, the Houses were being exceedingly polite. They honestly respected Higgs' savvy, courage, and wit. So much so that they treated him as an equal. Which means Ramses Higgs got to walk away and die in bed without 'attacked by wild dogs' as his obituary."

Jon's face turned paler than Marc's. "Holy shit. Really?"

Marc nodded slowly, toy abandoned. "Check the newspapers, it's all over the obituaries and tabloids. The 'wild dogs' and 'escaped zoo animal' angles are the most common cover story for the majority of Shifter related killings. Speaking of which, you ought to get a visit from the local authority, one Lieutenant Jerry Reiger. He runs interference on street level affairs, keeping a lid on things for the higher ups. Reiger makes sure no one asks any uncomfortable questions. At least, not more than once" Marc snapped his fingers under Jon's nose, dragging the blue-eyed lawyer away from visions of badges and mauled bodies dancing in his head. "Don't focus on that right now. I need you to pay attention and understand the people you are dealing with."

Two thumbs up confirmed Jon's attention, if not understanding, so the vampire continued.

"At any rate, Quarks Inc. goes under, Higgs puts his assets on the market, and both the Court and Senate bid on his property and holdings, using the usual backdoor methods to ensure the sweetest deal for them. But there were some complications." Marc looked around at the desks in the office, grief, hunger, and disgust warring on his face. "Higgs wasn't a gracious loser. He went to the grave cursing all Shifters, knowing full well they would descend like vultures before his body was cold. As a final "fuck you" to his enemies, Higgs laid out huge sums of his own money to poison the pot. He bogged the legal purchase down in a tar-pit of legal defense, all to get the Houses to go through less than legal channels. Not that they need a lot of prodding to do that. Higgs also paid to fudge the paperwork for the estate sale. Before anyone knew it, both D&D and Rising Sun claimed a piece of the pie. It was a mess."

Jon winced, connecting the dots. He did not like the picture it made. *Too much like a chalk outline at a murder scene.*

"Since neither one acquired it through honest means, nobody could present a paper trail to justify their purchase. The Beachfront property suddenly became a hot new battleground, not only because of its substantial net worth, insanely inflated due to the sunk costs of both Houses to acquire it, but because of pride. Neither the Court nor the Senate wanted to admit that Higgs got one over on them, and they sure as hell didn't want to cede it to their rivals. The Houses didn't want any kind of lengthy legal battle drawing outside attention. So they pulled in Arkadas to handle the deal. Arkadas is banker, broker, and money launderer for the Mythic polities here out west in the Sunset Lands."

Poor Jon, desperately trying to keep track of the pieces, shot his hand up on pure reflex, old Harvard habits kicking in. "Sunset Lands? What the hell is that?"

"It's what the Mythics call the West Coast. California and Mexico, mainly, though it stretches north and east a ways."

"Jesus. Does everything have to have a cutesy sinister nickname?"

"The Houses are a bunch of ancient shape shifting conspiracies claiming divine right to rule and with lineages stretching back into antiquity. Of course they have fancy names for everything and speak in code. Now, if you are done wasting air, let me finish."

Jon rolled his eyes but waved his friend on.

"Back to Arkadas. Almost everyone goes through him. They don't trust Arkadas, because the Senate and the Court aren't idiots, but they do trust in his greed. The old blowhard won't ruin a good deal. Arkadas knew there was only one way the Beachfront Case could end. Badly. So, in the continued interest of peace and profit, Arkadas & Associates hired a neutral, expendable, third party. You." Marc poked his friend in the chest hard enough to rock Jon back.

"Understand, they didn't do it because of your talent, good looks, or charm. You, yourself, are largely irrelevant. They chose someone close enough to Shifter blood to be useful to them and far enough removed from power that they wouldn't be missed. You aren't even really a consultant. Not to them. Your primary role in this is as a sacrificial lamb."

"Screw that. If these monstrous bastards agreed on this, why the hell can't they just abide by the outcome?" Jon grabbed the desk in a white knuckled rage. Despite the Harvard graduate's best efforts, the table remained frustratingly unflipped.

"They'll abide by it. Honor demands they accept it. But honor also demands the Houses make up for lost face. They do that by making an example out of whoever, or whatever, denied them. Which, in this scenario, happens to be you." Marc twisted a Rubik's Cube with blistering speed, hands a blur on the colored squares. "You happen to be low enough down the totem pole that you won't be missed, nor will your death offend anyone important. By that same token, you are still Blood, so your death counts toward balancing the scales."

"Why does everyone keep saying "blood" like that?"

Marc blinked. "Like what?"

"Like it's a codeword or a CIA acronym or something. So what if I have blood? Everyone does."

Marc shot his whining companion a blank stare.

"Umm, present company excluded."

"Blood, in this case, means that you have Mythic blood in you."

Jon scoffed. "No, I don't."

"Yes, you do."

"I don't! That's stupid, you're stupid, this whole thing is stupid!"

As Jon huffed and puffed in a display fit for a six old throwing a tantrum, Marc looked away, hand clamped on his mouth.

"First, calm down, Jon. Slow down your heartrate and get the blood pressure down. It's distracting. Second, your whining to the contrary, yes, you do have Mythic blood. Or rather your ancestors did. Why do you think you have the last name Doe? Where do you think all that money you spend so easily came from? Obviously, it's diluted but you still have enough Shifter in you to be the perfect catspaw for the Houses."

Jon groaned. "I'm the freaking Goldilocks of the Damned, is that it? Not too hot, not too cold…"

"…But just right. Exactly. The good news is that while you are a pawn, you are a valuable pawn. You won't be swept away until you reach the end of the board. Others haven't been so fortunate." Marc's gaze traveled the room, hand falling from his mouth. Jon got the distinct impression the scattered desks weren't empty because coworkers decide to use their saved-up vacation days. The vampire paper shuffler shoved the stack of Beachfront paper's into Jon's chest.

"For now, take the paperwork and look through it. Once you've read it and gotten a firm grip on the nuts and bolts, come back and we can strategize." Marc frowned, eyes moving as he rapidly sifted through his mental notes. His brows furrowed as he stumbled over some snag.

That's the "Oh crap" look. Here comes the really bad news.

"One last thing. You need to do this quick. We're on a time crunch."

"Why? Untangling legal snafus takes forever, especially with clusterfucks like this one. The big dogs live and breathe this stuff, they have to know that."

"Normally, yes. But with the current tensions, it's practically guaranteed both Houses need to resolve this mess quickly so they can back to business as usual. Arkadas left to meet with Aahmes Aegolius, correct?"

Jon thought back to his earlier meeting with the cigar smoking Arkadas. "Yeah. Right about now."

Marc nodded glumly. "That cinches it. The assassination attempt just kicked up the time table. The Houses are going to put on the pressure. We are at the eleventh hour. Better get reading, Jonny boy. Do or die. Literally."

CHAPTER 8

"THE SENATE has gone too far! They have violated the terms of the Truce. As such, I demand their claim to the Beachfront property be made forfeit and the deed granted to the Court, effective immediately." Aahmes Aegolius' voice rang with passion and authority, his fist pounding upon the elegant wood of the meeting table, the very image of a preacher or fiery judge. It was all quite tedious to Selina Aegolius sitting next to her wrathful brother. She'd heard it all before.

He needn't play so hard to the crowd. It's not as if there's much of one to play to. Selina thought wryly, looking across the table to Arkadas, the only other soul in the dark lit room. The broker had agreed to the late-night meeting to discuss the recent gaucherie at the Edfu estates. *An assassination attempt and one scared consultant. My, what a way to spend an evening. Hope the poor dear hasn't run for the hills.* Pushing the frightened Mr. Doe from her mind, she focused on the debate at hand.

"Hmm, a small and meagre list of demands. Is that all?" Arkadas puffed serenely upon his cigar, unmoved by the elder Aegolius' bluster.

Not that Aahmes honestly expected him to be. Selina watched the two posturing Shifters with a serene look which managed to convey a state between cool interest and intense scrutiny. The look had sent conspirators and interviewees alike sweating and stammering, so it always amused Selina to adopt it. *Always hide boredom behind poise and indifference. A valuable lesson learned at Court.*

"Due justice for their crimes. The Senate interfered with the impartial judgements of the representative by sending a harlot to lay with him."

"What of your invitation to an extravagant evening of wining and dining?"

"I simply wanted to explain the situation to the new consultant."

"And the kidnapping?"

Aahmes sniffed pointedly, the very image of poise and dignity, but Selina saw the minor tells that gave away the rage boiling inside. *My dear brother is not used to being defied.*

"Hardly worth mentioning in the face of the Senate' gross violation of the Truce. They attempted to assassinate my sister."

Arkadas took a long, lingering puff on his cigar, snubbing the remains in one of the ashtrays perennially present where the stodgy old beast went. "Some young hothead goes and does something stupid and gets gutted for their trouble. Business as usual, Mr. Aegolius. Hardly worth noting at this stage in the game. The dumb bastard's dead, leave it at that. Call it a wash."

Selina laughed quietly, hand on her brother's arm to forestall further outburst. "I see the wisdom in your suggestion, Mr. Arkadas, having said as much to my brother earlier. Yet his demands are not without merit. We expected the Truce to be held in good faith and it seems to be violated rather messily."

Her calm voice was met with a pointed "harrumph" from Arkadas. "I've already spoken to the Senate representatives. Nothing was sanctioned, it was a rogue agent."

Aahmes narrowed his eyes at Arkadas, leaning forward threateningly. "You took them at their word?"

"Given the amateur and sloppy nature of the attempt, I did."

The younger Aegolius held a hand before her, pointedly examining the same nails that had ripped the life from her assailant. "Arkadas, I'm almost hurt. Are you implying that I'm unable to fend off a few assassins?"

"No offense meant, Miss Aegolius, merely pointing out the respect I have for the talents of the Senate, and if I may, for the Court as well. Both of your Houses are far too talented for such pathetic half measures."

After a moment's consideration, Selina nodded, acknowledging the logic, while Aahmes continued to glare at Arkadas. "Have you no loyalty as a fellow child of the Sun?"

"I'm beloved of Athena, not Ra, my dear Aegolius. We tend to travel with the moon."

"A technicality. Ra is lord of all things of the air and that would entail a degree of obeisance on your part, Arkadas."

Selina cut the nascent theological argument short with a delicate cough, followed by a loud slap on the table when the two belligerents refused to heed her. "Focus, please. What of our new employee, Mr. Doe? I sent him to you, Arkadas. Is he still capable of performing his duty?"

"He's alive, if that's what you mean. Recovered quickly for a milkfaced nancy. I've given him over to Sipskos. The leech should bring him up to speed." Arkadas' venom laced tone told the Court siblings Arkadas' opinion of his vampire underling.

Selina nodded satisfied. "Thank you, Mr. Arkadas. We appreciate your understanding."

The talks dragged on, tensions defused, and spiraled into the usual pleasantries and promises to continue doing exactly what profited both parties. The Aegolius siblings walked from Arkadas' lair and slid into the armored shell of their limo. No sooner were they ensconced in the cream and gold metal Selina's eyes sparkled with mirth.

"Really, Aahmes? 'Have you no loyalty?' Laying it on a tad thick, don't you think?"

Aahmes held his calm mask for all of three seconds before a wide grin split his aquiline features. "I may have gone a bit far, freely admitted, but it was good fun nonetheless."

"This, dear brother, is why you never made leading role in the school plays."

"Perhaps, but I made a wonderful Mercutio."

Selina dismissed her brother's claim of thespian talent with a wave. "On that, we shall have to remain divided. Despite your dreadful performance, I think the talks went well."

"Indeed. We always suspected that Arkadas had spies in our ranks. This confirms it. He was prepared. He knew. Someone warned him ahead of time."

"Quite. Most likely the servants and certainly the guests."

Aahmes nodded, reaching for a bottle of bubbling water from the limo bar. "This narrows our search a bit. I'll spread word that we've ferreted out the traitors. Rumors of an Inquisition ought to send the cowards running. If not, there are always more direct methods of questioning." A sadistic hunger spread over Aahmes face. "The question that remains, however, is whether Jon Doe was complicit in the act."

Selina tapped one finger thoughtfully to her lips, a habit her brother's constant chiding never quite broke her of, and considered Doe's reaction at the party. "No. I took his measure. His fear was too real to be feigned. The poor fellow really is over his head."

"I should call off the Retribution Squads, then?"

Selina mouth drew down into a small moue of irritation. "Oh, goodness Aahmes you are incorrigible. This is a time for damage control not terror tactics. I'll send Reiger out to speak with our Mr. Doe. Please keep our killers on their leashes."

"Fear might make Doe more malleable."

"It might but I still hold that a softer touch is needed."

Aahmes nodded, accepting Selina's insistence. "As you say, dear sister. We shall try it your way. As your elder, I am only looking out for your wellbeing."

Selina smiled at her brother's protectiveness or what passed for it in their family. Amidst the literally cutthroat competition within the Aegolius ranks, Aahmes always held a soft spot for her, even going so far as to warn her of assassination attempts and playing favorites by eliminating her immediate rival family members. The smile faded as Selina thought back to Mr. Doe and his wide frightened eyes and her blood-stained reflection in them. Despite her best efforts to crush the wayward thought, the image lingered with her as the limo pulled away into the night.

§—§

Jon woke in his bed with a start, heart pounding in his chest. Confused and panicked, his eyes darted around his new room until Jon remembered he was in his new place in San Dominguez. Taking deep breaths, Jon struggled to calm down. *Holy crap, what a nightmare. Hob-knobbing with high-brow creatures from a cheap horror flick. I should write this shit down. It's garbage but I'm sure somebody in Hollywood would buy it. Feathers and claws.* Jon shuddered at the hazy memory, metallic talons covered in carmine. *God, those claws! Where did that come from? Must be the stress. That or someone slipped me some weird shit at the party.*

Just as the bleary-eyed legal consultant sat up, half convinced it had all been a dream, his eyes landed on a strange coat hanging on his doorknob. *The coat from the party.* Memories came flooding back. The party,

Selina, the attack. *All that blood.* The room began to spin, and a high-pitched ringing filled his ears. Clutching his stomach, the Harvard graduate ran to the bathroom and emptied bile into the toilet.

Clambering to the sink, Jon spat and cleaned his mouth first with water then with mouthwash. Then again with both.

Heart pounding in his chest, he snatched up his smartphone, prepared to get word out, letting all social media know that monsters existed…and froze. *What am I doing? What can I say?* Anything even resembling the truth could get Jon thrown in the looney bin.

At best.

At worst, the creatures that he worked for might decide slipping word to the authorities was a breach of client confidentiality and take it out of his hide. Literally. *No one would believe me.*

Jon Doe, practicing legal consultant, had a bit of a mental breakdown at the epiphany.

He kicked, he screamed, he cursed. He into his pillow. In short, he threw a tantrum.

Then, with a deep breath, Jonathan Augustus Doe set about his normal routine, getting up out of bed as if it were any other day. Shower, shave, brush. Style and gel. By the time Jon was done, he almost felt like himself again. Mr. Doe certainly looked the part, meticulous grooming as immaculate as ever. Jon took refuge in the normalcy of it, the sheer mundanity centering him.

Jon was so wrapped up in his routine that when the doorbell rang, the blue-eyed wunderkind paid it no mind. When the buzzer gave way to insistent rapping, Jon deigned to go investigate. By the time he reached the door to peek through the peephole, the rapping had become pounding.

On the other side of the door stood a tall, lanky man with a cigarette in his mouth, a hell of a lot of bags under his eyes, and a badge on his jacket proclaiming the letters SDPD.

Jon froze in shock at the sight of a servant of the law on his doorstep. *The police?! Shit. How, why?* More insistent pounding interrupted Jon's panicked inner monologue and the dulcet tones of a steady string of curses reached his ears. After a few breaths, Jon peeked again, disgust and surprise overtaking panic.

If this lanky bastard is police, standards must be dropping. Jon opened the door. *I'll just play it cool. No way would anyone with those monsters show up out of the blue in broad daylight.*

"Morning, Mr. Doe. Guess you aren't dead." The officer's tone made it clear that "good" didn't associate with "morning" very often, if ever. "I'm Lieutenant Jerry Reiger with the San Dominguez Police Department." The plainclothes officer took a deep drag of his cigarette, continuing without skipping a beat, pungent smoke chasing his words. "That's the day job anyway." Puff, exhale, puff. Reiger inhaled and exhaled with the regularity of a metronome.

This guy's a damn chimney. Grateful the cloying smoke was far from his expensive silk and cashmere wardrobe, Jon coughed into his fist and choked out a polite inquiry. "Welcome to *Casa de Jon*, Officer Reiger. What can I do for you?"

"Stop stirring up shit with the freaks, first of all. I've got enough work doing damage control as it stands without you kicking off Weird War III."

Jon froze, shocked at the casual mention of the monsters his poor mind was just now wrapping itself around. "I...I'm not sure what you are talking about..."

The officer pinched the bridge of his nose, and flipped Jon the bird. Clearing his throat, Reiger straightened his slouch and launched into a proclamation. "As a duly recognized agent of the Houses, may they reign eternal, and in the name of the Truce, I am here to ensure the chosen representative remains unsullied and able to perform his duties unimpeded." Though his words followed a ritualistic cadence, Reiger drawled like a bored Catholic priest laboring through a sermon. The chain-smoking avatar of law and order looked Jon up and down, snorted, and took Jon's dumbfounded silence for assent. "Looks like you're in one piece. Great. Now with that out of the way, my duty here is discharged."

As Reiger turned, the befuddled lawyer snagged his arm. "Wait." Jon snatched his hand under Reiger's frosty gaze. "You know about these... monsters." Jon hissed the last word, looking around like he was afraid the men in white coats were ready to jump out of the bushes. "You know what they've done. Can't you stop them? You're a freaking police officer." Though hardly of a fan of law and order due to his career choice, desperate times made for strange bedfellows.

A casual shake of Reiger's head dashed any nascent hope for an ally. "Sorry kid, above my paygrade. I'm just the middleman. My keepers called me to come check on you. That's it." Reiger turned to look at Jon. "Y'know they filled me in on your exploits, Doe. Not even a week here and you manage to get involved in an assassination attempt on a high-ranking Court official, sleep with a war hero of the Sunset Cohort, and up the time table on a monster blood bath. Gotta hand it to you, you screwed up big and you screwed up fast. Probably a record." Reiger gave a slow clap.

Jon gaped at the sarcastic bastard. "What the hell am I supposed to do now?"

"You got your books from Arkadas, right? Read the damn manual. Should lay everything out there." The lieutenant slinked over to his car, cigarette trailing smoke like a train. "You want my advice? Get your affairs in order, then start praying, if you're the type. Me, I'd be finding that red-headed wolf from the club and go out with a bang. Several if you can keep it up. Be seeing you."

The nicotine stained officer drove off without a second look. Jon stared in disbelief at the retreating vehicle, willing Reiger to turn around and do something useful. *Never a cop around when you need one.*

Something the lieutenant said bounced around in Jon's brain. *Red-headed wolf from the club? Oh, fuck me, did he mean Magda?* The strange insults of the big mook who had kidnapped Jon took a far more sinister air. With a distinct sense of paranoia skyrocketing, Jon rummaged around his bedroom until he found Magda's hastily scribbled number. Jon's hand shook as he dialed the number. With no response, he dialed again. His hands shook less the time after that. Five or six more times in as many minutes and Jon's hands still shook but now with frustration. *Why the hell are you going to give me your number if you don't answer the goddamn phone?*

Texts proved no better. Hissing in disgust, Jon tossed the phone aside and dragged out Marc's paperwork. He piled it alongside the offending jacket at his work desk in the living room. There they sat, alongside Arkadas' welcome packet. All the items that proved the impossible events of the last few days weren't figments of an unraveling mind.

After a lengthy trial period of sitting down, standing up, and then pacing about, Jon abandoned his efforts to confront the paperwork with a sigh. His stomach responded with a rumbling gurgle. *Screw this, I'm getting food.* Not for the first time in his life, the young Mr. Doe ignored his problems and hoped they'd sort themselves out while he enjoyed a bite to eat.

§——§

After some delicious savory morsels to quiet his stomach, the nagging sense of doom invaded Jon's culinary escapism amidst the trendy cafes and beachside dives of San Dominguez. *Fine, if the phones are out, let's see if we can find her the old-fashioned way.* Cruising around the city, Jon turned the outing into one-part casual stroll around town, one-part desperate hunt for a needle in a haystack.

Jon drove from the beachfront area with its tourist trap hybrid of indie businesses and cookie cutter fast food joints before crossing over into suburbia and its attempted hip-chic, vibrant and pastel colors doing nothing to hide the cookie cutter houses. Nestled like a diamond wedge between them, old downtown beckoned with its coffee shops and brightly lit storefronts. Jon prowled the tightly packed buildings, hunting for Magda.

How hard is it to find one brightly dyed red head?

Finally, he retraced his steps, returning to *Howl*. Though closed, a few club goers still lingered about, either hung over or still drunk from last night's debaucheries. Jon's inquiries with the fur and leather crowd revealed Magda hadn't been around for a night or two. The exuberance they showed, to say nothing of the fangs and horns on display, did nothing to calm Jon's nerves. Before, he would have simply chalked it up to some new fad. After recent events, the lawyer couldn't dismiss it as simply another strange twist of bad fashion sense.

Though painfully curious and desperate to find Magda, Jon decided against probing further after taking a second and third look at the crowd. Jeans and leather wearing loungers glared at his silk and pressed slacks with suspicion. *Better not press. Might be rude. Rude might get me dead.*

Even as Jon bemoaned the inherent unfairness of the universe, he couldn't shake the nagging feeling of being watched. Jon checked his rear view, drove in circles, and played every cliché trick he learned from bad cop shows and old black and white noir films to ferret out trackers. Unfortunately, it worked.

Jon saw the same oddly dressed people watching him go round and round. They weren't in a hurry to be anywhere and simply watched him. These impromptu spectators ranged from business men in suits that really enjoyed their extended lunch breaks to, to dog walkers oddly attached to certain streets, to men and women in overalls that tracked his car every time it went by. They grinned when they caught Jon looking back at them.

That's just creepy. A shiver went up Jon's spine and he turned his head to see a smaller man with tanned skin and a worn fedora and outdate suit sitting at a café. The man's dark eyes took in Jon and his audience, before raising his coffee in salute. His sleeve fell back to reveal a strange tattoo, a series of numbers in black ink, along his arm. Despite the jovial, almost fatherly face, Jon felt a palpable sense of malice and hate come from the seated man.

Discretion is definitely the better part of valor. Time to leave.

Getting out of downtown San Dominguez, Jon snapped up a coffee of his own and headed home to sulk by the beach, somewhat dejected at his fruitless search and pondered his next step while sipping a caffeinated treat and watching the waves go by.

The universe worked in mysterious ways, true, but some constants remained. Jon was already struggling to come to terms with several uncomfortable truths of late, many of them bloody. Even though recent revelations had turned his world upside down, other rules remained locked in place. Murphy's Law, for example.

Color Jon surprised when a tap on the shoulder revealed the object of his search. He nearly dropped his drink when he turned and saw Magda standing there like an answer to his prayers. A small bit of serendipity that instantly set Doe on edge. *I might be charming, handsome, and utterly irresistible, but nothing's that easy. From what Reiger said she's involved in all the crazy crap happening lately.* He eyed the punkess suspiciously and noticed something indelible had changed. A hard edge of watchfulness hung about Magda, her riotous hair now a war banner and studded leather jacket transformed into armor.

The silence stretched out uncomfortably as the two stood around like teenagers on an awkward date.

Looking up and down the beach, Magda frowned and spoke first, as if conceding a point and really pissed about it. "Yo."

"Hey." *Down to monosyllables by the second date. Wonderful. Par for the course, lately. What happened to me that I go from schmoozing my way past bouncers to this mess?*

The pair walked along the beach in awkward silence, seagulls cawing and fighting over scraps. Jon emptied the remains of drink at the noisy sea birds and threw the cup into a nearby trash bin.

"So, do you have a religious objection to answering your phone? Communication is essential in business and life."

Shoulders moving in what might have passed for a shrug, Magda barely looked at Jon, gaze sweeping right and left. "Dead phone. Crushed phone, really. Damn thing deserved it, chirping at me all the time. Never liked the things anyway. Besides, been busy."

"Busy with what?" Jon tried not to sound petty and almost succeeded.

"Work. Other shit. Besides, I went looking for you. You weren't home."

Even casually said, that tidbit of information brought Jon up short. He wasn't a fan of stalkers, especially given current events. "Wait, how do you know where I live?"

For all her fierceness, in that instant, Magda looked like a puppy. A pierced, guilty, sulky puppy in a leather jacket with mismatched eyes and a slightly crooked nose. "Anyone can find you since you're on the payroll. Just have to ask business services."

Well, that brought my paranoia level up to Defcon 1! "So everyone knows where I live?!"

Another stubborn grind of the shoulders. "If they care enough to look. Buck, this isn't easy for me, so if you could shut up for a moment and follow me, I won't have to knock your teeth out."

Throwing an arm around Jon's shoulders, Magda herded him further down the beach. The two cut off the winding sand-sprinkled slab, trudging through the golden seashore until they came under the shadow of the boardwalk. Concrete made a sloping hill to the boardwalk above and stout wooden beams created a little hideaway from the rest of the beach. It made a private alcove, a romantic hideaway tucked away in the shade of the concrete and wood. Given the nature of recent events, make out sessions weren't on Jon's mind. *Great place to stash a body, too. Crap, how it is that my life has come down to that being a thought I have around an interesting date?*

Taking a deep breath, Jon decided to address the proverbial elephant in the room. "Let me see."

The leather clad warrior's challenging smile showed a glimpse of the woman Jon met at *Howl.* "What? Here? Now? You first, Jonny boy. You show me yours, I'll show you mine. Then, maybe we'll see how well they fit together."

Shockingly tempted to take her up on the distraction, if only to focus on living bodies and not dead ones, Jon forced his attention to the problem at hand. *This is a job. Just like any other. Except my life is on the line. All the more reason to keep it cold-blooded.* "No. I mean what you really are."

"Oh? What exactly is that?"

"Don't gaslight me, lady. I've seen things since the club. Things I don't want to believe. Fur and claws and blood and other shit. I didn't have a damn clue when a whackjob with a knife mentioned sleeping with the enemy, but then I met him and his sister at a party…" Clamping his mouth shut, Jon pushed down the visions, the fear, pushing it away in his mind. *Eyes on the prize, as always.* "I've put a few things together. Let me see what you are. What you people really are."

Magda's mismatched eyes glittered with a strange mix of admiration, irritation, and concern. "Oh please. Buck, a stiff breeze could knock you over."

Jon plowed on. "A friend, honestly he's more like my brother because he's cared a lot than the rest of my family, gave me some advice

about time tables being upped. I may know jack shit about shapeshifting monsters but deadlines I understand. I also understand that it's my
ass on the chopping block. I'm damn near certain you're involved, been
involved since the beginning, and I'm nobody's sucker. I want to know
what I'm getting into. Let me see."

"No."

Jon stood around expectantly for almost a minute before his brain
registered the refusal. "What? I nearly get killed, witness some poor kid
get gutted, plus stalked by a one-night stand, who, I have been led to
believe, may howl at the moon for shits and giggles. I think I'm owed
some answers."

Jon's whining earned him another pained shrug and mono-syllabic
response. "No."

"What the hell? You came looking for me, right? Make with the
howling already."

"I came looking for you to send a warning, Jon. I'm not some pet
who does tricks. I'm a warrior, Jon, and I don't care much for diplomacy
and I don't take orders well." She grinned at him with all the fire she'd
shown on their first night. "For what it's worth, laddy buck, the club was
a happy accident. You looked like a good lay, that's all. We had our fun
and you were a great fling but know this…" Magda seemed to draw into
herself, throwing off the sulking slouch like a discarded coat, her leather
jacket transformed into armor and the red hair seemed a blood-stained
banner of defiance. "I am Magda Lahm Dearg, centurion of the Sunset
Cohort. You are of us, Jon, but you aren't one of us. You are not my people. Not Blood. And certainly not Cohort."

Jon would have been impressed if he wasn't three seconds from losing his shit. *As if ANY of that is supposed to mean a damn thing to me.*
Jon ground his teeth. *More ominous implied capitalization. What is with
these people? They could say "Hot Dog" with terrifying implications.* Regardless, stonewalling was stonewalling. There was no mistaking the pride in

Magda's voice when she spoke of her people. That was where Jon saw his opening. *Time to switch tactics.*

Arms crossed, Jon unloaded his full snark, a scathing, condescending tone that sent rival speech and debate teams into fits and jealous boyfriends reaching for baseball bats. "Cohort? Look, your hobbies are your own, but I think I'm entitled to answer whether or not I'm part of some acting group."

His willful ignorance got results, fast. Magda's pale face turned red enough to match her hair. She slammed a fist emphatically into her chest and Jon's sternum ached in sympathy. He knew how strong those arms were. "I am the sword of the Senate and proud to be so. I've fought enemies uncounted, triumphed through bloodshed and loss, and defeated them all, from abyss-spawned Fomorians to those arrogant Raptors. I've known pain and won glory for it." She spread her arms wide, only a torn crop top beneath her jacket, the scars that criss-crossed her lithe body proudly displayed, each one a symbol of victory.

Jon rewarded the grand gesture with a dismissive wave of his hand. "Yeah, I can see your little group plays rough. Big deal. Try remembering the safety word next time."

In the blink of an eye, Magda closed the gap between them until her hot breath washed over Jon's cheek. Mr. Doe didn't even flinch. *Go ahead and throw that punch. I've been abducted, jumped out of moving cars, and had to wipe the blood from a murder from my face. Let's see if I can get some answers.*

"We're the inheritors of Romulus and Remus, Jon. Children of the gods. Even before Rome, our imperium held true. We've been guardians of this world since before Odysseus sailed for Troy." A snarl echoed in her words, a strange Doppler effect that popped goosebumps on Jon's arms. A beast spoke within her and Jon couldn't tell which of the two sounded more dangerous.

Which, told Jon it was working. *Almost there. Can't stop now.* Jon's batted his eyes prettily with his lips drawn in an exaggerated pout. "I didn't know you were Italian."

The valley girl performance earned the mouthy lawyer an immediate response. With a howl, Magda hurled Jon into the air. Sharp pain shot up his back as he connected with the boardwalk's support beam and fell to the sand below. Stars danced in his eyes and he struggled to catch his breath. *Shit, pushed too far again!* Jon clutched his screaming back and looked up with teary eyes, expecting to see death coming for him.

Death, as it turned out, was focused on something else.

Instead of Magda closing in to finish Doe off, the punk warrior pawed at a metal blade lodged into her arm. Jon realized it would have slammed into him. *She tossed me out of the way.* With a harsh grunt, Magda yanked the knife, gleaming steel and gold, and threw it into the sand. Its filigreed hilt seemed familiar to Jon, though at the moment he couldn't be bothered to recall.

Coming out of the sea, three wetsuit-clad figures closed in, brandishing blades identical to the blood coated dagger lying in the sand. The punkess and lawyer were trapped between concrete and killers. Jon painfully swiveled from Magda, to the wetsuits, and back again.

Disbelief nearly overrode his panic. "Surfer assassins?"

"Retribution Squad." Savage hunger tinged her growl. A palpable joy; a berserker's lust for combat. Magda swelled, muscles flowing like wax, red fur sprouting across her body, patches of white fur honored her scars, badges of past triumphs. Within moments, the human woman vanished. In her place stood a lupine beast of sinew and slaughter which towered over Jon. "Come on then, cowardly Raptor scum. Let's stain the sands!"

The attackers obliged her rumbling challenge. Two wickedly curved knives flashed, low and high, forcing the Magda-beast to dodge. The lone assassin to her right took their opportunity, hands erupting into brass talons. *Just like Selina! Oh, fuck me, it's real. All of it's real!*

Jon sputtered a warning, but the red wolf-thing turned at the hip, grabbed the grossly exaggerated avian talons and pivoted like a dancer. A large, deadly, inhuman dancer. With a strangled squawk, the first attacker collided with the second, the two skidding across the sand. Smirking at her handiwork and stalking forward to finish the job, Magda failed to spot the final attacker diving from above.

A tad more inventive, the final assailant scuttled along the bottom of the boardwalk using its metallic claws, diving talon-first onto Magda's shoulders. The wolf maiden jumped about, attempting to dislodge her unwanted rider even as the surfer tried to shred her eyes. Tiring of the passenger, she drove both of her claws upward, describing a vicious pyramid, plunging through the ribs of her attacker. Howling madly, Magda pulled her claws apart, ripping the poor fool in two. Blood and viscera soaked her in a torrential explosion. The other two attackers, righting themselves, promptly fled at the sight of their dismembered friend. Jon cowered, eyes wide in horror at the gruesome sight. *My god. All that blood. Not again, not again, not again.*

The scarlet furred monstrosity turned Jon, covered in the blood of its enemies. Words forced from the muzzle, bestial throat struggling to shape the mewling sounds of the soft pink things that thought themselves masters of their world. "This is what I do. What I am. Warrior. Slayer. Ours is a world red in tooth and claw. You are not ready for such things. Leave. NOW."

Once again confronted with monsters, Jon ran.

CHAPTER 9

U NDER COLD FLORESCENT LIGHTS, Marc shuffled papers and dissected the contents of a dead man's office like a body on a slab, the realization of which brought him up short for a moment. *A dead man going through a dead man's things. Droll. Very droll.* Marc thumbed through the files of one late Kenneth Wheeler, formerly of Arkadas & Associates, previous account manager for the Beachfront Case, and current occupant of the police station morgue. Which left Mac holding the proverbial bag. Both Arkadas and Marc's undead sire, Lord Hynrich, expected imminent and spectacular results. Neither were renowned for their compassion or tolerance for failure. Unsurprisingly, working for two bosses sucked. *The stress alone is likely to kill me. Ha. Ha. Ha.*

With the personnel turnover, as Arkadas preferred to call it, it fell on Marc as resident specialist, trouble shooter, and barely tolerated support staff to get everything picked up and pretty for the new guy and their employers in the Houses. *Personnel turnover. What a colorful euphemism for your coworkers being horribly murdered.* Marc grumped to himself. That the new guy was his "long-time-no-see" best friend both excited and worried the anti-social vampire immensely. The arrival of the other half of their Harvard dynamic duo came as a pleasant, if bittersweet, surprise. Though it'd been nice to see Jon the other day, a nagging suspicion wouldn't leave Marc, squatting in his mind and annoying the taciturn executive assistant like a rock in the shoe or a row of books with one missing in the middle. Marc hated that kind of sloppy imbalance.

Like so often since their fateful reunion, Jon occupied Marc's thoughts.

Back at Harvard, Jon knew all the rules, even if he only learned them so he could break them properly. He'd taken Marc under his wing when they'd bumped into each other during freshman year. Jon hadn't taken kindly to Jonas Wendellton and his goons picking on Marc and doubly didn't care for the racist bullshit coming out of their mouths. Jon might be a prick, but he wasn't a bigot. Marc smiled at the memory, forgetting his extended fangs until they poked his lips. The two started up an impromptu Abbot and Castello routine until they'd befuddled the poor Wendellton boy into claiming responsibility for arson, murder, jaywalking, and pet abuse.

Jon and Marc been thick as thieves ever since, in no small part because nobody else could stand them. Jon came with both a prestigious pedigree and old money, a fact he never ceased to bitch about, but didn't play the game the way others wanted him to. The high-brow crowd looked at Marc as an up-jumped peasant because he arrived on a scholarship and not through the finest connections money could buy.

Marc and Jon played the game like masters, tweaking everyone's noses, from the Harvard Crimson sports teams to the deans, and coming out of it unscathed. Everyone either hated them or owed them, but they couldn't beat the combination of Jon's mouth and Marc's brain.

But that was then.

Jon knew the rules of the old Harvard game, he didn't seem to know a damn thing about this new one. Seeing his friend so off kilter shook Marc to his core. As roommates, Jon often groused and complained, incessantly lamenting his two favorite subjects: his series of unsuccessful romantic pursuits and his parents. Even when whining about his self-inflicted woes, Marc never knew Jon not to have a plan or scheme ready in his back pocket, a madcap gamble too crazy to work and too ludicrous to fail. Now it seemed the esteemed Mr. Doe was floundering, not knowing the faintest thing about the new game he'd been suckered into playing.

And not knowing the rules of the game might get him a lot more than docked pay or a suspension. A coffin made a hell of a penalty box.

Marc's confidence in his college buddy sank even lower when the aforementioned baby blue-eyed wunderkind slid through the old wooden door in a blur, babbling with fright.

"Ah. Jon. Back so soon? Guess you have changed. Wouldn't have expected you do the research, much less this quickly." Even as the panting lawyer struggled to catch his breath, a delectable odor seized Marc's attention. Seized it hard and didn't look ready to let go anytime soon.

Jon smelled of sand, surf, cold sweat, and the faint musk of Shifters. Several of them. Jon's heart beat rapidly, working overtime to pump rich oxygenated blood racing through his body. In short, Jon smelled disturbingly tasty, a rich cocktail of slaughter hung to him. *Lots of blood, none of it human. So, not his own.* Marc shook his head distractedly. He really didn't like imagining how his friend's blood tasted. Well, that wasn't true. Marc didn't like that he *did* enjoy imagining how his friend's blood tasted.

The shockingly mobile dead man mentally cursed and ran through the multitude of number exercises in his head to take his mind off wanting to devour his newly reunited companion. When that didn't work, Marc moved on to folding and filing papers. Anything to keep his hands moving and mid distracted. Marc had been so busy with work, racing to meet both Arkadas and his undead lord's demands, that he hadn't fed in hours. The accountant fought against his inhuman urges, actively battling against his hunger for life.

Marc was so wrapped up in his internal struggle to avoid cracking into Jon like a soft drink that Marc missed most of his friend's tale of woes. It was somewhat telling about Jon's state of mind, and the esteemed Mr. Doe's narcissism, that it took nearly half an hour for Jon to realize Marc had checked out.

"Are you even listening to me, Marc? Could you stop obsessing over your stupid paperwork or arranging your paper clips for five seconds? This is serious."

Marc's hands dug furrows into the worn wooden desk as he struggled to control his temper. Idiocy offended Marc on a good evening. Such idiocy coming from his friend, the same one whom Marc warned so very recently, set the vampire's fangs lengthening. *Of course, it's serious, Jon. This is exactly the thing I tried to tell you, you ass. But you never listen, do you?*

Oblivious to his friend's glare, the blood-coated lawyer paced back and forth, gibbering.

"Why me? I mean, I know I'm awesome, but come on. Sure, you and Reiger and Magda mentioned some kin and Blood stuff, but that's just stupid. They could go after some famous names, the real big wigs in the field." Jon stopped so fast he nearly fell over. "Oh. Names. Right. Probably noticed 'Doe' and signed me up. Great, just freaking great. Something else I can blame on the family legacy." Jon flipped a double deuce to the roof. "Thanks again, Mom and Dad. Glad you kept up tradition. Never around, but always messing with my life."

The all too familiar familial lamentation brought Marc's temper to the breaking point. *Surrounded by shapeshifting monsters and an undead friend eyeballing you like steak and you're still bitching about Mommy and*

Daddy? Jon, you goddamn idiot. You don't even understand the danger you are in. You can't see beyond your nose. And you smell delicious.

"It wasn't supposed to be like this! I didn't sign up for this, playing middleman for a bunch of freaking monsters."

It was the "M" word that did it.

Marc leapt from his desk to land in front of his friend, clearing the space in a heartbeat. The vampire's fangs plunged downward like two daggers and his eyes glowed red in the dark, ruddy and sinister. "Jon, would you shut the hell up!? I'm in the middle of something important, very hungry, and I'm trying really hard not to down you like a Slurpee right now."

Jon sputtered to a halt, diatribe forgotten, taking a good look at his old college buddy, taking in Marc's hellishly red gleaming eyes and his glistening ivory teeth. His sharp, pointy teeth.

"Shit. Marc. I...I'm sorry. I forgot."

"Did you, Jon? Well I didn't. Because I can't. Shall we discuss monsters, Jon? Here's a refresher course; I am one. I'm a walking talking corpse, I never get to see the sun, and I drink people!"

Jon's mouth dropped open in shock. *Hardly surprising. I've never laid into Jon like this before. He's only seen me get this worked up on one of my theories.* Thankfully, Jon did the smart thing and snapped his mouth shut with a click, shutting up and listening to the statue still Marc.

"I warned you earlier, but you didn't listen. First time didn't stick but now, finally, you realize how deep the rabbit hole is. But believe me my friend, you don't know enough to be properly frightened. And you need to know. Because there are worse things than death."

Marc felt a flicker of hope when realization dawned on Jon's face. Realization and empathy. "Marc, you don't need to talk about it."

"No, I think I do. How else can I get through that thick skull of yours?" Marc oozed back into his chair and snatched up one of his ever-present Rubix cubes. Giving his mind and hands something to work on helped him focus. Because his organized mind currently zigged and zagged crazily.

Jon needs to hear this and maybe I need to say this.

"Do you know what being turned does to you? It kills you. You do not go gently into that dark night. Forget the movies. Forget teeny bopper trash novels. It isn't sexy. It isn't smooth. You die. You choke, you panic, and you flail about desperate to escape, all while you feel your life being taken by something cold, unfeeling, and alien. And then this same inhuman thing rushes back in. It fills you. Overwrites you. It's a fragment of your sire, their essence digging and cutting deep, forcing the broken parts back together using the last flickering spark that won't give up on life. Then, when you come out the other side of that harrowing crucible, you are more *you* than ever before." Marc shuddered and hissed at the memory, fangs glinting in the wan light. For his part, Jon stood very quiet and very still.

"That alien thing, that piece of your sire? It winnows you, strips you down to your basics and then strengthens them, like polishing a stone, sharpening a sword, or going over something in big bright highlighter. That's why the Old Lords are very careful, paranoid even, about who they select for the honor. Ambition and daring are useful qualities in an underling but only in small doses. Too much of a good thing and your capable and loyal lieutenant suddenly isn't so loyal." Marc paused, exaggerated incisors chewing his lip. When Jon didn't say a thing, Marc took the silence as a good sign and pushed on. "You know my memory? My 'freakish recall' as you colorfully dubbed it, back in our sophomore years?"

Jon at least had the good grace to blush. "Hey, look, I'm sorry..."

Marc halted the useless apologies with a forestalling hand. "Eidetic memory. It got even sharper. Structures, systems, patterns. I see them. I understand them. All the pieces laid out in front of me. It's how I found the vampires first time, that's why Lord Hynrich chose me. Why he keeps me close. The courts... the other Elders..." Marc shuddered.

"Bet you'd make a killing in Vegas, huh?"

Marc brushed Jon's feeble joke aside and pressed on. "It's a boon and a curse, Jon. I can't forget. Ever. I've seen things that are seared into my mind. Things I'd give anything to forget. Horrors and wonders in equal measure. When your sire raises you, parts of them stick with you. It gives them a leash to control and command their offspring. When they speak, you listen. But the bonding works both ways. It also gives the childe glimpses of their elder." Marc looked directly at Jon, eyes haunted by the specter of whatever he witnessed in the secret heart of his undead sire. "I am the most recent childe of Lord Hynrich. And I know he will never stop and will allow nothing to stand in the way of his goals. Nothing and no one."

Silence reigned in the mausoleum office space, Marc stamped down old memories and new urges as Jon forced his confused thoughts into words. "This Lord Hynrich, even after all the terrible shit he did to you... it sounds like you respect him." Confusion turned the words into a question.

Marc's barking laughter broke into a coughing fit. *Huh, seems my lungs aren't used to laughing anymore. Guess I shouldn't be surprised.* Marc tried not think how long it'd been since he laughed. Too depressing. "Yes. Yes, I do. He also terrifies me. Lord Hynrich has ruled a piece of the world since the Crusades, Jon. He survived the Inquisition and their torches and Napoleon and his cannons. Not even the fires of the World Wars could end him. My elder thrived, where so many others fell." Pride filled Marc's voice, Jon listening open mouthed. "Lord Hynrich survived them all. Enemy after enemy, all dead. But not him. He outlived every last one. I've seen him, Jon. His flinty diamond hard core. Age hasn't dulled it, time has only made Lord Hynrich deadlier. His mind is razor sharp, his will is forged steel, and his word is unbreakable. My sire scares me, but I respect the survivor in him." Marc looked down at the many-colored cube, all sides matched, in his hands. "He also looks out for his own. I've been grateful for that. Especially now."

"What do you mean?"

"My sire knows something is coming. Something big. Lord Hynrich sees the signs, even if he can't see the whole picture. Like a good magpie, I get him scraps but we don't have all the pieces. Not yet."

"Something big enough to scare a vampire that made the Nazis run? Goddamn. So, this is our lives now, shapeshifter mafias and vampire nobles." Silence rushed in again as the two pondered the future. "But you've still got my back?" Jon's tentative plea cut Marc to the core worse that his whining ignorance ever did. Ruby tears filled Marc's eyes, the ashy substance clogging his vision. Vampires were not creatures made for remorse. Marc wasn't sure if he wanted to hug his old friend or throttle him.

"Your egoism is astounding, Jon. You really have to ask? Of course you do. I just need you to understand…if it were up to me, I'd back you to the end." Marc looked down, ashamed and afraid. "But it might not be up to me."

A moment of silence passed, the two friends lost in their thoughts.

"I had no idea. I thought I had it all figured it out, but I was wrong. You tried to warn me, and I didn't listen. I'm sorry." Jon held out his hand, but Marc knew what it was; an olive branch.

Marc grasped the proffered limb. "I've dealt with your rampant narcissism for years now. I'd be churlish to expect differently now."

Jon rolled his eyes. "Thanks, Mr. Thesaurus. Coming from anyone else that would be an insult."

The diminutive vampire shrugged "Simple unvarnished truth. You need you to check your living privilege around us Non-Living Persons."

"Wait, NLPs? Is that a thing? I call bullshit, you just made that up!"

Marc grinned back through a curtain of lanky midnight locks "Yep."

True, honest laughter echoed in the cavernous hall, a foreign sound in the grim office.

Marc idly tossed the completed Rubix cube to the side to join a pile of others just like it. "It's strange. I wasn't scared before. But ever since you arrived, I've been afraid. I knew I worked with some very bad people. Monsters, in the most literal sense. The world I...live...in is a very frightening place. Full of strange and powerful things. The difference is that I went looking for it."

Marc leaned back with a sepulchral sigh. "I knew that my old life, filled with its day to day minutia and trivial nonsense, would drag me under some day. The clothing, the posturing, the asinine concern over who was dating whom or what celebrity scandal was going on. It could only end with a bullet in my brain." The vampire mimed a gun with his hand, two fingers to the temple. "I understood the rules, Jon, but I didn't care enough to play the game. Not like you did anyway." Marc grinned at Jon, recalling their escapades at Harvard. "I went looking for something else, some kind of meaning. All those nights in front of the computer, the libraries, the searching and cross referencing. I dug deeper and deeper into the occult, looking for any shred of evidence to prove there was something more to this life. Then I found it. Rather, it found me. My search didn't go unnoticed. Very powerful forces watched my progress with interest. When the time was right, Lord Hynrich came for me. He elevated me."

Jon hung his head. "I never even noticed."

Marc slashed his hand, a harsh negation. "Under the bridge. You are who you are. You didn't want to notice. Most don't. Even if you had, I doubt you could even have brought yourself to believe it. Even here you are refusing to see what is right in front of your nose. What's important is that now you understand that such ignorance isn't a luxury available to you anymore. Here, ignorance is not bliss. It's fatal."

Marc leaned forward to hold Jon's gaze, eyes glowing like sullen embers in the dark. "You have to believe. Once you believe, you can start to understand just how far the rabbit hole goes. You just got your ass dunked into a very big pool and it's full of sharks. It's sink or swim time." Jon blinked, blues eyes lighting up at last, full attention on Marc. *Good. The old Harvard mantra worked.* "It's exciting and terrifying and I feel more alive than ever even though my heart doesn't beat. But now you've been sucked into that world. Helpless as a babe in the woods. You don't have any powers, Jon. You don't even have any backers."

A manic grin split across Jon's face. The vampire geek felt hope flicker in his breast. Marc knew that crazy grin. The same grin that Jon gave before winning a ridiculous bet with Professor Kao or talking his way out of a beating from the Harvard Crimson jocks. It was a grin that meant the impossible could be dared and won.

"Yeah I do. I got the biggest backer in the whole freaking world."

"Who?" Marc furrowed his brow, running through the catalog of potential allies and coming up dry.

Jon reached out and tapped Marc right on the forehead. "You."

Marc didn't want to admit it but his unbeating heart did a little hopskip of pride and love at Jon's first touch. The second tap only annoyed the vampire. Marc wasn't a touchy-feely person by any stretch of the imagination.

"You and your big ol' brain, Mr. Eidetic. This is nothing new. Listen to you, talking to me about big bad monsters, pfft. Hah! Buddy, did you forget? We took on lawyers, professors, and college rugby players! All of Harvard hated our guts and tried to kick us out or take us down. We beat them all! Survived and conquered, amigo. Lord Hynrich doesn't have shit on that. This is just another night on campus. You and me, against the odds, just like old times."

By the end of the speech Marc almost forgot his old friend came to him scared shitless. Even better, the vampire geek almost forgot his own fears.

"Team Supreme, back again?" Marc grinned, pointed fangs shining.

Jon didn't even flinch. He grinned right back at his undead amigo, pearly whites to pearly whites.

What the hell, Marc thought. *We might just make this work.* They'd tweak the nose of the biggest, meanest, scariest groups of immortal killing machines this side of the Pacific and come out smelling like roses.

CHAPTER 10

THE PENCIL HEAD BEAT the desk in a steady rhythm as Jonathan Augustus Doe stared at the legal documents from Arkadas with horrid fascination. Within the manila bound stack lay the totality of the Beachfront Case. It held all the sordid details and demands of his employers, its detailed legalese a host of black ink chains tied to Jon like puppet strings. The office files held the key to Jon's fate within them. *I might be able to figure a way of out this, if I could just bring myself to actually open the damn thing.* Jon watched the stack of paper the same way he'd watch a rattlesnake or a scorpion, expecting it to bite him at any time. Warily, the blue-eyed lawyer reached out and gingerly opened the binder. When the vicious stationary failed to attack, Jon shut it with a grunt.

Jon jammed the pencil into its holder in frustrated disgust and slumped into his plush office chair with a sigh. The last few days and nights ran in an endless loop, over and over, in his head. No new insight jumped out at him, no solutions to this insane situation he found himself in. Jon talked a big game to Marc but still struggled to come to grips with his bizarre life.

Why couldn't it have just been a spiked drink or some local pharmaceuticals? But a bad trip didn't explain away the packet of documents in front of him and the very real bruises inconsiderately ignoring any clever rationalizations.

I'm lucky to be alive after running into those monsters. Monsters. Better get used to the word. Cutthroat and ruthless as many of Jon's colleagues and contacts at Harvard had been, at least they were human. *Or so I thought. Maybe Old Bewford is really a mummy or something.*

The cryptic warnings from Bewford and his colleagues gained terrible weight in light of recent revelations. *They didn't touch the Beachfront deal because they knew something stank about the deal. Bewford and his cronies tried to wave me off the poisoned cup.* Instead, Jon blundered on, suckered by a shiny package and dreams of glory. The first big job of his career could possibly be his last as he tried to mediate a deal between two feuding monster clans. *Thank you, hindsight, for your 20/20 perspective.*

To top things off, Jon's best friend and only ally was an honest to god, pointy-fanged vampire. *Bella Lugosi would be proud.* The world of Jon Doe was so messed up he couldn't even categorize or rank it. On a scale of one to ten, things currently stood at a solid pear-shaped clusterfuck. Jon knew he promised Marc they'd nip this in the bud no problem, but the reality of the situation didn't match his initial optimistic expectation. *Every time I've tried sweet talking or tweaking the noses of these people, however loosely that term fits, they instantly go berserk. How can I negotiate when "disembowel" seems to be the default problem solving method?*

Mr. Doe paced about his now immaculate home. He'd dusted, swept, and mopped.

Twice.

He'd arranged and alphabetized his DVDs, books, and cereal boxes.

Twice.

Hell, Jon had even arranged his socks by color and fabric.

Twice.

Anything to distract himself from the work waiting on his desk and the poisonous deal it represented. Sadly, ignoring the problem didn't make it go away, leaving his mind racing frantically but going nowhere. It seemed he'd lost the Zen art of Chores.

Nope, screw this, I'm going around in circles. Time for a study break. The distressed lawyer grabbed his keys and punched up directions to the beach on his phone. Moments later, Jon tore off in his favorite toy, his BMW. Its familiar thundering roar calmed his nerves. *Nothing makes you feel like you can take on the world like a ludicrously over-engineered piece of machinery.*

Jon's hopes for a leisurely drive to ease his nerves burned away quickly. Navigating the unfamiliar mix of tourists, beach bums, and elderly yuppies made for a hectic stop and go ride. *Boston and Cambridge I can handle. New York? No problem!* He glared at the tanned beach goers as lackadaisically milling about. *These people don't know how to walk much less drive!* Jon narrowly avoided hitting a wandering punk band while looking for an open parking space after swerving to miss a skateboarder and her tanned surfboard toting companion running after her, looking for all the world like a Baywatch extra. *Goddamn West Coast crowd.* Jon worked his car in an intricate dance of down shifting, panicked stops, and sudden accelerations until the BMW pulled in miraculously unscathed to the boardwalk parking lot.

Jon looked over a sea of cars crammed side by side in countless rows. *Maybe I just have to get into the Pacifica groove of things.* Pulling on his Wayfarers, Doe watched the rides of the boardwalk, too far to hear the screams and laughs ringing out from the pier over the surf. The waves of the Pacific Ocean crashed against the shore with a steady rhythm, small rainbows shining in the spray. Children shrieked and ran from the foamy water chasing the receding ocean and running away when it returned. Surfers rode the cresting waves. On the sandy shores, people lounged in the sun, while board short and bikini clad beachgoers jogged down the sandy ways.

It could have been a post card picture. Sitting on the hood of his car, Jon relaxed and soaked in the California vibe.

The feeling lasted for about five minutes.

Bored now. Sliding off the high-end speedster, Doe walked down a gravely beach path looking for a bit of a respite from the bustling scenery. All the carefree merriment pissed him off in his current state of mind. No matter how he tried, Jon's tired mind kept wrestling with his current predicament. No amount of sun and surf was going to change that.

The winding seaside path cut down and round the coastal lines, moving away from the sandy expanse into rockier patches. Here the majestic waves carved out hard stone plateaus, far removed from the picturesque glittering expanses. The hustle and bustle of suntanned crowds faded leaving seagulls as Jon's only companions. After a mile, Doe began to regret his choice of shoes, wishing he'd traded his polished black office wear for some hiking boots. Chic and stylish, the sleek shoes didn't hold up as well to sauntering along a rocky coast. Feet aching and about to turn back, a thunderous crack and raucous laughter echoed from up ahead. *They don't have frat parties at demolition sites out here in California, do they?* Looking for any excuse to put off the mountain of paperwork lurking at home, to say nothing of facing up to literal monsters, Jon jogged around the bend.

Rather than a rowdy crowd of intoxicated youths, he found three people doing their best to make up for in volume what they lacked in number. However, Jon questioned if "people" applied here. A tanned bullheaded hulk, literally bullheaded with tall horns and glinting nose ring, stood out by the shore, pumping massively muscled arms up and down like he'd hit a home run. Hooting with laughter, a curvy goat lady lay doubled over, furry hooved forelocks kicking in the air. Her chest rivaled bull-head in size, despite the height difference. Directly beneath Jon, a coppery-skinned fellow with dreadlocks chugging a bottle of Sailor Jerry. He bounced a rock the size of a basketball in his hand, nearly as over muscled as his bovine companion. Almost normal, if you didn't look down. Below the waist, rock bouncer was a dappled horse.

Despite their differences, the trio shared the same taste in the jewelry. Gleaming bronze decorated horns, hoofs, and biceps on all of them, a reoccurring motif of eyes worked into the metal in blue and turquoise.

Jon raised his Wayfarers and rubbed his eyes in disbelief. The group remained after his double take, hooves and all. Cyclists whizzed by the stunned lawyer, yelling at Jon but didn't spare a glance at the cavorting trio. Jon grabbed a passing jogger by the arm and pointed down at the inhuman mythical creatures. "Hey, do you see that?"

The jogger looked from the unwelcome hand on his bicep and then down at the playful bunch. "Yeah?"

"You don't see anything wrong with this picture?"

"Should I?"

"You think maybe those people don't belong here?"

The joggers annoyed look turned cold. "Hey man, lay off. It's a public park and everyone is welcome. Even asshole bigots like you." The jogger shrugged out of Jon's grasp and pounded pavement, shooting Jon a glare as he did.

I really should be used to this by now. I really should. What's next, the Easter Bunny?

Horse-guy cantered to the side, polishing off his drink in one go before hurling the drained Sailor Jerry bottle aside. It joined an ever-growing pile, glass and metal creating a monument to their appetite for booze. More bottles and cans lay scattered about along with, Jon realized after a second, rock shards.

"You ready, Nate? You can't handle this fastball!"

The bovine fellow flattened a beer can against his skull and snorted. "Bring it, Ant-Man!"

I might be going crazy, but I still know the difference between a horse and an insect. Must be some kind of monster in-joke. More infectious laughter from the goat lady. Jon thought she really did have an excellent voice for a goat person. *Good pitch, great presence. Does eating cans result in a stellar falsetto? I could sell that to the Harvard drama club. New miracle diet!*

Winding up, the coppery horse fellow let fly, dreadlocks whipping about. The igneous missile sailed right for the Nate. The giant bull man surged forward and head-butted the flying rock, shattering it into a million shards with a deafening boom.

Mystery of the thunder, solved. Great job, gang. Now let's get Scooby a snack.

Having reduced another hapless rock to dust, the trio once again set about hooting in celebration, a rowdy affair of stamping hooves, fist bumps, and even more chugs of alcohol.

Brushing dust and pebbles from his head, Nate turned from a beaten old cooler with enough drinks to float a fleet of ships and the sailors aboard in his arm and spotted Jon on the path above. "Heads up, guys. Tourist." They smiled and waved at him, so Jon waved back at the walking, talking Greek myths. Seemed only polite, after all.

"Hey dude, wanna join in? Fast-ball special!" The centaur's grin seemed honest enough, but the bouncing rock in his palm wasn't near as welcoming.

Jon raised his hands in mock surrender. "Thanks, but I don't know if I can hang with you guys. Not sure I meet the dress code. No horns, no hooves, no service. Besides, I'd be pretty screwed when you chucked that little pebble my way."

As one, the trio's jaws dropped open. *Hah. Who knew that little revelation would knock Larry, Curly, and Moe here for a loop?*

Nate recovered first, bounding forward, bottles sloshing and jostling in his spectacular huge arms. "Wait, whoa, wait, whoa, whoa…Whoa!"

Such an erudite speech earned raised an eyebrow behind Jon's sunglasses. *Quite the charmer, aren't you, big guy?*

Undaunted by his rhetorical limitations, the minotaur plowed on. "You can see us? Like, *see* us, see us? Dude! You have got to come on down here and have a drink!" Nathan lifted aloft a bottle of vodka, dark bottled wine, and cheap brandy all in one massive mitt.

Jon halted a moment, weighing his options. *Well, they aren't trying to kill me. No blood, no blades, no problem, I guess. It's not like I have a whole lot of options. Besides none of the other monsters I've met offered me a drink. Except Selina.* Swiftly turning his train of thoughts away from the Edfu estates party, Jon meandered down the sloping path to the wave touched alcove. "Got any scotch?"

§——§

It turned out they didn't, so the Harvard graduate settled for some rum. The morning passed pleasantly into a balmy afternoon, with Jon getting to know his new friends. He even managed to forget his current deadly predicament. While Jon sipped at a bottle of the local brew, his hooved posse demolished the remaining liquor with gusto. He marveled at the resilience of their livers. *Pretty sure they went through half a liquor store of booze already.*

Despite kicking back a few with drinking buddies straight out of the Odyssey, the trio acted as though the esteemed Mr. Doe was the weird one. They bombarded him with questions, unable to grasp that he wasn't a vampire, Shifter, or some other unearthly critter. After running through an alphabet's worth of monsters, learning their A to Z's like good little children, Jon's hoofed companions finally seemed to accept his word on the matter.

"I'm a plain old, blue-eyed baby boy from Massachusetts." Jon re-plied for the thousandth time. *Not sure if I should credit the booze or the headbutts for the broken record questions. Maybe it's just their default setting. Is being a well-dressed gentleman really more of a unicorn than a unicorn for these…people?* He paused and thought about it. *Shit. Could be. Damn, I'm special even among legends.* Jon grinned to himself as his inflated sense of self-importance was reinforced.

Anthony, or "Ant-Man" as his buddies called the horse fellow in what passed for wit amongst the Three Stooges, shook his head with a gentle rattle of beads. "You sure, man? I mean we run into a lot of normies… oh shit."

Cries of "Dude!" and "Not cool" rang out as his companions looked at horse man, utterly aghast.

Jayne patted Jon's arm with a consoling "he didn't mean it like that," and Norman tried to cover for his buddy with an apologetic "he's not normally like this."

The centaur held up his hands like he'd committed a serious faux pau. "No offense! I mean, most normies are cool." There was an audible smack as Norman facepalmed his bovine head. "What I mean is, I'm down with your kind…"

Saving the horse man from himself, Jon grinned and wiggled his half empty bottle of rum good naturedly. Reassured that he was still cool with his new two-legged companion, the centaur continued. "Yeah, any-way, we run into them, like, a lot a lot. None of them can ever see us."

Anthony tapped the gleaming bronze band on his arm, rubbing the engraved eye lovingly. "These little beauties make sure normies, ummm, non-Mythics look elsewhere. Their eyes slide right off of us."

Jayne, the satyr in the group, leaned over to give her two cents, still gripping Jon's arm. Jon tried to focus on the words she spoke rather than the way her lips moved. The full-bodied woman proved very distracting. Her limbs moved with a rough elegance, like a curvy ballet dancer miming a wrestling match. "Yeah. Maybe you're a Mythic, on your mom's side? With a last name like Doe, do you suppose you've got some stag in you?"

Jon tried very hard to ignore the lovely view her chest presented or that her hand had traveled from his arm to massaging his shoulders. Jon focused on Jayne's soft brown eyes instead. Failing that, he looked to her black and blonde hair, curling ram horns poked out in the short cut. The sudden attraction bothered Jon a tad, given his previous disinterest in wildlife. *Sleeping with a werewolf doesn't change a thing! I mean, Jayne's got hooves, for pity's sake.*

"Pretty sure my parents were just very cruel or dumb. I mean, Jon Doe? I caught a lot of flak for that stupid name growing up in boarding schools." Jayne's brown eyes turned sympathetic and a comforting hand squeezed his thigh. *Nope. I am not going Discovery Channel.* Jon discreetly adjusted himself to escape the goat-lady's wandering hands. "I figured my folks regretted missing out on the 60's and decided to take it out on me with that name. Not my fault they didn't get to party at Woodstock."

It was like flipping a switch. At the mention of the famous counter-culture festival, Jayne went from sympathetic to excited in heartbeat.

"Woodstock! Wow! Yeah, they missed out! That was a hell of a time." Jayne apparently enjoyed the memories a lot, grinning dreamily into the sea, her clothes doing very interesting things with her curves as she stretched. Everything about her oozed sensuality and carnal indulgence. Which seemed like a hell of an accompishment when your legs looked like shag rugs.

No. No way am I turning into one of those guys on the internet.

Anthony interrupted her fun. "Just 'cause you smoked yourself re-tarded doesn't make you an honorary Woodstocker, Jayne."

"Ohhh, sick burn!" Nate, helping.

Flushing, Jayne flipped them both the bird "Eat me, you jerks."

As if on cue, both muscle bound louts swarmed over Jayne, making exaggerated nomming noises as they gently nipped at her ears, neck, and shoulder. They traveled to other parts of her anatomy and giggled shrieks lowered to whispered encouragement. About when Jon wondered if he should leave before the Monsters Gone Wild video unfolded further, a shrill beeping interrupted their fun.

"Tell me that's not what I think it is." Jayne's muffled groan rose from beneath the two walking slabs of man meat.

Anthony clopped over to a nearby backpack and pulled out a beeping smartphone, the tiny device anachronistic in the centaur's hand. "'Fraid so. Lunch is over. Time to get back to work."

Nate stood and scratched as his tall horns, face scrunched in concentration as his boozed addled mind pondered a deep mystery. "But how? Those surfer guys we hitched a ride out here with left a long time ago."

In unison, the hooved beach bums turned to Jon, freezing the lawyer's stealthy retreat.

Faced with three sets of puppy dog eyes from the stranded Mythics, Jon's resolve crumpled like wet tissue paper. *Everybody wants the D.* Jon thought forlornly.

Jon and his three inhuman hitchhikers paused only long enough for the beach bums to polish off the remaining booze with terrifying efficiency. After that, they directed Jon to their place of business with vague directions, descriptions of landmarks Jon couldn't possibly know of, and last minute directions yelled as they hit their turns. Their drive through San Dominguez traffic included highlights such dodging a Winnebago and no less than five desperate swerves and twice as many near misses. The bizarre peanut gallery crammed into Jon's luxury vehicle cheered the whole time, earning a sickly grin from their driver. Simply getting them into the car had been quite a feat of engineering. Jon scouldn't recall exactly how they managed it.

Jon made it absolutely clear if they scratched his pride and joy, their asses were grass. Despite his misgivings, the three pulled it off with nary a hoof misplaced. "It's a good thing we're so flexible." Jayne had winked at Jon while laying on Nathan's lap. Jon declined to comment on their good fortune.

A scant thirty minutes later Jon and the Terrible Trio, as he had come to think of his passengers, pulled up to the movie set. At this point, Jon figured he'd seen everything.

That the "movie set" turned out to be an old commercial airport hangar, Jon could deal with. That no one batted an eye as he drove his BMW with its down as three creatures out of Greek legends hung out of his car, Jon could deal with. Jon even accepted the surreal experience of Nate high-fiving Larry the security guard as he waved them through. About the time Jon and the Trio walked into the hangar the world went sideways once again for the blue-eyed wunderkind.

An honest-to-goodness office awaited them just inside the metal doors. The sight of which made Jon's heart do a little hiccup. He felt like he'd come home. *Familiar ground, at last.*

A high raised desk, colorful fish tank, and cheap chairs rested on a red carpet. Fuzzy prefabricated cubicle-style walls stretched out one either side behind it, ubiquitous nine to five drone cells, blocking their view farther into the facility. Beyond the corrugated metal ceiling and bare concrete floor, it could have been any white-collar workplace. *Reminds me of my intern days.*

Jon wasn't sure if booze or nostalgia made the tired, overworked, and underpaid days seem more palpable or if slaving away for the grumpy old Bewford just seemed nicer after meeting actual monsters.

An olive complexioned young woman sat behind the desk rapidly typing away at a computer. Jon found himself nodding approvingly at her attire. It was the first bit normalcy he'd enjoyed since arriving in San Dominguez. *Tasteful green jacket, paired ivory blouse. Minimal jewelry. Professionally neutral.* A pair of Oakley's on her narrow nose and a pony tail cinched it; this was a receptionist. No horns interrupted the swept back hair. Jon clutched at that tiny bit of familiarity like a drowning man to driftwood. *Every office needs a receptionist! Even offices inside hangars.*

"Yo, Cas-sea-day! How's it hanging?"

With a small sigh, Cassidy moved away from the computer. When she walked out from behind the desk, Jon's small lifeline of normalcy snapped. Cassidy hadn't been sitting at all. She'd been standing at the computer. On four legs, no less. From the waist down, speckled horse took the place of the expected human bits.

Gosh, that hair style seems terribly ironic all of sudden. The part of Jon's brain still operating on the crumbling premise of normality recognized the tell-tale sign of the "Do-You-Have-An-Appointment" speech. *The politest way to snowbank someone.* Jon reflexively defaulted to his best smile. It had opened many doors in the office and bedroom alike.

He needn't have bothered.

After glancing from the Terrible Trio to the clock, the harried filly's polite mask dropped, pure frustration bubbling through. *Familiar frustration, by the look of it. Not the first time these folks have been tardy.*

"Nathan, Anthony, Jayne. You are late." The strongly implied 'again' hung in the air like a flare. Cassidy coldly glared down at the only double X-chromosome bearer in their little band. "Jayne, Set Three on the double. They need more frolickers in the glen. And don't you dare stop at the food table on the way. Eat all the scones again and I'll have your butt in a sling."

Jayne gave a thunderous snort and rolled her eyes, which caused Jon to once again marvel at the lungs on the shorter lady.

The centauress wasn't having any of it. The office warden stomped the ground with a whinny, sparks flaring where front hooves met concrete, sending Jayne off into the cubicle labyrinth at a dead run.

The temperature of the room dropped a few degrees as Cassidy turned to regard the other centaur. "Anthony. Head directly over to the Red Room. Do not stop for anything. You're a warhorse again. Mount up."

Her four legged-counterpart let out a groan. "You know what I'd rather be mounting?"

Cassidy killed the work place harassment with a terse command. "MOVE IT."

With nary a "Yes ma'am," the coppery centaur raced off, following after Jayne.

The minotaur stood next in line. "Nathan, you're stunt double for *Terror of the Labyrinth 5*. Rocco doesn't want to get his hide dirty with the boiling lava scene. That means you're taking the dive." She emphasized the last part with a dagger like thrust of her pen.

"*Terror of the Labyrinth*? Those B-movie schlock fests?" Light bulbs flared in Jon's over stretched mind as he hazily recalled marathon drinking games set to the low budget films. "Marc and I loved those movies!" The Harvard graduate looked up with narrowed eyes and barely resisted the urge to tug on the bovine's horns. "I always thought it was rubber."

Nathan's genial slap on the back sent Jon pitching forward until he stabilized himself, embarrassingly enough, on Cassidy's flank. Realizing the anatomical implications of his faux pas, Jon hastily pulled back, red in the face and mouthing apologies. *That sort of thing starts lawsuits. I should know.* Their bovine companion remained good naturedly oblivious.

"Yeah, buddy! Movie magic. See, I'm wearing a mask of being a monster over me being a monster. It's genius." The final member of the three amigos announced this profound revelation. Jon failed to see the cosmic truth therein, looking to their equine greeter for assistance. Cassidy, tail flicking in agitation, pointedly cleared her throat to get the rambling minotaur's attention.

Nathan bobbed his head grinning, unfazed or unaware of both Jon's disinterest and Cassidy's impatience. "Jon, thanks for the ride, man. You're a lifesaver. Now if you'll excuse me, duty calls. Oh yeah, makeup! They're going to make me all pretty!" Pumping fists in the air in his best Rocky Balboa imitation, the swole bullman danced his way into the recesses of the hangar, humming the whole way. *If I didn't know better, I'd swear that was "I Feel So Pretty" from West Side Story.*

Alone, Jon now faced the full scrutiny of the office coordinator.

At least she isn't glaring at me like the Terrible Trio. After only a car ride with them, Jon sympathized with poor Cassidy. He imagined working with them was like herding cats. Giant, hormonal teenage cats. With hooves and horns.

"Do you have an appointment?" Nose scrunching, Cassidy turned her bespectacled gaze to her tablet. Jon mentally breathed a sigh of relief. *Familiar ground at last.* Gatekeepers were gatekeepers, on four legs or two.

Falling back on tried and true tactics, Jon flashed his most dazzling smile and sallied forth to meet the foe. "Doe, Jon Doe. Practicing Legal Counsel. Pleased to meet you" Jon reached out for a shake to start thawing the ice and decided to play a hunch. "I'm a friend of Archimedes Arkadas and Selina Aegolius." *Friend. Right. One can't stand me and the other's brother kidnapped me.*

Her eyes widened slightly at the name drops. The hunch played off. *At least I haven't lost my instincts entirely. The charm still works, well, like a charm. Time to seal the deal.*

"I was enjoying the local surf and turf when I saw the Terrible Trio stranded out there. They seemed an alright bunch, and I figured I'd lend a hand. I'd love to look around and get a feel for the place, new transplant and all. If you don't mind?" A cocked eyebrow and a slight tilt of the head joined the dazzling smile.

Cassidy vacillated, looking from him to the small screen before finally coming to a decision. Her face turned from disapproving frown to a smile that could have landed her a job at Disneyland in a heartbeat.

"Very well, Mr. Doe, my name is Cassidy Elafris, and it is my pleasure to be your guide today. Allow me to take you on a tour of Speculo Productions." Cassidy turned and waved toward the back of the vaulting building and Jon reflexively offered his arm. The lady horse seemed touched by the show of gallantry and accepted the proffered arm, made only slightly awkward by their height difference. Jon only came up to her collar bone and had to raise his elbow to compensate.

"Please, call me Jon." Arm in arm, or close enough, they plunged into the studio proper, where absolute pandemonium reigned.

As they walked through the studio, the goosebumps on Jon's skin weren't just because of the air conditioning. Barely controlled chaos filled the hangar-cum-studio as men, women, and monsters raced about in a frenzy of activity. Arguing seemed to be the common tongue of the bizarre menagerie.

The mix of living, breathing, beasts with everyday movie stage props, crates, and racks of wheeled wardrobe only reinforced the surreal experience. Jon cringed when a minotaur, barrel-chest covered with a blood-stained apron, threateningly waved a meat cleaver clutched in its meaty hand at some pencil necked geek in a tie. *Is that an honest to god pocket protector? That is hands down the weirdest thing I've seen yet.* The hook-nosed fellow stood utterly unfazed, reaching up to snap his fingers in front of the giant's face before yelling back, arms waving. The cleaver wielder slumped off, sniffling. Jon wasn't all that skilled at reading animal-people expressions, but Jon thought the big fellow actually looked hurt.

This is beyond surreal.

"Abram. Such a diva." Cassidy sighed, looking on with pity in her eyes.

"Actor?" Jon posited as he craned his head to track the retreating figure.

A brief shake of Cassidy's head sent her hair waving back and forth. Despite himself, horse analogies ran through Jon's mind. *Never did a mane seem so apt a description.* "Chef. Our actors have wildly varying diets and Abram prides himself on providing only the best for them all. But Mr. Chaucer... well." A slight hitch and a meaningful pause had Jon's ears perking up.

I know that tone. Professional disdain. Secretary doesn't care for the boss, eh? Office gossip really is the best way to get a feel for a place.

"Mr. Chaucer is our chief financial officer. Him and Abram argue on a regular basis about costs, quality control, deadlines, that sort of thing." She leaned in conspiratorially. "I think they have a thing for one another but just won't admit it. The scandal, you see. Birds and bulls."

Jon nodded solemnly as if he understood Mythic office politics and took it all in stride, including the fantastical inter-racial sexual tension. *Chef and the penny-pincher in torrid affair. Throw in a dash of "their kind" prejudice. Got it.* It all sounded like a bad daytime soap opera. Jon briefly wondered if he could sell the plot to the studio. *Art imitating life and all that.*

Dipping his head, Jon turned his baby blues on the secretary, commiserating with her struggles in running the office. "Romance is a tough business. The heart wants what the heart wants." Cassidy smiled and squeezed the smooth talker's arm a bit tighter. When she giggled, warning bells rang in Jon's head. He'd heard that particular titter more than once from a besotted college freshman or two. It never ended well.

Oh crap. Guess the Doe charm works across species. Time to pare back the usual moves. First, Jayne, now Cassidy. Jon found himself hip deep in attractive, if not quite human, ladies.

Panicking slightly, Jon looked closer at his guide. Her height, to say nothing of the horse bits, threw him off at first, but once past the professional attire, Jon realized she looked much younger than he first thought. *Probably barely out of college, pursuing her dreams in show business.* Jon had known several young ladies like her in his time. *Well, not quite like her. I can only imagine taking her home for the holidays. "Hey Mom, hey Dad, meet Cassidy. Say, do you think she could stay in the spare stable?"*

As Jon and his office guide passed a satyr bellowing stage directions through a megaphone, black beret one enunciated syllable from falling off, the full weight of the situation hit Jon. Jonathan Augustus Doe, practicing legal counsel, stood in the middle of a converted hangar, surrounded by movie making monster, as he flirted with a cute teen who wasn't even his species. All the while, the esteemed Mr. Doe was trapped in a Shakespearean feud between two secret societies of monsters, both of whom intended to turn him into a blue plate special if he crossed them. Jon firmly stamped down on the maniacal giggling welling up inside him and then firmly stamped it down again when it didn't take the hint.

Jon's sense of normality bent sideways and his grasp on sanity slipped a smidge closer to cuckoo-cloud lander status.

None of this mental turmoil passed his face though, hidden behind a rigidly plastered smile. *I'm still a professional, dammit.* Cassidy, unaware of his internal meltdown, nervously brushed an imaginary loose strand of hair back from her face.

"So, Jon, how long are you going to be in town?"

"Originally only for the extent of the job, though I'm looking to extend it a bit further out." A polite way of saying he wanted to outlive his current assignment.

"How lovely. What are your thoughts of San Dominguez so far?" She deftly maneuvered them between brightly colored sets and wardrobes passed in a riotous mishmash, noir atop comedy atop burlesque mixing with tin foil space suits.

"Well, it's definitely been exciting." *Which is certainly one way to describe kidnapping and murder.* "The community here is certainly more exotic than I'm used to"

Cassidy uttered something between a giggle and a whinny, stopping them behind a stage. On the other side, as Jon could hear shouting and the sounds of mock combat.

Belatedly, Jon realized his predicament. He'd been hoodwinked, hornswaggled, and herded neatly into a trap. Wardrobe and stage walls hemmed them in with no one in sight. Cassidy leaned in, intimately close. Even fourteen-year-old Jon knew where this was going. *Okay, nope. Pretty sure I'm not ready for inter-species dating at this point.*

Even as the blue-eyed wunderkind suggested they continue on, Cassidy insisted on her kiss, grabbing Jon firmly about the shoulders. Locked firm in place by her iron grip, Jon's mind raced for options shy of decking the centauress. *Which, given the hands of steel on my shoulders, might not get me out of this.*

Blessedly the panicked lawyer's salvation came in the form of a high-pitched battle cry and a furry object the size of Jon's couch crashing through the sound stage hiding Cassidy's amorous advances.

Cassidy pulled back, looking embarrassed and angry. Silhouetted by the lights beyond, a mighty figure stood triumphantly. Well, a mighty five-and-a-half feet tall figure. Tight denim jeans and midriff baring red crop top served as stand-ins for battle armor. Curly shoulder length blonde hair framed a heart shaped face with two arctic blue eyes set firmly in a good old, normal human-looking face atop a normal, albeit exceedingly fit, human body. The golden-haired newcomer could have been a fitness model. Though if the size of the brute she sent hurled backstage served as any kind of metric, "normal" only went skin deep. The blonde bombshell deftly ducked through the hole, stepping over the downed and dazed critter. Cassidy confronted the diminutive power-house, her irritation plain.

"Godsdammit, Zoe! Again?!" The heat in Cassidy's protests made Jon think the horse-lass referred to her interrupted seduction as much as the broken set.

"Sorry about that. Got a little overexcited. You know how that is, right Legs?" Despite Zoe's conciliatory words, the monster chucked looked amazingly unapologetic. Jon thought the wink and the nod might have something to do with it. Particularly impressive considering the actress faced scathing tirades from no less than four other coworkers, including the director, stage manager, and the poor shaggy sod she put through the wall.

"Guess I'll go freshen up. Don't worry about the new guy, I'll make sure he gets a great tour." Zoe nonchalantly wrapped an arm about Jon's waist and strolled off, leaving angry and sputtering movie makers in her wake. Cassidy looked positively apocalyptic.

As they walked, Zoe leaned up to Jon and conspiratorially whispered in his ear. "By the way, you're welcome. The little minx gets a little frisky around cute little normies. You wouldn't be the first pretty thing she's bagged."

The friendly pat incongruously reminded Jon of his Aunt Gertrude. *Never saw Aunt Gertrude put a werewolf through a wall, though.*

"You seem kind of new to the scene. Didn't want her sweeping you off your feet and ending it with a doc's visit for a broken pelvis."

Composure breaking for a minute, Jon almost got whiplash as he looked past the casually clad confidant toward his erstwhile guide behind them handling damage control. Jon let out a low whistle, honestly impressed. *Damn. Here I thought I was good. I fell hook, line, and sinker for her "little miss innocent" play. Shoulda taken notes.*

As if hearing his thoughts, Zoe went on. "Don't feel too bad. Cassidy means well. It's not an act, she really does get all skittish around cute guys. Falls head over heels, all four of 'em, for each new boyfriend. Cassidy just has a wandering, uh, heart, if you catch my drift. From what I hear, she could use a good harem. Nobody can keep up!"

Jon kept his winning grin up, even though Zoe's ribald guffaws made him want to sink into his shoes. *Almost another notch in the bedpost. Almost two for two. I mean, counting Magda...*

His thoughts skidded away from the fiery punkess as soon as he thought of her, images of their night of passion mixing with the visceral horror of a blood-stained berserker standing in the sands.

Eventually, Zoe stopped laughing at her coworkers love life and ambled over to a locker. "They are going to be a minute fixing that hole in the wall, not to mention old fluffy bun's ego. I've learned its best to clear out until they cool off. Want to snag some lunch?"

Jon looked askance at his exuberant companion, then shrugged. *The way my luck's going, she'll turn out to be robot from the future. What the hell. My life couldn't get any stranger.* "Know any good coffee places?"

CHAPTER 11

AFTER SCOOPING up her oversized backpack and leaving a hastily scribbled note at the front desk, the two hopped into Jon's BMW and drove off in search of the caffeinated nectar of the gods. Zoe directed him to Barry's Beanery, a burger and coffee joint known for its zany culinary experiments. The brilliantly blue box fit right into a host of equally vibrant houses, the entire row a riot of garish splashes of color. The whole thing spilled right onto the beach, the ocean side buildings forming a line of shops and boutiques, converted from pre-fabricated condominiums. The actress swore up and down it was to die for.

Jon was less than convinced. "Cozy."

"What?"

Jon sighed. "I'm used to…higher end bistros."

Zoe laughed and playfully elbowed Jon. "What are you, some kind of snob?"

Jon, rubbing his slightly bruised ribs, sniffed defensively. "Not at all. I just enjoy the finer things in life. Not something this kitschy. It looks like Starbucks' garage band days."

"Well, Mr. Silk Boxers and Too Much Hair Gel, think of it as an underground coffee joint."

"How'd you know I was wearing...?"

The blonde actress' smirked and Jon realized he'd been played. Again.

"I guessed. You looked the type Now shut up and come on. You'll like it."

"I use exactly enough hair gel, thank you very much," Jon muttered sulkily as he followed his guide inside.

Zoe chatted up the teenaged cashier like an old friend. His lip piercing shone as he grinned, clearly excited to see the blonde brawler, maybe even a bit star struck. Apparently, Zoe was a bit of a local celebrity and a regular at the beanery to boot. Without even looking at the chalk board menu, Jon's culinary guide opted for the Flamin' Cow, a slab of moo meat slathered with nearly every sweat inducing pepper known to mankind. Jon, figuring when in Rome, opted for the Peanut Butter Burger, which promised a savory-sweet combination of two childhood favorites.

All this being the menu's words, not Jon's. *I certainly would never have named my coffee something as atrocious as a "Mocha-vana."*

Zoe declined his gallant offer to pay, something Jon had insisted on for his knight in denim armor. Zoe threw it on her running tab and the two ducked out to park themselves in two fold-out chairs behind the converted condominium. With Zoe's oversized backpack resting heavily on the table between them, the lunch goers sat overlooking the beach surrounded by a forest of riotous colors. All around, the chairs and tables were painted different hues, copying the blaring and chaotic color scheme of the neighborhood. *Well, it's certainly unique. Suppose you could say it has an "authentic" charm.*

For the first time since his abduction, Jon truly relaxed. He wasn't sure why, but even without seeing the actress next to him put a mythical creature through a wall, Jon felt safe around the golden-tressed thespian. They sat in companionable silence, sipping pretentiously titled coffee and watching the tide come in.

Setting his cup down, Jon turned to his unlikely savior. "Thanks again. That could have been a bad scene back there. I'm not sure I want to be a father of fillies."

Zoe acknowledged the thanks with a nod between drags of coffee. "No problem. I kinda pegged you for a newbie."

"How? There is now way you saw me until fuzzy-lumpkins went through the wall."

Zoe grunted, tilting her cup back to drain the last of the bean juice. "True. But it's not a seeing or hearing sort of deal. We just know. It's a 'sixth sense' thing we have."

"We?" Jon leaned away from his coffee sipping companion. "I've been hearing way too much ominous implications from folks lately. Please tell me you aren't going to sprout wings or a new pair of arms or something?" Suddenly Jon was very afraid his joke might not be a joke at all. *The universe can't have that cruel a sense of humor.*

Jon was grateful for the distance a moment later when Zoe spit coffee over the table, laughing hard enough it hurt to watch.

"What? No!" Zoe tried to wipe up the coffee, took another look at Jon, and fell into more fits of laughter. She didn't stop until the waiter came with their food.

Calming down, she moved her giant bag to the deck with a weighty *thunk*, metallic something or others shifting inside of it, and tucked into her burnt offering of meat-things with gusto. "Heh, hey sorry about that. It's just, wow buddy, you really are new."

"I get that a lot. Mostly from people trying to kidnap or kill me."

Zoe shook her head vigorously mid-bite on her meal, its sauce so potent Jon could smell it from across the table, talking around a big chunk of masticated meat. "Sorry, dude. It's not like you broadcast it. Hell, you almost had me fooled. Except, I cheat." She waved absently with the burger, chili-sauce splattering the table. "Sixth sense."

Jon happily focused the conversation on something other than his complete ignorance of the horrific world he'd stumbled into. "Yeah, how does that work? You never did answer what 'we' meant. I doubt you suddenly stumbled into the royal 'we' for a second and you look a little young to be the Queen."

"You'd be surprised on that. Can't always count a Mythic's age by their frown lines." Zoe mumbled her answer between great chomping bites, inhaling her burger.

Good grief, she's already halfway through the thing and murdered the plate of fries. If she eats like that all the time, I don't know how she fits into those jeans. Guess hurling monsters burns a lot of calories. Jon promptly bit into the gooey morsel in front of him to make up for lost time. Turns out a peanut butter and meat sandwich worked just fine.

Zoe finished shoveling the last bits of food from her plate, greedily watching Jon chomp at his burger. "The 'we' in this case, meaning me and mine, are the Companions of Herakles." The Greek name rolled right of her tongue. "Remember all those all stories of monsters and myths you heard growing up as a kid? You saw for yourself just how real those are, up close and personal. Real personal."

Being the mature adult she was, Zoe paused to make kissy faces at Jon, in case her subtle point had sailed over the lawyer's head. Jon chose to eat his burger in dignified silence. When he failed to rise to the bait, Zoe continued her story with a sigh.

"Spoilsport. Anyway, for every Hydra, Griffon, or Harpy, you have an Odysseus, a Theseus, and a Perseus. That's us. Mortal scions of the gods and second cousins to demi-gods. We take our name from the most famous of 'em all, big bad Herakles himself!" Zoe stole a fry from Jon's plate and struck a dramatic pose, her greased spud thrust skyward like a shining sword. "Lets the other baddies know they shouldn't mess with us. We aren't the closest knit of groups, so the name helps remind the Mythics who they're screwing with."

Jon chimed in as Zoe swiped more fries from his plate "So throwing that guy through a wall, was that a warning to him to be on good behavior or something?"

Zoe almost choked on her stolen gold tater stick, laughing again. "Todd? Oh, sweet fates. No, no, no! Guy's a marshmallow. He's only a danger to a clothing store during a sale! Nah, that was just me doing what Companions do. See, everything in nature has a counterpoint, an opposite. Something to check it. Snakes might be bad news, but a hawk will swoop right down and snatch them up. Nothing exists in a void. When all those Centaurs roll up and start kidnapping some nubile young thing or other, one of us comes along to kick 'em in the nuts!" The actress demonstrated with a kick that sent a loose paper cup flying off into the sand. Jon watched in amazement as the crumpled container nearly beaned a low flying seagull.

Damn, she could always play some professional football if the wandering monster slayer-cum-actress thing doesn't pan out.

"Story goes that we Companions are descended from the Gods and their children. The gods loved sleeping around with mortals and it produced some stellar results. Example, Herakles." Jon nodded while fending off her attempts to snag the last of his fries.

"Well, the gods get randy, get it on with some mortal hotties, and pass on the lineage. Even though the godsblood is diluted, it's still there. And it is loud, let me tell you. The Olympian spark doesn't let us just sit down and lead a quiet life. It makes us get up and *do* something. Usually that means headstomping." Zoe's blond hairdo shook to and fro as she vigorously punched the air with what would have been a mean right hook.

"Every so often, usually when some clawed and jawed thing starts causing grief for normies, one of us Companions feels a tingling, a kind of pull to make us go check it out. We Companions named it the Call. Then, bam!" Fist met open palm with a loud smack. "I stepped up to the Call with vampires. Bloodsuckers wanted to get cute with some high schoolers. First, ew. Way too old to be messing around with something that young. Second, ew squared. I don't like the idea of dead things that move. Which is why it's so damn fun to put them back in the ground! That was an interesting Senior Prom, let me tell ya."

Wonder what she'd think of Marc. Eager to dodge sordid tales of her younger years, Jon used the last of his burger as a sacrifice to steer the conversation back to the Companions. He slid it across the table to a get a word in as Zoe fell upon it with vigor and gusto. "Back up a bit. Do you guys have a secret club badge or code names? How do you recognize one another and how does the pull work?"

Zoe stopped in her enthusiastic demolishing of his sacrificial offering to raise a finger as a point of correction. "The Call. It's the first time you get that itch. Something inside you just goes off and you have to step up. First time is always the worst. Feels like the heebie-jeebies up and down your spine and a fire alarm in your skull. You know, in your freaking bones, that something is wrong and it's up to you to do something about it." She slapped the table for emphasis, her enthusiastic slam sending innocent sauce packets flying.

"You get echoes of the Call after that. I knew, in the middle of my scene, that a normal human, which is you by the way, needed help near-by. The pull, it's like how you hear something that turns your head, something out of the corner of your eye that makes you jump. It's like… like…" Zoe paused, hands groping the air as she grabbed for words. Apparently the words were slippery devils because she gave up and shrugged. "It's something we just feel, a knowing deep in our gut. It isn't something we can really ignore."

"As for the spandex and tights thing... not exactly. It's a lot less Justice Friends and lot more fraternity, or hobby club. Freemasons, Motorcycle Clubs, that sort of thing. The Companions all know what we are and can recognize others like us. Common interests and experiences help build bridges. A lot of us do have a hard time of it, though. We can't always tell our families and have to be careful when we start getting outta hand with our strength. Just like Herakles." Zoe looked down and sighed. It was the first time since Jon had met her that her seemingly unstoppable energy drained away. "It's hard to hang onto any sort of normal life. In some ways, I guess, we're a support group for one another too. AA for ancient heroes reborn. Keeping 'em on the straight and narrow."

A moment later, the melancholy was gone, and the actress pointed at Jon. Jon leaned back, protective of his shirt. He knew where those fingers had been *Do not get those greasy digits anywhere near my pressed shirt, lady.*

"Which leads me to my next point. The majority of us don't go out of our way to hunt the Mythics. First off, there is a good chance we're related after all, since they're also descended from the gods. Friendly rivalry is our usual M.O. Taunting, challenges, pranks. Bets are super common, especially over some bit of honor or something. We call 'em 'Labors.'"

Jon perked up. "Example, Herakles."

Zoe tapped one sauce covered finger to the side of her nose, leaving a yellowish red mark. "Yep. See, honor and keeping your word are big freaking deals in our little community. A way to keep them and ourselves honest. That much power needs something to keep it grounded. Besides, when it isn't deadly serious, it's a lot of fun." The grin turned into a leer. "Ohhh, the things you can make 'em do to settle their bet. Works the other way, too. Settling a score with a score, am I right? Just like you and Cassidy, eh, eh, eh?"

With that, the conversation turned to another part of this brave new world Jon wasn't ready to think about. Mr. Doe ignored the figurative and literally ribbing of his eating buddy and subtly moved the conversation along. "So, movies! How did that happen?"

"Wuss. Well, if we're the soccer hooligans and vigilantes of the Mythic world, the Houses, your employers, are the crime syndicates and old business moguls. Godfather with Fangs. Old families with more money than Hades. They have their claws in all kinds of things. You told me on the ride over that you met the, uh, what did you call them, Terrible Trio?" Jon nodded. "Did you notice how other people didn't react to them?" A second nod. "That's because of charms, rituals, and spells cast on them. Notice those shiny baubles of theirs, with the eyes?"

Jon nodded a third time, earning full points in class. "Yeah, I got that part. They showed them off. Some sort of weird 'you can't see me' thing."

"Right. Those are part of their 'pay.' See, Mythics have always lived with humans and generally liked human things. Mostly the wine and wenching, but they diversify. Used to be Mythics could hang out in cabins deep in the woods, spooky towers, other horror movie sets waiting to happen without causing too much fuss. They'd head out at night and no one's the wiser. Things changed over the centuries."

"The miracles of modern technology didn't agree with them?"

"Yep. When video recording and camera phones started to crop up, the Houses used spells and charms to let the less human bunch wander out in public without causing a fuss. You don't want Fuzzy Lumpkins showing up in America's Funniest Home Videos. Those little jewelry bits on the Mythics throw up a 'shield' so normies won't notice the horns and hooves. So, it covers them on the looks department. Nothing's gonna stop folks from noticing the ruckus. They can party pretty hard on their own."

Jon's head bobbed vigorously, thinking of Anthony, Nathan, and Jayne. *I can only imagine a whole herd of the Trio running around.* A moment of pondering about his impromptu carpool buddies cost Jon the last of his fries to Zoe's nimble fingers. *She's like a mutant ninja pigeon. I am seriously rethinking that robot from the future angle. No one has that kind of mechanical precision.*

Chomping her way around a handful of her golden fried spoils, Zoe continued her lecture. "Anyway, the spell. The spells only work for so long. The bigger and better ones tending to take a lot of work and being renewed every so often."

"So, like a battery, or a license."

"Right! 'You must be this enchanted to go outside' sort of thing. Some of the rituals are very old school, with lots of clauses and specifics. Performed under the first new moon with a blade of quicksilver with an eye of newt cocktail. Real Merlin stuff." Her cherub face quirked into a smile, bits of fry poking out of one side of the mouth. "Some of them are a lot of fun, if you can get invited. The hoofers are unruly at the best of times, so they usually assign folks to keep an eye on them."

"Folks like you?"

Zoe's smile turned lecherous again. "Nah, I'm more of a bad influence. Anyway, the point is that they cloak 'em up so they can get out there and get a job. They give a stipend back, paying for their glamour, and everyone goes home happy. They use the money from that to… well…buy more stuff, expand their businesses, and make more money. That's how I got into acting. Decent pay, nice perks, and I get to hang out with some fun people. I even have time for night classes. Beats a desk job."

She quieted down as the waiter cleared their plates, giving Jon some time to process things.

"Recently though, weird stuff has been going down. Some of the rougher Mythics don't like the direction things have been going lately. These old schoolers think Shifters are getting too much like humans the past century or so, getting soft in the claw. They are worried all of them are going to turn out like Todd, the fuzzball I threw through the wall at the studio, all fluffy pillows, silk ties, and cologne. These hardliners, the Cull of Actaeon, want to romp and stomp and be where the wild things are all night long."

All trace of Jon's happy companion vanished, Zoe's bubbly soul replaced by an angel of vengeance. "They are dedicated to their ideals and have shed blood for their cause. The Shifter Houses aren't talking but all the Companions I know have been getting that certain itch more and more. It ain't stopping. Both the Senate and the Court of the Raptors keep telling the Companions to stay out of their business, saying everything is under control. But I heed the Call, not some monster in a three-piece suit. The Call is pulling. Hard. Something is going down, and if this keeps up, the Companions will step in. When that happens, the body count is only going to go up."

Jon swallowed a sudden lump in his throat. *Must be the greasy food.* "Damn. I think I'm right in the middle of that shit storm."

Zoe looked over, sympathy replacing the steel in her eyes. "Yeah, I had a feeling about that too."

There didn't seem to be much to say after that, so the two sat quietly and watched the sunlit tide. Silence reigned in the car all the way back to Speculo Productions. When Zoe hopped out of his speedster, huge backpack strapped to her back, she turned to Jon.

"Look, I can't promise anything, but for what it's worth, you have my sympathies and my support. You seem like an alright guy, Jon, for a sleazy, blood sucking, no-good, soulless lawyer. Numbers on the back if you need any help. Keep safe, okay?" Reaching into her backpack, Zoe handed him a small autographed glossy photo of herself before ducking inside, leaving Jon sitting alone in the parking lot with a shiny picture and his fears.

CHAPTER 12

FEW THINGS STOOD in Magda's way when her blood was up. Few were idiotic or brave enough to try. As Niall watched Brock talking the veteran down not three blocks from the Den, the greasy-haired youth idly wondered which category the two of them fell into.

"Out of my way, Brock! Blood has been shed this day and I intend to shed some more." Magda's beast simmered just beneath the surface, words growled through bared teeth.

She might as well have barked at a wall.

"No."

Niall winced at Brock's blank face and monosyllabic response. *Oh, very diplomatic. I can see we are well into opening a dialogue. That's a point solidly in the idiotic column.*

The vengeance hungry Cohort warrior jaw dropped at her line mate's response. "You would deny me my honor, my right as a warrior? Ohhh terribly sorry, shall I file a formal grievance?" Brock remained parade ground still, refusing to rise to Magda's taunts. "Know that a veteran of the Sunset Cohort has been assailed. Honor demands restitution. We'll take it out of the hides of those faithless feather dusters."

"Do you know for a fact it was the Court that did it?"

Brock's quiet question brought Magda up short, even her as she swelled to match the anvil-shouldered fellow in width, doing things to her wardrobe Niall would have appreciated in better circumstances. *Wow, that jacket is freaking durable. The pants, not so much. What's a few more holes?*

"A Raptor strike force ambushes myself and the neutral adjudicator and you ask me if the Court are to blame?" She now stood eye to eye with Brock, rippling musculature straining denim and cotton.

Niall waffled between amusement and worry, looking around anxiously. *Bad enough we're yelling damn near in the middle of the street, I don't want even to think about the nightmare we're gonna have to deal with if Magda goes full She-Hulk.*

Brock remained insufferably patient. "Stop for a moment. Analyze the situation. You say the squad attempted to kill the adjudicator. Why? Why not wait until he was vulnerable rather than accompanied by a seasoned warrior of the Cohort?"

"Huh, I didn't think of that..." Niall regretted his musings when he noticed Magda's glare rotate to him like the barrel of a cannon. *Not looking forward to another slap upside the head. She's likely to take it clean off in her current state.* The loose lipped youth held up his hands in surrender. Magda dismissed Niall before turning with back to Brock with a snarl.

"I'll add incompetence to their list of sins, right after cowardice."

"Retribution clades are neither and you know it. We both have the scars to prove it, Bannersworn." Magda flinched as though slapped at hearing her long-discarded rank. Brock's hand reflexively massaged his knee as he spoke of old memories and old pains. "Magda, please think about it. The most ruthless agents of the Court appear from ambush, allow you to see them, and then vanish without slaying either yourself or a vulnerable normie lawyer. That would certainly mean failure and disgrace, two things the elite enforcers of the Court do not suffer lightly. Unless…"

"Unless our deaths were never their goal." Magda picked up the thread, following where it led. "Unless it wasn't a sanctioned hit." Realization dawned on her face for a moment, before being replaced by sheer, unbridled rage. "Furies." Niall involuntarily took a step back. The amount of hatred and contempt Magda packed into a single word was staggering. "They wanted us to think they were a Retribution Squad. This is their handiwork. That damned Cull! The filth wanted to be seen. They wanted me to think the Raptors were guilty."

Brock nodded. "In order to incite retaliation from the Cohort. We strike back. More blood is spilled. The Court believes we struck first. The Senate believes the opposite. Negotiations break down. War erupts."

Niall jumped up excitedly. "Sure! Because they know how easy it is to get you whack jobs into a killing frenzy." When his elder companions looked at him for his offered insights, Niall quickly backpedaled. "I mean, 'us' whack jobs. Solidarity, right?" *One of these days I'll manage to open my mouth without inviting a backhand.*

Brock sighed heavily. "More accurately, they know our ways. The Cull knows honor demands a return strike."

"And if the Raptors didn't sanction it, it would appear as though we struck first. I cannot even name those who assaulted me." Calmer now, only a frustrated human snarl remained in Magda's voice.

Which is still enough to scare me. Niall watched Magda's hands shake. *That's not good either.*

As Niall worried over Magda, Brock continued. "Right. Both sides claim the other started it, the truce is broken, and we lash at each other's throats, further undermining the Houses' attempts at peace and, by extension, their authority. The resulting bloodbath would virtually assure the Cull's victory."

Niall blinked slowly at the speed at which Brock connected the dots. "Damn." No one shushed him this time, the older warriors agreeing with the sentiment.

"Well put, kid." Magda lightly slugged Niall in the arm.

A love tap. Only slight bruising. Despite the pain, Niall grinned goofily at the veteran's praise. *Good to see her smile, for once. Been pretty rare since her squad died.*

"I know you prefer open blades, Magda, but this is the battlefield we fight on here and now. We have to keep our cool and play our cards very close to our chest. The whole situation is a powder keg. Any spark can set it off."

"You mean like a respected Cohort veteran howling for blood?" Niall preemptively brought his guard up, expecting retaliation. *This is gonna hurt.*

The kid found himself pleasantly shocked when Magda doubled over with laughter.

"Niall, you are an irritating, daft little bastard but sometimes, just sometimes, you know what you're on about." The second slug of approval almost sent Niall off his feet.

Ouch. Hurts so good.

"Fine, Brock. I hear you. For now, we watch and wait. And when those bastards show their faces, we will paint the land with their traitorous blood." Murderous did not begin to describe the look on Magda's face. At that moment, Niall felt extremely happy that Magda was on his side. The blood lust transformed a moment later into a lunatic grin. "For now, who wants to get shit-faced with me? Fighting off fake assassins works up a hell of a thirst."

Without bothering to wait for an answer, Magda slung her arms about the two Legionnaires and marched them to the Den even as she laugher her heard off the whole way. As far as planning sessions went it wasn't very productive, but Niall thought they had a hell of a good time.

§—§

"Yes, I understand. Mr. Arkadas is a busy man. Well, when you can, tell him Jon Doe wishes to speak to him. Yes, again. Thank you, buh-bye." Jon's plastic smile melted the moment the secretary terminated the call.

Safe to say that well is bone dry. It had been over two weeks since Jon's talk with Zoe. Two weeks of increasingly stringent if politely word-ed requests from his employers for status updates. Two weeks of sweat-ing bullets that the next request might be made at claw point. Two weeks of getting to know the monsters he worked with.

Shockingly, more parallels existed between the law firms Jon knew so well and his current clientele. He surmised it might be because they were both staffed by slavering, flesh hungry beasts.

Jon discovered that office politics were office politics and the uni-versal rule of Cover Your Ass existed, whether you could turn into a feathered or fanged beastie or not. Requests for aid met polite refusals, an unwillingness to bother the boss, and a studious aversion to making more work for yourself. *Makes sense I suppose, if your boss might bite your head off. Literally.*

Arkadas proved, unsurprisingly, less than helpful. *The old bastard doesn't want to get his hands dirty. He knows I've got a target on my back and doesn't want to be anywhere near the fallout. Probably already written me off as dead.*

Waving his cellphone about, Jon puffed up his face, jowls pro-nounced, parroting the stuffy windbag for the benefit of his empty home. "What do you want from me, boy? That idiot, Sipskos, down in records should have given you everything you need. Figure it out!" Imaginary cigar stabbed at the air as Jon replicated Arkadas' pomposity. Though always up for a round of mocking mimicry, the blue-eyed wunderkind took no solace in his latest round of "make fun of your superiors."

Unjoweled, Jon moved on to the next item on his distressingly short list. *Marc. Well, maybe he has something I don't.* He summarily punched up his old college buddy. Problem was, like every other time Jon tried to reach the undead clerk, he only got the answering machine. *My life has become a waking nightmare of talking with unthinking machines and inhuman monsters.*

"Jon, I know it's you. Don't bother me. Research. You know the drill."

His unbreathing amigo's message lifted Jon's spirits a fraction. He remembered the dynamo of Marc at work back at Harvard. The lanky Sipskos forewent sleep, food, and sanity to follow threads of information through the most labyrinth of paper-trails until the puzzle pieces fit together. *Best to just sit back and let the wizard do his thing. Maybe this time I'll even take my own advice.*

Clutching at that guttering candle of hope, the lawyer returned to his list.

Reiger was emphatically out. The lawyer's one call to the office ended in abject failure. Not only did Jon's attempt at spy movie dialogue nearly have a squad sent to his house for prank calling the police, once he did drop Reiger's name, he was informed, in no uncertain terms, that the lieutenant would call Jon when Reiger was ready and not a moment sooner.

Jon seethed at the memory of the chain smoking Reiger. *Above his paygrade, my overly educated ass!* Jon could have sympathized with lieutenant it if wasn't Jon's neck on the line. Truthfully, Jon waffled between envy and respect for the cop. As the lawyer was discovering, working as a go-between for two bloodthirsty shapeshifting crime syndicates certainly demanded a careful balancing act and a cunning mind. The fact that Reiger still had all limbs intact yet spoke highly of his survival skills and ability to make the right play at the right time.

Unfortunately for Jon, the right play here meant throwing Mr. Doe to the wolves, bears, and whatever else tagged along for the ride.

Jon skipped over Magda and Selina with a small frown. He found himself reluctant to call either of the two Shifters for reasons he was unwilling to dwell on. Jon chalked the aversion up to the horrific violence and bloodshed last time he was near either of them. That rang hollow and a small part of Jon's mind chided him for his cowardice. *Wouldn't be the first time I've ignored the little voice.* Even though things were looking desperate, Jon couldn't bring himself to call.

Later, Jon told himself, not for the first time.

Down to the Z's of his contacts, Jon sighed forlornly. *Grasping at straws but let's give it a go.* Once again, Zoe's bubbly voice and surfer girl drawl formed a counterpoint to Jon's darkening mood.

"Hey Zoe, Jon again. When you're done smiting the forces of darkness or whatever, call me back." He thumbed the phone off with a sigh.

Jon rounded back to the last two names left to call. Two terrific women who just happened to be blood-soaked shapeshifting monsters. *What's a few dead bodies between friends, right?* The lawyer fought down a wave of butterflies in his stomach, which troublingly felt like it had little to do with the slaughter at the Edfu estate. Screwing up his courage, Jon went with Selina's number. *At least she should have a charged phone.*

A few rings later and a decidedly imperious masculine voice answered the phone. "Aahmes Aegolius, of the House of Aegolius. Speak."

Crap. Jon mentally kicked himself. *Of course, it wouldn't be a personal line.* Instantly, his shields came up, Jon's professional demeanor sliding into place like armor. His voice became smooth as butter, the legal mask firmly in place. "This is Jonathan Augustus Doe. Is Selina Aegolius available?"

Alas, Aahmes knew the game too. "Jon, how good to hear from you." Jon could practically hear the shit-eating grin on the man's hawk-nosed face.

Flashbacks of darkness, panicking, and sharp knives forced their way into Jon's head, which was rather new the lawyer. He seemed to have developed a veritable stockpile of trauma in a short time. *Play it cool.* "Thank you, Mr. Aegolius, but my business is with Selina. Is she in?"

"Not at the moment, but I assure you, Jon, anything you would say to her, you may say to me. Why, we can even meet to discuss this, face to face."

It took every ounce of Jon's control not to laugh in Aahmes' face. Or scream. *Not a chance, you psychotic windbag.* "Unfortunately, I don't believe that's possible at this time." *Because I intend to keep as far away from you as possible.* "You see, Selina is the primary point of contact, and this is highly sensitive information. I would be remiss in my duties to discuss any information with anyone unqualified to hear it."

"I am her brother and her elder. This project is the charge of my House. I am imminently qualified to be kept informed of any developments on the case."

"Then why is her name on the paper but not yours?" A perfectly innocuous question, but Aahmes' voice, frosty enough to chill the elder Aegolius' expensive champagne, told Jon he'd drawn blood.

"Mr. Doe, even taking your professed ignorance at face value, allow me to enlighten you as to how unwise your actions at this moment are. You do not want to stand against me. Now, tell me what you would tell me sister."

Jon cut him off with the politest smile, one so saccharine its sweetness oozed through the phone. "That would violate my contract. Please tell Selina I called and that I am awaiting her reply at earliest opportunity. Thank you for relaying the message."

Jon hung up with the spiteful glee of a six-year-old child. *You know, I might have just made a hell of an enemy, but damn that felt good.*

His audience thought so too.

"Hah, well done, buck! I knew you had guts in you somewhere."

Jon spun around with a strangled squawk to find Magda lounging insouciantly on his couch. When he saw his uninvited house guest's footwear that he truly panicked. *Her boots are on my couch!* A second louder squawk followed as he ran to slap her steel toed footwear off the expensive leather.

"Are you crazy?" he exclaimed. "Get your feet down! This is a Baker!" The punkess spread her hands and shrugged, baffled by her host's reaction. Jon wiped down the couch arm with the care normally reserved a wounded family member. "Never mind, you heathen. No respect for good upholstery. Wait, how did even you get in here?"

With the more pressing concern of smudged furniture handled, Jon's mind turned to consider the home invasion. He was surprised that Magda sneaking in didn't send him into a full panic, considering Jon had seen her transform into a bloodthirsty monster. When he looked at Magda now, he saw the same captivating person from their night at the club. Jon wondered if both of them were the real Magda; the beauty and the beast.

As Magda lacked mind reading capabilities, she ignored his internal musing and answered the spoken question. The Cohort centurion hiked a thumb toward the back end of the house. "Jimmied your window and snuck in."

"Of course." *Larceny on top of gruesome murder. Glad she has a well-rounded set of skills. Probably has jaywalking on the rap sheet, too.* "Since you took the time to get in here, what can I do for you?"

She grinned like the Cheshire Cat. *Or Cheshire Wolf, as the case may be.* "You've already given me a good laugh when you tweaked that pompous feather duster's nose! That is a fine gift. But no, my dear buck, this is about what I can do for you."

Jon arched an eyebrow. "Why do those words fill me with utter dread?"

Magda rolled her eyes. "That's some fine gratitude for you. I'm here to keep an eye on you, make sure the thrice damned Furies don't get to you."

"The what?"

"The Furies. The Cull of Actaeon. The ones who've cutting up innocent folks lately."

"Those guys. Zoe mentioned them." Jon waited a moment, but Magda simply sat with rear planted, looking around Casa de Jon. The blue-eyed lawyer coughed into his fist. Twice. "This is the part where you tell me where the hell have you been these last two weeks."

"Important as you might think you are, Jon, there are a lot of other duties that need attending. You recall that little scuff up on the beach?"

Jon shuddered. "Yeah."

"That skirmish damn near pushed the Houses to war. We've been running around playing nicey nice while looking for the bastards who really did it. All smiles and sheathed blades. It's hard work trying to be polite to folks who you're investigating for trying to kill you. In short, dear buck, you were bumped down on the priority list. Until now."

"Why?"

Magda grinned a lopsided smile. "Same reason your bosses... heh... our bosses have been breathing down both our necks. The clock's ticking on the Beachfront Case and that makes your sweet arse a prime target for the Cull."

"Fine, time crunch, angry bosses. So, what do these Cull guys want with me?"

Magda squinted at him in disbelief before shaking her head. "Oh, Jonny boy. I keep forgetting how ignorant you are."

Jon glared at the patronizing redhead. "You can blame yourself for that. I asked, and you fobbed me off, remember? I'm in the dark despite my best efforts to ask you weirdos for details about the crazy shit I'm neck deep in. You might want to cut it out with the secret password and club handshake smokescreen crap if you want me to do my job."

Magda laughed. "Thousands of years of ingrained tradition and practical application of hiding in plain sight, buck. Social camouflage. You don't shake something like that in a day." She looked at him, mirth fading. "But I'm thinking you are keen to ask about something else."

"Well, now that you mention it, yes! Forget about the freaking Cull. Is there any chance you can get your furry friends to not turn me into giblets? I'd consider it a big favor." A forlorn hope, Jon figured, but one he might as well ask.

"Now that's gratitude for you. Bite the hand that feeds you. I'm here to protect you, you idiot." Magda crossed her arms and looked off into a corner, trying for indignation.

Bullshit. Jon had been lied to by the best and knew deflection when he saw it. Jon eyes went cold. He steepled his fingers, elbows on knees. "Really? And if I made the call tomorrow that the Court can have the property? What would you do then?"

Magda jumped off the couch, glaring down at the lawyer, looming over him in a jangle of leather and metal studs. "You wouldn't dare!"

Jon's eyes were ice, even if his blood was on fire. "Wouldn't I? Why not? You aren't my protector, Magda, or else you would have been here from the start. No, you're my minder. Here and now, you were ready to lay into me if I didn't toe the party line. They don't care about me and you don't care about me. I'm just a means to an end. What really sucks is that the other guys are ready to do the same if I give it up to you, so I can't go running to them to save my ass."

A sad shake of Magda's dyed head only dropped Jon's morale further. "I cannot promise protection from your duty, Jon. It's bigger than that. This is a matter of honor."

Jon snorted. "Oh yes, very honorable. Murdering an innocent bystander you suckered into your twisted little games."

Barely restrained anger sent the warrior maiden pacing back and forth, her boots thudding on hardwood floors. "Jupiter's balls, man, have some dignity. This is your job, right? Damn well do it."

Without thinking, Jon stepped forward, nose to nose with Magda. "My job? My job is supposed to be handling paperwork, sipping martinis, and lying smoothly enough to a bunch of bored jurors to get rich snobs off the hook so I can collect a fat paycheck. It does not include choosing which side of psychopathic monsters gets to gut me, just to settle some stupid blood feud from before I was born."

One warning growl, low and guttural, escaped the Cohort solider. "Watch your tongue. I've bled for the cause and lost friends in our war. Don't push it, little man."

Jon ought to have backed down, used some of his supreme oratory skills to defuse the situation. Jon knew could. Jon knew he ought to. But he wouldn't.

Despair, fear, and anger can do ugly things to the mind. Jon had sailed well past the point of common sense. "Or what? You'll kill me right now? Go ahead! Might as well come from someone I thought cared about me, at least a little." Even as the words left his mouth Jon blinked a bit in surprise. *Where did that come from?*

Magda blinked as well, confusion mixing with her rage. "Care for? Come on, Jon. Surely you know it was only a bit of fun. A booty call, nothing more. I doubt you're a stranger to the club scene. How many romantic conquests have you had over the years?"

"Plenty, but that's not the point." The desperate lawyer hissed like a deflated balloon. "It just seemed that, for once, someone valued me for who I am, not just what me and my name can do for them. Guess you're just like Arkadas, Selina, and all the others. Abandoning me when it's convenient."

Magda's hand grabbed the front of his jacket, nearly tearing the fabric as she pulled. The smell of Jack Daniels on her breath washed over him. "I'm nothing like them." She softened her tone, loosening her death grip on Jon's shirt. "I do like you, buck, after a fashion. You've got more guts than sense, and I respect that. Throw in with us. Fully. I can speak to the Senate. They might be able to give you some protection." Even as Magda uttered the words, doubt and despair shone through her eyes, giving lie to the offer of sanctuary.

Suddenly tired, Jon gently removed her hands from his jacket. "Might? Sounds like I'd have better odds in Vegas. We both know the score, Magda. I'm here as a sacrificial lamb in your stupid war. A pawn to be discarded. Neither side is going to offer me protection. They only want to protect their interests. Expendable assets, I get it."

He herded her to the door, stepping outside. The fierce warrior looked deflated, not fighting the lawyer as they went. Jon looked up at the darkening skies. *Looks like rain.* He vaguely heard Magda muttering one last halfhearted attempt to dissuade him, though her eyes never met his.

"Thanks, but no thanks. I'll find my own way out of this. And if I don't, I hope they give me a lovely service. Send flowers. Maybe your duty will help wash your hands clean after all this."

Turning away from Magda, Jon trudged into town, spirits heavy and head full of worry.

Gray clouds loomed ominously overhead, threatening rain. Jon hunched down into his tailored charcoal Gucci pea coat. Catching his reflection in a mirror, Jon took stock of himself. Skies, coat, and mood all matched and he cut a handsome, if Byronic, figure. *Terrific. At least I look better than I feel.* He'd hoped to walk off his sour mood, but the recent week's events kept running through his mind, like a rat in a maze. Jon kept coming back to the same sorry conclusion: he couldn't escape any more than the rat. His dismal fate still loomed over his head like an executioner's blade.

His rapidly diminishing options consumed him, dimming Jon's enthusiasm for the trendy diners, coffee shops, and antique stores flanking him. Their glow and muted laughter deepened his sour mood as he trudged past. *Sure, laugh it up. They don't have to deal with bosses who will literally eat you for lunch over a missed deadline.*

A snarling growl, an animal's warning, tore Jon from his funk. A massive lupine creature, wine-dark pelt rippling like smoke on a midnight lake, crouched in a shadowed alleyway, eyes shining gold in the glow of the antique lampposts. Its threatening bulk filled the space between two trendy boutiques; the furred man-beast crouched on its haunches and still loomed above Jon.

Jon shivered in mortal dread as his primal hind brain picked out the scent of a predator. His nose caught the heady mix of matted fur, animal sweat, and the salty tang of blood. Doe recoiled from the beast, images of carnage he'd been struggling to ignore hammering to the forefront of his brain. With the visions of death came a tide of anger. Jon's simmering anger and frustration strangled his fear, burning through the foggy cloud of self-pity he'd been swimming in.

Everywhere I turn someone is trying to make me jump. Magda, Arkadas, Selina. Now this clown. Jon assumed one of his employers decided to up the ante. Possibly Aahmes, after Jon snubbed the aristocratic shit. Or maybe Magda, when he showed her the door. It did look like one of her crowd. *I wonder if this counts as a "gentle reminder" in their messed up world.* Fuming, Jon turned to unleash his ire at the slavering beastie.

"Look, if you want a biscuit, I'm afraid I don't have any." The savage monster cocked its head, a confused whine replacing its snarl, and Jon felt a brief thrill of victory as this specter of man's primal fear of the dark reared like a German Shepard. *Think you're scary, furball? Well, think again. I interned for legal firms!* Jon never cared for bullies, authority, or long-haired dogs. Having all three in one pushing him around sent his blood boiling.

Jon crossed his arms and adopted his well-practiced "cockier-than-god" stance used to square off against Harvard deans before laying into the shaggy bastard again.

"Hey, I get it. First the carrot, then the stick. A friendly face and some fluff talk aren't greasing the wheels so they send a big guy like you instead. If your bosses think flashing a little fang is going to get me to hurry this along, well pal, you can tell them it ain't happening. I've faced tougher and meaner bastards on college debate teams. Besides, you can't lay a paw on me. First rule of table talk, buddy. High pressure tactics don't mean much when the other guy knows you can't back them up. So why don't you run along and play fetch somewhere else before your leash gets yanked?"

The creature's growl rose in pitch, a whirring buzz-saw underscored by a truck engine's rumble. The lawyer gulped. He'd heard car stereos with less bass. Dread rapidly overwhelmed the flush of victory. Rain began to tumble from the heavens as the wolf thing spoke.

"Little man." The words emerged garbled and wrong, forced out of a muzzle unused to forming the pitiful mewling sounds of its soft pink prey. "You trespass against codes old when Babylon fell. Your arrogance offends me and your ignorance damns you. Know that my name, in your babbling tongue, is Ripper, for it is what I am and what I do. I am servant to neither the Senate nor the Court. My comrades and I reject their feeble decrees and revel in our gods-granted freedoms." Wolf eyes locked with very human, very terrified baby blues. "Namely, the freedom to hunt."

Brick shattered as the beast surged forward, claws outstretched for Jon's head. The butcher-knife talons missed their target by inches. The intended victim tore down the street as the monster wheeled, adrenaline granting the lawyer wings. Even as blood roared in his ears, the charnel house breath of the creature behind him washed over Jon. Desperately hurling himself into an alley, Jon narrowly avoided death at the creature's hands a second time, chunks of façade scattering.

Lungs burning, Jon raced past rusting garbage bins and barred doors, running through a maze-like warren of back alleys. Slipping and stumbling over slick concrete and stinking garbage, he skidded to a halt, fine shoes slipping on the wet alley. A wall reared up before him, brick and mortar barred his path. *Dead end.*

Escape denied, Jon dove into the piles of trash, desperately trying to hide amidst the detritus of high-end boutiques and fashionable cafes. Burrowing through the stinking refuse, the desperate lawyer spotted what may just be his salvation. A small basement window, rusting bars long since cut away and broken glass teeth set in a gaping portal. Scrambling through the filth, Jon tore through leaking trash bags to reach this slim chance of survival. Guttural laughter from the alley mouth interrupted his efforts. Despite himself, Jon turned to look. The creature filled the alley, blocking the only way out, monstrous bulk blotting out the city lights beyond.

"Digging in the trash, little worm? Pathetic scum. Coward! How typical of you, human filth! Crawl. Hide. You cannot escape from me! I will tear you open and devour your still beating heart. You will die amidst the waste of your degenerate people." Stalking forward, the beast trailed its talons along concrete wall of the alley, sparks reflecting in the rain.

Gibbering in fear, Jon frowned at the absurdity of the creature's monologue. Even in his panicked state a sense of unreal frustration rose up. *Death by cliché.* Tears streamed down his face as he threw himself at the narrow window. Bones ground and protested inside him as he struggled to fit through the narrow aperture. Daggers of glass cut into his flesh, rain and blood soaking his fine clothes as Jon forced himself, inch by panicked inch, through the rusty portal. With a final pull, Jon tumbled down into the moldy basement. Even as the harried lawyer fell into welcome darkness, a frustrated howl erupted behind him; the cry of a predator denied its prey. The hunter's quarry lay gasping for breath as the snarling beast raged above.

A massive arm followed the lawyer into the basement, talons tearing at the air as it blindly sought its victim. Rain drops flew from the dagger-like claws and soaked fur, glittering diamonds in the dark. Whimpering, Jon scuttled deeper into the decrepit space, staring in terror at the monster above. He blindly fumbled for anything he could use to drive off the beast snarling for his blood. Picking up a broken plank of wood in shaking hands, the consultant huddled against the slime-slicked walls. The beast raged and pressed harder against the window, the aging iron frame groaning and buckling under its assault. Without warning, the beast paused, like a hound picking up a scent. The taloned claws retreated, replaced with glistening fangs and a single baleful eye, shining in the basement darkness.

"Stay in your pit then, little worm. Burrow deep and hide in the filth and the dark. You may have escaped death at my hands this night but know this: you have only delayed the inevitable. I have your scent now, prey. If your blood does not stain the streets this night, it will soon enough. You will come to wish for so quick an end by my hands once your keepers decide you have outlived your usefulness. Treasure this night, o' pawn. Precious few remain."

With a final snarl, Ripper's nightmare face vanished, leaving Jon alone in the dank basement, with only wan moonlight shining through the narrow hole above.

CHAPTER 13

THE DOORS OF THE DEN SLAMMED open as Magda stormed in, bowling two Legionnaires over in the process. Ursus poked his head inside in her wake, holding the doors open by dint of his broad shoulders. Being a comradely fellow concerned for his fellow Cohort, the bear Shifter dragged both centurions to safety out in the cloudy evening, before the fools did anything to attract Magda's ire. Something had set the Bannersworn's blood afire and woe betide any who got in her way.

Magda's face was as cloudy as the weather outside as she stomped to her favorite table with a curt demand for stiff drinks. Try as she might, Jon's resigned desperation plagued her, the betrayal in his voice still stinging. *Damn his eyes! I was trying to help him! He made his choice. What does he know of duty?* Magda fumed as she snatched her drink from the hesitant waiter, who quickly slunk away. Anyone with a lick of sense gave the warrior a wide berth, allowing the sulking veteran her space.

Which is why it should come as little surprise that Niall sauntered up and unwisely joined her at the table, mocking smile on his lips and still damp from the downpour outside. "I take it negotiations didn't go well?"

"Shut up, Niall," Magda snarled between chugs of alcohol. The usual refrain did not deter the young Shifter.

"Ouch. Never heard that one before. Please, stop before you hurt my feelings." Niall's hands fiddled with his limply hanging locks. Hair gel and rain didn't mix, it seemed.

Magda glared silently, putting enough threat in her glare to send an army scurrying away in terror. When her young companions refused to take the hint, Magda huffed and leaned forward to gaze forlornly into her drink. "That damn fool lawyer. It's like Jon won't even try to save himself." She chugged the burning liquid, filling the silence as Niall listened, uncharacteristically quiet. "Bastard even had the gall to condemn me when I offered our aid. Won't even think of taking it, says we're as likely to kill him as those damned Court bastards." Anger fell away in a deep shuddering breath as the warrior faced the truth behind her rage, unable to fend off the shame and guilt any longer.

"Damn the man, he's not wrong. We would cut Jon off as soon as he ceased to be useful. Poor idiot got sucked into this without half a clue and now it's his head on the block. This isn't right. It's one thing to trample an enemy or to give one's life for the glory of the Cohort, but this is black-handed work for sure." Lips curled into snarl, she rolled the empty cup in her hands. "I fear my House, the great and glorious Senate, is going to kill an innocent."

If Magda was looking for a sympathetic ear, she was sorely disappointed. Niall snorted loudly at the end of her mournful soliloquy. "So what? Not like that's anything new."

Rolling her eyes, the elder squad member gave a disgruntled dismissal. "Not now, Niall."

Niall opened his mouth, then closed it, appearing to weigh his options. Common sense would have screamed not to poke the bear, though anyone who knew Niall, understood he and common sense shared a distant relationship. "I'm serious. Why does this one guy matter compared to all the other corpses piling up? Because you know him?" He snorted derisively. "What about all the other innocents who got killed over this inter-House crap?"

Another heavy sigh escaped the veteran. *I am not in the mood for Niall's shit right now.* She waved a hand dismissively. "That was different. We do what we can, but we can't save everyone. Besides, it was the Furies that killed them, not us."

Magda's dismissive reply snapped something in the young pup. Niall slammed two balled fists into the table, sending the veteran warrior scrambling to steady her cup and save the precious booze.

"Don't you get it? There's no difference! We are the Furies!"

Niall froze, seemingly realizing what he said and to whom and the danger he was in. Magda's gaze frosted over, cold and deadly as a killer's knife. She leaned toward Niall, faces scant inches apart, a situation that in other circumstances would have set Niall's heart pounding for very different reasons. "Recant yer words, pup. Now."

Niall blanched and swallowed hard but didn't back down. "No. You have to face facts. This shady crap is business as usual. We kill innocents all the time in our pointless, petty little wars. Our whole stupid system's broken. I mean, just look at us." He waved a hand at the bar full of disgruntled warriors, most of them blessedly ignoring Niall rambling, dismissing his and Magda's tête-à-tête as just one more of the mouthy pup's rants.

The young man sneered at them all which almost earned him a cuff from Magda. "The proud Cohort, all bent out of shape because we haven't had a chance to thump on something. Every time we skirmish, pick up ourselves up after a dust up and call honor settled, someone else dies for it. Someone who wasn't even a part of the battle and couldn't fight back. And for what? All because of some idiotic idea of 'honor?'" Words tumbled free from Niall's lips, a dam broken deep inside him.

"That's the damn problem; this blasé attitude toward dead innocents as fucking collateral damage and this over hyped machismo and paper-thin honor. We care only when we want to care, using people and treating them like disposable pawns. There is a sickness in the Houses. Peace is poisonous to us. It's why so many of us are joining the Cull. It's not for some higher cause. They want a chance to taste some blood. The Cohort is nothing more than a hit squad for the Senate. So many of us are signing up to hunt and kill because that's all they know. We're no different than the Furies."

Magda cut Niall's rant short with a rather unorthodox debate maneuver; she grabbed his shoulder and shoved the slender youth face first into the table. As Niall lay pinned, arm twisted in a painful hold, Magda's bared teeth came within inches of his face. "How dare you slander the House? After all they have done for you! It was the Sunset Cohort that took you in after your brother died! The Senate provides for us and we provide for it, and if that means bloodying our claws, so be it." Magda twisted harder, bone creaking and muscle bending under her hands. "Sean was one of us! Your own brother. He knew what it meant to be Cohort! He sacrificed his life for the House!"

Trapped under her unyielding grip, Niall hissed his defiance, spittle flying across the table. "Sacrifice? Is that what you call it when the Senate kills its own?"

Even as the words left his mouth Magda and Niall both froze mid-grapple. The two locked eyes, silent. Terror in Niall's eyes, confusion in Magda's.

"What did you say?"

After a small eternity, Niall continued quietly, sorrow replacing anger, fire drained from him. "Sean didn't sacrifice himself, the Senate killed him. He didn't believe. In the Cohort or the Senate. My brother told me things. Things he couldn't share with anyone else. About what he'd done. What he'd been ordered to do. The nightmares it gave him. Sometimes Sean would wake up in the middle of the night, screaming and sobbing." Tears gathered at the corners of Niall's eyes as he remembered.

"Sean hated what they made him do. How much blood he'd spilled. Sean was afraid they would take him out if he breathed a word of it. The night before he died, Sean woke me up. It was pitch black and I had no idea what was going on. Sean looked...haggard. Feverish. I've never been so scared as when I saw his face. My brother woke me up and told me to look after mom. He knew something bad was coming his way. Then, Sean was gone."

Even as Niall uttered his brother's secret, he tensed, body rigid, eyes looking up at Magda. Eyes that waited for the executioner's axe.

Magda balked as she realized her line mate was waiting for her to kill him right then and there. It hurt worse when she realized he was right. *Gods damn me, is this how far I've fallen?* A shadow of pain and regret washed over her, a familiar ache she thought she'd learned to live with, at least with a belly full of booze in her. "We all have nightmares." She eased off of her companion, eyes distant.

Shocked at the admission, to say nothing of his continued breathing, Niall awkwardly propped up on one elbow. "We don't have to. We can't just keep on killing like this. Something's gotta give."

Brock's tree-trunk arm squeezed between the two, his bulk physically separating them. "The only things giving right now are the table and my patience." The two Cohort warriors greeted his arrival with confused blinks. For such a large man, Brock could move with disturbing stealth. Then again, they had been somewhat distracted with their own conversation.

"Save the conversation for another day. For now, we have more immediate business. One of my informants just called in. Cull activity, another clerk of Arkadas' torn apart in an alley downtown. Sloppy work and still warm. Eye-witnesses testimony from Reiger's plainclothes places one of the renegades tearing after some dumb bastard who mouthed off to them. From the description, the killer sounds like Ripper himself." All ears perked up at the mention of the Furies' loudest firebrand.

Magda gripped Brock's vest, voice eager, almost hungry. "Ripper? You're sure?" The wolf Shifter was a powerful ideologue in the ranks of the Cull and one of the most vocal proponents the Furies' ideology.

The fanged monstrosity railed passionately against the Senate and Court, his rhetoric denouncing both as weak and blaming that weakness for the silence of the gods. Worse, Ripper was more than just talk. The renegade proved himself amongst the most brutal and active members of the Cull, slaying any perceived threat to their aims. Despite his notoriety, Ripper was a phantom. All knew of him, but the Cohort knew almost nothing about him.

All I want to know is where he is so I can kill him.

Brock gave a sage nod, unperturbed by Magda's death grip. "Best intelligence places him in downtown. I've been tracking his whereabouts with some contacts I have with the businesses in the area. If we move quickly, we may be able to end this tonight."

"Finally!" In the space between heartbeats, Magda's body swelled, the warrior barely slipping her leather jacket off as muscles bulged and her skeleton tortuously expanded. Carelessly hurling it against the wall in a jangle of metal, the wolfen-shaped warrior stalked to the door, Brock not two steps behind her, equally monstrous. "Let's mount the bastard's head on the fucking wall."

Dropping to all fours, they pounded out of the doors and into the stormy evening, nearly bowling over Ursus, who shouted after them about running out the front, that they had a dog door in the back for a reason.

Niall joined his pack in a burst of speed, human form making way for the wolf. Frowning and fretting, as much a lupine creature can, Niall trailed behind his line mates. Magda looked back with a wry grin. Even after the night, she didn't doubt for a second that he'd join them. They might fight, they might drive each other crazy, but they were still family, after all. *Ripper's a nasty piece of work. Niall's bleeding heart would be kicking him if he didn't do something. We put him down, that's one less Fury on the loose.* Three lupine shapes darted out of the Den, horns blaring as cars swerved to avoid what the drivers would swear up and down were three incredibly large dogs.

Howling like the damned, the Shifters tore into the night. The primordial cacophony touched a primal fear in those who heard it, sending shivers up their spines. It carried the reminder that despite all their cellphones and internet distractions, all their trappings of civilization, mankind was still prey. The howl promised a gruesome demise beneath razor-sharp claws and slavering fangs. Blood was in the air and something died tonight.

§—§

Jon sat huddled in the dark for a small eternity. He counted time in shuddering breaths and pounding heartbeats. With each pained exhale, he expected the nightmare of claws and fangs to return and finish what it started. Things scuttled and crawled over him. Jon kept slapping at his inquisitive many-legged neighbors, but his eyes never left the tiny bar of moonlight shining high above.

Have to get out of here, have to move. C'mon legs, up and at 'em! Move, damn you! Despite his mind's urgings, his body remained decidedly slow to respond. Unwrapping his aching arms, which clutched his legs in a death grip, Jon struggled to rise. Stranding proved a herculean task unto itself. As he forced his stiff legs to move, Jon stumbled forward into a puddle. Freezing at the noise, Jon looked up in panic to the basement window, expecting to see those terrible eyes still gazing at him. He tried to banish fear with reason. If the beast wanted him dead, it would have pushed through the bricked-up iron barred hole with its monstrous strength and then fell upon Jon, ripping and tearing with those terrible jaws.

Bile rose in Jon's throat at the visions of red massacre his mind conjured. *So much for rationalizing it.* Something about his failure to think it through struck the terrified man as hilarious. A desperate hiccupping laugh escaped the lawyer's tortured lungs. Choking back giggles, he stood again, only to have some chitinous thing slither down his back. Stifling a shriek, Jon shucked and danced until he couldn't feel it wriggling beneath his jacket. *Well. At least it took my mind off of the horrible creature waiting for me to climb out of this hole and snap me up like a rabbit.*

Rabbit. Stag. Prey. Through the terror, Jon felt another emotion rise; rage. *Way too many things calling me that lately. Goddamit, I am sick and tired of being jerked around by these monsters and I am completely sick and tired of this stupid last name dictating my life!*

He fed the flame of his anger, thinking of how he'd been pushed around, used, and manipulated, letting it grow, burning through the fear. Dragging out his battered phone with shaking hands, Jon struggled a few moments before turning on the flashlight function, stark beam piercing the dark. Dank mold covered the entirety of the sparse concrete pit, splotched and mottled across the wall in drunken lines and musty patches. Rotted wooden planks, rusting paint cans, and other odds and ends sat against one side of the bare cube, a home improvement project left abandoned, never to be finished. Rusted pipes ran along the ceiling, paint and stucco falling in cracks to show the ruined house beneath.

Jon turned, hoping for something more promising. Broken steps, jagged shards of moldering wood, led upwards. The phone's luminescent beam glittered off of a wrought iron screen at the top. Even with intact stairs, he wasn't getting out that way.

Light pierced the dark as he scanned the room. *There has got be a way out of here. Something I can use. Some way to call for help.* The trapped lawyer froze, a realization hitting his gut like a lead ball. *My phone. I'm holding my damn PHONE.* Flipping it over, the blue-eyed captive frantically scanned his contacts list, searching for the one person who might help him in his hour of need. He pounded frantically on the send button, spouting his plea for aid. "Marc! Pick up the phone, please man, it's Jon, I need help..." A flash and a beep interrupted Jon's call for help.

He held the gleaming screen to his face, glaring in disbelief. *No bars. No goddamn bars. I pay a tidy fortune for this plan and it won't even get any bars?!* Biting his lip until it bled, Jon raised the phone above his head, ready to throw the glowing brick into the wall. Then the light blipped out. Blinking in the sudden darkness, Jon's fury gave way to a cold numbness, beyond anger or sadness. *No bars, no service, and now, no energy.* Mechanically, he stumbled through the dark, hands grasping for rotten wood and moldy bits of construction material. Slowly, he piled the junk under the illuminated street window, dilapidated offerings to the portal above, building a moldering pile to climb his way to freedom or death.

{—}

Wind and rain beat down on the Shifters like the wrath of ancient gods, matting their fur and blinding them. They galloped at a breakneck pace, their heightened senses guiding them through the storm. The darkness was their ally. The masses of humans huddled inside their homes, away from the cold and damp, would be too busy staring at their light giving screens to notice the primordial killing machines in the wind and storm. Even those few out in the torrent would be hard pressed to notice the swift predators.

The pack raced through alleyways, bounded over fences, and slid past windows quick as nightmares. Brock, pelt gray and gold with muscles like stone slabs even in his wolfen form, led them through upscale streets of downtown, barreling past yuppie coffee chains and antique store designed to trap tourists with money to burn.

At last they found trace of their prey, the scent of blood on the wind.

As they traced the coppery smell, others flooded in; the deranged musk of the Shifter killer, the stink of man-fear, and a distinctively obnoxious perfume. One Magda recognized instantly. *Jon's cologne.* Letting out a short yip, she pulled ahead of Brock, taking the lead of the hunt. One look and he fell back in line, no questions asked. That's how it worked in the Cohort. You trusted your line mates. You had to. Hesitation in battle got you killed.

The pack swung around a corner, following the acrid mix of blood and cologne, and clawed to an abrupt halt, nearly stumbling over the mangled remains of the Fury's victim. Niall lashed out with a claw in frustration, connected with a dumpster in a thunderous boom, sending the steel box scraping along the concrete. Brock cuffed the young warrior about the ear, a rebuke for losing his temper, while Magda prowled forward, searching. She picked up Jon's scent, nearly hidden beneath the overwhelming stink of Ripper. With a yip they were off again, inhuman shadows in the storm.

The pack of not-beasts found Jon crawling through a small broken ground level window, rain soaked and bleeding, hands scrabbling for purchase on the wet concrete. When Brock moved toward the struggling lawyer, Niall whined and shook his shaggy muzzle, claw outstretched to pull him back.

Panting in the filthy alley, Jon heard the whine and sluggishly looked at the three monsters. Magda frowned, her lupine muzzle made a sinister mockery of the human expression. *Poor fool seems too tired to even flinch.*

"What? One of you furry bastards wasn't enough to take me out? You had to bring friends!?" He struggled to his feet and spread his arms wide, soaked and filthy as the rain poured down unrelentingly. "Come on! I'm done running! Eat me, you freaks! I hope you choke on it."

The empty bravado in the face of certain death saw Magda's frown curve into a broad grin, no less sinister in appearance. Once again it occurred to Magda that insanity and courage walked a fine line. *Crazy or brave, who can tell these days?*

Belatedly, she realized that an eight-foot-tall bundle of fur and fang wasn't the most reassuring image. "Jon, calm down. It's me, Magda." Even as she spoke, the words warbled and changed, shifting from a sonorous rumble to the warrior's usual cadence. Magda now took the place of a crimson furred death machine. Her companions took her cue and shifted to human as well, trying to reassure the bedraggled lawyer.

"Magda? What the hell are you doing here?" Suspicion, anger, and exhaustion coated Jon's words like heavy syrup.

Even as the shapeshifter moved to speak, Brock's hand tapped her shoulder. A moment of silent communication and Magda nodded, letting Brock step past. The big man cleared his throat. "Mr. Doe, my name is Brock Macintyre. You already know my associate, Magda."

Jon looked the jar headed wall of muscle up and down. "You don't look like a Macintyre."

An almost smile tugged at Brock's stoic face. Magda knew he got that a lot. *His phone appointments are always so surprised when they don't get the sprightly ginger they expected.*

"I have a unique family tree," Brock continued. "More relevant to your situation, however, is that I am a standing officer and representative with the Sunset Cohort. I wield the authority of the Senate in San Dominguez. As such, I am empowered to protect you from any enemies of the House until such a time as your obligations are discharged."

Blue eyes blinked a few times as the words took root in Jon's shell-shocked brain. "Well, that would have been very nice when that Ripper guy tried to decorate the basement with my fucking entrails!" Hysteria drove Jon's voice to a shrieking falsetto.

Brock remained unphased by the lawyer's outburst, remaining at parade stance despite the rain, his hands clasped behind his back as though giving a speech at a barracks or a presentation at a board meeting. Magda knew he had done both regularly, even if she made it a point to sneak out of them when possible. "We were unaware of any distress on your part, sir. Understand that had the Cohort known, all due haste would have been made to protect you. We came here tracking an enemy of the Houses, a rogue Shifter called Ripper. You've already met him. Congratulations on surviving. Few can claim that. You can thank Magda for the timely arrival that drove the renegade off. Magda picked up your scent and we followed the trail of blood to your location."

Even before Brock finished, Jon patted himself down in a panic "Blood? Where? Is it mine?"

Brock remained unmoving, merely one large shadow amidst many others in the storm shrouded alleyway. "That is a negative. It belonged to a previous victim of Ripper. An employee of Arkadas, we think, though we have not yet identified the body. You needn't worry, the victim wasn't of the Blood. Only human. No problems or repercussions that may impact your work."

Magda mentally groaned as the same argument she'd made in the Den left Brock's mouth. *Gods, does it really sound so callous?*

A wall came up behind Jon's eyes. Predictably, he didn't throw himself at Brock's feet in gratitude. "Only human? No one will miss him, huh?"

"Regrettably correct, as he was only a minor functionary. While unfortunate, casualties happen in war. Your ability to do your job remains unimpaired and there won't be any were-gild fines that would affect your pay or your employer."

Magda flushed as the stark brutality was laid out. *As a warrior of the House I know this is my duty. But to hear it spoken so, to a broken fool, it seems almost cruel.*

Jon sneered at Magda. "Protecting your investments huh? Always gotta watch your assets."

The growing sympathy for Jon vanished from Magda's mind. Hair's bristled from the warrior's body, rage welling inside her. A growl to put Ripper to shame erupted from Magda's throat. "Bite your tongue, Jon Doe! I offered you protection and you refused. You ran off on yer own accord. I had no way of knowing this would happen!"

Jon gathered what dignity he could, standing tall while dripping water and stained with blood and offal. "But you do know what will happen to me no matter which way I jump and you're alright with it. Fine. Good to know where we stand. Captain, sergeant, or whatever, you may consider yourself relieved of duty. I got this one from here." With a sloppy salute Jon walked stiffly past them out of the alley.

"That is your decision, Mr. Doe." Brock's monotone reply was harried by Magda's barked laugh as she threw up her hands.

"The gods preserve fools and madmen, Jon, but only for so long." She rounded on her line mates. "Centurions! To the hunt. We're going to find Ripper and end his madness. And I'm going to make a hat out of his guts while I'm at it."

Magda turned and ran for the alley's end. From one step to the next her body flowed and morphed. A giant wolf creature rather than a human woman hopped the fence followed by her allies. In moments, the monsters of legend vanished, leaving only broken glass and falling rain in an empty alley.

Jon staggered miserably along the street, wallowing in defeat and despair. *Nearly disemboweled by a wolf faced maniac, abandoned by the folks I might have called friends in this insane world, my designer jacket is ruined, and I currently smell like the back of a garbage truck. This job officially sucks.*

The warm glow of anger had long since faded to ashes, robbing Jon of his only shield against the sickening realization that he couldn't do a damn thing to stop his impending doom. Mortality pressed down inexorably, and it took everything Jon had to move one foot in front of the other.

Jon's stomach growled to remind him he hadn't eaten in forever. Everywhere he looked, closed cafes and bistros stood, beautiful facades empty and dark. *Restaurants, restaurants everywhere and not a crumb to eat. I'd kill for a croissant right now.* Cold, wet, and hungry, Jon trudged through the night.

A small eternity later, Jon saw salvation: a light in the distance. He beelined for the warm glow without hesitation, desperate to get out of the rain. Sanctuary came in the form of a paneled bay glass window, an aged stained-glass sign proclaiming the place "Copenhagen's," its lettering and design hailing from a simpler time.

Thank you, Copenhagen. Whoever the hell you were. Jon almost collapsed as he stepped through the door. He simply stood for a moment, focused solely on not falling over, and soaked in the warmth. Inside, wood paneling dominated the cozy restraint. Professional carpentry work marked the tables, chairs, and benches around a simple dining area, each hand-crafted piece of furniture a labor of love. Even the coat rack gleamed with all the signs of tender and meticulous care.

A large bar ran along the wall to his right. The bartender, a middle-aged man with a prodigious handlebar mustache that Jon thought some decades out style, squinted at the bedraggled lawyer as he walked in and immediately frowned.

"Last call has already passed. You'd best be on your way."

"I didn't ask for a drink, I just wanted to get out of the rain for a minute."

Bartender Handlebar Mustache set down his rag and stepped out from behind the polished bar. "I'm afraid that's not the sort of hospitality we offer, friend."

Any further threats were stopped by a salty voice from the floor.

"Eugene, please. Let the poor man breathe."

The drink slinger, Eugene, paused in his attack vector, turning to glance at the speaker walking up from another table. He had a weathered face, dark skin worn and tanned by the elements until it was the color of old leather. Laces of silver showed in his hair, but he moved with a remarkable strength and vibrancy. Though only coming up to the towering bartender's shoulder the old man carried himself with dignity and poise.

The elderly gentleman patted Eugene on the back with a smile. Laugh lines crinkled at the edge of twinkling eyes. "I dare say he needs a bit of warmth and a place to dry off. Two bowls of your chowder, on me."

Eugene's flinty expression melted and the mustachioed bartender backed off immediately. Jon marveled and worried at the about face. *That guy must be a local favorite. Or a mob boss. Given my luck, he's probably both.* The lawyer tried for panick but found only a numb sense of worry. Having to hide in a decrepit basement to avoid disembowelment tended to place other concerns in perspective.

With a resigned shrug, Jon hung his filthy coat on the rack, though with some reservations. It felt disrespectful to the elegant wood. Jon followed his benefactor to a table within kicking distance of the door. The bedraggled lawyer sat down warily, expecting the other shoe to drop. *Might be looking a gift horse in the mouth, but it's been one of those days.*

Compassionate eyes measured Jon and the younger fellow found it difficult to maintain his suspicions in the face of such an open gaze. "You have been cruelly used of late, it would seem. Sit a spell while I get some food." With more grace and ease than Jon expected from a man of his age, the kindly fellow rose and walked to the bar. True to his word, he returned with two steaming bowls of soup. Jon's stomach rumbled loudly as soon as the delectable scent hit his nose.

That smells divine. Jon tucked into the soup with gusto. His tongue cashed the check his nose wrote and then some.

The kindly stranger quietly watched as Jon devoured his meal. Unexpectedly, the old man rose and set his own jacket over Jon's shoulders. Jon jerked in surprise, leaning away from his salty benefactor's touch. But the old man simply walked back to his seat across from the young lawyer. "There. That should tide you over for the time being. Can't keep warm with that jacket you have. It's soaked right through. As the Lord says, 'Let he who has two coats, give to him who has none.'" Jon's tanned dinner companion extended a hand, a simple wooden cross dangling on his chest. "My name's Paul. I run a little place up the way where you can stay for a while if you have nowhere else to go. We can even get you cleaned up."

Jon paused, spoon halfway to his mouth as something clicked in his head. *They think I'm homeless or something. Handlebars at the counter probably thought he was turning away a drunk. Great, first I nearly get killed and now I'm mistake for some vagrant.*

Jon's cheeks flushed red in embarrassment as he belatedly shook the proffered hand. "I'm not...I mean that's ok. Name's Jon. I've got a place and I can pay for the soup. I've got a job. For however long it lasts."

"There's more, isn't there? What seems to be the trouble, my son?" Paul's eyes bored into him, not unkind but eerily insistent. Like he knew Jon had been lying and just wanted to hear him say it.

Holy shit, is this parenting? If feels like dad, if dad ever gave a shit enough to check on me.

Jon licked his lips and struggled to find the words. Paul seemed to be a good guy, but Jon couldn't simply blurt out that he was stuck between in a turf war between shapeshifting secret societies. "I have this... new job. I thought it was great. But the people I'm working for. Damn, I can't even call them people. They're fucking monsters!"

Paul frowned. "Language, young man. Troubled times is no cause for us to forget ourselves. But to your point. If you are unhappy with this new career, why don't you leave? Listen to your conscience. Nothing should force you to sacrifice your principles for your job."

Jon looked at the preacher across from him and blinked, his mind unable to register the foreign concept for a moment. *I can't take it.* Faced with the sheer earnestness in Paul's voice, Jon had a little break down. Jon's shoulder shook with repressed sobs. "I'd love to. You have no idea. But I can't. They literally won't let me. If I leave, I'm dead. But if I stay, I'm dead anyway. Even though I want to run, they would hunt me down like a... rabbit." A hitch choked off his last word, the snarling taunts of the monster in the basement window rearing in his mind.

Paul nudged the second warm bowl of soup toward Jon and the bedraggled lawyer set to it with vigor. It tasted just as delightful as the first. "Blessed are the meek, for they shall inherit the earth. But I do not believe this to true in your case, Jon. You clearly have been through a rough time, set upon by those of ill intent. Yet here you sit. Alive. Remember, where there is life, there is hope!"

Jon paused with spoon halfway to his mouth. "Hold on, preacher man. Was that Conan? Are you quoting Nietzsche at me?"

Paul's face lit up with an infectious grin, a mischievous glint in his eye. "Even a stopped clock is right twice a day. Besides, it's the Lord's world. I can call... dibs... I believe is the modern term used these days. Tell me, Jon, are you a man of faith?"

Jon grunted a negative as he scraped the bottom of the bowl with his spoon. "Afraid not, Paul. I always missed out on Sunday school."

Paul stood to place a companionable hand on Jon's shoulder, locking eyes with lawyer. "Then have faith in yourself. It will let you draw upon unfathomable reserves. There is power in faith. Use whatever words you like. God, Universe, Fate. Flying Spaghetti Monster if you must. But believe. In the darkest hours, we shine the brightest. That faith will carry you through the most taxing of times."

No one had ever spoken to Jon that way. Not his teachers, not his nannies, and certainly not his parents. Jon blinked away tears, throat tight. *Damn, must be the pepper.*

Standing up abruptly, Jon fished out his wallet and throws down a sodden stack of twenties. "Thanks. Soup's on me."

Smiling at the younger man's discomfort, Paul waved his hand. "Thank you, very kind, but not necessary. Pass it along to one who truly needs it. It's important for us limited humans to know we are not alone in these dark times, when we cannot grasp God's plan."

Jon's fatigued mind latched onto that last part with an iron grip. Synapses sparked and the proverbial light bulb flickered valiantly in the lawyer's mind. When struck with a bad case, getting the guilty off the hook; know your clients and play to the court.

Time to think crazy. A manic grin spread, pearly whites piercing through Jon's stained face.

"That's genius! Thanks, Paul!"

The kindly old man looked stunned at the abrupt change in his moody companion but smiled anyway. "You are quite welcome, Jon." Paul shoved a card at Jon as the lawyer ran for the door. "My place is just down the street. Doors are always open. Call if you ever need to talk again."

Jon snatched up the card and practically ran to the door. "I will! Maybe I'll show up for confession. But for now, put in a good word for me. I'm off to do the most ungodly amount of lawyering the big guy's ever seen!"

§——§

Magda, Brock, and Niall raced through the storm, desperate to snare their prey. The thrill of the hunt had long since passed. Their quarry knew every trick they did and then some. Ripper had doubled back, dove into water and garbage to hide his scent, and clambered dangerously close to the mewling man things in his bid to escape the Cohort's wrath.

For all his cunning, Ripper situation was hopeless, his fate sealed. Magda Lahm Dearg had sworn his end. No force in creation could save him now. Or so she kept telling herself.

In truth, though Magda hungered for the madman's end, the rage and anger she felt so keenly was but one thread of what roiled within her. The image of Jon, wet, blood splattered, and bereft of hope burned in her mind. Niall, pinned beneath her and prepared to die at her hand. *I was ready to slay my own line mate. The idiot's barely more than a child!* The thirst in Magda's throat cried out for something harsher than water and the realization of her need for drink sickened her more. *What have I become?*

Each time Magda forced the thoughts from her mind they crept back with insidious insistence, creeping vines of doubt. Something Magda could ill afford in the field. As the Cohort warriors scrambled in the shadowed corners of crowded rooftops, the furred hunters racing along as visions of children's nightmares passing unseen, Magda fell back to match Brock's stride.

Magda forced her words through fanged muzzle. It wasn't just the physical tongue that made the words halting and slow. She didn't want to face the simmering well of emotions but something compelled her. "You handled Jon pretty well back there."

Though panting, they understood one another well enough, the wind and rain small barrier to their keen ears. Brock replied, forcing language threw a mouth ill meant for soft human speak. "I've seen the thousand-yard stare in my soldiers enough times to recognize trauma when I see it."

Magda's head cocked to the side. "Then why the cold front?" Given Brock's admonishments to her and Niall to watch their harsh tongues, Magda couldn't believe Brock's blasé delivery had been anything but deliberate.

Brock's furred form gave a snort and a hitch of the tail, a wolfish equivalent of a shrug. "Sometimes a gentle touch is needed, other times a slap in the face. Pain manifests in different ways. For all of us."

Magda didn't miss the meaningful look directed at her. "You've some experience in this."

"Some. It does come up in my line of work."

Niall's yip brought them up short. The enemy had been found. There, in the gloom, stood their quarry, stalking out from an alley.

Ripper glanced over his shoulder before he dashed off. *Too late.* Magda face broke into a vicious smile. *We have you now, you twisted bastard. Damn, it's going to feel good to kill something!*

Descending from on high like primal emissaries of a savage god, the three werewolves hit the ground at a dead run, hounding Ripper. The chase, brief but intense, came to a sudden halt in the yard of a homeless shelter. Ripper stood with his back to the building as his enemies closed in.

"Spineless lickspittles. Catamites. Traitors!" Ripper's jaw snapped each word, fangs closing on air as if tearing each apart.

"Traitor? That's funny coming from the likes of you. Or did you just hit your head really hard and got loyal and maniac butcher mixed up? Easy mistake, happens to the best of us." Niall's lashing tongue at last found a target other than his comrades.

"I am true to myself. To what we are. It is our holy mission to thin the herd. The Houses have forgotten that we are the scourge of divinity.

We are meant to be hounds of the gods, not collared beasts. You Cohort scum are little more than dogs and jackals."

Dogs? I'll feed this scum his heart! Magda circled the pontificating Fury. "Enough of your blathering. Let's see you face warriors, not help-less innocents."

Ripper let loose a chocking laugh at Magda's snarled promise. It was a cold sound, full of hate rather than true mirth. "Innocents?! There are no innocents amongst mankind. I have seen first-hand the rancid heart of humanity and it is corrupt, blackened, and cruel. I witnessed this truth decades ago, when the world showed its true colors and went mad. *Arbeit Macht Frei*, my little Cohort friends."

Niall halted at the snarled German phrase. "Auschwitz?"

Even as Brock and Magda circled, Ripper raised his arm, hair receding and flesh shrinking, to display weathered forearm with a numbered tattoo scrawled in blackened ink. "Yes, little one. I was there. I smelt the ash in the air from the furnaces, tasted the dead on my tongue. Those bearing the crooked cross left me lying in a pile of corpses. It was in that moldering pit that the gods granted me a revelation. They showed me their holy design for us. The gods revealed to me what we are and what we must do."

Despite himself, Niall stood enthralled by the smoke furred renegade's words. Conviction suffused from Ripper's every word. This was a true believer.

Magda glanced at the boy for only a moment, snarling. *Dammit Niall, focus!* She lunched forward, taking a swipe at the pontificating killer, intending to end him. Ripper turned to Brock and Magda, snapping, biting, and growling, keeping the Cohort centurions at bay.

"This world is sick, corrupt. It must be purged, lanced like a boil. The gods are silent for we have forgotten our purpose. We must be the cutting blade and cull the herd. Too long we Shifters have waited, watching and silent, as man forgot the face of the divine. Humans have grown fat and weak and we have grown fat with them. The Senate and the Court are sick with the poison of modernity, trapped by their comforts and their petty politics. The gods have turned their backs upon them in shame. But some of us remain true. The Cull is the true path and we shall…"

Ripper's tirade ended abruptly as Magda leapt at him with a terrifying roar. The two crashed to the ground, rolling snarling and slashing. Brock and Niall moved to finish him, but Ripper pulled free, twisting from Magda's grip and losing a pound of flesh lodged in Magda's jaws for his troubles. The renegade vaulted over Brock, lashing out with hind talons to sever the big man's calves. Brock stumbled with a strangled scream as his calf was sliced in two. Brock's line mates rallied to their fallen as the Cohort officer rolled, desperately trying to put distance between himself and Ripper. Magda and Niall stood shoulder to shoulder to shield Brock as Ripper charged them.

Magda snapped at the air, eager to taste Ripper's blood. He claws flexed and thick drool feel from bared fangs. Magda's hate burned in her like a fire. *This is how it ends. How it always ends. Eye to eye, tooth to tooth!*

Focused as she was, Magda could only look in shock as the wine-dark furred Shifter leapt over their head to scramble up to the roof top.

"After him!" Brock painfully growled out, hopping ungainly to his feet, muscles already knitting thanks to regenerative powers of Shifter blood. Magda leapt after their quarry, following his scent. They traveled perhaps two blocks before pulling up short. "Brock arrived to find his teammates pacing the rooftops without the bloody corpse of their enemy.

"Where did he go?" Brock's furious tone brought Niall up short. It was the first time the pup had ever heard the stoic leader lose his temper.

Magda whirled and paced, lupine nose sifting bellows like lungful of air. "I don't know, I can't smell him anywhere."

"Try harder!"

"Don't you snap at me, Brock, or I'll cuff yer ears. I'm telling you I can't smell him. He's gone. We failed"

At Magda's doleful admission of defeat, Niall raised his head to the heavens and released a howl of rage and thwarted vengeance that echoed in the night. His elders looked on in surprise.

The pitch colored wolfman turned to his line mates. "What?"

Magda grinned widely. "You may not like it, pup, but you might be Cohort after all."

CHAPTER 14

I F MARC'S HEART could still beat, it would have been thumping out of his chest. Sucking in a breath through purely ancillary lungs, Marc chewed his lip and continued sifting through the mountain of files at his desk. Though paper stationary went out with the dinosaurs and despite having a heavily protected computerized database, Arkadas' firm still did things the old-fashioned way. With Jon's ass on the line, Marc performed his best archeologist imitation, digging through the ancient papers and desperately reviewing the data, looking for any way out of the iron maiden contract his college buddy was in.

So far, it wasn't looking good for the home team.

Pushing stringy hair out of his face for the hundredth time, Marc dove deeper into the minutiae of the contract. *That's where the chinks in the armor usually lay. The devil is in the details.* Even the best firms got lazy on that front. They banked on no one being willing to sift through the impenetrable wall of legal jargon to actually read the nitty gritty of a contract. Obtuse by intent.

Marc reveled in the convoluted language. It allowed the undead accountant to stretch his mind, unraveling puzzles of logic and triumphing over conundrums. This time, near panic rather than elation pushed him on.

Signatory hereby agrees to abide by all terms of the contract, et cetera. Standard legal boiler plate. Looks intact. Marc moved down the page. *Ah ha! Here we are. The dangerous stuff.* The Breach of Contract clause. Such a jewel of legal binding ensured practically no wiggle room and swift and terrible retribution to any who breached. Woe betide those who dishonored the contract! *It figures the only thing the Houses would agree on is bloodshed.*

The breach clause wording promised a messy end to anyone who crossed them. "Punished to the fullest extent of the law" in the legal jargon of the Western Concordat meant the offender could and would be reduced to roadkill. With this contract, the Houses could off Jon, send flowers and a card, and walk away hands clean and all honor satisfied. Worse, the wording of the contract combined with the sheer stakes involved with the land bid functionally guaranteed a lethal response. With the current political climate involving the Cull, neither the Senate nor the Court of Raptors dared show any weakness. They were legally obligated to murder in order to save face.

Archimedes K. Arkadas, fourth of his name, who absolutely hated it when Marc called him Hedwig, had caught wind of that at the outset of the Beachfront deal. He'd turned down what appeared to a very comfortable sum of money to hand it off to a third party. In this case, the inestimable Jon Doe.

I knew if Arkadas was turning down the chance to make a dollar, there must have been a hell of a catch. Marc hadn't known the catch in question involved brutal disembowelment by a howling crew of shapeshifting critters and assorted companions no matter who won the settlement.

Marc gulped at the thought of Jon's fate. Not in sympathy, but to swallow down bile. Ever since his lifestyle shifted to the solely nocturnal side of things, Marc had wrestled with the new appetites his changed physiology produced. It was easier when he'd been alone, but a familiar face only hammered home the gruesome hunger. Even thinking of his best friend's gory end roused up urges Marc would rather not acknowledge. *I refuse to think of my closest friend as an appetizer.*

Fumbling open the mini fridge, Marc pulled out a chilled blood pack and chomped through the plastic to get at the crimson liquid within. Thankfully his new condition included tools to cope with his appetites. *Palpability of the sanguine appetites aside, the vampire state comes well equipped to sate them. The fangs are can openers and hypodermic needles all in one. Excellent utility.* Slurping noisily, a habit not even his sire's compulsion could break him of, Marc returned to the matter at hand.

The only exit clause not involving a violent and gruesome end required voluntary dissolution of the contract by all parties. *Sadly, that seems about as likely finding a charming lady with a heartbeat to spend my evenings with.* Idly chewing on the empty pack, the undead accountant leaned back in his chair. *If the out clause proved dismal, time to look at it from a new angle.*

Kicking off from the desk, Marc wheeled his chair over to the filing cabinets, standing row upon row in regimented lines. Yanking out the document drawer with a clang, Marc thumbed through the folders. He dove through the original lease documents, property deeds, history of the property, and varied and sundry certifications, licenses, and other paperwork. Anything and everything, searching for a crack they could crowbar open.

His night dissolved into an endless parade of fine print, double speak, legalese, and little details. Fortunately, Marc thrived on such minutia. *The devil is always in the details.*

Hours later, Marc's exacting research yielded two things of note: a bloody conspiracy and a chance to save his friend. Marc flicked from file to file with lightning speed, burning through the company database... even the parts he wasn't supposed to have access to. *It's delightful being an "accountant" on the books. Everyone forgets I'm an eidetic computing machine with the best legal training money can buy.* Marc let out a dry, dusty laugh. *They never look past the superficial. You can cover all sorts of crimes with a badge and a title. A lovely bit of categorical feint, if I do say so myself.*

Plain as the daylight Marc couldn't walk in, multiple copies of the contract sat before him, identical save for a few crucial differences. That the contracts deeded ownership of the property to the Court and the Senate was to be expected. That there was a contract deeding it to Arkadas raised Marc's suspicions. It ceded the property to Arkadas in perpetuity like a fiefdom granted to a baron. *If Arkadas deferred the contract, why is there paperwork for the Beachfront property with his name on it? Why permanently? It should have been in keeping for one of the Houses. Stewardship, not ownership. This isn't simply sloppy bookkeeping. Arkadas is plotting something.*

As he dug deeper, Marc found Arakadas' guilt written in bloody, digital handprints. Emails showed one Zypresse Hain reaching out to Arkadas. Another red flag for Marc. *Arkadas never talks to anyone he doesn't have to, and that only means someone who can dos something for him. Funny, for a player with that level of money or influence, I've never heard of this Zypresse Hain.*

The two had discussed dates, locations, money, and names. In and of itself, it would be fairly innocuous. Except that all of the names listed were Marcus' dead co-workers. It seemed this Zypresse knew more about the dead staff than Marc did. It listed their ages, heights, and personal details. The files in the emails dug deeper, listing the allegiance of the workers, outing most as spies in service to either House, sent to keep an eye on Arkadas. For a disgustingly low sum, Zypresse offered to snuff them out to pave the way for the mysterious benefactor's own agents.

Arkadas seemed amiable to the whole affair.

Who are you, my dear Zypresse, that you would want to murder agents of the Houses? Marc paused. *Wrong question. Who are you that you would dare or have the means to murder agents of the Houses?* Marc pressed on through the digital archives, piercing barriers of encryption, revealing the conspiracy together piece by piece.

Though too canny, even in supposedly secure correspondence, to openly lay out the conspiracy, it was there in crimson markings between the lines. Zypresse spoke of the Houses with a passion, and his hatred could be read in each denunciation. The stranger's knowledge of their workings spoke of a familiarity beyond anything except someone with agents rooted deep within each camp. It all pointed to one simple truth: Arkadas was working with the Cull.

My boss killed my co-workers in a bid to control the Beachfront property. The Cull has access to insider information within both Houses and are feeding it to Arkadas even as he hands them all the dirty backdoor deals he's involved in. They can kill at will and with impunity and no one will even see the hand that did it.

The vampire dug deeper into Arkadas' ruthless machinations and focused on a small bit of legal clause in the contract. It was a small clause, but it was the crux which Arkadas' scheme rested upon.

The contract, with its blocky legalese, allowed for a third party to have control of the estates. It was this thin loophole that Arkadas wanted to take advantage of. Arkadas intended to be that third party. But he couldn't do it outright without making himself a target for both Houses. *Arkadas might be influential, but that influence won't do anything to stop the Cohort's claws or a Retribution Squad's blades.*

Instead, Arkadas intended to manipulate the situation to his advantage. Marc sucked a fetid breath into deflated lungs. An unnecessary act, but shock still produced engrained responses from Marc's living years. *Arkadas works with Zypresse and plants agents in key locations. They engage in chaos-based warfare, killing key operatives, and pushing the Court and Senate toward war. Once the bloodshed reaches critical mass, the two Houses will beg Arkadas to keep watch over the territory, if only to keep it out the hands of their enemies. Arkadas gains the land, gains influence, and comes out with both Houses indebted to him.*

However, this final option, which gave Arkadas the keys to the kingdom, also offered Marc hope. It was a loophole, a back door in the clause, which allowed Jon to choose a path between the two Houses without besmirching their honor. The steps necessary to make that happen, however, were problematic. It required not only the Houses' cooperation but also the signatories of neutral parties potent enough to have the respect and attention of the Shifters. The wording was clearly there as an afterthought, standard judicial boilerplate the legal juggernauts of the Houses ignored. In theory, it allowed a ceasefire to brokered. Functionally, it was as impossible as Marc flying to the moon and back.

Still, the few lines of legal wording offered a chance to save Jon's hide, albeit a forlorn one. *A solution and a problem both.* Though it offered a chance to get the esteemed Mr. Doe out of his present conundrum alive, it involved invoking greater powers than an office monkey like Marc could wield. It also meant calling down the attention of those mightier entities.

It meant Marc had to contact his sire. This was not something the vampire wanted to do.

Marc idly fiddled with a Rubik's Cube as he pondered his options. His boss was complicit in murder. His friend was on the chopping block. If Marc moved forward with the evidence, there was every chance he might be removed himself as an obstacle by Arkadas and the Cull. That left only one risk filled option. It wasn't a guarantee by any stretch of the imagination and involved a steep price. One that might risk Marc's immortal life.

Marc's prodigious mind turned the events over in his head, again and again, looking for another way out. Time and again, he came to the same inescapable conclusion; there wasn't any other choice. *I've got to contact Lord Hynrich.*

He had to take the chance, no matter how painful it might be. With decision made, Marc rose, setting aside his fears and doubts alongside a small mountain of paperwork. *Sooner began, sooner ended. As my Lord Hynrich always says, time waits for no one, not even immortals.*

Weaving through the office chaos with practiced ease, Marc opened a small side door half hidden behind filing cabinets. It might have been a broom closet, had it held anything in it. Utterly unadorned and bare of any furniture, any casual visitor might have dismissed it off hand except for one detail; the minute etchings scrawling across every inch of the room.

The arcane engravings traced along its floor, ceiling, walls, stopping only at the door Marc entered through. Complex diagrams of swirling lines described the arc of the heavenly bodies and detailed the march of ages. Alchemical symbols and runes press groaned with power, divine symbolism rampant in its intricate lines. A faint scent of burnt ash lingered in the space, the air oppressive and heavy.

Hardly expected in an office space, but the tiny room was an unnegotiable part of Marc's contract between Lord Hynrich and Arkadas. The ancient vampire insisted upon it.

Marc gulped, another vestigial habit from his living years. It helped him feel almost human. He strode to the complex diagram in the center, an astrologer's vision of the heavens in carved into wooden floor, this vault of the sky mirrored in the ceiling above. From here, one stood as the axis of all things, the unmoving mover, about which all celestial bodies moved. Drawing out a small blood red stone on a copper chain, Marc began to chant.

An unceasing mantra fell from his lips, spoken in a tongue long forgotten, claimed by his master to be the hidden language of the spheres. Slowly, wisps of smoke rose from the precise carvings. The arcane markings pulsed silently, clouds of smoke pouring forth to smother the undead speaker. Gathering speed like a storm could, the tempest pressed against the circle until with a great rush it surged inward, engulfing Marc utterly. The smoke slunk back into the mystical diagrams, leaving nothing but an empty room and a lingering stink of sulfur and brimstone.

For less than a heartbeat, Marc traversed the Land-Betwixt, a realm of no time, no place, and no sensation. Only a moment, yet an eternity pressed on him. The smoke vanished to reveal a rather more expansive tableau than the claustrophobic broom closet. Instead of four walls, a bleak windswept mountaintop greeted the vampire. Dark stone replaced the closet's wooden paneling, hard scrubbed grass and stunted tresses dotted the stark landscape. A cold wind howled past, rushing down the peak to the valley below.

Marc doubled over as pain suffused his entire body, grateful for his undead durability. He doubted any mortal creature could have survived such a journey. *Some things face eternity better than others.*

Standing upright, Marc's eyes were drawn inexorably upwards. A grim castle loomed above, the ancient stone bulwark hovering like a pitiless judge over all it surveyed. Having traveled through hell, the truly dangerous part of his quest now began. Marc would attend court and petition the master of the mountain fastness. His master and sire, the ancient vampire Lord Hynrich.

The bastion of Lord Hynrich jutted ominously upon jagged peak, a dagger thrust into the stormy skies, carved from the stone of the mountain itself. Centuries old, the forbidding monolith had endured the elements and war and stood worn but unbowed, having outlasted all of its master's enemies. It never failed to awe and terrorize Marc. Only a small dirt road led to its outer gate, a curtain wall providing ample opportunity in prior centuries to rain death upon anyone foolish enough to gain access without permission. The iron bound oaken doors opened soundlessly as Marc held aloft the small blood red gem. As he entered the keep's outer wall, Marc thought about what he hadn't told Jon about his new unlife. The perks, the powers, and the politics that made up his current nocturnal existence.

Vampires. *Stupidly powerful creatures with glaring weaknesses. I wonder if that makes us like Superman, just in reverse. Look it's a bird, it's a plane, it's coming to drain every last drop of your blood.* Marc tilted his head in thought as he walked the echoing halls. Shadowed things and unbreathing servitors darted out of Marc's way. With his symbol of office held before him, no servants, mortal or otherwise, barred his way, leaving Marc's mind free to wander. He had always been fascinated with the nobility of the night and joining their ranks dimmed none of his curiosity. If anything, it made them more interesting.

The sun utterly destroyed them and any of their works. Running water and holy ground diminished their strength. Didn't matter what faith, it still repelled them. That particular aspect didn't weigh in on any burning theological questions Marc and others might have. *None of the gods look favorably upon mortal upstarts claiming immortality, I suppose.* The lanky vampire always felt that didn't bode well for a vampire's chances in the afterlife. Fortunately for the undead, most were exceptionally skilled at cheating death.

In addition to natural boons in strength, speed, and senses conferred by turning into a vampire, they often developed reserves of occult power to draw upon. *All for the low cost of your mortal life and one hypothetical immortal soul.* These vampiric abilities only grew with time. Marc turned to look at the portraits of Hynrich's clan, mortal and undead alike, that hung in the long hallways. *Blood and bloodlines. Long lives tend to leave long lineages. Important to remember. Important too, to remember what you look like, I suppose, when mirrors aren't exactly our friends.*

Many of the ancient ones, especially those with ancestral holdings in the Mediterranean and Europe, established mystic links with the land to bolster their strength and making them near immortal upon their home soil. Lord Hynrich bound himself to this desolate range long ago, creating a near inviolate sanctuary against his enemies. However, while strengthened in the borders of his realm, it limited any movement abroad. They could not leave their lands without weakening themselves and even risking destruction. So, Lord Hynrich and other Elders used emissaries such as Marc.

Job security in a sense. Such vampires also bound their servants in the same way as the land. That was why Marc struggled to stay away from his sire as often as he could manage; having someone in your head sucked.

Marc knew his mental ramblings were only a distraction. *I can't think about what I'm doing. I might just run away screaming.* Looking at the broad double doors, painstakingly preserved against the elements, the undead pilgrim paused only a fraction of a second before pushing through.

Marc arrived to find court in session. Already a host of vampire lords stood in the cavernous space, cathedral walls arching to meet in vaulted shadows above. Gentle moonlight drifted through enormous stained-glass windows. Combined with the wavering torchlight from burning sconces along the vast hallway expanse, it gave just enough light for mortal eyes to see, but more than enough for a night predator to hunt.

Gathered in a throng, the Elevated stood garbed in splendor. Elaborate finery from across the ages adorned the undead nobles. Where a high lady wore a gauzy chiton fashionable in the court of King Minos, another lordling of lesser blood wore Tudor hose and a doublet with enough silk spilling from the wrists to veil a dozen brides. Silver and blood, the vassal colors of Lord Hynrich, dominated the court but here and there the colors of allies stood out like flowers in a moon and crimson field. Vassals and envoys from rival lords dotted the attending mob. *See also, spy, in the dictionary.*

Normally intrigue and politicking would be taking place in the cold hall to the sound of quiet chatter and muted conspiracy. Instead, the nobles murmured excitedly to themselves, a tittering susurrus of excitement. All eyes turned to the kneeling figure bowing before the master of the house.

Lord Hynrich sat upon an iron dark throne carved from the mountain's heart, an unmoving ivory statue. The ancient creature radiated power and authority, removed from the petty squabbling of his court.

The master of the castle glared at the cringing supplicant from his throne, a mask of disdain on his patrician features. The lord's eyes were sapphire shards in the flickering torchlight. Before him knelt the beleaguered Telemachus, an emissary and still-living member of Lord Hynrich's household.

His fine clothes were now stained and torn, the royal blue coat ruined with dirt and blood. The faint smell of smoke and the tangy odor of the sea hung about Telemachus. Marc frowned in confusion. *Telemachus is a seneschal, a bean counter. He shouldn't have been anywhere near a battlefield.* About them, the Elevated dukes and margraves looked on hungrily.

The seated master of the house raised a hand and the whispers died swiftly, only the crackle of the burning torches and the labored breathing of the harried emissary interrupting the sepulchral silence while the moon shone down in judgment through the high set windows.

"Telemachus, a fortnight ago we ordered you to manage your lands and tend to your herd in our Romanian holdings. You spoke to us of many woes, as a vassal should. These worries included a foe too terrible for you to face alone, shadowed raiders from the Black Sea. To ease your troubles, we sent forth our finest bondlings and their sworn warriors. A promise was given that our troubles would be alleviated. Yet only a few moons past you begged clemency and swore that with but more time you could deliver upon your promises." A sneer crossed the enthroned lord's features. "Yet here you kneel again, pleading for further boons. To compound your sins, our good servants inform us that warriors of our own Lineage lay slain upon the field, while your promise of good order in our lands remains unfulfilled. Why do you again presume upon our mercy?"

Marc's eyes widened. The "good servants" were the vampire lord's many informants. It meant that Telemachus had tried to hide something from Lord Hynrich.

Telemachus must have neglected to mention the casualties when he begged an audience of Lord Hynrich. Left out the detail that the master's own brood died fighting. Probably hoped to get in and get out before their master discovered his ruse and beg forgiveness rather permission. A stupid gamble, but Marc understood. All too well, given his own visit. *Desperate men do desperate things. Still, what could kill warriors of Lord Hynrich's household?*

A wince crossed Telemachus face, visible even in the soft torchlight. Pressing his sweat-dampened forehead to the floor, the distraught figure shuddered in vehement denial.

"Please, honored lord, it's not my fault!"

The room feel silent as the blurted protest echoed and faded, swallowed up by the pitiless stone walls. Marc chewed his lower lip. *Excuses and pleas rarely suffice in Lord Hynrich's presence. This can't end well.*

Hungry eyes turned to Lord Hynrich in anticipation.

A strange, alien sound shattered the unearthly stillness. It took those of the court, Marc amongst them, a moment to recognize the sound and mark its source. A rueful, rasping chuckle escaped the seated lord, stealing forth from behind a gate of sharp, pearly white teeth.

The ancient vampire was laughing.

Rising from his throne, the master of the house marched to stand before the kneeling Telemachus, who trembled like a rabbit in a snare, watching his master's approach.

Lord Hynrich knelt to gaze into Telemachus' eyes, sapphire to amber in the flicking flames of the torches. "Ah Telemachus, it is the thinnest of bloodlines that link you to our esteemed peerage. You may be family, but you are not Elevated. Not truly. As such you do not understand the burdens of leadership."

Lord Hynrich rested pale hands upon Telemachus' trembling shoulders and leaned forward, whispering into his vassal's ear.

"It is a mortal failing. Blame the seasons. Blame your enemies. Blame God. But when you *are* a god....ah." With each softly spoken word the prince leaned closer until the court strained to hear their master's tête-à-tête. "*Everything* is your fault."

Telemachus drew in a single breath; perhaps to scream, perhaps to plead or bargain, but found he could do neither as his liege's ivory hands clasped about his neck with inhuman strength. A twist and wrench saw poor Telemachus' head torn from his body, crimson vitae splattering the fine marble floor as the pale moon watched impassively above.

Muted laughter and hissed approval swept through the assembled gentry as the twitching corpse's final heartbeats played out. Marc struggled not to vomit on the floor. It would be a very poor start to presenting his case.

Lord Hynrich regarded the severed head of his former friend, a look of shock still etched on the grisly ornament's face. The ancient vampire frowned, as if whatever he saw in its lifeless features displeased him. "Life only allows so many mistakes, dear friend."

The matter settled, the vampire lord casually discarded the head and resumed his place upon the dark throne. Forcing down his discomfort and his hunger, Marc walked from the noble crowd and knelt before his sire. The young vampire studiously ignored the grisly remains of the previous supplicant next to him.

Marc knelt and said nothing, waiting for his master to speak.

"Childe Marcus," the ancient vampire started. "How good of you to join us. Your arrival is quite fortuitous. We find ourselves in need of trustworthy aides. The current help keeps losing their heads."

Cruel chuckles resounded throughout the hall at the morbid jest. It wasn't mere sycophancy either.

More form, more posturing. All for their amusement. I still can't believe immortals could be this shallow. Elevated court politics were razor-edged affairs, the rise and fall of players provided deadly entrainment for the jaded dead. Politics without blood was a drab business.

Marc focused inward and plotted his next move. He needed to play this to the hilt. "My life is yours to command, sire. My blood, your coin. My hands, your tools." *Focus on the words, use the script to your advantage. Play the rules and have a watertight case. Here, even more than with Arkadas, form matters.* "By Fortune's graces, my request this night shall hasten my current tasks' end that I might better attend to your needs."

Lord Hynrich lazily rested upon an arm of his throne, a bored expression writ across his face. "Your tasks begin and end by our will, childe. To presume otherwise would be both arrogant and unwise."

Marc pressed his head against the cold floor. "Of course, sire. It is in your service in the New World, in the Sunset Lands, I have chanced upon an opportunity to strengthen your forces."

"Do you believe our power requires bolstering from one such as yourself?"

Marc swallowed nervously, more involuntary remnants of his breathing days. *Please don't let him notice. He hates it when I act warm blooded.* "Not yours, my lord, but as your good servant I ever seek to provide for you. With Telemachus' failure and the loss of your house warriors, it may serve well to recoup those losses. Thus, I offer a chance for alliance amongst the Shifter Houses." The kneeling supplicant laid out his bait and waited.

Excited murmurs broke out amidst the nobility. Relationships with the shapeshifters always proved complicated throughout the centuries. Complications provided opportunities.

Lord Hynrich cut the air with a hand, a flash of power compelling the attending brood to silence. Mouths clacked shut as their sire exerted his influence over them. Even the guests stilled, as they stood within the vampire lord's sanctum. Lord Hynrich was the land and the land was he. "Intriguing, Marcus, particularly as we sent you as a gesture of good will to Arkadas to attend to finances. Establishing alliances with the changing breed oversteps the scope of your mission. It speaks of... ambition." The words dripped with menace. "An unworthy trait in a good servant."

Marc trembled as the force of his sire's will crashed over him, flooded him to the bone. "Indeed... but I saw a chance... certainly there would be risk but..." Marc's jaw slammed shut, chipping a tooth as Lord Hynrich's anger silenced him.

"Cease these pretenses, childe. We know your thoughts. You withhold your true intentions for this audience and your interest in such an alliance, provided it is more than a mere chimerical illusion, is not as a boon to myself. What do you truly pursue?"

Writhing upon the floor, mouth locked in a silent scream, Marc felt the ancient vampire's will drive into his mind like a blade, cutting through layers of self to scratch upon the very core of his being. Grasping the sides of his head, Marc rose to glare at his master.

"My friend... my brother... he's in trouble. I have to help him." Marc's nails dug bloody furrows into his skull as he confronted his lord, teeth bared in a pained grimace.

"For the sake of this friend, you would come before us, deceive us, and risk our wrath?" A dark pressure forced on Marc's mind as the vampire lord's gaze bore into the youngling.

"Yeesssss." Even as the tortured hiss left Marc's lips the cutting edge of Lord Hynrich's will abated, leaving Marc to gather himself on the blood-stained marble.

"Excellent. Your dedication is admirable. In light of such loyalty, we shall grant you this boon."

Marc twitched. Though he'd said nothing, the ancient lord had ripped Marc's request from his mind.

"We shall lend our name to your gamble but take heed." Lord Hynrich's eyes blazed and Marc quailed from the threat of his wrath. "Henceforth, all responsibility for this deed lies solely upon you. All acts, foul and fair, and their consequences rests upon your shoulders. Should you fail you will cast out and you shall find no succor within these walls nor aid from my house. Unspeakable agonies shall befall both you and this hapless mortal and we shall not lift a finger to aid you. Now go forth and carry out our will."

Marc raised himself and bowed stiffly. "As you command, sire." Slowly, Marc picked himself from the ground and limped away as the court parted before him like a perfumed sea. The assembled nobles looked at Marc like he was mad. No surprise, as despite Marc's lingering agony, his fangs were bared in a triumphant grin.

CHAPTER 15

BELLY WARMED by soup and desperation, Jon snuck back to the Arkadas property. He'd given serious thought to burning his clothes, but banked on Marc not caring for such social graces as not smelling like a dumpster. Jon still wasn't a hundred percent on his plan, but that had never stopped him before.

No more fearing these furred and fanged fucks. Monsters or not, they're still human deep down. And while that's scarier than anything else, it means I can make them jump.

All Jon had to do was find Marc. They'd figure something out. At least they could sand bag this thing to buy more time. Jon just needed to go on the offensive and start getting them to move for him, not the other way round. *I've been off my game since getting here. Time to do what they paid me for: win hearts and influence people.*

Jon squeaked through the backdoor with the key so kindly provided by Arkadas as part of his welcome packet. Shadows and silence were his only companions as Jon padded through the ancient structure, his footsteps painfully loud in the sepulchral halls.

He snuck through its eerily quiet halls, ears perked and eyes open for any sign of life.

So, Jon might be forgiven for screeching like a startled six-year-old when a mop hit him in the face. Flailing wildly, Jon calmed down after he realized his attacker was just a cleaning utensil. The sound of a slamming drawer made him jump again and an overall clad figure walked around the corner.

Feeling a little foolish, Jon tried to hide the mop behind his back. "Burning the midnight oil?"

With an ear-piercing shriek, the janitor turned into an oversized feather duster and rushed Jon, all beak and talons.

Pure luck saved Jon from a grisly end at the hands of the bird Shifter. He owed his life to a yellow mop bucket, as the frenzied janitor tripped over his own cleaning supplies in his rush to gut the lawyer. Jon ran past the thrashing beast deeper into the open-air office, running around the empty desks of Marc's lair.

They played a merry game of tag through the palatial office space. Jon fought an untimely urge to start humming the Scooby Doo theme song. *This would be funny if I wasn't about to be disemboweled by a freaking were-turkey!* Getting a desk between him and Beaky, the lawyer held the mop out like a spear at his avian attacker.

"Back off the D, buddy. In case you didn't know, I'm Jon Doe. Women want me and men want to be me. Shit, my shirts are worth more than your yearly salary." Unfortunately, Jon's bluster failed to have the desired effect.

"Doe? DOE?! Slave to the deniers of the gods! Creator of shackles. For thwarting the gods' plans, you deserve death. For the Cull! For the gods! For our freedom! Die, servant of the hated Houses!" Clearing the desk, the shrieking madman dove for Jon's throat.

With a panicked scream, Jon fell back, mop propped like a lamppost. The Shifter's momentum propelled it inexorably forward, impaling him on the wooden shaft. As the ranting Fury lay on the ground winded and gasping, Jon hopped to his feet. *This is bullshit. I'm not even safe at work.* The injured janitor started to rise, sending office supplies tumbling. Jon spotted a small side door and ran to it. He yanked it open to reveal an empty room, creepy doodles etched into bare wood from floor to ceiling.

Shock and outrage rooted him to the spot.

"What the hell?! Who has a room like this in their place of fucking business?"

Jon turned from what he assumed was the creative by-product of bored and drugged out office workers' lunch breaks to star at the beast creature as it rushed toward him, bronze claws outstretched. Beaky's victory shriek cut off abruptly as his head left his shoulders.

The janitor's shrinking body collapsed to one side as the head bounced and rolled into the shadows. Jon tumbled back into the closet. Betai stood, utterly poised, hard and deadly as the shining blade in her hand. She flicked the blood from it edge and smiled at him. It was then he noticed the orange and black striped fur. Gleaming yellow eyes shone with quiet mirth.

"Hello, Mr. Doe. Working late?"

As Marc stepped from the sulfurous portal chamber the coppery tang of blood hit the weary vampire's nose even through the acrid smoke. Too much to be a blood packet. *What happened while I was gone?* Creeping out of the arcane room, Marc peeked into the wider office. Of all the scenarios his prodigious mind concocted, Marc did not expect to see a bandaged and battered Jon Doe sitting at his desk, with the dark clad Daughter of Tigers cleaning her blade nearby. Marc pulled up short, taking in the absurd scene. *Seeing her without Mr. Vinara is strange enough, but Jon working*

late, that is truly bizarre. A large garbage bag and mop bucket sat off in a corner. Tired and hungry as Marc was, it smelled delicious. *At least not all of the blood is Jon's.*

Relief and a vague sense of triumph from surviving seeing his sire made Marc playful. "If you messed up my filing, I'll save the Houses the trouble and end you now."

Jon's aborted laughter had him hugging his sides. "Sue me. I know a good lawyer." Bloodshot eyes darted from Sipskos to the door and back again. "Did you just walk out of that closet?"

"Home office meeting." Marc settled into his chair, too tired to even bother with the niceties of forcing his lungs to huff air too look alive or answer Jon's befuddled look.

With no further information forthcoming from his undead co-conspirator, Jon raised a sardonic eyebrow at the laconic vampire. Marc didn't feel like explaining anything to Jon but surrendered to the inevitable as Jon went into pantomimes and exaggerated hand gestures to get his attention. *If anyone could grind down an immortal's patience, it would be the inestimable Mr. Doe. Might as get this over with now or he'll never stop bothering me.*

"I've been going over the contract and I may have found us an option," Marc said.

"Terrific! We'll have to compare notes. Looks like we've both had a hell of a day."

"Looks like. What happened to you?"

"Living the dream, you know how it goes. Life styles of the rich and desperate. No one returns my calls, which includes you, by the way. To top it off, Magda breaks into my house and puts her boots on my couch. She almost scuffed my Baker!"

Marc shook his head at the distress of his Harvard comrade. *Of course, he'd be worried about his couch. At least nothing happened to his car. I'd never hear the end of it.*

"I've dodged a crazy werewolf trying to gut me, told a bunch of the 'good' wolves to sniff some trees, had some amazing clam chowder, and came back here to find you and got attacked by the freaking janitor for my troubles," Jon continued. "Miss Chatty here saved my butt after the janitor tried to off me. On the plus side, I made some new friends. Movie stars. Gave me a free tour of Speculo Productions and even got an autograph from Zoe. Seems she's a local celebrity."

Marc perked up, practically vibrating is his chair. "Wait. You don't mean Zoe? *The* Zoe? The Blonde Brawler? I love her films! Did you get her number?"

Jon gave another one of his weapons' grade smirks. "Why yes, Marc, I'm fine as well. Thank you for asking. Of all the weird shit going down, you focus on the blonde."

Marc opened his mouth but shut it quickly. The irony of Jon's own statement flew over his head but that was nothing new. What had Marc's attention was Jon's eyes. The blue orbs glinted like their old Harvard days. *Our professors learned to fear that wicked shine.*

Jon put a hand to his chest with mock outrage. "You're drooling. It's enough to make a guy jealous."

"To be fair, she is a lot prettier than you." Marc instantly regretted the banter. Too much truth lay behind it. Marc had a crush on Zoe as deep as Lord Hynrich's dungeons. *Damn. I forgot the prime rule in Jon's wars of words. Do not engage. All I've done is give him confirmation.*

Jon homed in on the obvious interest with laser like precision. "Marc, buddy, I know I said we can do the impossible, but there are limits even to my greatness. Cheating death at the hands of eldritch shapeshifting monstrosities, no offense to any present company, is one thing but getting you a date is a whole other thing entirely. *Magnitudes* more difficult!" Jon spread his arms as wide as he could, grinning like an ass.

"Better try harder, you slacker. Might as well be good for something." Marc sat up stiffly, eyes like flint. "Besides, you owe me one. I called in some major favors to help."

"Yeah?"

"Yes. It came with a cost, though. My ass is on the line now, too. We are all in."

Jon pulled his chair forward, elbows propped on the edge of the desk. Marc did the same, the two falling into the "war room" habits that served them well when the good people of Harvard wanted both of them gone. *Let's hope you still have the old mojo, Jon. I'm banking on it.*

"Talk to me."

Marc recounted his journey from dusty archives to darkest file folder, the minor but nagging inconsistencies the lanky fellow continually ran into, getting more and more worked up over the fruits his investigative efforts. "I scoured every inch of what Arkadas held on site and the records simply didn't sync up. Contradictory reports, future dated time stamps, personnel shuffles before any openings, and an absurd amount of plain old misfiled papers. The Beachfront contract brought it together."

"What about it?" Jon asked. "Lots of firms have boiler plate and redundant contracts written up. Saves time."

"Yes, but none of them with Arkadas' name on it. Publicly, Arkadas knew it was a deathtrap, so he dropped the project without looking back. Even ensured he had an expendable third party to place in charge of it so he wouldn't lose one of his own assets. You don't go through all that effort to avoid the guillotine and then have papers drawn up to get you a front row seat. These mistakes couldn't be sloppy paperwork. I dug deeper."

Marc darted around the office in a frenzy, grabbing papers and hammering away at his computer to pull up the files, creating a tapestry of data, files, and findings.

"There? You see? Here, here, and..."

The manic glaze in his eyes died away as he saw his two companions' reactions. Jon leaned back in his chair, ready to bolt, while Betai crouched with sword at the ready, her skin covered in orange and black fur, eyes feline.

"What is wrong with you two?" Even as he asked, Marc knew the answer when his tongue touched sharp points. His fangs protruded past his lips, extended and ready to feast on crimson blood. Had he cast a reflection in the computer monitor, it would have revealed the full monstrous face of the vampire, eyes and fangs gleaming.

Marc had been so hungry and excited, he hadn't remembered to keep his mortal mask up.

Embarrassed, Marc withdrew his fangs with difficulty. "Sorry."

"Do not do that again." Betai did not move from her watchful position, blade drawn.

Mental note: do not make the holy warrior antsy. Betai does not care for me or mine.

Jon took a deep breath, which made Marc strangely jealous somehow. Then the lawyer let out a laugh. The crouching warrior seemed equally wary of Jon now, looking at him like he was a madman. "Damn, Marc. When we talked about going into business together, this is not how I thought it would go down."

Jon walked over to Marc and hugged him, despite Sipskos' muttered protestations.

"Jon, get back, I'm too hungry. I might..."

The young Doe pulled back with a grin. "Not a chance. I'm done being afraid of spooks and ghoulies. I wasn't there for you before buddy and I'm sorry. I think I get it now."

As soon as Jon's heartfelt declaration was over, Marc shoved him away and ran for the mini fridge, yanking out a blood packet and slurping it down in a violent frenzy of punctured plastic.

"Uggh gross. Thanks for ruining the moment."

"I warned you I was hungry."

"Not my fault you still haven't mastered table manners. Could you at least not slurp your meal?"

Feeling malicious, Marc waved the drained bag under Jon's face. "I could slurp you down if you prefer."

Jon didn't blanch like before and instead batted his eyelashes playfully. "Why, Marc! I didn't know you thought of me that way."

"Please. I have standards."

A cough interrupted their banter, causing them to jump. In their bonhomie, they'd forgotten about their sword wielding companion. "Gentlemen. As I saved your lives, I am responsible for them. I'd hate to end them so soon thereafter. So, please, may we get back to the task at hand?"

Jon gave his best jury-winning smile. "Just some gallows humor, Betty. Coping mechanisms."

Marc chucked the drained bag into a nearby trash bin. "Still, the Daughter of Tigers is correct. This is important. Arkadas is dirtier than we thought. He has plans for the Beachfront property and is collaborating the Cull."

"You mean the murderous yahoos who tried to kill me?"

"Tried to kill you, will still try to kill you, and have killed the staff here." Bitterness welled up in Marc as he extolled Arkadas' betrayal. "Arkadas sold them out. The Cull slaughtered them to make room their own agents, like our good friend chum bucket over there." Marc hiked a thumb toward the bloody remains of the deceased janitor.

"I know Arkadas wouldn't be above a bribe, but this is sick. Shouldn't the Cull hate him too?"

Betai interjected again, her word underscored by the scrape her blade on a whetstone. "For his excessive involvement in human affairs and perverse love of human trappings, yes. But such distaste pales compared to their rage against the Houses. The Cull holds that they are chosen of the gods and the Houses misuse their holy mandate. No matter how joined Arkadas is financially to the Court and Senate, he is still an outsider. Thus, the Cull may consider him a useful tool."

"So they save him for last. Gotcha."

Marc tapped his computer monitor. "Which is more or less the tone in the emails. This Zypresse character isn't exactly reverent with Arkadas. They're working together but there's no love lost."

Jon steepled his fingers, tapping the tips to his pursed lips as he thought. "Good to know. Pebbles, bandits, etc. That gives us an edge in our strategy. If only we could get an edge."

Marc made the effort of huffing in offense, making the air around him smell like pennies. "When have I ever failed to deliver?"

Jon held up his hands in concession to the point. "What ammo did your big old brain scrounge up?"

"The great and powerful of the Houses couldn't trust anyone from the other side to handle these affairs. Particularly not with the heightened tensions of the Truce. Hence, why they dragged you in."

"Yeah, got that part. Sacrificial lamb. Thanks for the reminder."

"Even though it is only for show and exceedingly temporary, the Houses still gave you final executive control. Anything you set up, if ratified by the respective parties, will be considered iron clad."

"Which is all fine and good, except they keep ducking my calls and I doubt they'd listen anyway"

Marc interrupted his friend's whining with a well time stress ball to the face. "Allow me my dramatic timing. Not all of us get to hog the floor like you do."

Jon rubbed at the red mark on his forehead. "Apologies, great sahib. This one begs forgiveness."

"As well you should, because I found a sub-clause. A very important sub-clause. Basically, an emergency out. Best I can figure, they never planned on using it."

Jon cocked his head and Marc resisted the urge to find a doggy treat. "Why?"

"Because it's less likely to happen than you keeping a partner for more than three weeks."

"Hey, low blow."

"The elders never intended to actually show up out here. It leaves them too vulnerable and far from their respective seats of power. They usually let their representatives do the talking. That is the key. Anyone can invoke *Dictatus*."

Marc waited for his old friend's applause. The vampire received a blank stare instead.

"Marc, if its any help, I am trying really hard not to make a dick joke right now."

"Ignorant heathen. You should know this from the Latin in our schooling." Marc shook his head. "*Dictatus* takes its cue from ancient Rome. For the Shifter Houses, it is the right of a representative to speak and act with the full authority of their superiors. It was an emergency measure in case tough decisions had to be made and there wasn't time to consult the top staff. It's also a great way to send someone more expendable than yourself to handle important affairs in case you suspect a trap. In short, we don't need the heads of the Houses, just anyone of sufficient rank to sign on the dotted line."

"Terrific. What's the catch?"

"Glad you are still paying attention. They didn't want to give any ambitious and wayward minions too much carte blanche. The House representatives could sign for them, so long as three neutral parties, all powerful enough to be recognized by the Houses, to sign off on the changes as well. We can use the redundancy and paranoia of the Houses to our advantage."

Marc turned to his old buddy, eyes still glowing in the dark. "That's why I took a gambit and went to Lord Hynrich to ask for his aid."

"Isn't that a conflict of interests?" Jon asked. "You are working for the Houses, after all."

Jon might not be able to tear his eyes off of anything in a mini-skirt but there is a brain in that head of his. "Technically, I work for Lord Hynrich as a loaner to Arkadas. Lord Hynrich is neutral, outside of internal Shifter politics. It's understood and expected that my master and the Houses are allies of convenience and nothing more. Everyone is always looking for ways to screw the others, so long as they can get away with it. That's partly my job here, to see if I can get any dirt dug up on the Senate and the Court."

"So that's why the Cull didn't target you."

"Correct. I'm spying for someone else *on* the Houses, not *for* the Houses. Though, Shifters don't take kindly to vampires very much." Marc nodded to Betai, whose hand hadn't strayed from her sword.

"We often resent those that lay outside the natural cycles, breathless one. Though your loyalty to your friend is commendable." She turned to Jon. "You are fortunate to have such a brave companion. He would risk his existence for yours."

The blue-eyed wunderkind looked down, a mix of pride and shame on his face. *Jon never was much good with feelings. For that matter, neither am I.* Marc saved him from any further awkwardness by carrying forward.

"Bottom line; Lord Hynrich has given his blessing, but only if this gambit works," Marc continued. "Anything goes wrong and we are on our own. I will be considered a traitor and a failure, and he doesn't care for either." Marc struggled to whisper the last words, fear and memories of pain choking in his throat.

Jon noticed and stepped up. "Hey, not to worry Marc, when we pull this off..."

"When?" *Such a small but important word choice.*

"You heard me. When we pull this off, Hynrich is going to be so happy he'll be doing backflips in his coffin."

Marc smiled them, incisors on full display, tiny crimson tears gleaming. *That's the old Jon I used to know and love.* "So, how are we going to do this?"

"We do what we always do, my good Marc. Win hearts and influence minds and make the puppets dance." Jon wrung his hands together in glee. "Now, get me a list of victims."

CHAPTER 16

AGDA, BROCK, AND NIALL RETURNED from their failed hunt sodden and frustrated. They forsook the familiar comfort of the Den to go their own way. Niall left for home, and Brock elected for his office, citing the need for a report.

"Paperwork?" Incredulous didn't begin to cover Magda's tone. The warrior shoved wet hair from her face, mohawk ruined beyond saving. "At this hour?"

"A tidy mind makes for a tidy ship."

"Ship? You're infantry, grunt."

"Quite true," Brock replied. "That's why I can beat up any wet ears who tries to object to me using the saying."

As Brock left, Magda found herself in the unenviable position of being alone with her thoughts. Given the current madness whirling in her life, her thoughts were the last thing she wanted to face.

Damn that Doe! He made his own bed, he can lie in it. Sadly, the mental protestation held no heat. The usual fire of rage, so long keeping the empty pit in her stomach at bay, no longer warmed as it once had. Magda paced along the damp concrete unseeing, lost in her own thoughts. Her attention drifted in the direction of the Den, her home away from home. Magda yearned for the light and laughter of drink and companions, anything to drive the now familiar ache in her heart to its corner. But as she hungered for amber liquid to sooth her woes, Niall's face burned into her mind; desperate, pained, ready to die. Die at her hands.

Gods, what have I become if my line mates fear me so? She let out a disgusted grunt and continued her aimless march, taking refuge from the torrent under a bus stop, seated next to a sleeping vagrant.

Magda held a fearsome reputation and reveled in it. She'd earned every pain-filled stitch of it. But what she'd seen in Niall's eyes had been a different beast entirely. The fear of a youth she held as a brother stopped her cold. Fear of her. *Justified fear.* Magda hung her head in shame. The realization that she'd been ready to kill a brother shattered her world.

Now, with no enemy nor drink nor warm bedmate to distract her, Magda faced that harsh reality. The growing rage, the many drinks, the endless dalliances all took on a new light.

Magda Lahm Dearg, Bannersworn of the Sunset Cohort, had been running. Running from the pain that still lingered ever since her fateful battle on the rocky coast of San Francisco.

Her snarl woke the bum sharing her plastic alcove, but Magda had already vanished by the time his bleary eyes cleared. She moved with a purpose previously absent in her wanderings. Guilt, anger, pride, and loss warred within her, their conflict no less fierce than the battles that left scars on her flesh.

Visions of her fallen comrades warred with Niall's face in her mind's eye. Every sideways glance her line mates shared as she downed another shot, the steps backward the centurions took in the Den when her ire was up, and the quiet whispers all took on darker meanings. They had feared Magda. *For the wrong reasons.*

Leaping fences, clambering escapes, and jumping between rooftops, Magda used every bit of urban terrain to her advantage. San Dominguez may have been a far cry from the urban jungles of New York or Los Angeles, but its squat and boxy skyline offered plenty of routes for an inventive Shifter to traverse the seaside city.

At last she came to an aging two-story affair, though not half as old as its neo-Victorian façade wanted people to believe. The sign planted out front announced it as "Wichita/Macintyre Counseling: Private, Personal, Family."

No matter how many times she saw it, Magda struggled to reconcile Brock's job as a counselor with the stoic war-leader she knew with. To see the man who gutted shell-backed creatures from the deep with a shattered sword then bend down and speak softly with troubled youths was a surreal experience. With a deep breath, Magda pushed inside, taking the stairs two at a time to reach his little office on the upper floor.

Her cognitive dissonance only deepened as she walked in to see him hunched over his desk, slender tools held in his powerful hands, eyes narrowed in concertation as he sought to raise the mast of a boat inside a glass bottle.

"Yes, Magda?"

His even tone snapped her back to reality. *That part remains unchanged at least.* But even as she opened her mouth to speak, she found the words slipping away. Instead, she took solace in familiar banter.

"I thought you had a report to do."

"Already finished and filed. The wonders of an electronic age."

"So you hide out here, playing with your toys?" The words slipped from her, the acid coating them turning a playful taunt into a hurtful insinuation of cowardice.

Brock maintained his even demeanor, making tiny corrections on his project. "Leadership is a heavy burden to bear, as you once knew. Everyone needs a pressure valve, some type of release, to cope with their duties."

Magda looked away, shame and anger warring insider her. "Sounds like a retreat."

"It's not a surrender to treat your wounds."

Magda knew Brock directed the last bit at her. The silence stretched on painfully, the burden on Magda to continue. The former Cohort officer hesitated, frightened to admit her weakness, if only for a moment. Then she squared her shoulders and puffed up with a large breath. *I've never been a coward before and I shan't be one now.*

"How long?"

Brock blinked at the blurted question, the only crack in his professional mask. "How long?"

"How long have you been watching me, waiting for me to snap? How long have I been battle-mad?"

"You aren't a berserker, Magda, just in pain. Loss affects us all."

"Niall thought I was going to kill him tonight."

"But you didn't."

Magda shot to her feet. "By a hair's breadth! He fully expected me to take his life right there in the Den, and I was ready to do it. Gods damn it, Brock. The Cohort is my family. Why would I...?" She trailed off, shoulders heaving and wracked with tears that could not be shed. Silence stretched as Magda continued to wage her silent internal war.

Brock's level tone broke the silence. "Sometimes, the scars we carry aren't visible to the naked eye. Not at first. The wounds are there, make no mistake, and you can see them if you know what to look for. But sometimes, the injured turn from the pain because it's too great. Because they can't stop fighting, because it would mean accepting the loss. They turn to drink, sex, whatever they can to take their eyes from the pain, since they can't bear to look at it. You asked to know when, Banner-sworn, and I say that you already know. You know when the shadows in your heart grew. When you gave up your command and wouldn't accept the loss of your friends in battle. You chose to fight your guilt and grief alone."

A second silence stretched, this one quieter, if no less fierce. Magda let out a slight hiccupping laugh. "Talking like that, no wonder you charge by the hour. I'm not sure I could afford your rates."

"Discounts for friends and family. And for good soldiers who need a hand."

The final silence held at least the promise of peace, no matter how distant. "How long?"

"How long until you've conquered your fears?" Brock shrugged. "Who can say? But I can say how it is measured. One day at a time."

Magda nodded and rose. "Then may the battle be joined, however long it lasts."

§——§

As the sky brightened with pre-dawn light, Jon and Marc discovered their options to be a very short list.

"That's all we have to work with?" Jon blinked in surprise. "We had better angles with the debate teams at Harvard."

"Those were nice and polite people. Here, you simply don't have the leverage. You're either not well known enough or too well known. Of the even remotely accessible House signatories, Deimos is a hardliner, Ariana's nearly vanished off the planet, and Athena is just plain paranoid."

Jon scoffed. "Fine, I'll just turn on the old Doe charm and the get the latest reps eating out of my hand."

Marc stared at Jon for a moment. "You do realize that the Court of Raptors' two most readily available signatories would be the Aegolius' siblings."

"Sure."

"Including Aahmes, who kidnapped you."

"Thanks, Marc, I think I remember that part."

"Whom you insulted at a public affair."

"So?"

"I'm saying Aahmes might be the easier one," Marc said. "You ran screaming from Selina."

"Dammit, Marc, I know. So what? Not the first time I've won over folks who didn't care for me."

"Yes, but none of them were attractive and powerful ladies who've had the misfortune of meeting you beforehand."

"What are you talking about? Ladies love me. Everybody wants the D."

Jon looked so hurt and confused, Marc actually did a double take. *He can't be serious. I knew Jon's delusions run deep and strong, but this is absurd.* Marc held a hand up and began to tick off fingers.

"Marline was a one-night stand. Jessica thought you were gay and wanted a shopping buddy. Leslie gave up when she realized she didn't have a sugar daddy. Susan stormed out, swearing you spent more time looking in the mirror than paying attention to her. Lauretta refused to listen to any more self-indulgent whining about your parents."

"Lauretta said she ended things because I was too clingy!" Jon paused as his brain caught up with his mouth. "Alright, I admit, I am much better at the launch than I am at the dismount. Sue me."

"What I'm getting at, Jon, is that you have been with these two ladies, these two powerful figures, a long time by your standards. Per your pattern, I suspect you have taken steps, intentional or otherwise, that have begun to drive them away. Given your history, any or all of the following are likely to have occurred."

Marc raised a second hand, once again counting off fingers. "Sharp and exaggerated judgements, distancing and isolation, harsh words from that weapon grades mouth of yours, and probably some blame cast that they didn't care enough about you, per whatever metric is in your head."

Jon squired in his seat, siganling Marc's words hit closer to home than the blue-eyed Casanova wanted to admit.

Still the Jon I knew and loved, warts and all. "My point is, how much good faith can we rely on you still having with them?"

Jon frowned. "I'm not sure. Selina's something special, though." Suddenly the old grin was back. "Don't worry about it. I'm sure I can talk them around. What about the other House representative?"

"Representatives. Plural. That would be Brock Macintyre and Magda Lahm Dearg."

"Oh. Right. Only met that Brock guy once, but I know Magda. She offered me help before. She might be willing to join in."

"Are you sure about that?"

Jon flashed another politician's smile. "I know people. Even when they aren't people."

"Fine. Benefit of the doubt. You sure you can handle Arkadas?"

"He is a greedy, power hungry, ruthless son of a bitch who will stop at nothing to get what he wants. Really isn't that different that the old bosses I used to intern for."

Marc arched an eyebrow at Jon's cavalier comparison. "Except for being an owl Shifter."

"Is he? I didn't notice."

"You never pissed him off enough to make him change. He hates ruining his three-piece suits."

Jon shrugged. "Alright, so he's an owl Shifter. I'll bring some tasty mice as a bribe. We've got enough blackmail to have Arkadas over a barrel. Done deal. We just need our deck stacked so he doesn't think of squirreling out of it."

"Wonderful metaphors, Jon. That still leaves us one short."

At this time Betai spoke again, voice even and strong despite her long silence. Jon jumped but Marc didn't flinch. The vampire never lost track of the sword wielding emissary.

"Might I suggest Ganesh? He has mentioned his admiration for your confidence and determination, Mr. Doe. We have spoken of your situation several times since our meeting in Arkadas' office."

Jon beamed, taking the compliment. "Why, thank you."

"I will tell him of your sacrifice as well, Mr. Sipskos." She nodded toward Marc before turning to Jon again. "If the Cycle-Broken is willing to risk dissolution at the hands of his creator for your sake, Mr. Doe, it speaks highly of both of you. I believe the esteemed ambassador would be receptive to your proposal."

Jon might have been gulled by the flattering words, but Marc was not.

"That is very kind, Daughter of Tigers, but why are you here?"

Jon looked at his brusque friend, outraged. "Marc! I think we can be a bit nicer to the kind lady who saved my life, don't you?"

"Betai Ka Bagha never does anything without a reason." Marc did not butcher her name as Jon did, giving full honor to the Daughter of Tigers. "It would be inefficient. She is oathed to guard Ganesh, but Ganesh isn't here." Marc turned to the tiger Shifter. "To save time, I'll ask plainly. Why are you here? What do you hope to gain? Why are you helping us?"

The Shifter's gaze took in her two companions, steely eyes weighting them. When she spoke, it was in the same conversational tone as before.

"I am a servant of the gods and enemy of their enemies. What the Cull does is a perversion of divine intent. I came to Arkadas because I sensed the hand of an even older enemy, a foe I have chased for some time. When I saw Mr. Doe under attack, I moved to protect an innocent. Arkadas has betrayed his word and seeks to plunge the Sunset Lands into chaos for his own gain. I have no desire to see that happen." Her amber eyes burned into the slender Sipskos. "Will that suffice, Cycle-Broken?"

Begrudgingly, Marc nodded, never once taking his eyes off her or her sword.

The tension was broken by the esteemed Mr. Doe clapping his hands together. The sound echoed like a gunshot in the cavernous space. "Wonderful! I'm glad we are all on the same page. Can we please get the conversation back to important things, like saving my hide? Thanks." Jon turned a doubtful look toward the sword wielding guardian. "Betty, not to look a gift horse in the mouth, but are you sure Ganesh wouldn't mind going against his old friend Arkadas?"

Betai gave a slight shake of her head, faint smile playing on her lips. "I cannot speak for Ganesh, Mr. Doe. The Tiger does not understand the Elephant. However, I believe he would have no objections to correcting his friend's ethical missteps. Ganesh is ever concerned with karmic debt."

"Sounds like we got a winner. I'm sure Ganesh will help us balance Arkadas' cosmic books."

Jon's grin was so infectious, Marc found himself caught in it as well, full fangs on display. "Lady and gentleman, we have ourselves a game plan."

Jon looked up and Marc eyes followed, something he instantly regretted as he caught sight of the brightening sky, tinted pink as night faded to morning. "Alright Marc, sun's up. You get some rest. I've got to lay some ground work. When you can, I need you to load me up with everything dirty you can get on Arkadas. I'm going to need that smoking gun."

Marc managed a tired nod, blinking sanguine tear-filled eyes. *I've got to feed or I'm no good to anyone. Hate to undermine Jon's confidence in me by draining him dry.* "I'll round up the evidence. Anything else you need?"

Jon cocked his head. "Marc, buddy, you might want to start polishing your resume. You may need a new job when this over."

CHAPTER 17

A CHORUS OF OUTRAGED VOICES echoed in the Den, full nearly to spilling. Columella dodged expertly through the frenzied warriors. It was enough to spark hope in Magda that the gods still watched over them. *The sot would need the blessings of Bacchus to get through this mess.*

Nothing else about the situation gave any such hope that the gods remained on their side.

Word of Ripper's assault on the duly authorized representative of the Houses and Magda's subsequent storm-swept chase spread like wildfire. Somehow, word became distorted through word of mouth and the two became mixed with recent Court activity. The rumor mill spat out a jumbled mess about the Cull and the Court colluding together, a mass of enemies that prowled around the Cohort, sniffing for weakness.

The warriors of the Sunset Cohort were mad. At the Cull, at the Senate, at the Court. It didn't matter who. The Cohort's blood was up, and they wanted their pound of flesh.

Magda applied her reliable methods of getting around; she blud-geoned anyone who stood in her way. The former officer shoved her way through the crowd, restoring order to the ranks almost on instinct. She caught herself in the midst of a prodigious dressing down, haranguing one poor unfortunate soul crushed like they were a new recruit on the parade grounds. *Jupiter's balls. It's true then. You can remove the centurion from command but you can't remove command from the centurion.*

Painful nostalgia rose inside Magda, faces of fallen comrades erupt-ing before her eyes. She shoved away from the knee knocking centurion to sit by Brody, surly and tired.

"I need a damned drink."

"Then have one."

Magda balked. "What? All that talk in your office and you just say 'have one?' Are you daft?"

"It will always be your choice. What you choose to do is what mat-ters."

Magda's teeth clenched so hard she saw spots. She placed her order through the same grimace. "Water."

Columella stumbled, eyes wide in shock. "My dear, are you feeling well?"

"Better than your ass will if you don't bring me what I damn well ordered!"

The portly barkeep nimbly danced away, an almost fatherly look of concern on his face.

Figures the drunk would care. Can't have yer best customer go dry on ya. Fah, maybe he thought he was grooming another devotee of the Ruler of the Vine all this time. Can't stand to see my faith waver.

"Now was that so hard?"

"You sound like Niall."

Brock let Magda simmer as her water came back. She sipped it des-ultorily.

"How the hell do you manage this, Brock?"

"One day at a time, Magda," he replied. "One day at a time."

Cheers of approbation and loud thumps drew their attention to another table.

"What is that all about?" Magda muttered.

Brock grunted. "Nothing good."

The roar in the Den grew louder, a rising tide of arguments, shouts, and fraying tempers. The dam was about to burst as the Cohort's repressed frustration came to a head.

"I'm telling you, it's the damn Court! Those feather dusters can't be trusted. We should go out and..."

"Damn Cull! Freaks and traitors! Hunt them all down. How do we know they aren't here, watching and laughing at us?"

"We need a show of strength, teach 'em all no one messes with us."

"Godsdamn Senate, tying our hands together when we're needed most. They can't even protect their precious pawn, whatsisname? The buck kid."

"Doe?"

"That's the one. Heard the Furies made a hit on him. Ripper was two inches from his throat. Ask me, maybe it's time for a change."

The last one drew cries of outrage. Terrifyingly, it also drew cries of support.

"Shut your traitorous mouth!"

"You're the traitor! Feeding right into the Court's plots."

"Liar! That's Cull speak if ever I heard it."

Magda saw the end coming and rose to stop it but was only halfway to her feet when the first punch was thrown. With a juvenile cry of "who you calling a bitch, bitch?" one of the centurions knocked her comrade flying.

Chaos erupted as the Cohort of the Sunset Lands turned on itself.

Magda waded into the carnage, shouting orders and cracking heads. Her attempts to reign in the rioting warriors became a fight to stay alive.

On any battlefield, there was a chaotic order to things, pushing and pulling, forces arrayed against one another to do violence and claim victory. Magda had read the ebb and flow of such things many times. This held little similarity with that. The grand melee was without order or reason, closer to the murderous final phase of a battle than its orderly start.

Like a drowning swimmer, Magda struggled to keep her head above water. She ducked a chair and punished the attacker with a thunderous jab to the kidneys. Even as the chair-wielder dropped, a heavy form tackled her from behind. Snarling a curse, Magda rolled with it, writhing around to grab the attacker's hand. She bit savagely on the extended limb, tasting blood. Kicking free, Magda rolled under a table to spit out the blood in her mouth and catch her breath.

Her throat burned, her head ached, and she'd had enough.

Magda rose with a savage road, tipping table and the centurions atop to the floor. In the blink of an eye, Magda grew, the wolf loosed and howling loud enough to shake the timbers above.

"Enough! Are you soldiers or squabbling children?!" Her lupine eyes scanned the room, quieting the brawlers around her who looked up in awe. Deimos and a tight knot of officers were pushing through the mob in a phalanx, separating the combatants and clubbing the worst offenders that didn't take the hint to calm down.

Magda glared down and cuffed anyone around her who looked stupid enough to keep fighting. "We are Cohort! Family! We are better than this!"

"Very true." Brock's voice cut through the air like a steel knife. "We are the Cohort of the Sunset Lands. Sword of the Senate. We will not brawl in the dirt like drunks and game-cocks."

The Shifters shuffled about like guilty school children. Brock cleared his throat and continued. "Hear me now, for I speak with the voice of the Senate. They are aware of the actions of the traitors and of the Court. Know that in three days, the Senate will demand a response from the representative. We will have the Beachfront property. Should Jonathan Doe fail to reach this reasonable and just conclusion, the Cohort has full authorization to render justice and march against our treacherous foes. *Ave Senatus!*"

The cheers of the warriors shook the Den harder than Magda's howl even as her anger vanished, swallowed into a cold pit in her gut. Magda sat down hard and stared a bottle of wine, miraculously unbroken in the scuffle, shaking hands clenched tightly in her lap. *Brock, you bastard, what have you done? You didn't have to throw Jon to the wolves!*

But Magda couldn't lie to herself. She knew the truth. The Cohort was too far gone. In these times of poisonous peace, the warrior band threatened to tear itself apart. Brock did the smart play and took the path of least resistance. This way needed the smallest price of blood to restore unity. Unit at the cost of one life.

Jon Doe, the sacrificial lamb, exactly as the lawyer said.

Niall's condemnations, Brock's announcement, and Jon's accusations rang in Magda's ears. *Damn him. Damn him for a fool.* She didn't know which of them she meant. *Damn me, too.*

CHAPTER 18

ITTING IN HER THRONE LIKE CHAIR in the Petitioners Hall of the Edfu Estates, Selina Aegolius looked down at her polished nails and for what felt like the hundredth time considered how they would look covered in the blood of the blustering fool in front of her. Peter Kapnos, Exalted of the Court of Raptors, strutted about in his sky-blue suit, pinched face contorted with the efforts of his rambling, pale hair waving with the exertions of his tirade. Kapnos was in rare form, pontificating for all he was worth to sway the esteemed and noble peerage of the Court of Raptors gathered in session to discuss current events. Though Selina was currently first amongst equals, the jealous and ambitious nobility were entitled and due their right to watch and discuss the proper course of action for their House.

The elite of the Court had met to discuss the tumultuous Beachfront session and as a high-ranking member, Kapnos was allowed to have his say. No matter how boorish, dim witted, and tiresome that say might be.

Of course, Selina allowed none of her homicidal thoughts to slip her mask as Kapnos rambled on the perceived inadequacies of the current state of affairs and thus, by proxy, her own actions. *He may be an arrogant little worm, but he has the ear of too many factions at Court to gut. More's the pity.*

"Inexcusable! Their accusations are simply inexcusable. Imagine, our Retribution Squads violating the Truce. Unthinkable! The Court would never sanction such an action. Our honor is beyond reproach." Puffed up with pride and indignant rage, Kapnos turned from haranguing the seated great and good of the Court to face the regal Selina with an imploring look upon his face. "We cannot permit our lessers to slander us so. This cannot be allowed to continue."

"Indeed, Exalted Kapnos," Selina replied. "Which is precisely why we are taking all steps to handle the situation. In the spirit of the Truce, I suggest you calm yourself. Rise above the lesser beasts' growls."

"Yes, but..." The pompous Court noble was poised to begin another rant before Selina cut him off.

"Excuse me, Exalted Kapnos, but this petition is over. Other duties demand my attention." Without waiting for a reply, the younger Aegolius sibling rose from her imperious chair and strode from the petition hall. She marched past long hallways of marble, silver, and amber without seeing their beauty, long since inured to their beauty. Such opulence was commonplace and expected to one such as Selina. She reached her brother's office and strode inside after a perfunctory knock, locking the door behind her and sitting primly at his rich mahogany desk.

Aahmes looked up from his laptop to, piercing eyes looking at Selina over a pair of half-rim spectacles. "My, my. If I didn't know better, I'd say you were in a tiff, dear sister."

"A tiff? Never, dear Aahmes. Because that would indicate losing control and to lose control..."

Aahmes finished the saying with a smile. "… is to be imperfect. And that is something we never are. Still, petitioners are rather taxing. Tea?"

"Please."

Her brother crossed to the sterling tea set, prepping her tea the way Selina liked it. *He ought to know my tastes after all those years of making our own food when the servants couldn't be trusted not to try and poison us. Ah, simpler times.* Selina smiled a bit. *Goodness, aren't I feeling nostalgic?*

"I'm grateful to have a brother who looks out for me."

"What else is family for?"

"You mean other than plotting, scheming, and extra hands to bury the bodies?"

"Well, yes, of course, other than that."

Selina chuckled to herself and leaned back. "It is extremely tiring that they squawk about the same affairs over and over again. Such petty nothingness."

Aahmes looked at her over his cup. "Large problems often arise from small concerns."

"We have it under control," she said. "Things are proceeding apace."

"It is not about what is, dear sister. It is about the *perception* of what is."

Sensing a lecture arising, Selina cut it off as quickly as she could. "The point, please, dear brother. I do have things to attend to in my lifetime."

"Simply then. Whether all matters are in hand, that any dispute raises the worry that things are not. If a thing is said enough times, it takes on a life of its own. The worry takes hold and the phantom becomes reality. By saying and believing a thing, our esteemed colleagues of the Court will act as though it were the truth. Thus, perception of weakness equals weakness."

Selina sighed heavily. "Politics."

Aahmes raised the cup in a toast. "Quite so."

"Aahmes?" Selina reached out, resting a hand lightly on her brother's arm, halting the cup inches from his lips. "Did you put almond in this drink?"

Aahmes eyes widened and he dashed the cup to the ground. The two siblings rose with astonishing speed, standing the center of the room, back to back. As if on cue, black-clothed figures burst through the door, rushing at Aahmes and Selina.

She recognized their sinuous motions, the smooth killer's grace. These were Retribution Squads, elite agents of the Court and supposedly loyal killers who would take their own lives rather than let any noble of the Court of Raptors come to harm. Now they approached two of the highest-ranking representatives in the Sunset Lands with murder in their eyes.

The poor damned fools never stood a chance.

Selina touched the gold and topaz charm at her wrist and the Oath Blades, the knives that symbolized the Retributions Squads holy mandate as the Court's punishing hand, thudded into the floor as though pulled by chains.

Most dragged the attackers with them. In a moment, Selina was amongst them, her hands replaced with brass talons. Each strike was precise, gouging eyes or slitting throats as they killers struggled to right themselves. It might have been a dance, the flowing strike and retreat. The last came crashing to the ground, concussed by a swhirling disc hurled from behind.

Only Selina and Aahmes remained standing. She turned to her brother, exasperated. "Really? The tea plates?"

Aahmes stood on a pile of slain of his own, fingering a rip in his jacket. "I needn't have resorted to that if you hadn't drawn my blade into the floor."

"One for nearly a dozen seems a good trade, Aahmes."

Aahmes sniffed. "Perhaps. Still, that was well done, sister dear."

"Thank you. You'd think, after all this time, my esteemed peerage would have abandoned assassination attempts. How very unimaginative."

Aahmes retrieved his blade with a graceful sweep. "Honestly? I am half given to think it is merely the Court showing its displeasure."

She flicked blood from her wrist, frowning. "Then I am insulted at the waste of Court resources."

"Nevertheless, this polite insistence does mean we will have to increase our time table. The representative must make a decision and soon."

Selina's phone rang and she smiled at the contact number. "Speak of the devil. Yes, Jon?" She blinked a few times at the lawyer's words. "Tomorrow? I'll check my calendar but that should be fine. Yes, I know the place. Excellent, I'll see you there."

She turned to her brother with a triumphant smile. "Seems I am to meet with the esteemed Mr. Doe after all. He has invited me to brunch."

CHAPTER 19

A RISING SUN found Jonathan Augustus Doe, lawyer extraordinaire for extraordinary clients, sitting anxiously on the back patio of Barry's Beanery. Sunlight turned baking sand dunes into hills of gold and glinted majestically off the gentle waves. A wonderful sea breeze drifted in, cooling the day from sweltering to just about perfect. Only a constant rapping noise distracted Jon from the picturesque view, and it took the Harvard graduate a moment to locate the source: his own rapidly tapping foot on the patio.

Jon frowned down at the offending appendage. *This is ridiculous. I've eaten worse opponents for breakfast. It's not like I'm arranging a meeting that will make or break my desperate gambit to keep breathing. With the same woman I saw disembowel someone with her bare hands-cum-talons. The clincher being she has a brother I snubbed who's demonstrated a penchant for kidnapping. Nothing to be nervous about at all.*

After Marc had snagged Selina's personal number from Arkadas' database, Jon set out on the first step of his diabolical plan; he'd invited the younger Aegolius to brunch. Jon looked about Barry's and indulged in a slight frown of culinary snobbery. *Hardly the highest end bistro or candle-lit restaurant, but it'll do.* Jon had required a neutral space for the meeting, and Barry's fit the bill. Open, public, and lots of escape routes.

If he was being honest, the memories of Zoe comforted him too. *Wish the one-woman wrecking crew was around. It's amazing how much safer you feel when your lunch buddy can make a slavering beastie say uncle. Fortunately, I came prepared for a different kind of brawl.* The blue-eyed wunderkind looked down at the suitcase resting near him and grinned. He had everything he need inside to bring Selina to their side. *Thank you, Marc. You always deliver.*

With the stage set, armed, and ready, Jon waited for his brunch date to arrive.

Fortunately for Mr. Doe, Selina Aegolius was ever punctual. Anything else would have been imperfect.

As the lawyer nursed his cup of caffeinated nirvana on the back patio, he heard the Court representative long before he saw her. Her arrival set off muttered conversations in a ripple through the blue shack. She simply had that effect on people. The awe-struck stammers of the pierced-faced teenager heralded the Mediterranean debutante's approach long before Selina's cultured accent reached Jon's ears.

Selina appearance did not disappoint. Wearing a casual black dress and matching black jacket, Selina walked with such poise that the simple ensemble may as well have been queen's attire. Jon almost envied that level of charisma. He definitely envied the expert tailoring. *I'm willing to bet even I could make that dress look good with her tailor.*

"Selina, kind of you to show."

The representative of the Court of Raptors sat down and gave Jon a genuine smile. "Hello, Jon. It's good to see you doing well. I've heard rumors of late. You seem to lead a very interesting and very charmed life."

"Not by choice. I'm living in interesting times, though I'd say I'm hardly alone in that."

"Oh? How do you mean?" The faintest shadow of a smirk gleamed behind an impassive façade, the Aegolius sibling not giving an inch.

Not bad. Jon made a show of checking the files in front of him. "The list is fairly comprehensive, I wouldn't want to keep you here until dinner."

"I can't say I'd mind that, Jon."

Jon matched her smile with a dazzling one of his own. "I agree, but I am on the clock and have some sense of professional ethics."

"As a lawyer? How strange."

Jon gave a chiding cluck of his tongue. "Another lawyer joke? You'll have to do better than that, Selina."

"Simply easing you into things, Jon. Don't want to overwhelm you. Call it an act of mercy. You've had a rough time, of late."

"Duly noted. Now, to the matter at hand."

"Spoilsport."

Fires burned in Jon's eyes as he locked gazes with the grinning Aegolius. "Selina, your company is amongst the most enjoyable I've had since taking this job. While I would love nothing more than to banter with you until the sun went down, I am on a deadline. Emphasis on the dead."

A faint turn of the head. Denial or acknowledgement, it might have been either. *Damn, she's good. I have to be better.*

"Now, I could list the lies, blackmail, and falsified documents, but that would only count as business as usual for the Houses. Instead, I'd like to begin with the most important part: a simple list of names. Rupert Evans, Eliza Maki, Virginia Demas, and Robert Turo. All murdered in the last few months. There are others, of course, but these are the most prominent."

"Tragic. The police really ought to do something."

"They might, if the Houses weren't actively having Reiger covering it up."

Selina gave an imperceptible shrug, showing as much concern as if a waiter forgot to bring an appetizer before the main meal. Still, it was a reaction, however small. Jon counted his victories.

"I agree this is hardly peace in our times," Selina said. "Though I'm certain you've heard the phrase 'tempest in a teacup?' The Court has endured far worse in its long history. This too shall pass. Our victory is as assured as the sunrise, Jon. We've ever been able to outmaneuver the Senate when their brutish tactics fail them."

Jon shook his head, smile long faded. "Though I may not have been born to your, ah, lifestyle, Selina, I am more than capable of reading the waters. This whole Beachfront snafu has been anything but business as usual for the Houses. Inviting in outsiders, rashes of murders, confused records, attempted assassinations, and even your own people joining the Cull..."

"What did you say?" Her icy words halted the conversation as surely as a snowbank.

"Joining the Cull. Jumping in bed with the enemy. Going rogue. Pick whatever euphemism suits you. One of them personally tried to kill me. It seems the Senate aren't the only ones who engage in brutish tactics."

Selina's calculating gaze matched her brother's. "That is quite an accusation. It is the official position of the Courts that the renegade band is the product of the less civilized Mythics. That mad man, Ripper, is ample evidence of that, being their most vocal and active proponent."

"Not an accusation, Selina, it is a fact. Another fact that might surprise you is that Arkadas has betrayed both Houses and is working with the Furies."

Time seemed to stand still, only the crash of waves counting the seconds as Jon watched his counterpart. Then Selina's face twisted up. Its contortions continued into a series of choked snickers. The esteemed representative of the Court of Raptor's eventually descended into a full-blown giggle fit.

"Gods, Jon. You continue to surprise me. Such a bold statement. One might even say absolutely ludicrous." She paused to sip a bit of her cooling coffee. "It is a well-known truth that Arkadas loves one thing and one thing alone: money. He wouldn't risk the substantial sums we provide him for a handful of malcontents. No sense in killing the goose that lays the golden egg... metaphorically of course." A hint of smile still danced in her dark eyes.

"Well, then, it appears you have a fox loose in the hen house... I presume metaphorically, but who can tell these days?" Jon slid the files he'd been reading across the table. "See for yourself."

Selina flipped through the folder, smile melting away. By the end, all hints of emotion hid behind a thick impassive pane of glass, all windows to the soul barred and shut. Jon truly understood how open she had been until this point and just how precious a thing he had lost. It shouldn't hurt as much as it did. Though it pained Jon, the lawyer never let his own mask waver. *Do or die time.*

"Quite a cunning fabrication you have here, Mr. Doe. Congratulations to your little vampire friend. His handiwork, I'm sure. The risks of mixing outside help and sensitive data."

"You know I'm not lying. You and your brother pride yourselves on smelling out lies."

"True, though it seems you have deceived Aahmes before. Perhaps you are doing the same to me." She sneered at Jon, a centuries' long lineage of arrogance resting upon her like a mantle. "It seems to me that a man in your position would go to great lengths to save their skin. How convenient to obtain this sudden evidence of treachery by our long-term financial partner. It seems a rather contrived smokescreen, a deflection, your attempt to throw pebbles amongst bandits." A crisp British accent emerged, intentional and ruthless, each enunciation dagger sharp.

Jon Doe, practicing legal consul, didn't bleed at the scathing assertion.

The lawyer leaned back, a smug grin plastered on his face. "If I fabricated something, it'd be far cleverer than this. You should hear what Marc and I got up to back in Harvard. Did I ever tell you about the Crimson fiasco? By which I mean *all* of the Harvard teams. My handiwork, though you'd never know.".

A flicker of amusement rose and died on Selina's face, though that may have been a desperate hope-fueled hallucination on Jon's part "Your collegiate antics are of little concern at the moment. Your relationship with Marc Sipskos, however, is of great concern to us. As you have prior history with this fellow, quite close it seems, he is in the perfect position to manipulate, alter, or outright fabricate data. Considering the data is internal to Arkadas & Associates, we could have no means of corroborating. Having an inside man casts doubt on your claims rather than reinforcing them."

Courtroom defense, is it? Perfect. "That's twisting the facts. My own self-admitted ignorance, to say nothing of your acknowledgement of such, of all Mythic society precludes a collusion with Marc to set this up. He discovered this of his own accord and independently of my actions. I'm simply bringing it to light."

"Perhaps you are a better actor than we gave you credit for. Perhaps you are a fast learner. You have displayed a remarkably ability to think on your feet. Either way, your cleverness damns you."

"If I had sufficient foreknowledge, hell any inkling at all, of what I was getting myself into, I wouldn't have taken this job. Even if I had a grudge against the Houses, nothing is worth tweaking the noses of a bunch of psychotic inhuman killers. Hardly worth yelling 'gotcha' when the noose is around your neck."

Selina's frosty eyes thawed slightly, considering his argument. Jon could practically hear the train of thought. *Considering the threat of gory demise, there seemed little motivation for this sort of pre-planned scheme. Point for the defense.*

"You're right about one thing, Selina," Jon continued. "I am clever. Clever and desperate. Don't forget, I'm just plain old human me. I have to be somewhat clever to last ten minutes around you people since I can't grow fangs or claws or whatever. Now, if I were really clever, I'd never have come here and risk brutal dismemberment by a slavering beast." Jon tapped two fingers on the folder in front of Selina. "But I am clever enough to have outed Arkadas, and I'm just clever enough to have way out of this mess with my skin intact. I need you to pull it off."

"Very well Jon. Let us temporarily consider that this information is real. Why come to me?"

"Because I am done being a tool and a pawn. Time to be a player again."

"A laudable goal. I repeat, why come to me?"

Jon could practically taste Selina's suspicion. *Good. Her caution justifies the risk. Because Selina didn't leap at this chance, she's less likely to sell us out later. Still, no guarantees.*

"First, please understand and appreciate I've been completely honest with you so far, which is a rare thing for a practicing lawyer," Jon said. "I respect you, and I think we understand one another despite the differences in the circles we operate in. You are intelligent, connected, and not as entrenched in your hatred of anything with the Senate on it."

Selina frowned at the mention of her House's ancient rivals. "I will not betray the Court, Jon."

"Then it's a good thing I'm not asking you to. The Court stands to benefit from this if we play our cards right. But none of this can reach the ears of anyone outside our group."

"Why would that be, if you aren't asking me to betray my House?"

"Because I'm proposing a compromise with the Senate. A joint ownership of the Beachfront property brokered by yours truly with me as keeper of deed. A common, mutually beneficial trust."

Selina frowned, tapping one delicate finger to her lips in thought as she calculated the ramifications of Jon's plan. "Ah, I see. Aahmes would never agree to such a thing nor would any others in his camp. Particularly not if approached by someone so far below them. No offense."

"None taken. I might be the new guy, but the one thing that's been hammered into me since I arrived at San Dominguez is that the two Houses can't go five minutes without whipping out a measuring stick to see whose stick is bigger."

Selina didn't bat an eye at the crude metaphor. She ceased her tapping and regarded Jon with her piecing gaze once again. Caution was there, but interest as well. "Tell me about this plan."

"I've been empowered to broker the deal but only if the Houses sign off on it..." He left the unsaid hanging in the air, outstretched hand passing it on to her.

A slow grin spread over Selina's face, rows of pearl shining against her dusky skin. "The Houses... or their representatives."

"Exactly. We need you on board to make it work. The contract also demands neutral parties sign off as well on any deviations to the contract or any plans proposed by me. The great and good of the Houses probably included that little clause to discourage any conspiracies like this from cropping up. Joke's on them. We already have Marc's sire on board." Jon paused here, gauging her reaction to a dark lord of the night being one of their business partners and having a hand in the property.

Fortunately, Selina nodded, finger returning to its thoughtful tapping. "Lord Hynrich is noted to have an ironclad sense of honor. His word is his bond. More importantly, he is notorious at seeing grudges fulfilled to their bitter ends. It will cause anyone seeking to contest the plan to reconsider how far they wish to pursue such actions."

Jon's admiration grew. The well-dressed Shifter understood exactly what they were in for and calculated possible outcomes. *The best plans always had Cover Your Ass clauses in them.*

"Who else do you have in mind?" Selina asked.

She's in. Selina never said anything, nothing that would hold up in court, simply asked a question. But Jon had closed enough deals to know when someone signed on.

Despite his urge to do a backflip out of joy, Jon settled for leaning forward conspiratorially. Mr. Doe did have a flair for the dramatic. *Besides, it's fitting, since a conspiracy is exactly what we're doing.* "With you and ol' lord sun shy backing us, I'm moving on to the other House representative. I've got an angle."

Her smile, her real smile, returned with dazzling brilliance. "Oh? What angle is that?"

Jon beamed back "We throw a party, of course."

§——§

Standing in the Den barely twenty-four hours later, Jon congratulated himself, looking proudly about the dingy drinking establishment. He set a mean spread. Suckling pig, slabs of steaming roast beef, and roasted chicken sat steaming away on platters while a bewildering array of alcohol stood on display. Amber beer sat in metal kegs, while wooden barrels held wine. Sangria and sweet drinks sat in clear bowls, the light shining on their many colors. Rosemary, sage, and other delectable scents floated in the air.

Of course, I didn't cook a bit of it.

That honor belonged the flamboyantly dressed owner and proprietor of the dive bar, a fellow named Columella. When Jon arrived, with Selina and a bundled up and slightly smoking Marc in tow, the proprietor Columella was less than pleased. Seemed the Den was the local watering hole for Magda and her furry Cohort buddies. No one who wasn't Cohort showed up there unless they were looking for a fight. Everybody knew that.

Except me of course. So, when a representative of "the enemy" showed up, Columella told them in no uncertain terms they walked into the wrong neighborhood.

You know this town is messed up when a gorgeous dusky beauty bothers the barkeep more than a walking, talking, blood-drinking corpse. Poor guy must really like his bar, considering he kept calling it a temple.

Only after Selina swore to honor the "sanctity" of the place and uphold the "Values of Ivy and Donkey" did the satyr nod grudgingly and graciously accept copious amounts of their money

As the portly fellow cooked up a storm, drinking, laughing, and singing as he went about his culinary dark arts, Selina watched with rapt attention. "He truly is an exemplar of his faith."

Jon took her breather admiration at face value. *Looks more like Uncle Steve let loose at Thanksgiving.* Despite Jon's misgivings, the result was stunning, a true delight for the senses.

Jon rubbed his hands together, manic grin plastered on his face. "Now, all we need is for our star to arrive."

Selina tapped finger to lips. "You do know the former Bannersworn is rarely without her companions?"

"I know. Brock and the kid. Met them once. Nice folks for hairy monsters. It was all in the dossier."

That raised one of Selina's immaculately styled eyebrows. "You have dossier files on Cohort soldiery? Why was I not made privy to this?"

"I'm not that cheap, Selina. I don't put out on the first date."

Marc snorted behind him. "Since when?"

Jon flipped his college buddy the bird. Matters of friendship handled, Jon returned his attention to the esteemed Miss Aegolius. "What I mean is that the more cards I hold to my chest, the better. Besides, I know damn well you haven't given up all of your secrets. I'm willing to bet you have more than one out clause to protect your own interests. Just in case, of course."

"Mmm. Quite."

"Hopefully, Magda should be arriving any minute now."

True to the blue-eyed wunderkind's prediction, Magda Lahm Dearg burst through the door. The warrior paced forward like a wary beast, shoulders hunched and ready to battle. As soon as Magda's mismatched eyes fell over the seated Jon a lighting fast array of emotions blurred across her face. Unfortunately, once she registered his companions, nothing but hurt and rage remained.

Like a train picking up speed, the former Bannersworn powered toward their table.

"Magda, if you could just take a deep breath and have a seat, we can talk about thisNOTTHEFACE!" Magda's kick launched Jon from his chair, tumbling to the floor. Columella poked his head out with a scowl before seeing Magda. With a nod, the holy man ducked back into the kitchen, satisfied everything was business as usual.

Jon admired the lovely lights dancing in front of his eyes as Magda loomed over him, fists clenched and trembling with rage. Marc stood frozen in uncertainty, fangs bright in the bar lights. Jon was happy Marc stayed out of it. *I don't care what cool new perks being dead's given him, the guy's never been in a fight in his life, unless you count being shoved into lockers. I've seen what Magda can do. Marc would be road kill.*

"You bastard. Desperation can drive people to foul things, but I thought better of you. Couldn't you have stood and fought with your last breath instead of resorting to... this?" Magda hissed the words as she waved dismissively at Selina. For her part, the Court representative watched the proceedings with a mask of aristocratic detachment.

Jon spat out blood onto the floor, tonguing a loose tooth. "I'm a lawyer, Magda. Not a fighter. Definitely not a Shifter. You plainly pointed that out in our little chat at the beach." Jon wiped a last bit of blood from his busted lip with a pocket handkerchief. "I'm only trying to survive this shit show."

"Coward. I thought since that night in the rain you had the courage to do more."

"I'm doing everything I can to win, Magda. I'm working for both of the Houses at gun point. I don't give a shit what either of the Senate or the Court thinks of me. You and I both know I'm only a pawn to them. Both of them will hang me out to dry and not shed a tear. I'm working with the few people I can trust. People like my undead brother, the good Ms. Aegolius, and yourself. At least, I damn well hope I can trust you."

Magda reared back in disgust. "I won't betray my House. Unlike others here."

Turning her eyes to Selina, Magda stalked toward the dusky Court representative, muscles swelling as the beast awoke within her. Selina responded in kind, hands morphing into monstrous metallic claws.

Jon staggered to his feet, standing between the two Shifters. It would have been rather comical, the idea of the Harvard graduate stopping the two shapeshifting creatures, were it not so desperate and sad.

"Enough! Magda, back off. Selina is here at my request."

"Stand aside, buck."

"Not gonna happen."

"Move or die!"

Magda stood head and shoulders above Jon, an abhorrent mix of the bestial and human, voice contorted with rage and forced out of a muzzle barely suited for the mewlings of weak pink things. Jon didn't even flinch.

"I told you, not gonna happen."

No sooner did the words leave his lips, Magda struck. Pain flared in Jon's side as the warrior's fist cannoned into his ribs. He flew back, staggering into a table.

Magda looked down at him, succumbing to the red tide of her rage. She turned to Selina, intent on slaying the Court Shifter.

"Get your ass back here, Magda!" Jon wheezed out. "Might as well finish the job."

Magda froze at Jon's sputtered taunt and turned to the gasping lawyer.

"No, I mean it. You've already got the blood of innocents on your claws, what's one more?"

"Shut up."

"Or what? You'll kill me? Thought that was the plan."

"SHUT UP!"

Magda hauled Jon into the air. Jon frantically waved Marc back, seeing his friend stepping forward with a chair raised in marble white hands, fangs extended and eyes crimson. Jon looked down at Magda, her face shifting between wolf and woman.

"Go on, do it. Kill me. It wouldn't be the first time you've killed someone who can't fight back."

"I've never slain any who wasn't an enemy."

"Bullshit. Your precious House and your Cohort buddies do it all the time. I'm just the last sucker in line. Whether you like it or not, your hands are as soaked in blood as theirs. I'm offering you a chance to change that. A chance to make things right. So, you can either listen to what I have to say or kill me right now."

Jon's voice never wavered, never once showing his pain or the panic inside. *Now or never.*

Slowly, Magda lowered Jon to the floor.

"I won't betray my House." Her voice dwindled to a defiant whisper, an oath to the last unsullied part of her soul and pride in a brotherhood she once thought noble beyond reproach.

"I'm not asking you to," Jon said. "I'm asking you to help your House. There is too much blood between the Court and the Senate, too many of the old guard entrenched in their ways. With your help, we can start a new way, make space for some new blood."

Magda laughed, a sour sound, hollow and devoid of true mirth, an alien noise from the hero who loved and hated with such honesty and passion. "Buck, I AM the old guard. I've fought and killed for the Senate for decades, waded knee deep in blood and bodies to tear at my foes. I've stood shoulder to shoulder with the bravest souls you can imagine and stared down horrors that would kill you with but a look. I won't turn my back on the Cohort. They're family."

Jon gritted his teeth in frustration and pain. "Family can be assholes. Trust me, I'm an expert. Also, they can be wrong. If you actually care about them, you'll help me." Seeing she was wavering Jon sat down heavily in a chair. "Look, hear me out and then decide."

Without giving Magda a chance to respond, Jon launched into his pitch, laying out the contract loophole, Marc's sire, Arkadas' collusion with the Cull, and the conspirators need for backers, including Magda.

"All you would have to do is sign on as representative of the Senate," Jon concluded. "The House would actually profit from it. You'd prevent needless bloodshed, most importantly my own. None of your comrades have to die and no more innocents caught in the crossfire."

"You're wrong on one account, buck. My comrades would still die."

"What are you talking about?"

"The Cohort's ready to tear itself apart. The Senate upped the time table. You've got maybe two days before the Senate demands a decision. Then, they make an example of you."

Jon leaned back with a laugh. "Oh, is that all?"

"What?"

"All part of the plan. We already know Arkadas is backing the Cull and their bloody little games were working on pushing everyone to war."

Magda rubbed her temples. "Get to the point Jon, I don't want to listen to your grandstanding."

"The point, dear Magda, is that we are going to throw the proverbial pebble amongst the bandits. With Arkadas in our pocket, the Cull is going to find itself without allies. Two birds, one stone. Meanwhile, the Senate spins it as all part of the plan, none can gainsay their ineffable wisdom, and the Cohort will go back to thumping heads as usual and feeling real proud of themselves."

Magda heaved a defeated sigh. "Couldn't help you even if I wanted to."

"What do you mean? I watched how those two lug nuts acted around you. They followed your lead. Selina even called you a Bannersworn. From what I read, that makes you a big damn hero and a big damn deal."

"I *was* Bannersworn, Jon. I led my line mates with pride. Life and death in my hands. But after the fog and the blood... I stepped down from command. I can no longer invoke *Dictatus*, the authority of the House. Now I'm just a centurion. A fist. I'll kill anything that stands against the Cohort, but I won't be responsible for others' lives any longer. It hurts too much to do otherwise."

"Wouldn't want to you feel bad as your murderous companions floss their teeth with my entrails."

Jon nearly flinched at the raw pain in Magda's eyes but held his ground. *Does that hurt? Too bad. I'll be as much of an asshole as I have to be to push you through this.*

She held his eyes before sinking to the table. It was the only time Jon had ever seen Magda so defeated. "Damn you, Jon. The worst thing is, you're right. We would gut you without a second thought should you aid those damn feather dusters. Because you are disposable. Because it's easier to kill. Merciful gods, how long have we been like this? How long have I been like this?"

"If you actually want to change something, Magda, start now."

"I can't get you what you need. I don't speak for my House in the Sunset Lands. I have no right to *Dictatus*."

Jon watched her silently for a minute, biting his tongue. It was one of the longest two minutes of his life. *I've pushed as much as I can. Now she has to do the rest.*

Finally, Magda looked up. "I can't sign, but I know who can. Brock Macintyre. He was with me that night in the rain. Despite being a pain in the ass and a stickler for protocol, Brock's a wise fellow and a ranking officer of the Sunset Cohort. I'd trust him above any other, even with this… conspiracy. If we could convince Brock to aid in this mad scheme, he could invoke *Dictatus* and stand as signatory."

"You're with us?"

"Aye, for now. I'm not doing this for you, Jon. You're not that good in bed." Magda stretched a crooked smile, and Jon at least had the good grace to blush as Marc cackled and Selina coughed politely into her hand to cover a grin. "I'm doing this to redeem the soul of my brothers and sisters. There is nothing I won't do to save them." Cold eyes turned to Selina. "Even work with a faithless Raptor."

"I'm doing this for the good of my House as well, my dear Bannersworn. A truce, nothing more."

Jon quickly stood up to prevent his little cabal from tearing itself apart. "Excellent. Glad that's settled. Now, if you could please remember that for the next 48 hours, that'd be great. I won't have my plans upset because of your grudges."

Magda savagely bit into a turkey leg, talking about a mouthful of deliciously seasoned poultry. "Plans? What nonsense are you going on about?"

Jon's grinned a madcap grin. More than one Harvard professor learned to dread that grin. "You'll see."

CHAPTER 20

MANY BLOCKS AWAY from the imposing Arkadas & Associates manor, Jon looked down dubiously at a shining golden amulet, shaped like a blazing sun, in his hand. "This thing will really work?"

Selina only responded with an indignant sniff. "Mr. Doe, that 'thing' is a prized relic blessed by the gods with boons of command and pure sunlight. It is a holy icon of incalculable worth. Yes, it will work. Simply hold the disc aloft, speak the words as I told you, and it will produce an immense power, protecting you from harm and imbuing you with the authority of the gods."

"Sounds like magic."

"That's because it is."

Jon shoved the golden disc back at the Aegolius sibling. "Bullshit."

"Jon, after all you have seen, do you truly have a problem believing in magic?"

Jon opened his mouth, gaped like a fish, then closed it again. For once in his life, Jon was utterly at a loss for words. *Good thing Marc isn't here. He'd never let me live it down.*

"Well, here's hoping. I'm going to need to protect myself," he finally said.

"It will work. Our other partners need only hold up their end."

The blue-eyed Mr. Doe beamed at her. "Don't worry about it. Marc and Magda will handle their parts. We just have to do ours."

Selina waved a hand idly, as if it were already done. "Good luck, Jon. Remember, should your attempt to blackmail one of the most powerful figures on the West Coast fail, we never had this conversation."

§——§

Arkadas glared at Jon across his imposing desk, stodgy and irate. "You must be joking."

Jon's patented shit-eating grin never slipped. "Not at all, Arkadas. I'm quite serious."

"Then you're insane," Arkadas snapped. "Why on earth would I sign that thing?"

"Firstly, you stand to gain a great deal of income and influence. Second, you get to walk away alive."

The burly legal magnate guffawed in Jon's face. "Boy, you've got balls to threaten me. Balls, but no brains."

"Arkadas, please. I'm a very busy man and your bluster is tedious. I've got..." Jon looked down at a nonexistent watch, "... a million other things to set my plan into action and this is taking up far too much of my time. Simply agree to the terms and we all go home happy."

"I'll ask again, boy, since you've clearly lost your mind. Why would I do that?"

"Because you've meddled with the Beachfront property documents to bring the Houses' resolution to a grinding halt. You've printed copies that give you sole ownership of the territory, to whip out when convenient. You've sold out your own employees, sending them to their deaths in the name of your own greed. But I understand. None of that bothers you. Your soul is already blackened enough, what's a few more sins? No, what you should be worried about is that you've betrayed both of the Houses, killed their servants and conspired with the Furies to undermine the Truce, all in the name of making a buck. Well, several bucks, really. Because if they're too busy with one another, no one questions how you ended up the hero and watching over the Beachfront property."

Jon tossed a bound packet of documents onto Arkadas' desk, photographs, printed emails, and other damning evidence spilling out. A blueprint for murder, all lined out in black ink and red tape.

"Quite the smoking gun, wouldn't you say?"

Arkadas glanced at the pile of documents and back at Jon. His face grew redder and redder, a storm of rage darkening it. "You little shit. You think you can just come in here and threaten me?"

Jon stepped back as Arkadas stood up, jowls rippling like water, something threatening to burst forth from beneath the skin. "Well, I was hoping you'd understand the severity of your situation. Before you do something drastic, know that I've taken steps to release this evidence if I don't walk out of here in one piece."

"Relying on Sipskos, are you? Hah. You backed the wrong horse, my boy. No one will believe the leech."

A small beep sounded from Jon's pocket followed by several more in rapid succession. Jon's grin grew even larger. "I wouldn't be so sure. I've got more friends than you realize. Besides, your Cull buddies aren't going to be happy knowing that we're meeting so you ca sell them out to the Houses."

Arkadas' momentary confusion bought Jon the precious second he needed to jump behind one of the oversized chairs as the ceiling collapsed.

Bone chilling howls and shrieks echoed in the room as three monstrous Shifters poured through the hole. A mix of fur, fangs, and feathers, the newcomers looked from Arkadas to Jon half hidden behind his chair, before turning their full rage upon the suit-clad broker.

"Traitor!" The howling zealots piled onto Arkadas, intent on carving their pound of flesh.

Slouched behind cover, Jon breathed a sigh of relief that they'd chosen the juicier target.

If they'd hoped to find Arkadas easy prey, they were sorely disabused.

Without wasting a word, Arkadas transformed into a gigantic owl, his prodigious bulk nearly doubling. Jon gulped. The Harvard graduate never thought of owls as terrifying. Cute, maybe creepy, but never terrifying. He'd never considered one the size of a small car. Hunter's eyes glinted above a razor-sharp beak that looked able to slice through a car door. Gleaming brass claws, same as Selina's, glinted against a body old and gray.

Cull and Arkadas met in a swirling struggle, shrieks and screams echoing loudly in the cramped quarters. The old bastard clawed and punched, moving like a boxer in a ring. A dog-like fellow fell back with a yelp, his ear torn to shreds and blood flowing over his eye. The feathered attacker grabbed at Arkadas only to have the old owl slam the plumed critter into his other amigo, a weasel looking thing.

Despite his stubbornness, Arkadas was outnumbered, old, and out of practice. Numbers and youth turned the tide quickly.

Bleeding and enraged, the Cull fanatics forewent any strategy, hurling themselves at the elder Shifter without grace or form, tackling him to the floor. They clawed and tore, sprays of crimson staining the office. Arkadas' outraged roars shook the destroyed office.

"ENOUGH!" A voice of thunders spoke, even as golden light filled the room. The Mythics froze mid struggle, muscles straining as their eyes dashed about in panic. Try as they might, they couldn't help but obey the stentorian command, trapped in the prison of their own bodies. Slowly, agonizingly, they turned to the source of their bondage.

In the center of the light stood Jon Doe, practicing legal counsel. One hand held aloft Selina's amulet, gleaming with the color of a summer sky. The light faded, and the terrible voice receded to become the very human timbre of Jon Doe. "That's my meal ticket you're attacking. I need him alive, so you three are going to have to find someone else to bleed today." The pitiful human voice broke the spell and the Cull gathered themselves to tear the impudent fool apart. Even as they leapt from their prone victim, the light returned, as did the terrible otherworldly voice. "IN THE NAME OF THE IMPERISHABLE SUN, LEAVE. GO NOW, INTO THE DUST AND SKY. DO NOT TROUBLE THIS ONE ANY FURTHER."

Shrieking, the Furies clambered over one another, fleeing in terror. In panicked, ungainly bounds, they leapt out of the ruined ceiling and scrambled out of sight.

Arkadas, bloodied and savaged, stared at Jon in shock.

"I told you I had more friends than you realized, Arkadas." Jon shrugged casually. "Both the Senate and the Court are in my pocket."

Arkadas spat blood and staggered to his feet. "Bullshit. If that were true, you wouldn't need me, would you?"

The large owl Shifter rushed Jon, pinning the blue-eyed wunderkind to the wall, brazen claws a simple flex from tearing Jon's throat out. "No, the Houses don't care about you."

"But they *do* care about being betrayed, Arkadas."

Another gobbet of blood hit the floor as the old man cleared his throat. "Who's betraying anyone? Your dead body is my ticket back into the Houses' good graces. Shame the Furies killed you. Tragic, really. I tried my best, go the scars to prove it, but it wasn't enough."

"What about the evidence?"

Arkadas grinned evilly. "You won't be around to testify. The Houses will believe me. After I point them in the direction of one another, they'll be too busy trying to tear each apart to even look my way."

"Still won't save you from the Furies."

"Perhaps, but I'd say your mangled body will make a good peace offering. Especially with Ripper. Oh, my boy, he hates you. I think you might be the only one to have ever gotten away from old Zypresse." Arkadas leaned in close, skin crawling and reknitting the torn flesh even as Jon watched. "Congratulations."

"Thank you. I do feel rather proud of myself right now." Jon's madcap grin brought Arkadas up short. Slowly, Jon pulled his other hand, the one that had been hidden behind his back the entire time. In it, a small cellphone blinked happily. "Remember that smoking gun? With this, you won't have any rock to hide under. Everyone will come for looking for their pound of flesh. All we had to do was give you enough rope to hang yourself."

Arkadas waffled only a moment before lowering Jon to the ground.

"Thank you. I knew you'd see it my way," Jon continued. "Now, here is exactly what you are going to say at the signing ceremony tomorrow…"

§——§

It wasn't until Jon strolled out of Arkadas' ruined office, down the iron staircase, bent by the passing of some large creature, and leaned against the back wall of deli some blocks distant that he took his trembling hands out of his pockets.

I just successfully blackmailed one of the most powerful men on the West Coast. Only took getting within an inch of death to do it. Jon flinched at the memory of those terrible claws around his neck, each breath brushing against razor-sharp edges. *I might have won this round, but I'm going to have to watch my back very carefully from here on out.*

Jon rapped on the backdoor of the deli three times in rapid succession even as he dialed Selina Aegolius. Selina's cultured tones came through.

"Jon! Since you are alive and well enough to call, I presume the negotiations went well?"

"The rumors worked like a charm. Marc let slip that I was meeting with Arkadas and the Furies showed up like clockwork. They didn't even give old bastard a chance to explain."

"As expected."

"Yeah, fanatics are funny that way." Jon had to control his hands as they started to shake again, remembering the wall of monsters surging forward, slavering for blood. "Arkadas is on board with our plan. The warning over the phone let me get out of the way when the lunatics burst through."

"Wonderful. As an added bonus, we narrowed down the informants in our ranks."

"What are you going to do about that?"

"Best you didn't ask, Jon. Our Inquisitors' methods are... thorough."

Jon shuddered at the cold-blooded words delivered in such a conversational, even chipper, tone.

"Win for all sides then. Except those poor bastards. Which reminds me, thank you for the amulet." Jon glanced at the gold and sapphire icon wrapped about his arm. "I'm going to hang onto it until the ceremony, as insurance." Jon didn't mention it was insurance against Selina backing out of their deal. He didn't have to. *Not like it's her first rodeo.*

"Of course, Jon. Do be careful. As I said, the Voice of Ra is no cheap bauble or tourist's trinket. I'd hate for you to lose it. Aahmes would most certainly have a word with you."

"Good to know." Jon marveled how parched his throat was. "You move forward on your end. Let me know how it goes and if you need any help."

"Jon, please, don't insult me. I'll have it all wrapped up, neat and tidy. We can only hope that little Cohort miscreant completes her task."

As Jon thumbed off the phone, Marc popped his head out of the door into the dim alleyway, squinting at the sun's light, not even bothering to brush limp hair out of his face. *He looks like hell. Keeping going with the sun out must be a nightmare for him.*

The haggard vampire blinked a few times at Jon. "So?"

"It worked."

Marc did not look happy at the revelation. Neither did Jon, for that matter. "You know, this only makes him more dangerous, not less."

"Yeah, I know. Having dirt on merciless shapeshifting business moguls is not going to make sleeping any easier. Holy shit, have you seen his claws? For an old guy, he's as fast as any of the monsters I've seen."

Marc slumped a little further against the door frame. "I told you, age makes Mythics more dangerous, not less. Besides, disembowelment is the least of the things he could do to you."

Jon smirked at his gaunt friend. "Sure, he could send lawyers after us. By the way, why did you want to meet here? Scratch that, how did you even get here?"

"Tunnels."

Jon scowled at his laconic companion. "Okay." *As if that answers anything. Better not ask. He'll give me a week long lecture complete with diagrams on how it's the most efficient and logical choice. Then nag me when I don't take notes.* "How did you even find this place? I thought you couldn't eat real food."

Marc couldn't meet his friend's eyes. "There is some variety in my all liquid diet, Jon. Sometimes I get so wrapped up in work, I forget to stock up on food. I raid their freezer when needed."

The way his old friend spoke about sneaking through tunnels to get his blood fix, as if he were picking up pizza during their college dorm days, made Jon's heart sink. *I'm going to help you, buddy, just as soon as we get this shit handled.*

Jon patted Marc on the shoulder consolingly. Awkwardly, but consolingly. "I'm going to get myself presentable for our appointment with Ganesh. We're cutting it close, buddy. Let's hope Selina and Magda have their fronts handled."

§——§

Once again, Selina found herself wishing the assembled great and good of the Court of Raptors had but one neck so she could throttle it. Particularly as her esteemed peerage squabbled like turkeys around the circular meeting table. She sat upon her raised seat, a queen over an unruly court. Aahmes sat amidst the crowd, one of the peers but not, currently, elevated above them.

Officially, anyway.

Most knew the Aegolius siblings formed a powerful alliance, likely to back one another's decrees. Most of the Court Exalted would respect that and tread with caution. Not so Peter Kapnos.

"Outrageous!" Kapnos shouted. "You cannot possibly expect us to believe that the Cull of Actaeon has infiltrated our ranks!"

Selina kept her claws from erupting into talons at the sneer on Kapnos' face. Everything he did seemed designed to enrage her. Which, Selina, knew, was exactly the point. Any loss of control would undermine her position. *I'll not let that preening twit get the best of me.*

"That is precisely what I demand you understand."

"Preposterous! It is the official stance of the Court that the Cull is the result of less civilized Shifters. None of our ilk would join that rabble."

"The official stance is wrong."

That statement caused another uproar. Selina cut through squabbling with a slam of her fist on the long table.

"We are well aware of the Court's penchant to shape perception to mold reality to fit our superior vision, but that luxury is no longer afforded to us. Aahmes and I have uncovered knowledge that the Furies have infiltrated our ranks."

A subtle nod to her brother made clear the formidable political bloc of the Aegolius siblings. Sadly, this didn't cow the noisy petitioner.

"Ah yes, the latest round of unwarranted interrogations your agents have made." Kapnos sneered.

"Our investigations have been utterly justified and necessary as you can see by the results."

"More likely fabrications to justify your political jockeying. You may be an Exarch, Ms. Aegolius, but neither you nor your brother may act unilaterally. Your witch hunts prove nothing but your own unseemly lust for power."

Selina could not have hoped for a better moment. The dusky stateswoman gave a silent hand signal to her brother. Behind him, Ptolemy could not see the cruel grin growing across Aahmes face. The elder Aegolius loosened his blade in its holding and pointedly ignored the cracked door as figures crept silently in to the supposedly secure meeting. The blustering fool gave all the cover the intruders needed.

Peter Kapnos' tirade was cut short by a crimson smile drawn across his neck. Before his hands could staunch the bloody spray a second vicious cut emptied his entrails onto the elaborate carpet.

Panic erupted as the Court reacted to the assassins in their midst. The attackers uttered no sound, no proclamation or battle-cry. Their shining daggers and brazen claws spoke volumes.

They were Court. Worse, they were a Retribution Squad.

Shrieks and screams filled the courtroom, quite different than the prior roars. Bloodlust and agony replaced outrage and dying gurgles, and last gasps replaced whispered plotting.

Aahmes and Selina fought back to back, claws and daggers driving off their opponents. Blood stained the rich upholstery, crimson on purple, sapphire, and cream. The nobles fought with anything at hand, from fine blades to ink pens and pitchers of water.

Then, as suddenly as it began, the attack ended, the mysterious assailants retreated, leaving only the dead, dying, and the survivors.

The injured attacker gave a cry of "glory to the Cull" before slitting his own throat. He expired with a wet gurgle, life blood spilling onto the expensive rug.

"I trust this satisfies all parties as to the validity of my investigations." None dared challenge Selina's wintery gaze. "Excellent. Aahmes and I will continue our search. Rest assured, the guilty parties shall be rooted out and justice shall be met."

Leaving the Shifter elite to gather themselves, the Aegolius siblings strode imperiously from the room.

They marched through the airy estate, taking its opulence as their due. When they reached Aahmes' study, Selina allowed a satisfied smile to come to her face.

"Well, that worked out rather well, don't you think?" she said.

"Indeed. With our peers stumbling over themselves in the wake of the 'Cull' attack, none will question our actions. They will presume it will be just and proper in the name of the Court. Shame about Lennox, though."

"The Squads knew the risks. All are prepared to lay down their lives for the good of the Court."

"Quite. But none are eager to do so. Nor do I like losing assets."

"Calm yourself, Aahmes. As I said, this deal will yield tremendous wealth for our House."

"Presuming your pretty little puppet can pull this off."

Selina grinned at Aahmes' rather disparaging description of Jon. "Mr. Doe has proven remarkably resourceful. He approached me with this gambit and, may I remind you, is the source of the inspiration for this 'Cull' attack? Utilizing the Court's own Retribution Squads, carefully screened for those most loyal to our faction, to throw suspicion onto our enemies is brilliant."

Aahmes barely halted in rolling his eyes. "Yes, dear sister, how could I forget? You've only reminded me a half dozen times."

"Then trust in me, dear brother. With our faked attack and our blackmail on Arkadas, we stand to capitalize immensely on the Beachfront property."

"And should Mr. Doe's gambit fail?"

"Then we do as honor demands and eliminate any threats to the House. For the glory of the Court." Selina spoke with a conviction she didn't feel and found herself wishing to avoid the worst-case scenario. One that likely involved the gutting of one Jonathan Doe.

Selina turned from her brother and strode from the room, a precautionary measure to remove any assertions of conspiracy. As she walked, she considered the young Mr. Doe. Though Selina had only known him for a short time, the Aegolius sibling increasingly found herself impressed with the resourceful mortal. *He has no knowledge, no backing, and no abilities save a quick mind and a formidable sense of self-worth. Why should I care if he lives or dies?*

Tapping her finger to her lip, a habit that Aahmes detested, Selina pondered the situation.

Romantic interest was so utterly anathema to the collected Shifter, such a foreign concept in her guarded life at the heights of power, Selina instantly discarded such an errant thought. With that discarded, a flicker of nostalgia, a dash of intrigue, and a helpful dose of curiosity was all that remained. *Jon reminds me of myself, in a way, when I was a child, amidst the razor-edged politics of the Court.* A wistful smile crossed Selina's face. *I shall be for Jon as Aahmes was for myself. I'm helping this new comer grow, that is all.*

Still, the interest lingered, the shadow of an affection she didn't care for. *Perhaps, if he survives this gamble and proves himself a worthy peer, we might see what benefits an alliance with Jon Doe might yield. If he survives, of course. Yes, the potential benefits certainly justify my efforts to protect an asset.*

Pleased that the conundrum had been resolved, the esteemed Selina Aegolius moved forward to the next phase of her conspiracy.

CHAPTER 21

FOR ONCE IN HER LIFE, Magda dearly wished for a cellphone. Or possibly a car. She'd been hunting high and low for Brock, stomping through half of San Dominguez to no avail. No one at the Den knew where Brock might be, and his office was locked up tight. When she'd wrenched a cellphone from one of the Cohort, she was struck with the terrible dilemma. She couldn't remember his number for the life of her.

The fact that she never once called it may have had something to do with it.

None of the line seemed to have it either. *The bastard always kept it in the phones he gave me.* All of which were currently crushed and useless due to Magda's stubborn refusal to carry them.

In the process of walking back and forth between his last known locations, Magda grappled with a rising sense of frustration. Old habits reared their heads, particularly ones she so recently swore off. More than once she found herself winding her way back to the Den only to swerve away from the front door at the last second. Ursus wisely declined from commenting each time. Magda knew if she walked through those doors again, there was no coming out. *Finding something to punch, shag, and drink under the table is not going to solve my problems!*

It took some convincing to drag her mind from its dark place to the matter at hand: finding Brock. Without him on board, their plan fell apart. The thought of it twisted her lips. *"Our" plan. Gods, up to my neck in skulking about.* Only by framing it as a broader battleplan kept Magda moving. Even a whiff of politics would risk sending her well clear. *I must redeem the Cohort. And just maybe myself.* Without other options, Magda hatched a desperate scheme.

She paid Niall Taggerty a visit.

Niall lived with his mother in a two-story slice of suburbia. Within spitting distance of the beach, like so much of San Dominguez, its fading paint showed the hallmarks of sea breeze and blinding sun. Magda rapped on the front door and politely waited. When Niall's mother, Lily Taggerty, answered the door Magda bowed. Petite with midnight hair and sad eyes, the t-shirt and jeans wearing woman took it in stride. Regardless of Niall's revelations, Sean was a hero of the Cohort and his family deserved all due respect and courtesy. Well, Lily did anyway. Niall was a centurion and a pest and deserved his lumps. Besides, it built character.

"Good afternoon, Mrs. Taggerty. Is Niall home?"

The warrior could see the walls go up in Lily's eyes, no surprise considering her eldest died in service to the Sunset Cohort. Having one of their revered battle heroes boded ill for the survival of her youngest.

"I'm not here for a mission, ma'am," Magda said gently. "I just want to speak to Niall about a friend."

"Very well then, Bannersworn. Please come in." As soon as Magda crossed the threshold, Lily changed. For one, she became much louder. "NIALL! Get down here right now. A friend is here."

Magda smothered the urge to grin. *Mother Taggerty could be a hell of a centurion with those lungs. Heh, Deimos would be spitting green with envy. Or ask to marry her on the spot.*

A great thundering heralded the young man rumbling down the stairs. "Mom, what is it? I'm in the middle of..." Whatever Niall was about to say was utterly destroyed when the he saw Magda.

Magda let loose the laughter she'd struggled to hold back a moment earlier.

Niall had come roaring down the stairs in only his boxers, which just so happened to be a reflective red with little matte hearts all about them. Seeing the object of his crush standing in his living room, Niall turned as red as his boxers before thundering back up the stairs.

"Thank you, Mrs. Taggerty. I'll take it from here."

"That's fine, Bannersworn. Leave the door open."

Still a mom. "Yes ma'am."

Magda raced after her fleeing line mate. She barged into his room just in time to see him frantically closing his computer, a pair of jeans half way up his legs. A much loved and beaten up desk sat under a window, bed crammed into a corner with clothes piled atop it in a little nest. Posters of heavy metal bands, all black and shiny chrome, dotted the walls. Pride of place went to a weathered if anachronistic poster of James Dean, the rebel without a cause smirking out at the cozy space.

"Hiding the evidence isn't going to help you, lad. Wonder what I'd see if I popped that open?"

Niall whirled, panic written on his face, eyes darting between Magda and the computer. The poor fool's distress sets off a new bout of giggle in the punk-tressed warrior.

"Oh Niall! Your face! Heh. Priceless. Fortunately for your purity, dear sweet Niall, I'm not here to raid your porn. I only need your phone."

"My what?" Still standing in his boxers, Niall looked utterly confused, not sure where to look or what to do next.

I'm willing to be he never thought of me in his room quite like this.

"Your phone. I'm trying to track down Brock, but I can't find the fellow."

"Um, ok, sure...stupid zipper...but why?" Niall jumped around trying to fit into his jeans while having some obvious anatomical difficulty.

"Because you have his number and I know where to find you."

"No, I didn't mean why me. I meant why do you need to talk to Brock? He always has to hound you down just to have you show up to anything. Shit, if you weren't at the Den getting soused half the time, he'd never find you."

I'm going to let that one slide. For now. Boy still needs some discipline. "Dammit Niall, shut up and give me your phone."

Niall, jeans affixed at last, turned to face Magda. "Sure. Just tell me why."

Magda rubbed the corners of her temples as a massive headache came knocking. "I told you. To call Brock. Can't find him, you have the number and a phone. Fork it over."

"Why?"

"Because I said so, damn your eyes!"

"I will. Just tell me why."

Magda glared at the lanky youth, hands clenching and unclenching into fists. *Dammit, I don't want to bring in anyone else into this mess. Who would back such an insane scheme?* Magda stopped dead as realization hit here like Jupiter's lightning bolts. *Wait. No one except Niall. He's always yapping about how we should take more care for the little people.* She looked at him again, eyeballing him carefully. *But that's no excuse for mouthing off to a superior!* Magda's glare lasted a moment longer then transformed into the grin that so often send enemies screaming for the hills. Niall audibly gulped. *I won't thump on him. Turning a new leaf and all that. Besides, he's too used to it by now. He needs a more creative punishment.*

Jumping at Niall, Magda quickly grappled him onto the bed, using his arm as leverage. Niall protested the compromising position with a yelp. No sooner did the thud resound than Mrs. Taggerty's voice called up at them.

"I know the sound of my son's bed creaking, Bannersworn. What's going on up there?"

Magda grinned as Niall froze. "Nothing to worry about, Mrs. Taggerty. Your son's a pest is all. He won't listen to common sense." Her free hand snaked into Niall's pants pocket, ostensibly reaching for the cell phone outline she saw, but ensuring she brushed by the other bulge she'd witnessed on the way.

Lily, for all her mom powers, didn't seem to have X-Ray vision and remained oblivious to the shenanigans overhead. "Understood. Niall's bright but a handful."

Magda laughed aloud. "More than you know!"

Niall froze in mortified terror. Magda could practically hear the thoughts grinding in his head. The idea of his mother walking in on him like this just about killed the poor fellow. Magda took pity on the lad. Cellphone claimed as booty, she left him sprawled on the bed.

"What the hell, Magda?" Niall hissed with tears of frustration and embarrassment in his eyes.

"Don't go crying now. Jon got a lot worse at the club. By the way, what's the code for your phone?" Niall gave it without even the need for another arm bar. Magda nodded with satisfaction. "You might want to deal with that though. Looks a bit uncomfortable."

Niall's gaze followed the nod of her head, blushed, and promptly stomped out of the room. Magda felt a little bad. A little. *At least now I can make a call in peace. And maybe that damned crush has finally been stamped out.*

Decidedly ignoring the impulse to dig through Niall's phone to find more ammo to torment him with, Magda brought up Brock's number. A stoic, though worn, voice answered. "What did you do this time, Niall?"

"I've suddenly become a warrior many times smarter than both of her packmates."

"Magda? How? What? Why?"

It was the first and only time Magda could recall the unflappable Brock sound confused.

"Where in the name of Neptune's soggy arse are you?"

"I do have a profession, Magda. I made a house call, visited a client, and enjoyed an extended lunch. The perks of one's own business. You should know that, if you ever stopped by to teach your classes at the gym."

Magda pinched the bridge of her nose, familiar frustration rising. She'd utterly lost track of the days and her obligations outside of Cohort business. *Between attempts on my life, hunting Ripper, uncovering conspiracies, and running about with Jon on his madcap scheme, I've forgot what day it is. Probably been fired and didn't even know it.* The thought only spiked her rage hotter. *I'm going to take this out of Ripper's hide when I find him!*

"Never mind that," Magda said. "I need your help."

"You have it. What do you need?"

"I'd rather not say over the phone."

Brock paused a moment. "Fine. Be careful, Magda. If you are at Niall's, I can only assume you've already been traipsing up and down town on a wild goose chase and probably raised hell in the Den. That raises flags. When everyone is looking for traitors, that can be dangerous."

Gods. I knew the Court played such games, but I believed us above this. Politics is one thing, but this suspicion is unworthy of us. Rather than diminish her resolve, it only bolstered Magda's focus. "I will. Just be in your office."

"Excellent." Brock killed the line.

Magda took a moment let the magnitude of what she was going to ask of Brock sink in. Which left her a bit shocked when a voice spoke up behind her.

"What was that about?"

Magda whirled, foot lashing out instinctively only to miss Niall's head by inches. "You little fiend! How long have you been there?"

Niall shrugged. "Pretty much the whole time."

"Have you no shame?"

"Funny considering what you did to me just a minute ago. Also, this is my room and that's my phone. Now gimme." Magda lobbed the device at him harder than strictly necessary. "Seriously, what do you need to talk to Brock about and how can I help?"

Magda growled, stepping in very, very close to Niall. "Niall, stand down."

Shockingly, despite Magda assuming her beatings had done their job, but Niall's stubborn streak remained. The young man met her gaze evenly.

"No. Magda, you're in trouble and somethings going on. I want to help." His eyes softened for a moment. "Please. You can trust me."

Magda blinked in stunned silence. *Little bastard is persistent.* "Niall, for all that is good for you, don't follow me and don't get involved. If I can, I'll fill you in after the fact. But for now, I need you to stay put.

"No promises."

Stomping down the stairs, Magda barked out a farewell to Lily. "Your son's a pest."

As Magda stormed out the door, Lily smiled sadly. "That he is."

§——§

Magda was no coward. She'd kill anyone who said otherwise. Of course, it was hard to avoid thinking it when she'd paced back and forth in front of Brock's office more times than she could count. Hard to decide who to punch when the accusation rang in your own mind.

This is idiotic! I'll just march and there and demand the grunt stand and invoke Dictatus. Simple. Then why can't I open the blasted door?

In her heart, Magda knew why. The burden was painfully familiar. The burden of responsibility. She'd spent countless hours drinking, fighting, and fucking to forget it. *If I do this, I'm responsible for the fate of my Cohort brethren. Their blood and breath, from this moment on.*

Even as she raised her hand to knock, the door opened to show Brock's stocky frame. "Magda. I heard someone stalking and muttering outside my door. I expected my six o'clock had shown up earlier, not you. Why don't you come inside and tell me what's on your mind."

"Not sure I should. If you heard me outside, your walls must be pretty thin."

"Years of practice. I can read the creaks and groans of this place like radio signals." The two sat down in Brock's office, sturdy desk between them. "What brings you to my office? Is it about what we talked about before?"

"No. Yes. Godsdammit, Brock, why did you do it?"

"You'll have to be more specific."

"Offer up Jon as sacrifice! He's no threat to the Senate or Cohort. Jupiter's balls, Jon barely knows his head from his ass when it comes to the Houses."

Brock shook his head sadly. "Wrong question, Magda. You know why. I did what I had to do to hold us together. You've done the same. Cohort first and always. You saw the bloodlust in our comrades' eyes. The Cohort needed focus. It needed an enemy."

Magda opened her mouth to speak but no words came out. Brock leaned back in his chair, a stature as unflinching as the earth itself. "Ask what you really want to ask."

Digging her fingers through the cheap stuffing of the chair, Magda ground her words through gritted teeth. "How long? How many innocents have we slaughtered in our wars?"

"Countless." Brock's face might have been carved from stone as he uttered the words.

The red headed warrior white knuckled grip threatened to tear padded arm rests to shreds. "I believed in what we did, Brock. All the enemies of the House deserved death at my hands, for we were good and noble and just. We were defending the world, godsdammit. Now you tell me it's all been a lie?"

"We are what we have always been, Magda. An army. The sword of the Senate. Nothing has changed. We also killed as was needed. You simply refused to see it before."

Magda rose in a fury, chair launched across the room in her haste. "Damn us! Damn you! Damn me!"

"While your outrage is laudable, in a sense, it is far too late. Hard choices have to be made, Magda. You know this all too well. You've made them yourself. But you've stepped down. Left that burden on someone else's shoudlers. Someone had to make the call, Bannersworn."

Tension settled in the air like an early morning frost, crisp and brittle. The clock ticked unerringly on the wall.

Begrudgingly, words leaked out of Magda. "I've got an alternative."

"Let's hear it."

Magda poured out Jon's mad gambit, the technical loophole they'd exploit to neuter the Cull's influence, trap Arkadas, and keep the Truce.

Brock listened to it all, eyes never flinching. "Clever. But not enough. I won't do it on the word of a thin-Blood relative."

"Not on his word. On mine."

Brock leaned forward. "Now, at last, we come to what matters."

"I say we back this gambit."

"Well, that is a reasonable suggestion, centurion, but I'm not sure a rank and file soldier has the best grasp of the larger picture."

Damn you for making me do this Brock. "I am Magda Lahm Dearg, Bannersworn of the Sunset Cohort, and I demand we take this action."

"If I agree to this, will you formally petition to be returned to rank? No more running?"

"Yes, damn your eyes. Invoke *Dictatus,* speak with the authority of the Senate to uphold this compromise, and I'll lead the Cohort again. Back out on your word and I'll gut you like a fish."

Brocks eyes sparkled with satisfaction. "Well done, Bannersworn. It seems you've learned diplomacy after all."

CHAPTER 22

JON LOOKED DOWN ANXIOUSLY at his watch. He paced. He groused. He slumped. None of which made his companions magically appear before him. The blue-eyed wunderkind stood outside of Ganesh' office, some blocks distant from Arkadas' own. Unlike Arkadas' anachronistic estate, this was a modern high rise, no different than any of its neighbors crammed next to it.

No rush, guys. Barely two days to go and it's not like I'm a dead man if this doesn't work. Oh wait, I am.

Jon fumed and paced, but all his sound and fury amounted to very little. Marc told him as such from his perch in the shadows of the stoop. "You do realize your pacing achieves exactly nothing?"

"You do realize pointing out the obvious is equally asinine?"

Marc shrugged and went back to dodging the vanishing sun.

Selina and Magda arrived, virtually at the same time though in very different ways. Magda sauntered up, hands crammed into her jacket, yet the red-haired warrior seemed a different person. She walked without her sullen slouch, her eyes were brighter and more alive than Jon ever remembered seeing.

Selina's arrival, via cream and gold Rolls-Royce, completely obliterated Jon's focus on Magda. Even in his anxious state, Jon drooled at the four wheeled marvel. As Selina elegantly exited the vehicle, the lawyer wasn't sure which he was more enamored with: the beauty in business casual or the opulent car.

Magda snorted, less impressed. "How much blood money did you need to buy that eyesore?"

"More than you're worth, my dear. I doubt you can count that high."

Jon sighed audibly. "Not now. Kill each other on your own time. Right now, saving my life is the priority. Magda, is your war buddy on board?"

"Aye, Jon. Brock will invoke *Dictatus*." She rolled her shoulders back and stood proud. "He does so at the behest of a Bannersworn of the Sunset Cohort."

Marc gave a low whistle at the revelation and even Selina's cool mask broke in surprise. Jon might have been the new guy, but even he realized the importance of Magda once again taking up the burden of leadership. He remembered the pain in her voice during their argument at the Den. *Holy shit. That's gotta hurt like hell.*

"Thank you."

Magda snorted. "I didn't do it for you, Jon. I did it for my brothers and sisters."

"Still... thanks. Selina, I won't insult you by asking if you succeeded."

"Was there ever any doubt?"

"Excellent! Now, let's go get Ganesh on board and wrap this up, nice and neat."

Jon led the march into Ganesh's office, their band escorted by Betai, manic grin plastered on the lawyer's face.

Ganesh's office cum living space was small, tasteful, and inviting.

Little more than an exaggerated rectangle, soft warming colors dominated the space. The faint scent of sandalwood lingered. An array of brightly colored lounge chairs and ottomans fanned out, forming two semi circles that faced one another with Ganesh's desk as the anchor point.

Ganesh sat at a low desk, drinking some tea and looking as if he hadn't a care in the world.

Lucky bastard.

The garishly dressed man smiled and rose to greet his guests. "Hello my friends! Glad you could come."

Jon grinned back, teeth blinding. He was in full court room mode. "Howdy, Ganesh. Thanks for seeing us."

"It is nothing. I am glad to see you doing well. Betai speaks well of you and told me you had something of great importance to tell me."

"You better believe it. Sit down and let me tell you a tale."

Jon spoke with as much zeal and gusto as any of his practice trials. Mr. Doe poured every ounce of his charisma, charm, and talent in rhetoric into his telling. Jon told a tale of deceit and betrayal, of unjust persecution, and a chance to make a real positive change.

So, it took him a moment to register Ganesh's simple reply of "No."

White noise rushed in Jon's ears, like the sea waves crashing over him. He rammed the palm of his hand against his ear a few times, as if trying to dislodge something stuck there. "I'm sorry, Ganesh, I'm not sure I got that right. Could you repeat that for me?"

The diplomat stood unmoving, a benevolent and aloof monolith. "You heard correctly the first time, my friend. My answer is no."

"No?" The unreasoning static grew louder and louder in Jon's ears.

"No. Jon, I sympathize with your plight, but I cannot risk this endeavor."

Jon slumped down into a lemony colored chair, its cushions embracing him with a *whumph*.

He glanced around the lovely décor of Ganesh's office, a far cry from the grotesque Victorian parody that were Arkadas' offices. The soothing colors and friendly vibe did little to lift Jon's mood as he rubbed his temples to drive away a throbbing headache. "But Betty said you'd join."

Jon glared at the lethal bodyguard just over Ganesh's shoulder. *Ganesh should have been on board.* But when they came in and laid it all out, a damn sight more politely than with Arkadas might he add, the kind-hearted Shifter responded with a polite but unequivocal refusal.

Their host's eyes shone with regret, compassion, and determination. "I am sympathetic to your plight. No one with a heart could not feel for you. But I cannot forget my duty to my people. I am their servant and their interests must come first and foremost." He turned to regard his lethal companion. "The Daughter of Tigers, for all her many strengths, gives greater credence to her sacred quest and ancient prophecy. She cares little for the minutia of politics or bonds of governance."

"Wise woman. Sounds reasonable to me," Magda muttered, perched on an old travel chest drummed into service as an end table.

The steel in Ganesh's voice and the iron in his eyes hammered home an old quote Jon once heard; compassion does not equal weakness. "Be that as it may, she places her divine quest beyond all other concerns. She considers any ensuing bloodshed a worthy sacrifice, should it mean keeping the Ancients at bay."

The words meant nothing to Jon but Magda, Selina, and Marc all stood on edge like cats catching scent of a large a dog. Frustrated and sick of being the odd man out Jon opened his mouth. "Mind sharing with the new kid in class? What 'Ancients?'"

Ganesh looked to Betai, whose amber eyes shown with passion. Still, the warrior simply shook her and gestured brusquely for Ganesh to tell the tale.

"In days long past, the gods walked more freely amidst their children. Wonders and horrors abounded. Old powers touched the earth and the servants of such powers clashed. Many of these old titans were banished in mighty conflicts long ago. So too were their servants locked away. Bloody ages resigned to myth in your world but very much our histories. Your companion, Magda, earned much glory in stemming the Atlanteans' recent advances upon the surface world."

Eyes haunted, Magda grunted a halfhearted acknowledgement of the compliment. Jon did not take it so quietly.

"Atlanteans? As in, lost continent? Disney film? Aquaman?"

"Yes, Jon, though they are hardly as benevolent as modernity portrays them. Nostalgia, I suppose. Remember, in more than a few of those tales, the gods themselves condemned Atlantis to sink beneath the waves. They punished the Atlanteans for their evil ways, drowning their homeland in a single night."

Betai strode forward, picking up Ganesh's tale. "But they were not destroyed. The dark powers they courted prevented their total destruction. Half trapped in their abyssal prison, the Atlanteans are deranged and twisted beyond reckoning."

"Fomorians."

Jon started at Magda's growl. The redhead could pack immense amounts of emotion into a single word but nothing, not even her contempt of Selina and the Court of Raptors, held a candle to such pure, undiluted, hate. Betai inclined her heard, hand on the sword as though ready to draw. The two shared a moment of shared animosity against their foes in the depths.

"Even now, old powers roam the land, donning new guises in their diminished form. I fight a war millennia old. Their servants take on many faces, but their evil remains as foul as in ancient days. I see the ancient foe's hand at work in San Dominguez, and I aim to burn them out."

Ganesh sighed. "In truth, she sees their shadowy tendrils everywhere, but I give credence to such rumors in this instance. There has been much darkness of late."

Magda flexed and paced. "You think Arkadas is working with the Fomorians? I'll use his entrails for bait!"

Ganesh gently placed a hand on the violence-strung Bannersworn, showing a bravery Jon didn't think he could ever match. "I do not know for certain. A jackal and a vulture may desire the same meal and not work together. There is bloodshed and sorrow aplenty without attributing it to the machinations of the ancient foe." Ganesh's eyes grew sad and distant, and Jon sensed he felt each loss as keenly, as if he knew the murdered fellows. "It pains me that Arkadas is complicit in such deals. I knew my friend had his faults, but this is worse than I ever credited him."

Jon pounced at his opening. "If you won't do it for me, do it for Arkadas."

"Pardon?"

"Without you to check him, Arkadas will keep murdering and lying and funding those Cull lunatics. If you help us, we can keep him on the straight and narrow and help balance the karmic books."

"I cannot. You come to me as a neutral party, and I am humbled you would trust me so. But the fact is, to your Houses, I am an outsider," Ganesh said. "I cannot be seen to check Arkadas or even openly defy the Houses. They would view my actions as undermining their authority. An opportunistic power grab at best, an infiltration or preparation for a larger attack at worst. Such an action undermines my credibility and thus my future ability to negotiate. While I appreciate a chance to prevent needless bloodshed, being associated with this audacious plan of yours risks my ability to ease tensions between the Houses and my own people. I cannot forsake the greater good on a gamble, no matter my own heart on the matter."

Jon threw up his hands. "Fine then. You are a man of your word. Seen werewolves, vampires, and other crazy shit, why not that? Guess I'm due for a unicorn soon." He turned his head to Betai, who remained characteristically laconic. "Hey, Ms. Tiger. Care to join us in our doomed endeavor?"

Betai and Ganesh locked eyes for a moment and tension filled the room.

With a sigh, Betai looked away. "Though I would add my sword to your cause, I cannot. To do so would violate other oaths."

Ganesh turned toward the motley band. "She is constrained as I am, though her holy quest may wish it to be otherwise. The Daughter of Tigers is well known and tied to my own person. If she aids you, it would appear as though it is with my sanction. This cannot be."

Marc spoke up before Jon could utter a word. "Siddartha, please."

"My decision is final. My compassion must extend to my own charges. I will not risk their lives in this. I am sorry. My sympathies are with you, but you must find another to aid you in this. Betai, please remain here. There are matters we must discuss. Jon, you have my deepest sympathies. May you go with the gods' protection."

Silent as a funerary march, the band of supplicants left Ganesh's office, each step one closer to the gallows.

Jon threw up his hands. "Fine then. You are a man of your word. Seen werewolves, vampires, and other crazy shit, why not that? Guess I'm due for a unicorn soon." He turned his head to Betai, who remained characteristically laconic. "Hey, Ms. Tiger. Care to join us in our doomed endeavor?"

Betai and Ganesh locked eyes for a moment and tension filled the room.

With a sigh, Betai looked away. "Though I would add my sword to your cause, I cannot. To do so would violate other oaths."

Ganesh turned toward the motley band. "She is constrained as I am, though her holy quest may wish it to be otherwise. The Daughter of Tigers is well known and tied to my own person. If she aids you, it would appear as though it is with my sanction. This cannot be."

Marc spoke up before Jon could utter a word. "Siddartha, please."

"My decision is final. My compassion must extend to my own charges. I will not risk their lives in this. I am sorry. My sympathies are with you, but you must find another to aid you in this. Betai, please remain here. There are matters we must discuss. Jon, you have my deepest sympathies. May you go with the gods' protection."

Silent as a funerary march, the band of supplicants left Ganesh's office, each step one closer to the gallows.

CHAPTER 23

"**S**HIT." Marc spat the word, which neatly summed up the spirit of the group.

Jon sat on the front steps, listless and drained, his dynamism and charm swallowed by bleak despair. *So close. We were so close. Dammit, it's not fair!*

He looked up at his co-conspirators. Magda paced while Selina studied her phone, brow furrowed as though trying to unravel a puzzle.

Marc stared at Jon with a hungry intensity, skin pinking under the fading rays of the sun, now just a sullen glow on the horizon. "What next?"

Jon looked around before it clicked that Marc asked him. "What do you mean?"

"Simple question, Jon. What next?"

"Why are you asking me?"

"Because you always have something in your back pocket. Another plan, ploy, gamble. You've talked your way out of worst scrapes than this."

Jon laughed, short and hollow. "Flatterer."

"I don't do flattery, Jon. Just the facts." Marc's mortuary breath washed over Jon as he leaned in close. "What. Do. We. Do. Next?"

Jon jumped up from the stoop, angry now. "I don't know, Marc. Yeah, normally I'd pull another rabbit out of my hat, but this was it. The Hail Mary pass. The last push."

"Screw that, Jon. It's my ass on the line too. There is always something else."

"You think I haven't been looking at this thing since some jackasses abducted me off the street? I know damn well I'm gonna be gutted like a fish if we don't come up with something. I've got nothing! We've got a day left and no one else we can go to. All the big players are off the board. Heh, maybe I could snag the Terrible Trio and have them vouch for me. Do you think a bunch of hooved hooligans count as good character witnesses?"

Jon's gallows humor failed to elicit laughter from his comrades. Instead, his co-conspirators shared significant glances.

"Don't any of you dare hold out on me now. Starlight's burning. Spill."

For the first time since backing Jon on his hare-brained scheme, the three co-conspirators looked nervous. Selina played spokeswoman for the group.

"Well, Jon, you mentioned the hoofers. An idea emerges, though it's a bit silly, crazy even." Selina's voice was sweet enough to woo an angry bull. Pity she was dealing with a desperate Jon Doe instead.

"Silly is good. Crazy is even better. Tell me."

"We might recruit the hoofers." Each word sounded like it was being pulled from Selina with barbed wire.

Jon scratched his head, thinking of the three drunks he carted to Speculo Productions. "Wait, you mean those guys have pull in this town?"

"Well, they aren't really an organized entity, per se," Selina said. "They tend to be distant from not just human politics but politics in general. Short attention span, if you will."

Marc snorted. "That's putting it politely. Bunch of good for nothing louts."

"Wow, Marc," Jon said, rolling his eyes. "Way to go full Harvard. You going to talk about 'those people' now?"

Marc opened and closed his hands in a frustrated gesture. "Jon, you haven't had to work with them. Payroll alone is a nightmare! Centaurs, minotaurs, satyrs, they're like hormone-ridden teenagers with ADHD but built like linebackers and fuzzy supermodels. Sometimes both!"

Jon rushed to his feet, hopeful for the first time since leaving Ganesh's place. "Perfect! I speak fluent meathead!"

Marc pinched the bridge of his nose. "You're not listening, Jon. They really *don't* care."

Magda nodded her support. "Good for a party or moving your furniture, but not much else."

"Marc's right, Jon," Selina said, chiming in her assessment. "Most of them don't hoard power or jockey for position, outside of the occasional wrestling match or some such to establish a pecking order to attract a mate or equally base pastimes. They are content with what they have and do not trouble themselves with the heights of power or deeper mysteries."

Jon hissed like a tea kettle. "Then why bring them up at all if it's useless?"

His three co-conspirators shared another round of nervous glances before Selina spoke again. "Chiron."

"Wonderful, except *I have no idea who you're talking about!*" Jon's shriek may have sounded like a six-year-old upset over spilled ice cream, but he was far too worked up to care.

"Chiron is a centaur, a noted public speaker, and quite civilized... at least for hoofer standards." Selina coughed into a manicured hand.

"So, what's the issue?"

Magda snorted. "The horseman isn't exactly loved by all. He's a fire-brand, always arguing for hoofer's rights and such and snubbing his nose at good, honest traditions. Some amongst the Houses think he's one step from being as bad as the Furies."

Jon blanched. "Is he going to try and kill me too?"

Selina picked up the thread with a small shake of her heard. "Oh no, Jon. While his rhetoric may be populist drivel, he is an honest man. His word is his bond. Which is rather the problem. He's been immune to any number of table talks." Her soft moue of distaste sent Magda laughing and Marc looking elsewhere.

"What the featherduster means is that he's refused any number of bribes, blackmails, and anything else besides."

"Quite. Thank you, Bannersworn."

Jon rubbed his hands together, manic grin crawling across his face, blue eyes alight. "This Chiron hasn't met me yet. Get ready to kiss hands and shake babies, folks. It's schmoozing time."

Marc sighed in a gust of sepulchral air. "Jon, you understand that not only is Chiron seen as a rabble rouser and trouble maker, notoriously mistrustful of outside deals, this all rides on getting the Houses to even recognize the hoofer as an equal peer worthy of being a signatory."

"Do we even have a choice?"

Silence reigned as each of the conspirators considered the weight of what they faced. At last, Selina broke the silence.

"No. We are committed. We have already dallied too long. Arkadas will never forget our blackmail. He'll deduce who supplied you with that amulet. It won't be long before our failure to recruit Ganesh is revealed to Arkadas. Either we move now or cede initiative." Selina's eyes came to stare intently at Magda. "Bannersworn, can you be trusted to do the same on your end?"

"In the name of all that I was, all that I am, this task shall be undertaken, no matter the ruination I must bring about to make it happen. So speaks Magda Lahm Dearg." Her fist clashed violently on her chest in the style of ancient Rome.

Marc opened his mouth, but Jon forestalled his no doubt prosaic response with a brotherly embrace. Utter shock made Marc pop his fangs.

"Thank you, Marc."

The raw sincerity may have been new ground both Jon and Marc but understanding flowed between them like the days of old. Or so Jon thought until Marc grinned, flashing full fangs at his living companion.

"Putting my immortal existence on the line, not a peep of gratitude. Promise to make a call to a bunch of frat boys with delusions of politics, he hugs me."

The sheer galled offense on Jon's face sent his companions into fits of laughter. Despite Marc's gallows humor, none amongst them failed to understand the dire magnitude of their situation. Their fates danced on a razor's edge and they had one last desperate chance to make things right.

Rather than feel crushed by the weight, Jon felt his anxiety fall away, not gone, merely distant, overtaken under clear focus. *High stakes, life and death, one shot, nothing new. Just one more chance to beat the odds.*

§——§

Harried mythical creatures in suits and ties shouted across the room, a constant clang of phones, printers, and computers rang out, and folks ran, trotted, or jumped hither and thither on cloven feet narrowly missing one another by hair's breadth. The whole affair resembled nothing more than a vaguely organized riot, with farm animals in formal dress thrown in for good measure.

The office clamor instantly brought Jon back to his temping days for legal firms, right down to the battered second-hand furniture supplanted with the finest of out-of-date electronic equipment. *I'm willing to bet most of these computers are old enough to vote.*

It all smelled of the scrappy underdog, right down to the chipped name plate out front. With recent events being what they were, Jon felt a slight tingle of kinship.

Once Marc pulled up their files, it had been a hop, skip, and a short drive downtown to reach the office. It shocked Jon a bit that so many Mythics could work amidst humans without raising any problems. But then again, he'd never noticed his roommate turning into a room temperature walking corpse with an aversion to sunlight. *Bit of magic and a dash of good old human tunnel vision works wonders.*

Not a hair stood out of place as Jon strutted through the mayhem in his best power suit, ready to pitch his case. A minotaur with hair done up in a 1950's beehive never looked up from her furious typing when she greeted him without a preamble.

"Do you have an appointment?"

Ah, those dreaded words. Hello, gatekeeper. With any luck I won't have to fend off amorous advances this time.

"Good morning. My name is Doe, Jon Doe, practicing legal representative. I've got a meeting scheduled with Mr. Chiron. I'm currently with Mr. Arkadas' office."

The old buzzard's name drop backfired on Jon. The ambient degrees dropped from coolly neutral to downright frosty.

"Unfortunately, sir, I can't seem to find you in our calendar. I'm afraid you'll have to come back later."

Jon's smile could have been in a toothpaste commercial. "I'm certain Mr. Chiron will want to see me."

"I'm sorry, sir." Her tone assured him quite the opposite. "You'll have to leave and come back with an appointment."

"I'm afraid I'm going to have to insist."

"Then, I'm going to insist you leave. Now."

"Not going to happen, my dear."

Madame desk-jockey rose to tower over the obstinate lawyer. Blood-shot eyes glared at Jon, and her pink dress threatened to split open with each raged filled snort. Jon never stopped smiling and didn't budge an inch.

I'm not going anywhere, lady. Even if you kill me, it's only beating the competition by a few hours.

Even as gigantic hands reached to throttle him, Jon spotted a familiar face in the madhouse. Nathan, a tie awkwardly wrapped around his thick neck and button-up threating to explode, moved carefully around the office.

"Nathan! Hey!" Even at the top of his lungs, the lawyer's voice barely made a dent in the din. Fortunately, the big lug's ears perked up and he looked over to notice Jon's frantic arm waves.

The good-natured bovine thundered over with a grin plastered on his face oblivious to his office companion's mitts clamped around Jon's jacket. "Good to see you, buddy! I got this one, Pearl."

The clerical assistant gave an un-enthused grunt but let Jon go. Nathan draped his arm around Jon's shoulders and dragged him away.

"What brings you here? Trying to break into showbiz the back way?"

Jon hop skipped along to keep up with the Terrible Trio's long legs.

"I'm looking for Chiron. Got something big I think he'd like to get in on."

"Chiron!? Hang on pal, I'll take you right to him."

They weaved past several clusters of desks crammed together to make workstations in the open office. At least the lazily whirring fans weren't low enough to risk Nathan's horns. The sea of bodybuilders part-ed and Jon got a good look at his last hope.

Chiron sat at a desk no different than any other on the floor. Only a ten-foot void, clear of any other desks, file cabinets or other office detritus, marked him out. His salt-and-pepper hair was drawn back into a stern braids which fell down past his shoulders, stopping just shy of where man became horse. Brass-rimmed half-frame glasses rested on a bold nose. His olive-bronze complexion looked like a swimmer or farm-er, one used to the sun.

While still impressively built like his kindred—apparently all the hoofed Mythics ate their Wheaties—the centaur carried himself with the bearing of an elderly professor or a dignified statesman. When Chiron nodded at the pair, Nathan crossed the invisible boundary.

Jon extended his hand. "Mr. Chiron, I presume? How's Achilles these days?"

Chiron laughed, hearty and without fear. "Happy in retirement, or so I hear, legends notwithstanding. I do strive to be a teacher of heroes like my namesake." The centaur took Jon's hand in a firm double shake. To Jon's eye, Nathan's boss seemed a figure of dignity and poise. Jon's struggled to keep his face even as his stomach sunk in despair.

Shit. Bitter, desperate, or greedy I could work with. Didn't count on an honest politician. Gotta figure out an angle. Playing for time, Jon opened with niceties.

"I appreciate you being willing to meet with me on such short no-tice."

"You come highly recommended. Nathan speaks well of you, Mr. Doe, and of your driving."

Chiron's eyes twinkled. Nathan gave a long-distance fist bump to Jon, sending a blush across his cheeks.

"Just lending a hand where I could."

"You aided those in need. Such decency is commendable. Few help our kind without strings attached."

Chiron's veiled warning rang loud and clear to Jon. *Hugs, kisses, and don't screw with me? Thanks very much.*

"I'm sorry to hear that. I understand you are a bit of a representative for the neutral Mythics in the area?"

"Essentially correct. I and other like-minded Mythics push for change in our society and to rectify certain inequalities amidst both the Senate and the Court."

"That's a noble sentiment," Jon said. "I believe we can help each other on this front."

"Indeed?" Chiron responded with all the warmth of a glacier.

"I'm about to make a powerful change in how things are done in San Dominguez, something that will give you real pull with the Houses."

"I suppose all I have to do is sign on the dotted line?"

Jon beamed his winning smile at the centaur. "Actually, yes."

Chiron listened as Jon outlined his plan, judiciously edited for brevity and to avoid painting Chiron as the option of last resort. Nathan eavesdropped on the entire conversation, almost stapling his tie to the desk as he clumsily pretended to do office work. A small spellbound cluster of hooved Mythics joined around him, captivated by the lawyer's rhetoric.

"So, you see, Chiron, you would be a signatory, recognized as an official peer of the Houses. You would be in a position to truly change the face of San Dominguez and receive recognition for the plight of your people."

The dusky centaur stood as firm as a rock in the face of Jon's charisma, face blank as professional poker player as he considered Jon's words.

"Mr. Doe, I appreciate your sentiment, but I cannot agree to this."

The crowd murmured, and Jon's stomach sank further into his feet. *No, not like Ganesh. Not again.*

"Chiron, I'm urging you to reconsider. This is an excellent deal for both us."

"I've found 'mutually beneficial' bargains with the Houses rarely helps my kind as much as the Shifters. History teaches us to be wary of Greek gifts and wooden horses."

"I'm not here representing the Houses."

"Please, Mr. Doe, don't insult me. You work for them. Simultaneously, in fact. A rare feat."

The fact that such employment was about to end in a brutal and bloody end erupted in Jon's mind. "It's complicated. I'm here in good faith. This is an honest to goodness game changer we've got here."

"That may make it worse then."

"Chiron, this is a unique situation."

Chiron stomped once firmly, giving Jon the impression of a nervous tick. "I will not sign on with your plan without stronger guarantees. Should this fail, it will simply reinforce what they already say about us. To be associated with such a debacle will hurt my people and our cause profoundly. We will be seen as selling out to the Houses by many of our supporters as well as weak by many of our opponents by failing at such a... human... scheme."

Nathan stepped in just before Jon unwisely attempted to strangle the bespectacled quadruped.

Quietly, almost bashfully, Nathan spoke up. "We can do this." The two turned to Nathan, both somewhat shocked that the minotaur could speak without yelling.

Clearing his throat, the bovine spoke more confidently with every word. "Boss, we got this! You said it yourself. 'There is nothing we cannot achieve if set our minds to it.'" The agitated office worker practically hopped up and down in place. "Jon seems like a good guy. Sure, he's petty and egotistical and stresses over his car's upholstery too much, but... this seems like a good chance to make headway." Nathan looked between his mentor and the petitioning lawyer, who frowned at the uncharacteristically astute description of his failings from the B movie actor. "Besides, when have we ever let a little screw up stop us?"

Both Jon and Chiron stood stunned at their strapping office companion for a moment. One could hear a pin drop, if not for the ambient roar of Mythic cubicle drones.

Jon swallowed and inspiration hit him. *Wait, Chiron isn't Arkadas. Time to play on the heart strings.* "Chiron, please understand. I may not have lived with the injustices of the Houses my whole life, but I am as much a victim here as your constituents. My head is literally on the chopping block. I can't offer you any more guarantees than I have. But I can offer a chance for recognition and justice."

Jon held out his hand imploringly, every ounce of his bent toward looking innocent and trustworthy. Chiron frowned for nearly half a minute before his composure broke down into gut busting laughter.

"Hah! From the mouths of babes! To have my own creed thrown back at me. Hoisted by own petard, was it?" He removed his glasses to wipe tears from his eyes. "Very well then, good sir. What would you need from me for this fanciful scheme?"

"A little song and dance and smile pretty for the cameras." Jon flashed the pearly whites as Chiron took his hand.

Chiron grinned back exultantly; half glasses nearly thrust from his face. "Mr. Doe, you have yourself a deal."

CHAPTER 24

THE BEACHFRONT PROPERTY itself sat deserted some miles out from San Dominguez proper. Its drab, functional buildings stood as unremarkable sentinels of Corporate America, flanking a large central parking area on three sides. Sandy dunes came right to the concrete, the sea just a sparkle at the edge of sight. The sun blazed in the sky, baking cracked concrete. Closed and shuttered for some time, a chain link fence encircled the shuttered office building.

Though long unused, it stood ready to host many esteemed, if bizarre, guests.

A large stage had been erected in the weed choked parking lot, rows of folding chairs separated by an aisle down the middle. In the name of peace, clear battle lines had been drawn. Crews bustled about, handling the thousand menial tasks needed to set up any large gathering. Guards patrolled the edges even as workers set up tents and laid water and food.

Jon and company watched the hustle and bustle from the stage. Marc looked around, but Jon doubted his eyes were really on the workers. The undead's eyes were wide and every so often, he'd look up to the blazing sun, awe writ across his face. The joy on his friend's face made Jon's heart ache. *I've never seen Marc so excited over something so simple. It usually takes a murder mystery or quantum physics to get him going. Who knew walking in daylight could be so exciting?*

Jon turned his own face to the sun, shades keeping blindness at bay. *Something so simple. Something I take for granted. Damn. If I live through this, maybe I'll appreciate the little things a bit more.*

Jon crushed the nascent anxiety and brought his razor focus to the fore. His eyes swept the bustling lot with a winning smile plastered onto his face. He felt electric. Anticiaption made everything sing, like whenever Jon stepped into a courtroom or debate podium. Only this time, amplified tenfold. *Biggest court case of them all; Jon vs. the freaking world.* He flicked at glance at his gaping undead companion. *Well, Jon and company.* They'd debated and schemed, hashing out the finer details.

The trap was in place. They just had to see it through.

The first of the line of cars drove through the chain link fences at a quarter past noon. The spacious parking lot, only slightly cracked with green shoots poking through, held all the visiting dignitaries' vehicles and their security detail. And there was *quite* a security detail. *Trust seems to be in short supply. Can't blame them. You don't live for centuries without a healthy dose of paranoia.* Besides, in the cases of the Houses' leadership, everyone really was out to get them.

Jon could relate, even if he didn't sympathize.

The sleek and elegant vehicles of the Shifter dignitaries imitated a secret service block party in their all-black paint schemes. The Aegolius siblings' Rolls-Royce broke the tedium. The siblings stepped out, as impressive as their vehicle. Sharp power suits, modern business sleekness contrasted with the archaic ornaments hanging from them. Lapis lazuli, gold, and sterling silver hung about their arms, chest, and hair. A winged Ankh dangled about Selina's neck, symbol of her office.

After a few polite rounds, Selina broke off from her Court minders to stand on the stage near Jon.

"Glad to see you looking well, Jon."

"Same to you, Selina. Looking forward to the show?"

"Indeed." Her eyes stopped on Marc. More specifically, on the sun amulet wrapped around Marc's neck. "Is that the Voice of Ra?"

"Yes." Jon grinned and nodded.

"The holy relic I provided to you in confidence for safekeeping?"

"The very same."

"A symbol of the imperishable sun hung about a creature of the night?"

"Accurate." Jon's grin never faded.

Selina stopped for a moment, dumbfounded at the audacity of not only casually handing over a priceless relic, but giving it to a blood sucking nocturnal creature.

"Quit your whining, featherduster. The bloodsucker has proven himself. He's earned a few moments in the sun." Magda, dressed in her usual attire despite the momentous occasion, had crept up to the stage from behind, arriving with the Cohort contingent sticking to the Senate officials like furry secret service. By contrast, Brock's purple button-up shirt and slacks looked outright regal.

Then again, maybe the man makes the clothes in this case.

Niall completed the trio, hanging back in a black and white ensemble that looked better suited for a funeral. With the Shifters having securely claimed their territory, the neutral parties trickled in.

The non-House officials' wheels bucked the all black cliché. Chiron unfolded himself from the back of a simple Volkswagen, a true horseman of the people. By contrast, Arkadas' Bentley limousine, complete with uniformed chauffeur, seemed remarkably garish and vulgar.

Ganesh surprised Jon by riding up on a BMW bike with his stoic bodyguard shadowing him on one of her own.

"Why did you invite Ganesh? Has he changed his mind about signing?" Selina asked quietly, hand casually screening her mouth. Jon figured being around her peers kicked in ingrained habits, likely in the name of self-preservation.

Jon kept the beaming smile plastered to his face, sunglasses shielding his eyes from the midday sun. All around them, the looming decrepit buildings of the old tech company bore mute witness to the proceedings, observers but not participants to their own fate.

"Nope, but I figured it'd be nice gesture to invite him and Betty. No hard feelings and all that."

"That, and you owed the Daughter of Tigers, since she saved your sweet ass," Magda chimed in.

Niall piped up from behind her, "She cuts a mighty fine figure in riding leathers, too."

Jon couldn't help but agree but declined to comment as Brock and Magda ordered their young companion to shut his trap and show some respect in a way that only family could. The three Cohort warriors stood with Jon, Selina, and Marc upon the stage. Their conspiracy may not have been readily apparent, despite their cluster.

Can't see what you aren't looking for. Not a one of these monsters thinks a plain old blue-eyed human boy can outsmart them.

Every moment raised Jon's tension, the razor edge of adrenaline, waiting before the trap snapped shut. He hoped Selina's assurance of Aahmes' assistance would be proven later but the evidence for Magda's side of things stood by them in the form of Brock Macintyre, representative of the Senate in the Sunset Lands.

Jon still wasn't privy to the finer details, but it sounded like the soldier signed on simply because Magda backed their insane scheme. *He puts a lot of faith in her.*

Best Jon could tell, Niall, youngest of the trio, was there for moral support. Despite her obvious irritation with him, Magda trusted the teen-aged Shifter, which was good enough for Jon. *I like the guy's mouth. Reminds me of me. Fairly sane too, for a Shifter. Hope mountains of bloodshed don't wear down that spark.*

By now, the gathered great and powerful of the Senate and the Court, rivals and enemies for years uncounted, ancient conspiracies who watched civilizations rise and fall to dust, filed in and sat in cheap fold-out chairs to hear a struggling legal consultant dictate terms to them. Most Shifters came strutting and sneering at their opponents on the other side of the aisle.

They should be, Jon smirked to himself. *Since I told each and every one of them that they were the prettiest princesses at the ball.*

Only a few frowned at the unorthodox nature of the meeting. They smelled a trap, whereas the rest flashed smug grins. Both the Court and the Senate believed the promises fed to them by their representatives. Only once they noticed Jon's other guests did the whispers stir up.

Jon waited for the appropriate dramatic timing, letting the confused murmurs build. Finally, in no small part to Marc's gentle nudging, Jon stepped up and tapped the microphone.

"Thank you all for coming, I realize this is a bit unusual, but given the series of events surrounding this whole affair, I figured a party is necessary to clear the air. What's a little kidnapping between friends, right?"

Forced chuckles echoed around the empty concrete square. Jon engaged in a bit more showboating, ran through a few more formalities, working the crowd and making them sweat.

"Now, at last, the moment you have all been waiting for. Due to the troubled nature of this case, it took some time to determine the proper result. By consulting all relevant parties and reviewing the data, I have a resolution to the Beachfront case. As a show of good faith and in full accordance with my duties and responsibilities toward both Houses, I declare joint ownership, under the jurisdiction of regional representative from both the Senate and the Court of Raptors. To ensure neutrality, I will oversee development as a neutral third party to facilitate any ongoing negotiations, until such a time as my services are deemed fulfilled." As he held his breath, his movie star smile never wavered, prepared for the first objection. He didn't wait long.

Fortunately, it came from an expected quarter. Aahmes Aegolius shot to his feet, blade in fist and voice ringing with outrage. "You worthless jackal! Your services are no longer required, nor is your head!" Others around him echoed the sentiment, with inventive variations of the same theme. Disembowling, decapitations, and several other messy ends were enthusiastically suggested.

Even though he was prepared for the elder Aegolius' outburst, the venom in it took Jon back a bit. *Damn, it really does sound like he wants to kill me. Good.* Jon scanned the crowd, watching the angry Shifters. *Aahmes played his part. Now for the others. The show must go on.*

Good performance art needed multiple players to spice it up. Selina stepped forward with the grace of a queen. "Calm down, dear brother. I have already given my full support of this action in the name of the Court." She turned to address her brethren, badges of office gleaming in the sunlight, reminding all of her authority. "I have spoken with Mr. Doe and his proposition seemed imminently reasonable. It is simply an extension of our existing Truce." The reinforcement of the unpopular agreement quelled most death threats. The great and powerful of the Houses couldn't argue against their own plan, not without losing face. "Rather than drain our resources, the alliance secures profits for both parties. The fiscal burdens are diminished, and we may ensure the raids by our common foe are further neutralized. Thus is the measure weighed and its worth taken."

She turned to Jon, hand outstretched. "I invest Jonathan Augustus Doe with oath of office for this land. Let it be *sacrum*. So speaks Exarch

Aegolius, Highest of the Carnelian Ring, Voice of the High Council. Let those who walk in the light, hear and obey. And may those who walk in the dark, beware." Pronounced with the authority of a judge passing sentence, no one uttered a protest. Satisfied, Selina allowed the next representative to speak.

Brock tromped across stage and stood before the microphone with hands clasped as though in a debriefing.

You can take the man out of the military, but you can't take the military out of the man.

"I have been presented with the full details and intent of this contract. Upon advisement by my trusted subordinates, coupled with thorough examination, we have determined this is a noble endeavor and worthy of our support. If we are to garner the security of the region, we shall set aside our feud with Court and focus our attentions of malcontents and renegades who slay those under our protection."

Growls piped up from the Cohort members at the veiled reference to the Cull of Actaeon's recent blood-stained rampage. It was a clever rhetorical trick, focusing the Cohort's ire on a shared enemy, a follow-up to Selina's own invocation of the Truce.

"Thus, the Senate recognizes the Court and its servants as *Auxilia Fidus Amicus*, as was the case against the Fomorian threat during the San Francisco Incursion. We extend this honor to the broker and holder of this treaty as well. Thus do I invoke *Dictatus* and ratify this agreement. I invest Jonathan Augustus Doe with oath of office for this land. Let it be *sacrum*. My word is iron. By the glory of the Senate and the honor of the Sunset Cohort, let it be so."

Cowed by Selina's poise and faced with such an earnest speech from one of their own, none of the Shifters dared voice a complaint. A handful of the Senate guards even slammed their fists to their hearts with quiet but earnest calls of *Ave Senatus*.

Jon stepped forward once again, taking the stage from Brock. The suspicious mutterings of the House representatives were muted and sullen as they started to put two and two together. They'd been caught in a coup by their own representatives.

Thanks for giving me the rope, guys. Hope you enjoy hanging from it.

The idea had been brewing since Marc first mentioned the fate of the former Beachfront property owner. The House leaders might be monsters, but they had to play by the rules, otherwise the whole system they'd built crashed around them. Faced with the threat of a civil war within the Cohort and an ascendant Cull, neither the Court nor the Senate could risk showing any weakness.

For the time being, these terrifyingly powerful men and women would have to play along or admit that they'd lost control of their pawn, outsmarted by a snot nosed know-nothing punk from Harvard.

Jon kept as much of his internal gloating out of his voice as he continued dictating terms. "In light of this new union, there is another facet we would like to address. With the new building opportunities, the Houses will be involving the sizable support and population of our hoofed brethren in the greater San Dominguez area. Mobilizing them will increase productivity and enable us to finish all future construction in record time at minimal cost to the Houses. As recognition for this concerted and concentrated effort, they will be entitled to certain privileges and recognition within the Sunset territories. Chiron will act as representative for their demands and functioning liaison between the newly created Hoofer League and both Houses."

That stirred up one hell of a shit storm.

Arkadas' eyes nearly bulged out of his head, and even Jon's conspirators blanched. Shouts rang across the parking, the hoofers hollering and cheering while the Shifters screamed slurs and insults back until they remembered they were supposed to be better than their non-Shifter counterparts. None of the old powers had any respect for the hoofed brethren, and the establishment of what seemed to be a pocket kingdom of the rowdy bunch didn't go down easy.

I can imagine those pompous Shifter pricks' thoughts on the matter. Filthy peasants! How dare they not be grateful! Of course, all I've done is unionize the hoofers but it's a great start. The proverbial cherry on the equally pro-verbial sundae was that Chiron acted as the nominally unified hoofers' representative. *I'm sure it offends the Court and Senate's delicate sensibilities to have to play ball with a rabble rouser like Chiron. Time to smooth some feathers and convince them everything was still business as usual.*

"However, it would be unseemly not to include a venerable pillar of the community," Jon continued. "The esteemed Arkadas will be ensuring the contracts are all above board and suitable to all parties. His experi-ence and familiarity with the Beachfront Case will be invaluable."

Arkadas had been sulking in his chair but nodded slowly and rose to his feet. He didn't like being in front of his employers and selling them out to Jon, but he decided it was better than aforementioned employers finding out he had really sold them out to the Cull of Actaeon.

Persona non grata is a hell of a lot more bearable than being dead. Guess Arkadas and I have something in common now. Lucky us.

Jon wisely gave Arkadas a wide berth as he relinquished the stage. He wanted to avoid any unhappy accidents.

"After careful review of the facts and measuring all variables, I have determined this to the best course of action. I, Archibald K. Arkadas, hereby ratify this action." Arkadas glared daggers at Jon and walked stiff-backed off the stage.

Well, that wasn't the script I gave him, but close enough.

Jon grinned savagely. He'd saved the best for last. "The final neu-tral signatory shall be Lord Hynrich, whose impeccable code should be known to all. His emissary shall sign in his place."

The crowd exploded at the mention of the ancient vampire lord's name; shouts of shock, awe, and even fear. As Marc stepped into the sunlight, the cries only redoubled. Some Shifters openly exploded into balls of furs, feathers, fangs, and claws. Vampires were NOT supposed to do that. The guards and even the attending bigwigs stood ready to end the abomination post-haste, until Selina spread word that it was Court magics allowing the vampire to avoid immolation via UV rays.

It was only polite, after all, to allow an emissary to speak without bursting into flames.

The lanky haired accountant-cum-spy calmly addressed the august body.

"I, investing my Sire, in body and will, do hereby sign in the name of Lord Hynrich, Master of the Carpathians, Holder of the Forgotten Keys and Warder of the Grey, eternal is his vigil." For a moment, Marc's eyes fluttered shut and an unearthly gale swirled around him. When his eyes opened something else lurked behind them. Something ancient and powerful and hungry. The voice emerging from Marc was cold as the grave, unyielding as granite, and harsh with the passage of centuries. "This do we decree and none may challenge our herald's word. Defy this proclamation at your peril."

With that the alien presence of the ancient vampire receded and Marc shuffled away from the podium, unwilling to look at Jon as though ashamed. The blue-eyed lawyer wanted to console his old friend but knew it would have to wait.

Time to strike while the iron is hot.

"Thus it is signed and recognized. By the powers granted to me by the Houses, we move forward into a new era of unity and prosperity. If any seek to challenge this contract, know that they stand against the unified forces of all signatories."

He paused fractionally, to allow any final protests or attempts to derail their gambit. Behind his smile, Jon sweated bullets as the moment of truth arrived. No shots rang out, no howls of rage, and no bronze claws glinted.

Looks like I get to live!

"For further details, we have provided copies of the contract for each of you. With the formalities over, please enjoy the provided refreshments and mingle. Thank you all for coming. We have a lot of work ahead of us."

The celebration afterward seemed almost anti-climactic. Jon and company retreated off the stage as the Houses hesitantly and awkwardly trailed over to rows of food and drink waiting for them under shaded awnings. Court and Senate rubbed elbows and, for the moment, upheld the new and expanded Truce, even finding common ground in grousing about the upstart human and his hoofer allies. While certainly counter conspiracies would be brewing, it seemed that, for now, the leaders of the Houses were too in shock to react.

Chiron trotted up to Jon behind the state with Nathan in tow. "You have made history this day. My people will finally begin to gain the leverage and respect we deserve, to stand amongst the Houses as equals." As he shook Jon's hand, the erudite centaur leaned in closely. "Be wary, Jon. They won't let this slight go unanswered."

Warning delivered, Chiron trotted off to join in the festivities. Nathan shook Jon's hand, huge mitts that dwarfed the human's pink mittens, with tears in his eyes.

As the two Mythics left, Jon turned to see Arkadas, who stood in the wings nearby.

Laughing.

This isn't good. Arkadas waved Jon over and the lawyer warily trotted toward the owl Shifter. Their secret co-conspirator had made no effort to hide his contempt and rage until now. The about face was disconcerting and promised no end of trouble for Mr. Doe.

"Hello, Arkadas, glad to see you in high spirits. Surprised, but still glad."

Jon's verbal jab only sent Arkadas into greater fits of laughter, jowls rolling with mirth. "My boy. You are crazier than I ever imagined."

"Pretty sure I knew that already. Why are you busting a gut over it?"

The owl Shifter wiped tears from his eyes and gather himself. "Because you have single-handedly managed to anger every person of interest in the entirety of the Sunset Lands with your gamble today. The Senate and the Court won't stand for this snub, even if they won't publicly acknowledge it. Assuming the Houses or Cull don't reduce you to a bloody smear, you'll be lucky to survive your allies. Hoofers would be enough, but that butcher Magda and the Aegolius snakes? You're as good as dead."

Jon failed to see the humor in the situation and stayed silent as Arkadas continued his merry gloating. "I imagined a thousand terrible fates for you. Endless torments and catastrophes that you wouldn't even appreciate until years after they'd befallen you." Arkadas grinned an ugly grin, the grin a sick child gives before killing a cat or pulling wings off butterflys. "Then you went and involved those damn hoofers. Credit where credit is due, I'd never thought it possible, but here we are."

"Yes, it's quite an achievement and I'm amazing. How is that a bad thing?"

"Don't you get it, boy? They're hoofers! They love you now, but one slip-up and you have a mob of unruly, passion-driven meatheads with more muscles than brains. Hell, their parties are as likely to kill you as their riots. Worse still, you signed up an ancient vampire in your little conspiracy! You bargained with a lord of the undead. That, my boy, takes a special kind of stupid."

Jon squirmed. "You made a deal with him too."

The weak protest earned Jon a wagged finger, a teacher reprimanding a slow schoolboy. "That was business, pure and simple. I didn't place myself in debt to the bloodsucker, didn't flaunt my agreement before the world, and I sure as hell didn't have the unmitigated stupidity to shove that pact in the way of both Houses' ambitions."

"The Court and the Senate can't touch me." Jon wished he felt as sure as he sounded.

Arkadas sneered at Jon. "You think you're the first one to flaunt tradition or use the letter of the law to gain an advantage? Boy, they have been making and breaking contracts written in blood for centuries. You won a hand and think the game is over. My dear Mr. Doe, you have no idea the depths of danger you are in. I don't need to lift a finger. You've signed your own death warrant. I'll just sit back and enjoy the show. You're going to have the Senate and the Court united around destroying you and everything you care for. Don't worry, when you die, I'll be sure to send flowers. It's only polite."

Arkadas slammed a meaty hand against Jon's back and walked off with a guffaw, no doubt delighted by visions of Jon's grisly and untimely end.

Brock, who had quietly convened with his Cohort companion while Chiron spoke with Jon, brushed past Arkadas to speak with Jon, Magda giving a withering glare to the departing owl Shifter. Brock stood before Jon, hands behind his back as though at parade at the barracks.

"Mr. Doe. Magda tells me I can trust you, and I trust Magda with my life. With all our lives, actually. You should know she takes on the burden of command once more for your sake. I hope her faith in you is deserved." Brock saluted Jon, fist to heart, before dragging Niall away to confer with his superiors.

Magda kissed Jon fiercely, tongue dancing, claiming, and tasting him like their first night in the club. With one last passionate growl, she turned and raced after her battle brothers. Selina pointedly looked elsewhere, having drifted into their earshot at some point.

Jon reeled in the wake of her assault. *Huh. That was nice. Still don't know where we stand though.*

As he readjusted mussed hair and sunglasses, Jon turned to Marc who had been lurking about. "Thanks, man. That was really brave of you today. I understand how hard it is to have him in there, now. Just wanted to say thank you."

Marc looked bedraggled, and Jon suddenly noticed the undead accountant was smoking in the setting sun. The vampire looked down at the golden amulet, its metal surface warping and cracking in his pale hands. "I think I broke it."

Selina examined the relic with a frown. "Your master's presence devoured its arcane energies. It was never meant for such a powerful entity, certainly not one so directly anathema to it."

Oh crap. We just broke her holiest of holies. Without thinking, Jon stepped between Marc and Selina, ready to defend his undead amigo. Jon didn't realize he'd been willing to take a claw for his friend until it was too late.

Oddly, Selina face lit up in sympathy, rather than rage. "The light is denied to you once again, Marc. I'm so sorry."

The vampire smiled tiredly. "Don't be. I got to see the sun again. To see all the colors of light... and did you see Arkadas' face during the speech? No regrets. For now, I'm off to find a nice shady spot to not combust."

Jon stood for a moment, basking in their amazing victory. Selina remained by his side, eyes scanning the milling and retreating crowd. Jon quirked an eyebrow as he wondered why she had not run off to join the festivities, before remembering the clandestine nature of her deal with Aahmes. *Right, can hardly break out the champagne with your secret ally in front of everyone you just swindled. She has to play the "villain" in our little drama.*

"So, your brother's on board with our mad cap scheme. Kind of surprised. Pleasantly so, but still..."

Again, that almost smile touched her lips and Jon mirrored it without thinking. "Yes, well, he does have a bit of sentimental streak in him when it comes to his sister. Though you must see it in the eyes of our own internal politics. In this way, should it fail, he loses nothing and appears vindicated. If it succeeds, the Court is raised up and, more importantly, so too do the Aegolius' fortunes." Selina leaned closer and whispered a final bit of gossip. "He also promised to use his influence to mitigate any fallout on my position. One can hardly fault the exuberant ambition of a younger sibling, after all. He'll assure them that my heart was in the right place." Selina smirked at the last.

"Huh. Call me biased, but I did not peg my kidnapper as the kindly sort."

"Yes, I was always his favorite. His assassination attempts against me as a child were never half as bad as he gave my other siblings." Selina said it casually, with the same nostalgic wistfulness others reserved for memories of blowing out candles on birthday cakes.

Unsure of how to respond, Jon kept his mouth shut, showing astonishing maturity.

Marc would be proud.

Selina's aristocratic tones broke the growing silence. "You know, Jon, Chiron is correct. You embarrassed the Houses today. They will find a way to strike back at you in the future."

Jon shrugged still riding the high of his victory. "The future is the future. I'm alive today and that's what counts. Let them come. We can take them."

Shockingly Jon found that he meant every word. *For once in my life, I've got people backing me. They believe in me and not just the family name.* Together, his unlikely allies pulled off an impossible scheme. Together, they had denied death by the skin of their teeth. Today, they could dance and sing, and tomorrow? They'd leave tomorrow's worries for another day.

"Selina, thank you. Not just for what you did for me, but for what you did for Marc as well."

"You are quite welcome Jon. Though I hadn't intended for our relic to be used in such an... unorthodox manner, it was rather miraculous to allow a nightwalker to be blessed by the sun. Besides, you and your friend make life just a bit more interesting in San Dominguez."

Grinning like a madman, Jon stepped out from behind the stage to look at the crowd of tentative allies and certain enemies. "My dear Selina, you haven't seen anything yet. This is just the beginning."

ABOUT THE AUTHOR

Nicholas Walls is a long-term enthusiast of sci-fiction and fantasy. If a story had a fantastical element, Nick devoured the story. A historian by training, Nick also brings the past to life through the Facebook page *History In Five*. His debut novels, *The Butcher's Tale* and *Primal Real Estate*, alongside his other literary offerings, can be found at his website, nwallsauthor.com.

www.ingramcontent.com/pod-product-compliance
Lightning Source LLC
Chambersburg PA
CBHW071753110726
47908CB00006B/1791